Praise fo

“Victoria Laurie ha ... tale in this latest Psychic Eye M... ...ere are few things in life that upset Abb... ...ooper, but ghosts and her parents feature high on her list . . . giving the reader a few real frights and a lot of laughs.”

—Fresh Fiction

“A fabulous whodunit. . . . Fans will highly praise this fine ghostly murder mystery.”

—The Best Reviews

Acclaim for the Psychic Eye Mystery Series

“A great new series . . . plenty of action.”

—*Midwest Book Review*

“An invigorating entry into the cozy mystery realm. . . . I cannot wait for the next book.”

—Roundtable Reviews

“Well written and unpredictable. Everything about this book is highly original. . . . A fun protagonist with just enough bravado to keep her going.”

—*Romantic Times*

“The characters are all realistically drawn and the situations go from interesting, to amusing, to laugh-out-loud funny. The best thing a person can do to while away the cold winter is to cuddle up in front of a fire with this wonderful book.”

—The Best Reviews

“Victoria Laurie has talent to spare—she’s a writer to watch.”

—J. A. Konrath, author of *Bloody Mary*

Other Psychic Eye Mysteries

Abby Cooper, Psychic Eye
Better Read Than Dead
A Vision of Murder

Best wishes!

KILLER INSIGHT

A Psychic Eye Mystery

Victoria Laurie

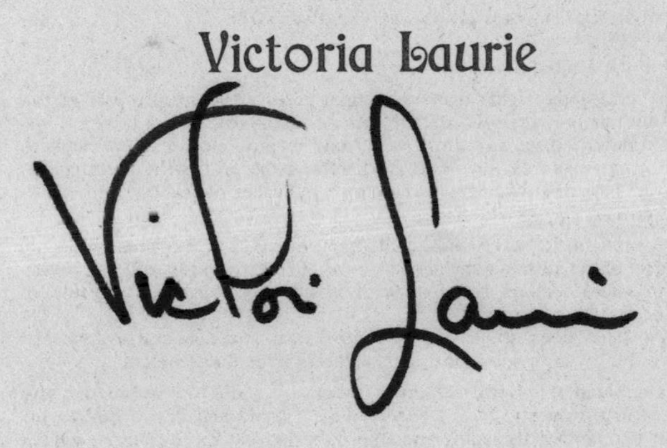

A SIGNET BOOK

SIGNET
Published by New American Library, a division of
Penguin Group (USA) Inc., 375 Hudson Street,
New York, New York 10014, USA
Penguin Group (Canada), 90 Eglinton Avenue East, Suite 700, Toronto,
Ontario M4P 2Y3, Canada (a division of Pearson Penguin Canada Inc.)
Penguin Books Ltd., 80 Strand, London WC2R 0RL, England
Penguin Ireland, 25 St. Stephen's Green, Dublin 2,
Ireland (a division of Penguin Books Ltd.)
Penguin Group (Australia), 250 Camberwell Road, Camberwell, Victoria 3124,
Australia (a division of Pearson Australia Group Pty. Ltd.)
Penguin Books India Pvt. Ltd., 11 Community Centre, Panchsheel Park,
New Delhi - 110 017, India
Penguin Group (NZ), cnr Airborne and Rosedale Roads, Albany,
Auckland 1310, New Zealand (a division of Pearson New Zealand Ltd.)
Penguin Books (South Africa) (Pty.) Ltd., 24 Sturdee Avenue,
Rosebank, Johannesburg 2196, South Africa

Penguin Books Ltd., Registered Offices:
80 Strand, London WC2R 0RL, England

First published by Signet, an imprint of New American Library,
a division of Penguin Group (USA) Inc.

First Printing, September 2006
10 9 8 7 6 5 4

Printed in the United States of America

For Alice Johns (Inga Brault)
From the bottom of my heart, I thank you
for a friendship that saved my life.

Acknowledgments

This novel was inspired by a childhood friendship. And as I've worked to complete this particular Abby Cooper installment, I realize how many friendships have actually gone into the story's creation. It's these special relationships that I would like to acknowledge here:

First and foremost, I would like to thank my childhood friend Alice Johns and her family for taking in a lonely little runt like me and forever modifying my perspective on friendship and family. Thank God I had you—Alice, John, Eric, Nina and Jimmy—to shape and model what a true, loving family can be. Nearly thirty years later, I still hold you all so close to my heart.

Speaking of family, I would like to acknowledge my brother, Jon, and my sister-in-law, Naoko. Thank you so much for your love and friendship. I treasure the both of you.

Next is my very dear friend and agent Jim McCarthy, who always brightens my day with his wit, charm, encouragement and support. I know you must be sick of hearing it, mon cher, but I simply adore you! Also, along with Jim, I would like to thank Jane Dystel and the entire staff of Dystel and Goderich, who are like my guardian angels. I feel so secure in your care, and please know that I get how lucky I am to have your representation.

Thanks also go to my fantabulous editor, Martha Bushko. Martha, I can hardly express to you my gratitude for all that you've taught me, and what a diamond in the rough you are. I have grown so much in just two short years under your wise guidance. Thank you for pushing me, thank you for your patience, and most especially, thank you for your friendship and care. I will miss you so much—be good, be well, be prosperous and remember to drop me a line. I always knew you were a rising star—can't wait to see you shine, girl!

As Martha says good-bye, I now inherit Molly Boyle. Molly, I'm absolutely thrilled to have landed with you, and look forward to a terrific partnership. Thank you for your assistance thus far, and cheers to the future!

Of course I can't leave out the legion of friends who have inspired characters, helped with the research, and religiously read this series while offering their amazing support and encouragement. They are Karen Ditmars, Leanne Tierney, Dell Chase, Silas Hudson, Dave McKenzie, Sandy Upham, Laurie Combs, Rebecca Rosen, Thomas Robinson, Maureen Febo, Alison Alsobrook, Joan Rogers, Debbie Huntley, Nora Brosseau, Kristen Laprade, Patty Healy, Suzanne Parsons, Kate Norton-Edge, Renee Camara, Beverly Ring, Dr. Stephani Amstadter, Dr. Stephen Pap, Jaa Nawtaisong, and the rest of my peeps out there. You guys rock!

Moving on to my crew (yes, just like Abby, I've got one too), I would like to acknowledge the support and love I receive from the Other Side. My crew's guidance has steered me to some amazing opportunities, and—for the most part—kept me out of trouble. Thank you, my guides and angels. I love you so much.

And last, but certainly not least, I would like to

thank every single fan who has e-mailed or written a letter to let me know you're enjoying this series. You have no idea what all your support has done for me, and how much it thrills me to read your lovely words. I'm inspired by each and every one of you. Thank you for making my day, and especially for passing Abby on to friends and relatives. Due to your efforts, word of mouth is spreading, guys—I'm so grateful for your help and please, keep it up! ☺

Chapter One

As I looked down the black barrel of the .38 pointed directly at my chest, and into the familiar eyes of my killer, all I could think was, *I'm a friggin'* psychic, *for Pete's sake! Why didn't I know it was* you *all along?!*

I never got a chance to ponder that answer, because at that exact moment an explosion shattered all thought as a bullet ripped open my chest and sent me hurtling backward to land faceup looking wide-eyed and panicked at the big blue sky.

For the record, getting shot is nothing like they show in the movies, which, if you believe the actors, must feel something like a cross between a pinprick and a mosquito bite. The truth is, taking a bullet hurts like a mother.

Dying is also not all it's cracked up to be, but more on that in a moment. For now let me tell you that from the second I landed on the ground I knew only the intense, searing heat filling my chest like a vat of molten lava and a pain so intense it stole my breath away. All I could do was beg that big blue sky for mercy. A moment later the sky was blocked out by the face of my killer, who again aimed the gun at me.

Now, you have to appreciate the agony I was in. Looking up at that barrel, I knew it was both my destruction and salvation. I just couldn't take the pain, so I nodded in acquiescence. *Please, just make it stop!* my mind screamed. A moment later, with the sound of a second explosion, I got my wish.

When they tell you that your whole life flashes before your eyes when you die, that is actually true. Well almost. In my case, I was privy to only the last week leading up to my death, but I've always been a *Reader's Digest* kind of gal, so keeping it short and to the point was fine by me. The fact that my review began on Valentine's Day, just before a major breakup with my commitment-phobic boyfriend, simply confirms my belief that the Universe, for all its wisdom and glory, really does have one gigantic sense of humor.

As I trotted off to heaven, a sensation of being in a theater and watching a movie played across my consciousness, and the opening scene began in the middle of a client reading. Yes, I'm not only psychic; I'm a professional. And during this particular session I was having a bit of a translation problem. "Okay, Janet, now they're showing me a checkbook, and I get the feeling of newness with it. Are you opening up a new checking account?"

My client, Janet, shook her head no, her face scrunched up in confusion.

Inwardly I groaned. This had been the pattern of the entire reading. I'd say something; Janet would say no, that didn't fit; then I'd fish my intuition for more clues and eventually it would click. It was a lot of extra work, and, as we were only twenty minutes into a forty-minute session, I was already tired. "Well, my guides are making me feel like you *are* opening up a new checking account, and they're also saying something about travel. So do you know if your bank is offering any kind of travel perks for opening up a new checking account? Like, open an account and get frequent-flier miles or something?"

Again, a head shake no from Janet. "Abby, I'm

really not opening a new checking account. The one I have is fine."

I smiled politely and in my head I reached out to my spirit guides, collectively called "the crew," and said, *Hey! Can we please get it together here? Give me something she can recognize! She keeps saying no.* Immediately I got the thought, *mother* . . . in my head. I shrugged and asked, "Janet, has your mother asked you to open up a checking account? Or would she ask you to open up a joint account? Maybe it's her bank that's having the special on travel, because they are pointing to your mom and saying 'travel' and 'account.' "

"Ohmigod!" Janet squealed as she made the connection. "Abby! I'm so sorry! I *am* opening up a new account, but it's an equity line that I've already applied for, and the purpose is because I want to send my mother on her dream vacation to Bermuda!"

I sat back in my chair and let out a sigh. "Yeah, those equity lines usually come with checkbooks," I said with a smile.

Janet laughed. "I know; how obvious can you be, huh?"

"Mmmm," I said noncommittally, and leaned in again, focusing on a new topic. "All right, now they're talking about where you work, and they're saying there's something about a fracture. They're showing me two halves with a line down the middle, and saying that there's some frustration here, or problems between the two halves. So, I think they're saying that your company may have a division of power and the two halves might not be getting along. Do you know what I'm talking about?"

Again, Janet scrunched her features up, giving me the confused face.

I dug a little deeper and said, "They keep insisting there's a split, and it's something about a division within your company. I have group A over here and group B over there, and I feel like the two halves aren't talking to each other, like there's confusion communicating or something. . . ." I looked up to see if this was registering with Janet, but her brows only lowered and the frown deepened. "Not ringing any bells, huh?"

"No. I don't know about any problems with leadership within the company I work for. We've had the same president and CEO for years, and all the VPs seem to interact well with him and with each other. And I'm sure we would have heard if there'd been some sort of division."

I rubbed my forehead with my palm, mentally asking my crew to help me out here. They replied by showing me a building, then splitting the building in half and moving each side of the building to the right and left alternatively. I wasn't wrong. There was a split within this company. "Janet, they're not backing off of this message. My crew is insisting that there's been some kind of a change or split or *move* within your company recently."

"Oh! Like a *real* move?" she asked me, the scrunchy face lightening up.

"Yes, that fits," I said, coaxing her to make the connection.

"In that case there *has* been a division. We just moved the IT, marketing and accounting departments across the street to another building because we were starting to run out of room."

I resisted the urge to get up and slap Janet. "And is this causing some problems in communication?" I asked, feeling rather exasperated.

"Now that I know we're talking about a *literal* move, the phone system doesn't seem to be working between the two buildings. We also had a virus within our company's network on Friday which took down the whole e-mail system, so no one was really doing much communicating at all," she said with a laugh.

I smiled and reminded myself for the billionth time that while the planet Mercury was in a retrograde pattern I could expect a few more readings to go exactly like this one. "So as I was saying, about this division, did it cause a small shift in power? Did your boss perhaps go over to the other building and you guys are on your own for the moment?"

Scrunchy face again. "No . . ." Janet said.

I took a deep, calming breath and asked, "So who's head of the IT, marketing and accounting departments?"

"That would be our VP, Jim Delouche. He's my boss's boss."

"And did he stay in your building?"

"No, he moved over to the new site."

"Janet?"

"Yeah?"

"Any chance you could put your thinking cap on here and help me out?"

She smiled sheepishly and said, "I'm taking you too literally, aren't I?"

"Just a tad."

Our session ended ten minutes later with only three more scrunchy faces and one zinger of a headache over my right eye. I saw Janet out the door and headed into my office, just off the room I use to read clients. My office had been trashed by a wacko about three weeks earlier, and I was still trying to put the pieces back together. The most arduous task—of going through all the files from my filing cabinet that'd been tossed around like confetti—I'd saved for last. However, since I needed to get my paperwork in order for my accountant, I'd slowly started going through the mess in between sessions and on my lunch break.

Today I had a good hour before my next client, so I grabbed my PB and J sandwich out of the small fridge in my office, took a stack of files and paperwork, sat down akimbo on the floor and began to sort them into little piles. About fifteen minutes later I heard the front door of my suite open and a deep baritone call out, "Abby? You in here?"

"Back here, Dutch!" I said loudly, a small grin already forming at the corners of my mouth. Dutch Rivers used to be a detective with the Royal Oak, Michigan, police, before joining the FBI. He was currently stationed out of the local Troy Bureau office, and over the past few months Dutch and I'd had a few opportunities to work together—my natural talent meshing nicely with his detective skills. He appeared in the doorway, and, despite the fact that we'd been dating for a while now, my breath caught at the sight of him.

"Hey, there, sweethot," he said, doing his best Humphrey Bogart.

I would have whistled if my mouth weren't so dry. Dutch is six feet, three inches of gorgeousness with light blond hair, square features, a nice straight nose, midnight-blue eyes, and a body like Adonis. Today he was dressed in black Dockers, a crisp white shirt unbuttoned at the neck and a black leather jacket. He looked good enough to eat. "Hey, yourself," I said, giving him a quick hair toss and what I hoped was a seductive smile. "We still on for tonight?"

"Mmm-hmm," he said, squatting down in front of me and fingering one of the piles I'd set out. "What time should I be over?"

"Sixish." I'd gone to the grocery store this morning and purchased steaks, potatoes and green beans, which were all Dutch's favorites. I'm much better at breakfast than I am at dinner, but I figured it shouldn't be too hard to grill a couple of steaks and bake some potatoes. In the back of my mind I wondered if you could microwave green beans.

"So what's the occasion?" he asked playfully, picking up a folder from another pile.

"You're joking, right?" I asked, looking for a hint of it on his face. Something in the folder caught Dutch's attention, and he didn't answer me right away.

I couldn't see what he was reading, so I nudged him with my foot. "Hello? Earth to Dutch."

Dutch snapped his head up and said, "What? I'm sorry, what did you say the occasion was?"

Now I knew he wasn't kidding, and I worked hard to hide my disappointment. "It's Valentine's Day," I said quietly.

Dutch paused and blinked his eyes twice rapidly, then glanced at his watch, noted the time, looked back up at me and said, "Gotcha!"

I forced a smile and said, "You sure did!"

Dutch's face was slightly pale as he set the file aside and got up from his squat position. "So, I need to run. Just wanted to check in. I'll see you at six then?"

"Bring your appetite," I said with another flirtatious smile.

Dutch nodded. He seemed distracted, or concerned, or something. "Okay."

"Hey, cowboy," I said as he turned to go. "You okay?"

"Yeah," he said, not turning back to me. "I just got a lot on my mind. See you tonight." And he was out the door.

"Weird," I said when I heard the door close. My intuition buzzed and my eye fell on the folder Dutch had been looking at when he went all pale and sweaty. I picked it up and my jaw fell open in horror. "Oh, *shit*!" I said. "Of all the folders littering my office floor, Dutch had to pick up my wedding folder. You know, that folder that many of us single gals start about age ten, filled with cutouts and clippings that get added every time we come across a wedding gown, bridesmaid dress, wedding cake, engagement ring or honeymoon hot spot we like? Yeah. That one. "Ugh . . ." I said, and slapped my forehead. Wrong move when you've already got a good headache going.

I got up and went around to my desk, fishing through the drawers for some Tylenol. Finding the bottle I opened it and chugged two capsules down, my face doing its own scrunchy thing. After a few minutes I shrugged my shoulders. Dutch had to know that the file didn't mean anything. Right? I'd had that folder for years, and just because I kept it didn't mean I wanted to marry him or anything. Okay, so it didn't mean I wanted to marry him *tomorrow*. I tried to laugh. He was a levelheaded, reasonable guy. A simple folder with some wedding stuff wasn't gonna scare him off that easily, right?

I plopped into my chair behind the desk and laid my pounding head on the desk. "I'm so totally screwed," I said to the empty room. To add insult to injury, my right side took on a light and airy feeling, my sign for, *You bet your tuchus.*

Later that night I was whacking the smoke detector off the ceiling with a broom to stop the *eeeeeeeeeeep!* sound when I felt a breeze of cold air behind me. The kitchen was full of smoke, and it was a little hard to see the smoke detector, so I just kept whacking in the general area I thought it was in when Dutch came up behind me and gently took the broom from my hand. Reaching up, he unscrewed the cap of the detector and removed the battery. "Ringing the dinner bell, I see?" he said with a smile.

"Hey, cowboy," I said over my shoulder as I hurried to unlatch the windows and open the back door. Seeing the open door, my miniature dachshund, Eggy, raced outside, most likely to get away from the choking smell of crispified steak.

Dutch poked his head in the oven and smirked as he looked at the blackened meat still smoking away on the grill. "How long have these been in here?" he asked, turning to me.

I managed a shrug as I fanned the door to let the good air in and suck the bad air out. "I dunno. About forty minutes?"

"Ah," Dutch said, standing up. "I think they're done."

"Great," I said, and sped around him to grab two plates off the counter. "How about you load up the plates with the meat and potatoes and I'll get the green beans."

Dutch looked at the stovetop, a question forming on his features. "What green beans?"

"In here," I said, and opened up the microwave. Shriveled green globs stared back at me. Did I mention I'm much better at breakfast? Grabbing a towel, I carefully extracted the bowl they were sitting in and carried them to my dining room table. Behind me I heard a *plunk!* and asked. "What was that?"

"The baked potato. Abby, how long were they in the oven?"

"I put them in the moment I got home from work."

"How long ago was that?"

"About an hour and forty-five minutes ago," I said, glancing at the clock. Muffled laughter wafted its way from the kitchen to the dining room. "You're not laughing at me, are you?" I snapped.

The muffled laughter abruptly stopped. "No. No, of course not." *Liar, liar . . . pants on fire . . .*

I rolled my eyes and pulled a pack of matches out of my pocket, lighting the two red candles on the table. I'd worked hard to set a romantic table, with maroon cloth place mats and matching napkins. I'd spread tiny confetti hearts on the tabletop and had set a small bouquet of red roses in a Waterford vase between the two candles. Dutch walked in carrying the plates with what looked like two large hunks of charcoal and shriveled brown pieces of dung next to them. My heart sank as I saw our dinner on the plates. "Crap," I said as Dutch hovered the plates over the table.

"Aww. Don't worry about it, Edgar," he said, using his favorite nickname for me after famed psychic

Edgar Cayce. "I like my steak well-done, and I'm sure it'll taste better than it looks." *Liar, liar . . . pants on fire. . . .*

I sighed and gave him a half-smile. "I wanted this to be special."

"So sit down already," he said, putting down the plates and giving me a wink.

I beamed at him and was about to pull out my chair when something about him caught my attention. I looked at him for a long moment, my head turned slightly to one side. Something was different.

"You okay?" he asked after taking his seat and flipping open his napkin to put it on his lap.

"Yeah . . ." I said, and shook my head. "Did you get a haircut?" I asked as I pulled out my own chair and sat down.

"Couple weeks ago," he said as he picked up the A.1. and began to drown his dead steak in it. "Actually, I'm due."

"Huh," I said, picking up my fork and knife. There was a cold wet nudge on my leg, and I looked down to see Eggy sitting next to me, and the moment we made eye contact, his skinny tail began to thump on the floor. "Hey, buddy," I said, and started to cut him a piece of my steak. It took a while, but eventually I sawed off a small burned edge and lowered it to the floor. Eggy sniffed at it, picked it up in his mouth, then promptly spit it back out again. He nudged me again, and I gave him a look and said, "Sorry, pal, beggars can't be choosers."

"So tell me about your day," Dutch asked as he too worked to saw off a small piece of steak.

"Ugh!" I said, remembering what a toughie it had been. "I swear, with this whole Mercury-retrograde thing going on, I'm working hard for the money."

"Mercury what?" he asked.

"Retrograde," I answered, and put a small piece of steak in my mouth. Like Eggy, I too had the urge to spit it right back out, but to save face I forced myself to swallow the bite. After chasing that with a gulp of water I explained, "Three times a year the planet Mercury goes into a retrograde pattern, meaning that in the night sky the planet appears to be moving backward in relation to Earth's orbit. It's not really moving backward; it's just that it looks like it from the ground. And since Mercury is the planet of communication, it means that during this period of time we don't have its help with things like how we talk to each other. In other words, things can be misunderstood or miscommunicated." As I spoke to him I couldn't quit the feeling that something about him was definitely off. It bugged me enough to segue into asking him, "Did you part your hair different or something?"

He shook his head. "No. Same part. Nothing's changed. So, you had a tough day, huh?"

"Yeah, but oh! I almost forgot. Ellie called about an hour ago to make sure we were still coming. Did you find out if you can fly out with me next Thursday?" Ellie was a childhood friend of mine who lived next door to me from the age of one to the age of eleven before her father took a job in Colorado and moved the family there. Her wedding was the following Friday, and I'd been invited, which meant Dutch was my date.

Dutch looked at his plate and made a show of splitting open his shriveled potato and slathering it with butter, which the dehydrated vegetable soaked up like water on the Sahara. "I don't think I can get the time off," he said, avoiding my eyes.

"What?" I demanded. "But, Dutch! You have to come with me! It's a wedding; I can't go *alone*!"

"I tried, babe. Really. But this case I'm working on needs my full attention, and it doesn't look like it'll be wrapped up in time to make your friend's wedding."

I looked at him for a minute, not sure of what the change in attitude was about. A mere three weeks ago he'd told me to reply to the RSVP that both of us would be attending. "What's going on?" I asked, setting down my fork and knife.

"Nothing," he said too quickly. "Hey!" he offered, changing the subject. "I got you something." And before I could corner him, he was out of his chair and into the kitchen. He came back a moment later with a shopping bag and handed it to me.

I couldn't help it; I had to smile. I'd grill him about Ellie's wedding later. "I got you something too," I said, and raced into the study to get several boxes all wrapped in red tissue paper with pink bows.

"Hey," he said, looking at the stack. "You went all out."

I smiled and we exchanged presents. I motioned for him to go first, and with a smile he obliged. I watched eagerly as Dutch lifted the lid off a small rectangular box and said, "Whoa, Abby, you shouldn't have."

I grinned and gave a small clap of my hands, "Try it on!"

Dutch pulled out the new TAG Heuer Formula 1 watch I'd spent a small fortune on and gave me a rather pained look. "You spent too much, Edgar."

"I did a few extra readings last week; it's nothing," I said. "Now try it on already!"

Dutch did, and I gave another clap. "Next one!" I said, really enjoying this.

Dutch gave an eyebrow shrug and moved on to his second present, a cashmere sweater, and his third, a Coach wallet. His fourth and fifth presents were a box of flavored massage oils, and a coupon booklet good for things like a free back massage, breakfast in bed, and one night of wild, hot monkey love. I was hoping he would cash in that particular coupon this very evening.

"I think you went a little overboard here," he said as he looked at the collection of presents on the table.

"You're easy to shop for," I said as I took out the small box wrapped in plain purple wrapping, sans bow, that he'd given to me. "Did you wrap this yourself?" I kidded.

"Sorry, I've been busy," Dutch said, that same pained look on his face. "I didn't know Valentine's Day was such a big deal to you. I would have gotten something more if I'd known. . . ."

"Hush!" I said, and shook the box. I was secretly hoping for jewelry. Nothing too fancy, maybe a bracelet or some earrings to match the pendant he'd given me for my birthday. As I shook the box something knocked around inside, and excitedly I tore the wrapping off and held up my very own, incredibly thoughtful and wonderfully romantic . . . cell phone. "Ah . . ." I said as I looked at the packaging, the air going right out of my sails. "It's a cell phone," I said woodenly. "But I already have a cell phone." Ungrateful, party of one—right here!

"Yeah, I know," Dutch was quick to explain. "But this isn't just any cell phone; it's got a built-in GPS locator."

"Uh-huh. Well, that's just *so* much better!" I said my voice going up several screechy octaves.

"See, this way you can never get lost, Abby. It's got a satellite sensor that lets you know exactly where you are anywhere in the world. And it comes with this hands-free earpiece; that's Bluetooth technology, state-of-the-art stuff!"

"Gee, I thought the ones with the built-in cameras were cool," I deadpanned.

"And you're always complaining that your other cell never stays charged. This baby's got over a hundred hours of standby time. Now, I couldn't port your old number over to this one, because the contract is in your name and you weren't with me when I bought it, and I wanted you to have service right away, so I had them give you a new number, and paid for one year of unlimited minutes. All the paperwork's there. It's a great deal."

"So . . . new cell phone, new service plan and new phone number. Yippee."

Dutch wasn't noting my reaction. He was too excited by the gadget. "And they had a two-for-one special going on, so I got the same model, see?" he said, holding up his own brand-new cell phone with a big grin on his face.

"Excuse me? What was that?" I asked, giving him a sharp look.

"I got the same model?" he said, his voice going up in a question mark as he finally took notice of the glare I was giving him.

"No, not that. You said something about a two-for-one special?"

"Yeah. The store was having a sale—"

I held up my hand in a stop motion and cut him off. "So tell me the truth, Dutch, who did you really buy this phone for, me? Or you?"

"You, sweethot," he said, looking nervous. "I mean, I needed one too; the Bureau recommends them for all their field agents. . . ."

My head cocked to the side and my eyebrows lowered. "You're *kidding* me with this, aren't you?"

"No! I thought it was a great gift. I just happened to need one too, and it was a lucky coincidence that the store was having a terrific sale."

"And this whole buying me a year of unlimited minutes—that get you any discounts?" I demanded.

"Uh . . . only a little one."

"How little?" I said, crossing my arms.

"Buy-one-year's-worth-of-talk-time-for-the-first-phone-get-the-other-one-free kind of little."

"You are *unbelievable*!" I snapped and picked up the phone to shove it back in its box, then stood up to collect our plates.

"Abby," Dutch began. "Come on, don't be that way."

"What way?" I asked, looking at him as the hurt over such a stupid, unsentimental and unromantic gift welled up inside me. "Just because I went to so much trouble to make tonight special and romantic for you doesn't mean you have to return the favor, after all."

"Edgar . . ." he said with an exasperated sigh.

"What's up with you lately?" I asked him. Dutch had been a little distant the past week, and I wondered what was going on with him.

Dutch shrugged and twirled the napkin in his lap, but didn't answer me.

I stared at him for a long time, and just as I was about to turn away, something dawned on me that made me set the plates back down on the table and suck in a breath as I was taken by surprise.

"What?" he asked as he looked up at me, his expression uncomfortable.

"I know what's different about you," I whispered as a wave of fear gripped my insides. "It's missing. I don't know why I didn't see it sooner. But it's not there anymore."

"What's missing?" he asked.

"Me," I said simply. "I'm not in your energy."

We all carry people we're close to in our energy, and when I intuitively looked at Dutch, I always saw a faceless brunette with long hair over his left shoulder. I'd come to learn that the brunette was me, and it always made me feel safe that he carried me around like that, tucked safely over his left shoulder. Tonight, however, I wasn't there. The spot I usually occupied was empty.

Dutch stared at his feet for the longest moment, and then he finally spoke, and his words broke my heart. "I just think we're moving a little fast here, Abby. I mean, I'm new at the Bureau, and these assignments come with a lot of pressure. I need to be focused. I can't allow myself to become distracted when so much depends on the outcome. I just want you to consider slowing things down for a little while, until I've put in a little time at the office, okay?"

"It was the wedding file, wasn't it?" I asked.

"I'm not ready to get tied down again, Edgar," Dutch explained, his eyes downcast. "I mean, someday, yes. But I just got divorced."

I nodded dumbly, and the silence played out between us for a long time. I thought about trying to explain the file—that I'd had it forever, and that just because I kept it up-to-date didn't mean I thought we should get married. It simply meant I was prepared when and if the moment ever arrived. But then, as I looked at him and that hole over his left shoulder where I used to be, I knew that explaining the file wouldn't do a damn bit of good. His mind was made up. We were *finito*.

Finally, I bent low and picked up Eggy, biting my lip to hold in the sob threatening to burble out. With effort I managed to say, "Please leave."

Dutch's head snapped up. "Leave? But I thought we could spend some time together tonight. Don't you want to talk this through?"

"No. I want you to go. Now. Please." Dutch held my eyes for a long moment, his face unreadable. Then he stood up and started to take off his new watch when I said, "You might as well keep it. I can't take it back now. It's engraved."

"You had it engraved?"

"Look at it in the car, Dutch. I don't care. Just leave. . . ." and the sob that I'd managed to hold in check burbled up anyway.

Dutch stepped forward and grabbed me, hugging me and Eggy. "Hey, there," he said as I sobbed into his shirt. "Come on, Edgar, don't do that. Listen to me. All I'm saying is that I need a little room to focus on my job. Some time to concentrate on what I need to do until things quiet down a bit. And I'd really like you to be okay with that, please?"

I sniffed loudly into his shirt. The void in his energy told me more than any words that there was no future for us, so his even bothering to ask if I was okay with giving him some space was nothing but a waste of time. "Just go," I said as I pulled back from his chest and pointed to the door.

Dutch tried to make eye contact with me but I turned away. Finally, he hung his head and walked to the front door. He paused there for the longest moment, and I watched his back while silently begging him to change his mind and stay anyway. Then with a sigh he opened the door and walked out.

Chapter Two

"Hello?" I said into the phone the next morning, my swollen eyes making it tough to read the caller ID.

"Abs?" came a familiar female voice.

"Hey, Ellie," I managed, my voice sounding hoarse from so much crying.

"You sound bad, girl! What'd you and that hunka hunka burnin' love *do* last night?"

"We broke up," I said, sitting up and squinting at the clock. It read ten A.M.

"Ha! Funny! No, really, what'd you do?"

I sighed heavily and let the silence speak for itself.

"Ohmigod! He *really* broke up with you?" Ellie asked.

"He said he needed some space. Wanted to slow the train down."

"On *Valentine's Day*?!"

"Dutch always did have great timing."

"Bastard!"

"Yeah, and the worst part is, he was really nice about it. He even gave me a hug. What guy hugs you when he breaks your heart?"

"Aww, Abs, I'm so sorry!"

"What can you do? It happens," I said as the waterworks started again.

"Get your butt on a plane and come to Colorado. I need you anyway. One of my bridesmaids took off with her boyfriend and now I'm one short."

I closed my eyes and let my head fall forward. I'd forgotten about the wedding. What was that phrase? Always the bridesmaid? "Ellie, I don't know that I'm up for that right now. . . ."

"Abigail Cooper, you listen to me. The worst thing you can do is sit in your house and mope around about this guy. What you need is a change of scenery. Something with gorgeous views and lots of activity, and I know just the place and just the party. Now get out of bed, pack your bag and hop on a plane already!"

"Ellie," I said.

"Yeah?"

"You really need to try the decaf."

"So you'll come?"

"I'll think about it. I'll call you tomorrow."

"Chin up, sweetie. 'Kay?" she said, and we disconnected.

I tossed the phone to the other side of the bed, then pulled the covers over my head and curled up around Eggy again. He snuggled up under my chin and let out a heavy sigh. I couldn't agree more.

A few hours later, Eggy and I were both downstairs when a small knock came on my back door. I looked down at my disheveled self, in my baggy sweats, raggedy robe and socks that didn't match, and thought about not answering it. Then the knock came again. Moaning, I shuffled over to the door and peeked through the curtain. A Hell's Angel grinned back. Rolling my eyes, I opened the door a crack and said, "Hey, Dave."

"Hey, honey! You ready to go look at another property?"

Dave McKenzie was my former handyman and current business partner. Recently we'd purchased one of those "handyman specials" which is a cute real estate term for "condemned—enter at your own risk." However, due to the house's rather spooky condition, Dave refused to go near the place and had hired a crew to fix it up so we could sell it. That didn't stop him from looking for another property to invest in. His thinking was that if I went with him before we actually bought a prospective fixer-upper, perhaps we could avoid such haunted circumstances again.

"Not today, Dave. I'm not feelin' so hot."

"You got a cold or something?" he asked, taking a step forward to inspect me through the crack.

"Or something."

Dave nodded his head and said, "Yeah, you look like hell, girl. Dutch give it to you?"

"In a manner of speaking."

"Want me to get you some chicken soup?" he offered helpfully.

"Naw, I'm okay," I said. Just then Eggy, who'd been clawing at the door, anxious to greet Dave, wiggled his way through the small opening and began jumping up and down by Dave's feet.

Dave bent over, picked up my pooch and got a faceful of wet, slobbery kisses. "Hey, there, buddy," he said in between licks as he eyed me curiously. "You sure you're okay?" he asked as he stepped forward expectantly, and I had no choice but to open the door wide and let him in.

"The truth?" I asked.

"Bring it," Dave said as he crossed the threshold and shut the door with his foot.

"Dutch broke up with me last night and I'm kind of a wreck."

"He *what*?" Dave said, setting Eggy down.

"He broke up with me."

"But you two just got back from Toronto. I thought everything was great."

"Me too," I mumbled as I pulled down a mug from the cabinet and poured Dave some coffee.

"So what happened?" he asked, nodding as he accepted the mug and reached for the sugar bowl.

"I'm not really sure. I mean, yesterday Dutch happened to catch a glimpse of my wedding file—"

"Your what?"

I did a combo heavy sigh and eye roll as I explained. "My wedding file. It's a file that girls keep so that when you guys get down on bended knee we are fully prepared to walk down that aisle one year later. It takes a lot of preplanning, ya know."

"You keep a *file*?"

"Oh, get over it, David," I chastised. "Of course we keep a friggin' file. It doesn't mean we want to get married *tomorrow*; it just means that we are prepared should the occasion arise . . . you know . . . someday . . . down the road . . . a ways away. . . ."

"And you're wondering why Dutch got a little cagey?"

"No. I can see it from his perspective. I mean, *he* doesn't know that my file is about a hundred years old, so I'm assuming he thinks I've been hoarding these clippings and pictures ever since we met. For the record, though, I've only cut out two photos and clipped one article in the past few months."

Dave was making a face at me that seemed a cross between "yikes" and "what were you thinking?"

"It's not like I let him see it on purpose!" I said rather loudly as the tears started and I began to sniffle.

"Okay, okay," he said, setting down his cup of coffee and hurrying over to fold me into a hug. "Listen," he said in a soothing tone as he patted me on the back, "I'm sure all he needs is a little time. He'll start missing you, and wondering what he was all worked up about. Then he'll call and want to talk, and before you know it the two of you will be back together again."

"Is that what you'd do in the same situation?" I asked.

"Hell, no, I'd run like hell and never look back," Dave said.

I shoved away from him. "Thanks, that makes me feel *so* much better, Dave!"

"Yeah, but that's me, Abby. That's not Dutch. I never wanted to make it official."

"You don't get it," I said as I plopped down in one of my kitchen chairs.

Dave picked up his coffee and came over to the table. "What don't I get?"

"I'm not in his energy, Dave. I'm gone."

"Come again?"

I sighed, searching for a way to explain. "It's like this. You know how you carry photos of your wife and kids in your wallet?"

"I don't have any kids," Dave said.

"Not *you,* Dave," I groused. "*Normal* people. You know, how *normal people* carry around pictures of their family in their wallet?"

"I'm with ya."

"Well, it's like that. When I look at you intuitively, I get this picture in my head of your basic outline, and then over your left shoulder is this woman with blond hair, who I assume is, uh . . . what's her name?"

"My old lady," Dave said with a sly smile. Dave had never shared the name of his common-law wife with me, and I'd been trying to trick him into telling me ever since I'd heard him use the term. It was our little game, and so far he was winning.

I rolled my eyes at him and continued. "Your significant other is located right there over your left shoulder, and that's how, when I do readings, I can tell if someone's attached or not. They carry the imprint of their lover in their energy field."

"Tell me about how this relates to Dutch," Dave said.

My shoulders slumped again and my smile faded. "Just like you, Dutch used to carry me in his energy. Only last night I was completely gone. I mean, it was as if I'd never even been part of his life, like he'd erased even the memory of me."

"You sure you weren't just having an off night?"

I drew in a deep breath and let it out again as I thought about that. "Anything's possible," I said. "But I checked his energy a couple of times. I might have gotten it wrong once, but not several times. He's removed me from his life. . . ." And with that I began to cry . . . again.

"Hey," Dave said as he rubbed my shoulder, "I'm sure that with a little time, he'll come around. I mean, Abby, you're the whole package. You got looks, brains and superpowers. How could any guy resist all that?"

I sniffled into the sleeve of my robe and blinked back some tears. "I don't know, Dave. I really thought we made a good pair. I guess there were signs, and maybe I missed them. Maybe I was just projecting that our relationship was progressing."

Dave gave me an awkward pat on the head, and offered, "You know what you need?"

"Some Kleenex?"

He smiled. "That, and a vacation. Sometimes getting the hell outta Dodge helps give you some perspective."

"Funny you should say that," I said. "My friend Ellie's getting married in ten days, and she's invited me to Colorado to take my mind off things."

"So go."

"It's more complicated than just up and going," I said.

"How ya figure?"

"I have clients who have waited weeks for an appointment. I can't cancel on them."

"Reschedule them, or arrange for phone readings. My sister's been going on and on about how good you are over the phone." Dave's sister, Annie, lived in Texas and was married to some rich oil tycoon. I'd given her a phone reading two weeks earlier. The difference between the siblings had given me a whole new perspective on Dave.

"Then there's Eggy. I can't simply dump some dog food in a bowl and leave him." At the mention of his name, my pooch came over and put his front paws on my knees, nudging my hand with his nose. I bent down and picked him up, cradling him in my arms.

"I can cover you with that," Dave offered. "My old lady's grown fond of him and it wouldn't be any trouble. He's a good little guy."

I scowled at him. He was making this way too easy. "I don't know. I just don't think it's a great time to go away right now."

Dave sat back in the chair for a moment and studied me. "You're thinking Dutch may change his mind and come knocking, and what if you're not around, am I right?"

I avoided his eyes and buried my face into Eggy's fur. "Yeah. Something like that," I mumbled after a minute.

"If Dutch wants to get a hold of you, he's got your number, Abby. The more you sit around here and wait for that phone to ring, the more depressed you're gonna get when it doesn't. I'm with your friend Ellie. Get the hell outta here. Go to Colorado and get your head on straight."

I looked up into Dave's gray-blue eyes for a long moment, wavering. Finally, I nodded and said, "Yeah, okay."

"Good girl. Let me know when you want me to pick up the munchkin and I'll come back over. In the meantime, chin up, kiddo."

I saw Dave out and laid my head against the door, depression thick and heavy all around me. Getting dumped was always such a struggle for me. It was an ancient war wound. I'd been rejected by my parents as a child, so every time I was faced with this particular karmic issue I had to fight that "what's wrong with me?" battle all over again. Maybe Dave and Ellie were right. Maybe what I needed was a big fat distraction until I had a little distance; then I could face the music that Dutch and I were finished.

Anyway, I'd be helping out a friend. Ellie had actually called me a month or two earlier, when she was planning her wedding, and asked me if I'd like to be one of her bridesmaids. I'd been flattered, but I'd politely declined, since I wanted to bring Dutch and show him off, and I felt he would feel uncomfortable if I were seated with the wedding party and he was stuck next to someone's aunt Gertrude.

Besides, Ellie had always been there when I needed her most. When it had become clear that my parents wanted nothing to do with me, I'd found comfort and solace in her friendship. And even more than that, Ellie's whole family had taken me in as a sort of surrogate daughter. Yes, going to Colorado might be just what the doctor ordered.

With new determination, I stepped away from the door and walked into my study, flipped on the computer and logged on to a discount travel Web site. As I searched the cheapest fares, I felt my intuition buzzing in the background of my thoughts. I didn't answer the buzz. I didn't want to hear from my crew right now; I simply wanted to get away. If only I'd listened, I might have avoided the whole death thing in the first place.

Chapter Three

"Ladies and gentlemen, we will be docking at gate six-A momentarily. Current temperature at Denver International Airport is an unseasonably balmy fifty-six degrees, and the time is five P.M. Please remain seated until the airplane has come to a complete stop at the gate. However, it is now safe to use your cell phones and other electronic devices. As always, we appreciate your choosing to fly the friendly skies with American Airlines, and hope you'll fly with us again real soon."

I closed the magazine I'd been flipping through and pulled out my carry-on bag from underneath the seat in front of me. Sifting through it, I pulled out my new cell phone, flipped it open and pressed the ON switch. I watched the display light up with a map marked with a small red star, designating my exact location. I clicked a button, which made the map disappear, and looked for the little envelope to appear in the right-hand corner. *Crap.* I had no new messages.

I frowned and closed the lid. Dutch hadn't called. Not that I really expected him to. It was just that I was trying to hold on to this little speck of hope that we'd get back together. That speck was getting smaller by the minute, as it had now been three whole days without a word from the guy.

I shook my head, trying to focus on the positive, and stared out the window. It would be good to see Ellie again. It had been a long time for us, nearly three years. Just then the plane came to a stop and the internal lights clicked on. I moved out into the aisle to stand cramped there between the other passengers until the doors opened and we could exit.

A man to my right knocked against me as he pulled his bag from the overhead compartment. "Sorry," he said, his face blushing. "Tight quarters in here."

"No problem, and make sure you let your wife know that this move is only temporary. You'll be back home in no time."

The man smiled at me as he turned his head away, then whipped it back in my direction. "Excuse me, but *what* did you just say?"

"Hmm?" I asked, then realized that I'd just blurted out a bit of intuitive insight.

"What you just said, that bit about my moving. How did you know that?"

I smiled gamely at him as other people stared at us. The man's voice was a tad on the alarmed side. "It's okay," I reassured him. "I'm a professional psychic."

"I don't believe in psychics," he said warily.

"No problem," I said, putting up my hands in a surrendering motion and giving him my best Bo Peep smile. "Good luck in California, and tell your wife that she can find a nursing job anywhere. Oh, and don't worry about your daughter. She'll make new friends. Especially with her love for theatrics. California's the place to be if she wants to be an actress. And one last thing," I said, turning the volume up on my intuition. "Your house will be sold within the month. It's the family with the army connection. They love what you've done with the studio over the garage."

The man stood there staring at me for the longest

moment, his eyes large and round and his mouth hanging open stupidly as someone from behind me said, "Hey, can you move it forward? I gotta use the john."

Shaking himself out of his shocked state, the man turned and bolted off the plane. I allowed myself a small chuckle and followed at a slower pace. I made my way to baggage claim, where I spotted Ellie. I shouted her name as I crossed the terminal, and we crashed together, squeezing each other in a gigantic bear hug. "Ohmigod!" she said as she pulled back from me and held me at arm's length. "Look at how gorgeous you've gotten!"

The way she was looking me over made me laugh heartily for the first time in days. "Me? What about *you*?" Ellie had been a swan since childhood. Tall and elegant, she had gorgeous smooth skin a shade or two darker than mine, big brown eyes the shape and color of almonds, long blond hair and a smile that could light up any dark room.

She was one of those people you simply liked to stare at—just supremely pretty in a natural, earthy way. Her personality matched her good looks, and she always had a horde of friends, both male and female alike. She made everyone around her feel at ease, and she had a knack for remembering all of the small details that made you believe she was genuinely interested in you.

I had always told her that someday, when I grew up, I wanted to be just like her, and seeing her now only reinforced that idea. "God, you look good!"

"It's Eddie," she said, her brilliant smile lighting up with extra wattage. "He's responsible."

"Does he come in a bottle?" I asked as she took my arm and led me over to the baggage carousel.

"Better," she said with a mischievous grin. "He comes in a snack size, and I'm always hungry, if you catch my drift."

I giggled. "Still the same unfiltered Ellie, I see."

"Still the same blushing Abby, I see."

"Some things never change."

"Some things should! Now, let's get your bag and blow this Popsicle stand."

We waited by the carousel for about fifteen minutes before bags from my plane began making their slow turn around the line. I kept my eyes peeled for the big blue suitcase I'd packed full enough to pop the zipper. "There it is," I said, finally seeing it tumble down the chute.

"Hey, Abs?"

"Yeah?" I said, as I moved in closer to the conveyor belt.

"I don't want to alarm you, but there's a guy over there who won't stop giving you the evil eye." I looked up from the belt to where Ellie was staring and caught sight of the guy from the plane whom I'd freaked out. When our eyes met he glared at me for several seconds before disappearing into the crowd. "Yikes," Ellie said as he turned away. "What the hell did you do to him?"

"Introduced him to my crew," I said as I pulled my bag from the carousel.

"Ah," Ellie said. "I'm thinking he didn't much care for their opinion?"

"Not so much their opinion as their very existence," I replied with a smile. "I think, however, I might just have given him some good food for thought. You ready?"

"This way," she said, and we headed out of the terminal.

A short walk later we stopped in front of her shiny brand-new Lexus SC 430 and I whistled low in appreciation. "Biotech sales must be up lately," I said as Ellie opened the trunk.

"I did pretty good this year," Ellie said, rubbing her palm along the back quarter panel.

"I'll bet," I said as we got into the car. "You still drive like a crazy person?"

"Is there any other way to drive?" she asked with a grin as she zipped out of the parking space.

I said a few prayers as we took corners at alarming speed before coming to an abrupt stop behind a few cars in line to pay the garage attendant. "So, about where to put you," Ellie began while I took deep, calming breaths. "You could stay at my condo, but Eddie's sister is flying in from Utah and she's got the guest bedroom. That leaves a blow-up bed in the living room, which would be okay for a night or two, but not for a week. So I was thinking you could stay at Aunt Viv's."

"She's still alive?" I asked in surprise. Ellie's aunt Vivian was actually her great-aunt on her father's side, who had lived on the North Carolina coastline for as many years as I could remember. During the summers Vivian would come and stay with Ellie's parents, driving her mother crazy and treating her father like the little boy she had raised after his parents were both killed when he was six. One spring, before Viv's annual visit to Michigan, Ellie and I had been invited to her house for a week. I still remember the glorious old home placed scenically on a bluff that had withstood so many hurricanes and tropical storms. She lived in a gigantic old Victorian on top of a cliff, and the view from nearly every window was spectacular. A half dozen years ago, Viv had moved to Colorado, her old home finally too much for her to keep up with.

"Yeah, she's still going strong. You'd never know how old she is by her energy level; that woman is as spry as a someone half her age! And in case you thought she'd softened in her old age, let me assure you she's as mean as ever, but I figure you can take her," Ellie said, cutting me a sideways wink.

I chuckled. What I remembered of Vivian was that she had never felt restricted by the rules of polite society. If she had an opinion about anything, she certainly wasn't afraid to share it. I had always liked the old woman, so I was willing to give the sleeping arrangements a try. "Okay, I'm not a big fan of blow-up mattresses anyway."

"Cool. How about we go to my place and grab some grub first? After that we'll hike on over to Viv's and get you settled, okay?" Ellie said as she gave her ticket and some money to the attendant.

"Sounds like a plan—Ohmigod Ellie! Friggin' slow down!" I exclaimed as she squealed out of the garage and zoomed down the ramp toward the freeway.

"Relax, Abby. It's not like I'm gonna kill us," she said, and the moment she said that I got the worst feeling. I shivered, then cinched my seat belt even tighter and held on to the dashboard for dear life.

We arrived at Ellie's condo thirty minutes and about fifteen more shrieks from me later. I jumped out of her car almost before it had come to a complete stop and bent over to touch terra firma. "Safe ground!" I said.

"Drama queen," Ellie said with a hearty laugh as she got out on her side.

"*Who* taught you how to drive?" I demanded as I stood back up.

"My brother. Why?"

"I'm going to hunt him down and shoot him! Ellie, is your car registered as a lethal weapon?"

Just then I heard Ellie's front door open and a male voice said, "Is that little Abby Cooper?"

I turned and my jaw dropped. Ellie's older and astonishingly gorgeous brother Duffy stood on her front porch with a huge grin and his arms full of beer. "Yeah," Ellie said as she pulled my bag from her trunk. "And she's talking about shooting you."

"Already? Gee, that was quick. Even for me," he said, his grin widening as he handed off the beer to someone behind him and came marching down the steps.

As he closed in I regained my composure—a little—and smoothed out my hair. I'd known Duffy since before I could remember, and I'd had a crush on him for equally long. When I had visited here three years earlier, Duffy had been away on an oil rig in Kuwait, making oodles of cash and dodging bullets as he worked to restore the oil flow to a country ravaged by Saddam Hussein. I hadn't seen him since I was seventeen and hc was twenty-one, and I never remembered him looking *this* good. "Hey, Duff," I said as he wrapped me in his arms and gave me a squeeze that made breathing difficult.

"Abster!" he exclaimed as he hugged me. "Jesus, what's it been—fifteen years?"

"Give or take," I said when he set me down and I had a chance to look him over. Duffy McGinnis was in the neighborhood of six feet with thick gorgeous brown hair that had a hint of curl at the ends. His eyes were dark brown and, like his sister, his skin was olive toned. He had ridiculously broad shoulders and an itty-bitty waist with, from what I remembered, one of the best asses ever to fill out a pair of Levi's. His build was much thicker than I remembered, and his sweater bulged in all the right places. "You been workin' out?" I asked, reaching up to squeeze a bicep.

Duffy flexed and gave Ellie a wink. "See?" he said to her. "Women like muscles."

"Do *not* encourage him, Abby. He spends way too much time in the gym as it is."

"She's only mad 'cause I'm draggin' Eddie with me," he said as he put his big arm across my shoulders and took my bag away from Ellie. "Come on, gals, we got a whole roomful of people dyin' to meet the psychic."

I gave Ellie a sideways glance. "El . . ." I moaned.

"I may have let it slip to a few of my friends, but I swear if anyone bothers you I will personally set them straight."

I was always a little apprehensive to meet people in a social situation who knew what I did for a living. What can I say? A lifetime of being seen as "different," and subsequently ostracized, had me slightly sensitive.

Ellie and her family, in fact, were just about the only people who had never made much fuss about my abilities. Ellie's mother, Nina, had sat me down when I was seven for a heart-to-heart talk. "Abby," she'd said, "you know not many people can appreciate it when someone like you comes into the mix. But I want you to know that we understand how special, bright and gifted you are. If you ever want to come over and hear how much we love you and your gifts, you just knock on my door. Okay?"

I never forgot Mrs. McGinnis's kindness, or the warmth that the entire family always had for me.

Duffy walked me up the front stairs and into Ellie's condo, setting my bag by the stairs, and, turning with me still in the crook of his arm, he announced to an entire roomful of strangers, "Hey, everyone, this is Abby Cooper. Abby, this is everyone."

I gulped and waved shyly to all the pairs of eyes on me, and everyone in the room waved back.

"Come on, Abby," Ellie said. "I'll introduce you around. Duff, we'll be ready to eat anytime the burgers are done."

"Give me ten more minutes, El," Duffy said as he let go of me and headed out toward the back of the condo.

"Duffy looks good," I said casually as Ellie took my hand and began to lead me into her living room.

"Yes, and he's single again," she said with a sideways glance.

"What happened to Rachel?"

"Dumped him, just like you said she would in that reading you gave me a year ago."

"Oh, yeah! I remember a little bit of that reading. Wow, I know you said he was really into her. What happened?"

"Do you remember telling me that something to do with travel was going to come between Duffy and his girlfriend?" I didn't, but for the sake of argument I nodded my head. "She cheated on him with a pilot," Ellie said.

"Get out!" I said, surprised at the connection.

"It was awful, Abby. She and Duffy were living together at the time, and we think he was even working up the nerve to pop the question."

"How'd he find out?"

"My mother saw Rachel and some guy in a pilot's uniform doing the lip-lock at a restaurant and told Duffy. He had Rachel's stuff moved out onto the lawn by the time she got home."

"He always was a man of action," I said, looking through the kitchen to the outside, where Duff stood with a group of guys around a grill.

"Did you know he's a sheriff now?"

"What? Getting shot at in Kuwait wasn't high-risk enough for him?"

Ellie chuckled. "I know. I swear he's going to give Mom a heart attack one of these days."

"Where is your mom?" I asked, looking around the room.

"She and Daddy are at the club. They wanted to have breakfast with us in the morning. Mom especially can't wait to see you."

I smiled and was about to comment when someone next to me said, "Well, don't hog her, Ellie! Let everyone else get a chance to say hello."

I turned and looked at a very pretty redhead a little taller than Ellie offering a plate of hors d'oeuvres to me. "Hello," I said, taking the plate. "Are these for me?"

"Yes, Ellie made them, and they're delicious. I'm Sara, one of the bridesmaids. I hear you've come to save the day so that we don't have an extra groomsman."

"And thank God for that!" Ellie exclaimed. "I swear, when I catch up with Gina I am going to wring her skinny little neck!"

"What's the scoop with Gina, anyway?" I asked.

"She took off after her ex-boyfriend," Sara said.

"So out of character for her too. And even though I'm pissed that she chose this time to do it, I'm secretly proud of her, because this isn't something Gina would normally do," Ellie commented.

"Gina's boyfriend moved to California about two months ago," Sara explained. "He asked her to go, but she said no. Gina's sort of into her career right now. Anyhoo, he sends her flowers for a couple of weeks, calls her on the phone a bunch and keeps asking her to quit her job already and come out there. Then one day the flowers stop coming and the phone calls dwindle to nothing, and Gina decides she can't live without him. So Kelly—uh, that's Kelly over there," Sara said, pointing to a petite brunette by the fireplace, "gets this call late at night last week and it's Gina. She's boarding a plane and headed to California, and she's not sure when or even *if* she'll be back."

"Wow," I said. "That does take guts. I hope they end up working it out."

"Still, it would have been nice if she'd waited until after the wedding," Ellie said. "She's one of my best friends, and I can't believe she's going to miss my big day."

"She'll be there in spirit, honey," Sara said, and something about the way she said it sent big alarm bells clanging through my head.

I turned my head slightly to try to focus on the message coming in through my intuition, but just then Duffy announced from the back porch, "Dinner's ready!" and Ellie grabbed my hand. "Come on, Abby. You can sit next to me. Eddie won't be here until late—his shift doesn't end till nine, and I'll be lonely. You can keep me company."

"Cool," I said as we headed over to the sliding glass door. "We're eating outside?" I asked, seeing a huge picnic table out back with table settings and dishes.

"Don't worry; it's still pretty warm out, and we have

a couple of heaters placed around the picnic table. Trust me, with your coat on you won't be cold."

Luckily, Ellie was right, and after everyone was seated she introduced me around the table. I nodded to every new face, concentrating on committing their names to memory. There were only three other bridesmaids besides myself, and with relief I noticed that they had easy names: Kelly, Sara and Christina, each smiling at me as Ellie said her name.

After the introductions were made, we all piled our plates with food and listened to Duffy, who was sitting on the other side of me while he entertained everyone with wild stories about our childhood. He talked about things I'd completely forgotten about, like my getting stuck on the roof after Duff had dared me to climb out a window and then locked it behind me the moment I turned around. Or the time he fell out of the tree house in a neighbor's yard and broke his arm. He made a point to let everyone know that "little Abby Cooper was the one who ran and got my mom—even though Abby hadn't been anywhere near me when I fell. She had no way of knowing that I'd broken my arm, but she was the first one to raise the alarm."

He was right. I remembered being three houses down in Brittany Johns's basement playing a game of *Sorry!* with her and Ellie when I'd suddenly bolted to my feet and announced, "Ellie! Your brother's hurt!" It was shortly after that incident, in fact, that Mrs. McGinnis had given me the speech about being special.

After dinner we all helped with the plates and dishes, and Ellie got busy in the kitchen putting the finishing touches on dessert. I had a chance then to take a little tour of her condo, which I remembered she and Eddie had purchased the year before.

I wandered to the stairs and looked up the hallway. A gallery of framed photographs lined most of the entire wall leading to the upstairs. I found myself taking a slow tour up the steps looking at the photos of

Ellie, Duff, her parents and all of Ellie's friends. There were a few of the two of us when we were little, and this made me smile.

About three-quarters of the way up the stairs I paused at a photo of Ellie and another beautiful blonde. The photo seemed recent—it captured Ellie's current hairstyle, and it caught me off guard because the image of the woman in the photo next to Ellie appeared flat and one-dimensional. That's my way of knowing someone has crossed over. Whenever I see a photo of someone who has died, they appear almost flat next to others who are still alive. I searched the other photos and found the same woman in one with Ellie and a group of friends on a ski trip that I'd heard about. If I remembered correctly, the photo was taken just this past Christmas.

I scanned my memory banks. Ellie and I talked on the phone about once every few months and e-mailed each other at least once every couple of weeks. I couldn't remember her talking about having a girlfriend pass away.

"There you are," I heard from the bottom of the stairs.

I turned and smiled at Duffy.

"Ellie's almost ready with the dessert. You want some?"

"Sure. Hey, Duff?" I said, turning back toward the picture.

"Yeah?" he said, coming up a few stairs.

"Who's this friend of Ellie's who died?"

Duffy cocked his head and gave me a funny look, then looked to where I pointed and said, "Aw, that's Gina, our runaway bridesmaid. Did someone tell you she died? 'Cause I'm sure Ellie's gonna kill her when she gets back into town for missing the big event."

I sucked in a breath. "*This* is Gina?" I asked in a hushed voice.

"Yeah. Cute, isn't she?"

I sat down on the stair and stared up at the photo,

willing the image to change, to grow in thickness and take on the same vibrancy of the other images in the photo. "Oh, God . . ." I said.

"Abby, you okay?" Duffy said, coming the rest of the way up the stairs and squatting down in front of me, a concerned look on his face.

"Duff . . ." I said, my eyes pleading. "Oh, God, Duff . . ."

"Abby, talk to me," he said, stroking my arm. "Tell me what's going on."

"It's Gina . . . she's not . . . she's . . ."

"Hey, guys!" Ellie said from the bottom of the stairs. "Come on, dessert's on the . . . Abby? Are you okay?"

"I'm fine," I said quickly. "I think it's just the altitude or something. Maybe I just need some air. Duffy, will you help me outside?"

"Sure," Duffy said, locking eyes with me. "Ellie, don't wait for us. We'll be there in a few minutes."

"Can I do anything?" Ellie said as we came down the stairs, me leaning on Duffy and looking anywhere but at her.

"No," I said as we got to the landing. "Really, I just need some air."

Duffy and I got outside and I took some shaky steps down the driveway. As we walked he held my arm as I took deep breaths, trying not to hyperventilate. When we got to the road I sat down and put my hands to my face. "Abster, come on, girl. Talk to me," Duffy said, hunkering down next to me.

"I have this talent," I said through my fingers.

"You're psychic," he offered when I paused.

I raised my head. "Yes, but it's more than that. I can look at a photo and know when someone is dead. And when I look at Gina's photo . . ."

"She's dead?" Duffy asked me, his face registering real alarm.

I nodded, "Yes. I'm sorry but it's the same for every

photo she's in. I know it sounds crazy, but Duff, I just know she's gone."

"Jesus." He rubbed his fingers through his hair, then looked toward the house. "Ellie's gonna come apart. She and Gina were tight."

"Listen," I said, grabbing his arm. "You can't tell her until we're sure. We need to check with her boyfriend. Maybe there was a car accident in California or something and we just haven't heard about it yet."

"Is that what you're getting?"

"I haven't even tuned in on it beyond the fact that she's dead. Let's check with her boyfriend and get some answers, okay?"

Duffy looked at me with such intenseness that I felt a moment of supreme self-consciousness. "You're sure?" he finally asked me.

"Am I sure about waiting to tell Ellie or that Gina's dead?"

"Both."

I sighed heavily. "In my gut I know Gina's dead. But on the off chance that the altitude is throwing off my antennae, I think we should wait until we've had a chance to confirm it before we say anything. I mean, this is Ellie's wedding week, after all."

"Christ," he said, and squeezed my hand. "Okay. Come on. I'm gonna take you to Viv's tonight myself. If Ellie sees you right now she'll know something's up." He stood up, taking me with him. We began walking toward a shiny red Mustang when a light cut through the darkness in the driveway. We both stopped as a car pulled in and parked behind Ellie's.

A tall, good-looking man got out and waved to Duffy. "Hey, stranger, is the party over?"

Duffy squeezed my hand and gave me a quick glance that said, "Hang in there," as he answered. "Hey, Eddie. Nope, the party's still goin'. You're just in time for dessert—I think Ellie made her famous peach cobbler."

"My favorite," Eddie said as he came over to us. "Hi," he said to me as he extended his hand. "You must be Abby. Ellie and Duff have told me all about you."

"Nice to meet you, Eddie." I shook his hand and did my best not to look shaken.

"You two coming in?" he asked as he turned toward the door.

"Uh, Abby's not feeling so good, so I'm going to get her to Viv's for the night."

"You want me to take a look at her?" Eddie asked, swiveling back. It was then that I took in his surgical scrubs and remembered that he was a surgical resident at the hospital.

"No!" I said, then immediately offered, "I think I'm just really tired."

"Uh . . . okay," Eddie said, slightly startled by my initial reaction. "Listen, I'll tell Ellie that you guys are headed off to Viv's."

"While I get her settled in the car, would you mind bringing out her bag from near the stairs?" Duffy asked as he wheeled me to the passenger-side door.

A few minutes later we were safely away from Ellie's, and I turned to him and said, "I forgot how kind you could be."

"Say what?" Duffy asked as he looked sideways at me.

"Kind. I remember one summer afternoon when Chris Newburgh pushed me down and I skinned my knees, and you came running and beat him to a pulp. Then you picked me up and carried me home and put Bactine and a Band-Aid on each knee."

"You always were a skinny little kid. You hardly weighed more than my cat," Duffy said with a grin.

"So what's the plan?" I said, changing the subject again.

"I met Gina's boyfriend a couple of times. His name is Mark Weaver, and I know he went to work for Microsoft. I'll run a search tomorrow, see if I can't track him down, and ask him if something's happened to Gina . . . that is, as long as nothing's happened to him too."

I nodded soberly and said, "I hadn't considered that maybe they've both been involved in something terrible."

"I can start with him and see where that leads. Gina's parents live somewhere in Europe—Switzerland, I think—so finding them could be a little tricky. But if we can't track Mark down, then we'll need to figure out how we can get her parents' whereabouts from Ellie without causing too much panic, just to see if maybe they've heard from their daughter in the past few days."

"Do you know the last time Ellie heard from Gina?"

"The day before she took off to California, which was last Tuesday. Ellie's been calling her every day and leaving messages, but Gina hasn't returned her calls. From what I know about Gina, that's not atypical. She's known for not returning calls. Kind of into herself."

I sighed heavily and sat back in my seat, thinking that sometimes it just sucked being psychic. I was always the first to get the bad news. The first to know that something wasn't going to turn out well. Granted, I got the good news too, but still, every once in a while it would be nice to be surprised like everyone else.

"Here we are," Duffy said, shaking me from my thoughts as we pulled into the circular driveway of a lovely Tudor-style home. "And I see Aunt Viv's let the birds out," he added, indicating a flock of six pink plastic flamingos on Vivian's front lawn, all posing with one leg curled up under their bodies.

"Tropical," I said as we came to a stop and opened the door.

"Stone-cold crazy is more like it," Duffy mumbled just as the front door opened and a small, bent figure hovered in the doorway.

"Is that you, Duffy?" came a warbling voice.

"Hi, Viv," Duffy called back as he went round to the trunk and extracted my bag. "I brought little Abby Cooper over," he said, giving me a wink.

Vivian squinted in my direction, "She's hardly *little* anymore, Duffy. Perhaps you need an eye test."

I hid the urge to smile as I headed up the walkway. "So good to see you again, Vivian. How've you been?"

She smiled at me and said, "Well enough. Although my grand-nephew thinks I'm off my nutty," she added, looking reproachfully at Duffy.

"Aww, Viv, you're giving yourself too much credit," he joked.

"And you need a haircut," she said, poking him good-naturedly in the ribs. "Are you staying?" she asked when he'd set my bag down in the front hall.

"Wish I could, but that would only give you an opportunity to nag at me about living the good life of a bachelor, so I'm gonna have to take a rain check."

"You're too old to be single," Viv chastised, undaunted by Duffy's sarcasm.

"I appreciate the expert advice on things too old," Duffy said, and I let out a giggle in spite of myself.

"Don't encourage him," Viv said, rounding on me.

"Sorry," I said, and cleared my throat.

"What about that nice girl you were dating; what was her name?"

"Time to go," Duffy said, and bent to kiss his great-aunt.

"You wait too long and your swimmers won't be able to paddle water," Vivian said as she swatted him on the bottom. "Then what will you do? No one's going to want to marry a man who can't get his swimmers to paddle water. Women want men who can hang in the deep end, you know."

"Good luck," Duffy said, and gave my cheek a kiss; then he turned and without a backward glance headed to his car.

Vivian closed the door as he backed out of the

driveway, and gave an irritated growl. "That one will never learn. Now let's have a look at you," she said, pulling herself up as much as her small, bent frame would allow.

In spite of myself, I stood up straighter under her scrutiny. "How do I look?" I asked.

"Like hell. What's happened?"

My shoulders slumped. "You name it," I said without elaborating.

"Man trouble," Viv said, her head nodding in her own affirmation. "I'd recommend Duffy but I *know* him, and I *like* you," she said, giving me a wink.

I chuckled. "Same old Viv."

Waving me into the living room, she asked, "You still got the sight?"

"Last time I checked," I said, pulling my suitcase behind me.

"Good for you. We always knew you were special. Now, there are two rooms for you to pick from. My bedroom's that way, but I gotta be honest; I'm a hell of a snorer. You'd probably get more sleep in the bedroom at the other end of the house."

"Anywhere you'd like to put me would be fine," I said as I took a gander at her furnishings and tried not to gape. Viv's living room was jam-packed with furniture. It was like a two-pound box stuffed with five pounds' worth of things.

"I've had to trim down lately," Viv said, indicating the living room. "Just got rid of all sorts of crap. You into that feng shui? I'm trying to get this place more in line with some good energy flow. See that?" She pointed to a very narrow path that wound around the couches, chairs and tables squished together within the room. "That's my energy river. See how it twists and turns around the furniture? That's how you get good chi."

"Ah," I said, desperately trying to hold in a chuckle. The room was an energy disaster, but hell if I was going to be the one to point it out to her.

"Yeah, I read a book on it. Well, not the whole book. Maybe just one chapter, but I think I got the hang of it. Anyway, your room is down this way." She headed out of the living room and down a corridor.

We stopped at the end of the hall just off the laundry room, and Viv opened the door. "Here we are. You should be comfortable in here."

I looked over her head at the room with slight trepidation. There was no telling what Viv had done with the excess furniture from her living room. I was pleasantly surprised to find that the room contained only a double bed, two nightstands, a bookshelf, an armoire and a dresser. Every wall was occupied with something up against it, but if I was careful I could probably navigate the room in the dark without stubbing my toe more than once or twice. "This is great, thanks, Viv."

"I wake early," she said in answer as she turned to head back down the hall. "Bathroom's off the kitchen down this way if you need it."

I smiled at her back, shaking my head, and only hoped I was half as eccentric when I reached my golden years. With a sigh I pulled my luggage into the room and began to unpack. After I'd hung the clothes that didn't look too wrinkled, I grabbed my cell phone out of my purse and stared at the readout. No calls. I scowled, then punched in a number and waited while it rang.

"Hello?" my sister, Cat, said.

"Hey, it's me," I said.

"Hey, me," Cat chuckled. "You made it to Denver safe and sound?"

"Yeah. What day are you and Tommy coming in again?"

"Tuesday. Ellie said I could bring the boys as well."

"That's great. I miss them, and I'd love to see them." There was a pause on Cat's end of the line, and for a moment I thought I'd lost her. "Cat? You still there?"

"Yes. Uh, Abby, there's something that I need to tell you, but I don't want you to get mad at me."

Uh oh. Sentences that started out that way never ended well, especially where Cat was concerned. "I'm sufficiently braced. What did you do?"

I heard Cat take a big breath and say, "I may have let it slip to Claire and Sam that Ellie was getting married this week."

"You what?!" Claire and Sam were my parents . . . at least biologically speaking. We'd had a rather contentious relationship from the get-go, and things hadn't improved with age. If they knew that Ellie was getting married, they'd find some way to crash the party.

"Abby, I had to!" Cat insisted. "They've been living in my guesthouse for two months and they've been sucking me dry! I've *got* to get them out of here!"

I pulled the phone away from my ear and rubbed my face with my hand in frustration. After I'd counted to ten I lifted the phone back to my ear and said, "Catherine Cooper-Masters I am so annoyed with you I could thump you on the head! You know they've probably already booked a flight! They'll be out here in, like, a day!"

"More like two," she said timidly.

"I'm gonna kill you," I said.

"Abby, there was no other way! I had to get them on a plane. And this way, once the wedding is over they can head back to South Carolina and I can get back to normal."

"How do you know they won't fly right back to Boston?" I demanded.

"Because I booked their flights. Again, it was the only way I could ensure that at the end of the trip they'd have a one-way ticket back to their house. And you know they're too cheap to pay for another ticket."

"I'm gonna kill you . . . *slow,* Catherine."

"Abby, come on! Be reasonable. . . ."

"Over and out," I snapped, and slammed the lid to

the cell phone closed. This was a disaster. The last time I'd been in close proximity to my parents, I'd actually considered taking up drinking as a recreational sport. They drove me crazy with their fake affection in public and their frosty demeanor in private. Just knowing they were going to be here brought up every disenfranchised feeling I'd had with them as a child. Cat knew better, and because she couldn't grow a backbone, I had to suffer. I groused on the bed for a while and finally got undressed, slipping into a T-shirt and shorts and getting under the covers. As exhausted as I was, sleep was a long time coming.

Chapter Four

"Abby-gabby! Abby-gabby, come to the phone!" I heard a woman's soft voice call me from my dreams. I knew that voice, and I knew that nickname, but my sleep-fogged brain was slow to make the connection. "Come on, Abigail, wake up and come to the phone!" she called again.

I fought my way up to full consciousness and opened one tired lid, looking around a room I didn't recognize. I sat up in bed with a start and tried to remember where I was. My eye lit on a photo across the room of Ellie and Duffy when they were little kids, and everything clicked into place . . . except the voice that had woken me. It sounded like it came from the hallway, and even though I knew it was impossible that the owner of the voice could be there, I got up to check anyway. I opened the door and nearly bumped into Vivian. "Oh!" I said with a start. "Morning, Viv."

"Phone's for you," she said, shoving the phone at me.

"Thanks. Were you the one calling me to come to the phone?" I asked wondering how on earth she knew the special nickname only my deceased grandmother had used for me.

"No. I answered it in the kitchen and brought the

phone down the hallway. I was about to knock when you pulled the door open."

"You sure you didn't call me?" I asked again, convinced I'd heard my name being called from the hall.

"Positive. Now don't be rude, girl; talk to Ellie." She thrust the phone at me and trotted off down the hall.

I blushed and put the phone to my ear as I turned back into my room. "Morning, El."

"Good morning, Abs. Is your stomach better this morning?"

"Huh?" I asked.

"Eddie said that Duffy took you to Viv's 'cause your stomach was upset. I hope it wasn't anything you ate."

"Oh, yeah, I'm fine," I said, remembering the night before. "I think it was just all the travel and stuff. So what's going on?"

"Well, Mom and Dad really want to see you, so I thought we'd have breakfast with them this morning. How about I pick you up in an hour and we can meet them at the club?"

"I'll be ready, Freddy."

Ellie chuckled. "And by the way, don't tell Viv that we're eating at the club. She'll want to come along, and the last time she ate with us she stole most of the food off the buffet table and swiped a couple sets of the silverware. Mom was so embarrassed."

"No sweat. See you in sixty."

I disconnected, grabbed some clothes and headed to the bathroom, where I took a luxuriously long shower and spent time curling my long hair. I emerged an hour later wearing an ankle-length chocolate suede skirt with an off-the-shoulder cream sweater loosely belted with a chocolate belt and matching suede boots. As I trotted back to my room for my purse, I caught sight of Viv dressed in her Sunday best, a huge handbag on her arm and her nose poking through the curtain as she kept a watch on the driveway.

"You headed out?" I asked casually.

"Yep. I figure Ellie's taking you to the club with her folks, and I don't want to miss a good spread. They have the best prime rib in town."

Uh-oh. "What makes you think we're going to the club?" I asked.

Viv pulled her nose out of the curtain and twisted her head in my direction. "Cut the crap, Abigail. I know damn well where you're headed, and I'm not gonna be left behind. Besides, I could use some silverware. Did you know they use real sterling flatware? I only managed to sneak two sets out the last time. I figure I need at least two more to round out my collection." Before I had a chance to protest we both heard gravel crunching. "There's our taxi!" Viv announced, and out the door she flew faster than I would have expected a ninety-one-year-old could move.

I darted into my bedroom, grabbed my coat and purse, then chased after Viv. When I got outside, Viv was tugging on the door handle of Ellie's car and shouting, "Eleanor McGinnis, you open this door!"

Ellie was inside the car, and through a small crack in the window I heard her shout, "Aunt Viv, please! I can't take you with me! There's no room!"

Viv stopped pulling on the handle long enough to peer through the glass at the teensy-weensy backseat of the Lexus. "I can fit back there!" she shouted, and started tugging on the handle again.

"Aunt Viv, be reasonable!" Ellie said, her voice an octave higher than normal. "Mom will *kill* me if I show up with you. Remember the last time?"

"Oh, please, like that snooty club would really cancel your parents' membership," Viv said. "I'll be good this time, I swear!" *Liar, liar . . . pants on fire . . .*

"Vivian," I said from behind her, catching her attention. "What if I promise to bring you back something from the buffet? Wouldn't you like a whole container of prime rib?"

"Don't you coddle me, Abigail!" she snapped. "I'm

going and that's that. Now you two can take me, or I'll call a cab and meet you there. But if you make me resort to that then I won't be on my best behavior."

Ellie and I looked at each other through the glass for a moment, weighing that option, when finally Ellie popped the lock and Vivian jumped in . . . to the front seat. When she was comfortably nestled in, she looked at me and then at the backseat as if to say, *You're not actually going to make a little old lady sit back there, are you?*

I rolled my eyes and asked, "Viv, can you at least move your seat up so I can squeeze into the back-seat?"

"I aim to please," she said dryly and pushed a button on the side of the seat sliding her forward with a soft humming sound.

"I am so sorry," Ellie said while I squished into the back.

"No problem," I said. "But just so you know, she guessed where we were going. I never breathed a word, I swear."

"I'm in the car, you know," Vivian said, pulling the door closed. "It's not like I can't hear you, sheesh!"

"Oh, we are *very* aware that you're with us," Ellie deadpanned, and gunned the motor. "Might want to buckle up, Viv. You know how I drive."

"Damn skippy. Let's see what this baby can do! Yee-ha!"

We arrived at the Valley Hill Country Club a mere fifteen minutes and six or seven *yee-ha*s later. As I unfolded my bent frame from the backseat I wondered if it was too early to order alcohol. "You okay?" Ellie said as we made our way inside.

"A little cramped but I'll be fine. So how bad is this going to be?" I asked, gesturing toward Vivian's back as she scrambled up the stairs, the clasp on her giant handbag already open.

"*Nightmare on Elm Street* bad," Ellie said with a groan. "Mom's gonna freak."

"Maybe Viv will behave herself," I offered, but as soon as I said that my left side felt thick and heavy—my sign for, *You can forget about it.*

"You two go ahead," Viv said over her shoulder. "I gotta hit the powder room. They have the best little soaps in there," she added as she pulled her purse open wide and darted through a doorway marked, LADIES.

"Say, Abby, I wanted to ask you something . . ." Ellie said as we crossed through the front lobby. "I know you must be tired and all, but I was wondering if later you might be up for giving me a reading?"

"Absolutely," I said without pause. One of the great pleasures about being psychic was offering it up as a gift to my close friends. It always made Christmas and birthdays easier.

"You are a doll," she said, beaming. "I just want to know that Eddie and I will be happy together. I mean, I know we will, but it'll be nice to have you tell me—Oh, look! There's Mom and Dad!"

While Ellie was talking about her life with Eddie, I got an incredibly loud buzzing sensation as my intuitive phone went haywire. I tried to focus on the message coming in, but was distracted by the sight of Ellie's parents. Figuring I could simply give her a reading later and pick up on what the message was, I pushed it aside and hurried forward to greet Nina and Jimmy McGinnis.

Nina opened her arms wide and I rushed in for a hug. I squeezed her tight, then stepped back to look her over. Nina was about the size of my sister, Cat, right around five-foot-nothing. She had a pleasant round plumpness to her, and a mischievous twinkle in her eye. A native of Iceland, she still spoke with an accent that made her *S*s a little longer and her *W*s like they had an *H* attached. She hadn't changed much from my childhood memories, just a few more white hairs where salt and pepper had once been, but for the most part she looked exactly the same. "Abigail," she said warmly. "It's so good to see you! Look at how beautiful you've gotten!"

"Right back at you, Nina," I said with a broad smile.

"Hey, don't forget about me," Jimmy said to my right as he threw out his own arms. I smiled playfully, then launched into his warm embrace, noting that he'd grown a bit thicker around his very tall frame, but for the most part he too still looked the same.

As I backed away from Jimmy I heard Nina give a gasp, then whisper, "Oh, God. Tell me you didn't bring *her*!"

Without turning around, Ellie knew who her mother was talking about and hurried to explain. "Mom, I tried, I really did, but she practically climbed on top of my car!"

I turned just as Viv reached us. "Hello, Nina. Jimmy," Viv said with a friendly wave. "What're you all standing around out here for? Let's eat!" And she shuffled toward the dining hall, the light scent of bath soap flowing from her purse.

"Ellie!" Nina hissed, trying to keep her voice down. It was no secret that Nina and Viv had never quite gotten along. The fact that for many years Vivian had lived with Nina and Jimmy over the summers was testament to her patience. The kicker was that *everyone* got along with Nina. She was loved by just about all who knew her. Her patience and motherly nature were legendary. But Viv was perhaps the one person in the world who could push her over the edge.

"Mom, really, I'm *sorry*!" Ellie tried.

"I'll keep my eye on her, Nina," Jimmy said as he hurried after his aunt.

Nina watched him go, then turned back to us. "Should we make a run for it?" she said. "Maybe find another place to have breakfast?" I laughed, but it sounded like Nina was halfway serious.

"You mean leave Dad *alone* with her? Mom, come on, we can't do that to him," Ellie said.

Nina heaved a great sigh. "Good point, honey. I suppose we might as well get this over with. Just be prepared to bolt if there's trouble."

We headed into the dining room and spotted Viv and Jimmy right away. Jimmy was carrying a plate for his aunt as she piled it with enough food to feed three people. He caught our eye and nodded his head to a table nearby, and we walked over and sat down. As I looked around the beautifully set table, I noticed one of the places was missing its silverware. A moment later a waiter stepped forward and filled our water glasses, then set an extra set of flatware down next to a cup of coffee. "For the madam at the buffet table who was missing her silverware," he said by way of explanation, then took our drink orders.

After he'd gone I said, "Viv's planning on stealing that flatware. She mentioned something about wanting a full set back at her house."

Nina groaned. "Oh, yes, Vivian never misses the opportunity to pinch a place setting or two. That woman is going to be the death of me. But I don't want to dwell on her. Abby, tell me all about your life, and don't leave anything out. Ellie says that your practice is booming, and I hear you've just bought a new house."

I caught Nina up to speed on my life of the past three years—leaving out the parts that involved crazed killers, mafia hit men and serial rapists . . . oh, and, of course, I left out the part about my recent breakup with Mr. Not-right-now-I-need-to-focus-on-my-job. I figured Nina had enough to worry about with Vivian at the table. Why distract her with so much bad news?

"Aunt *Viv,*" Jimmy said across the table, and we all turned to look.

"What?" she replied, pausing in folding up three huge slices of prime rib into her linen napkin.

"Can I at least get you a to-go box?" he said.

"Hell, no!" Viv replied as she wadded up the meat

and stuffed it into her purse. "They take half your food when you give it to them to wrap up. This way I know I get what I pay for."

"So you're paying today?" Jimmy asked, narrowing his eyes.

"What's that?" Vivian said, cocking her head. "Sorry, Jimmy. Think my hearing's going. I'm headed back to the buffet line for some of that dessert. You coming?"

The question was more a command, and after a warning look from Nina, Jimmy obediently got up from the table to follow Viv.

"So guess who I heard from the day before yesterday!" Nina said, turning back to me.

"Who?" I asked.

"Your parents. Claire called me out of the blue. I haven't heard from her in ages. And of course I told her about Ellie's big day, and wouldn't you know, your parents would love to come!"

"Wow. How about that," I said woodenly. Nina had no idea how much my relationship with my parents had declined over the years.

"Yes, I believe they're flying in on Tuesday. It's been so long since I've seen them. How do they look?" she asked me.

"About the same," I said. Truth was, I hadn't seen them in years, so how could I know?

"It will be wonderful to have the old gang back again."

Ellie sneaked me a look that said, *Sorry!* and I nodded that it was okay. Just then her cell phone chirped and she dug it out of her purse to look at the readout. "Hey, big brother," she said. "Where are you? We're all here at the club." There was a pause; then Ellie said, "Yes, she's right here; hold on a sec," and handed me her phone.

I gave her a puzzled look and she shrugged her shoulders in an "I don't know" gesture, so I took the phone and said, "Hello, Duffy. What's up?"

"I found Mark Weaver," he said without preamble.

Working hard not to give anything away to Ellie and Nina, who were both watching me intently, I said, "Uh-huh. Did you get the answer you were looking for?"

"Not really. Listen, I'm gonna swing by there and pick you up. I may need your help on this."

"Uh . . . okay."

"But don't tell Ellie or my mom what's up yet, okay? Not till we know something for sure."

"Right. Okay, see you in a few," I said, and clicked off, wondering how I was going to explain my need to leave.

"Is Duffy coming?" Ellie asked.

"Yeah. He and I have an errand to run," I said, trying not to look nervous.

"Really?" Nina and Ellie both said together, their eyebrows raised.

"Yeah. Something for the wedding that Duffy needs some help on. But I can't tell you, because it's a surprise."

"Ahhhh . . ." both women said together again, and nodded to each other with little grins.

"So, I'd better eat while I can, 'cause I think he'll be here real soon," I said, getting up and heading over to the buffet line. On the way I caught sight of Viv and Jimmy by the dessert table, near a huge plate of sugar cookies. Vivian looked covertly around, then pulled Jimmy in by his suit coat and hid behind him. After a moment she stepped away, hugging her bulging handbag closely. Jimmy followed after her with a pained look on his face.

I was joined a moment later by Nina and Ellie, who were chatting about what still needed to be done before the wedding. "The caterer called this morning, Ellie," Nina said. "She said she's switched the spinach soufflés for the stuffed mushrooms, so Eddie will be happy."

"I'm about to marry the man and I never knew he had such an aversion to spinach." Ellie chuckled.

"Oh, don't worry, honey; there was plenty I didn't know about your father before I married him."

"Like what?" I asked, turning around to join in the conversation.

"Like the fact that he had an aunt Vivian," Nina said, a half scowl on her face. Turning to me she explained. "Jimmy and I met when he was a marine stationed in Iceland. We had a whirlwind courtship and eloped only three weeks after we met."

"Don't tell me; let me guess," I said. "He never got around to mentioning his eccentric aunt until you guys came stateside."

"Bingo," she said, and turned back to Ellie. "Trust me, if I had known about her before I said 'I do,' you'd have a different father, Ellie."

We all giggled, then Ellie smacked her forehead. "Oh! Abby, I almost forgot. We have to get you fitted for that bridesmaid dress. Gina never picked hers up from the bridal shop, so all we'll have to do is a few alterations. Shouldn't be anything too dramatic. You two are about the same size."

"Speaking of Gina," Nina said, "has anyone heard from her yet?"

I turned back to the buffet table, afraid the look on my face would give me away as Ellie said, "No. That superfreak hasn't returned one of my calls. Not that that's anything new. I don't even know why she carries a cell phone. She never answers it and she never returns a voice mail."

"At least Abby was able to take her place in the end. All's well that ends well," Nina said, and for some reason I felt a shiver go through me.

"You cold, Abby?" Ellie said, noticing.

"A little. I'm going to head back to the table. See you two in a minute." And I darted away.

I ate in earnest, anticipating Duffy's arrival, and it was a good thing I did, because just as I was polishing off some potatoes I felt a hand on my shoulder and a throaty voice said, "Hey, gang. What's shakin'?"

Everyone at the table looked up and gave Duffy a warm smile in greeting. Everyone, that is, except Vivian. "How're your swimmers?" she asked him.

"Still paddling," he said, looking her in the eye.

"Hmmph," she replied. "That won't last, you know."

"Viv," Duffy said in answer. "Is that your purse that's leaking?" And we all looked over at the puddle on the table forming by Vivian's handbag.

"Time to go," Jimmy said, standing up and hovering over Vivian's chair. "Nina, why don't you catch a ride back with Ellie while I make sure Viv gets home safe and sound?"

"Thank you, Jimmy," Nina replied gratefully.

"But I'm not finished yet!" Vivian protested when her chair was pulled out by her nephew. As she was tugged away from the table, she made a lunge for the salt and pepper shakers, and Jimmy had to wrestle them out of her bony hands. Not about to give up, she snatched an extra set of silverware before he had a chance to stop her, shoved them into her overstuffed purse, then held up her hands karate style. "Stand back!" she barked. "My hands are like weapons!"

"Easy, Viv. Let's get your coat and go," Jimmy said with gritted teeth. His face began to turn a pinkish hue.

"Fine," Viv said, pushing the contents of her purse down so she could get the clasp closed. "This party wasn't all that fun anyway. You people need to lighten up!"

After they'd left the table Nina sighed audibly. "Thank the Lord that's over. Duffy, are you going to stay for something to eat?"

"Sorry, Mom, can't. Abby and I have an errand to run."

"Well, stop by tonight for dinner, or are you working the afternoon shift again?"

"'Fraid so," Duffy said as he bent to give his mother a kiss on the cheek. "I'll call you tomorrow so you don't worry, okay?"

"And when will you have Abby back?" Ellie

wanted to know, the curiosity on her face evident as she looked from me to Duffy for any sign of a clue as to what we were up to.

"I'll need her for a little while. Why? You two have plans?"

"I have to take her to the bridal shop for a fitting. Can you have her back by one?"

"You got it," Duffy said, then leaned over and kissed her on the top of her head. "Call me if you need anything. Okay?" he said, his voice tender and his eyes pinched.

"Uh . . . sure," she said, looking at him with a puzzled expression. "Duff, you okay?"

"I'm cool," he said, regaining his composure. "Come on, Abby; let's roll."

I excused myself and followed after him. As we got outside, Duffy handed his valet ticket to one of the attendants and gave me a glance. Then he did a double take.

"What?" I asked feeling self-conscious.

"You clean up nice, you know that?" he said with a grin.

I felt my cheeks grow hot. "You giving me a line?" I asked him, narrowing my eyes.

"No," he said as his Mustang arrived. "No line. It's the truth. If I'da thought way back when that you would turn out to be a looker, I never would have picked on you so much."

"Good to know," I said with a grin as we got in the car. "So where are we headed?"

"To Gina's," he replied as he turned the ignition.

"What did Mark say?" I asked.

"He said the last time he heard from Gina was two nights before she disappeared. She never called to tell him she was on her way, and as far as he knew the last conversation they had was their last one for good. He said he told her that he'd met someone and was moving on. He doesn't know anything about her booking a flight to LA."

"*Did* she book a flight?" I asked.

Duffy nodded. "That was my next call. And yes, she did book a flight, but she never checked in and never boarded the plane."

"Something happened," I said.

"Sure looks that way."

"How about where Gina worked? Have you been able to talk to her boss, or someone who may have known what she was up to?"

"Not yet. But if we don't find anything at Gina's apartment, then that's the next place we'll go."

There was a pause as we drove in silence for a minute, and then I asked, "Duffy?"

"Yeah?"

"Why am I along? I mean, I'm flattered and all, but you're a trained cop. Shouldn't you be doing this alone?"

Duffy gave me a sideways glance and said, "Abby, come on. Ellie's told me all about how you worked with your local police department. Didn't you help nab that serial killer?"

"Yeah," I said, rubbing my arm subconsciously, remembering the stab wound from the serial killer I'd helped the police catch.

"And when we were kids, who helped Mrs. Tracer find her cat?"

"Oh, yeah," I said, smiling, "I remember that."

"And who helped the Robertsons find Collin?"

The Robertson family had lived on the opposite side of the McGinnises. Collin was the youngest member. One day he was playing hide-and-seek with a bunch of us kids from the neighborhood, and somewhere in the middle of the game he'd disappeared. Someone finally noticed that he was missing and had raised the alarm. While his frantic mother and other parents scoured the neighborhood, I'd suddenly had a vision of Collin in the Fishmans' attic, two doors down. I'd told Collin's mother what I'd seen and sure enough she found him exactly where I'd said he'd be. He must have sneaked into the house when no one was looking, made his way upstairs to the attic and fallen asleep on some old quilts.

"And your point is?" I asked.

"Hell, you're better than a bloodhound, Abs. If we have a prayer of finding Gina, something tells me your radar's gonna get it done."

"Gotcha," I said, a smile creeping onto my face.

A little while later we pulled into a rather sizeable apartment complex laid out in one big loop of large block buildings. We cruised around the place, finally locating the rental office on the opposite side of the complex.

After a brief explanation to the woman behind the desk at the rental office, and the flashing of Duffy's badge, we were given a key and directions to Gina's building. "Did you want to come with us?" Duffy asked the portly woman with carrot-red hair.

"No way. The last time you guys came through here looking for someone who hadn't shown up for work, I was the first person through the door and the first to see he'd blown his brains out. There's no way I'm going to repeat that nightmare. Just tell me what you find," she said, and turned back to her computer.

Duffy and I headed back into the car, drove the short distance to Gina's apartment and parked. Duffy didn't get out right away; instead, he turned to me and said, "You can stay here, you know. You don't have to come in."

"You think she might have killed herself?" I asked.

"It's possible. I mean, I really thought Gina had her act together, but hearing that someone you love has found someone else can be a pretty tough thing to handle."

I smiled at him. "Sounds like you're talking from experience."

"Yeah, anyway . . ." he said, looking at the key in his hand. "You want to stay here?"

"No. If she's not in there I might be able to get a bead on her energy. I'll just keep a safe distance until we know for sure."

"Okay then," Duffy said, and we got out of the car. We headed up to the second floor and Duffy knocked loudly on the door, his head bent, listening for any noise from inside. We waited a couple of beats and he tried knocking again. "Gina? It's Duffy. You in there?"

Nothing happened, so he inserted the key and opened the door. We walked into her apartment, and I'll admit I was a little apprehensive. It seemed such an invasion of privacy to enter someone's home uninvited.

Gina's apartment was laid out in a somewhat classic design. We entered into her living room, a small kitchen and dining area off to our left. Straight ahead at the end of a hallway we could see into a bedroom, and I could just make out a door off either side of the corridor, one for what must be a bathroom and the other for a possible second bedroom.

"Sit tight," Duffy said over his shoulder and moved through the living room. "Gina?" he called again. "Gina, it's Duffy. Are you here?"

I watched as he made his way down the hallway, only now noticing that he'd tucked his hand under his jacket. I assumed he had it resting on his holstered gun, and with a pang of remorse I remembered sharing a similar experience with another cop.

Duffy paused at the door to his left, then opened it slowly. He disappeared through the doorway, and a moment later I heard the sound of a shower curtain being pulled to the side. After a beat he appeared again. "Nothing there that shouldn't be," he said to me before opening the other door directly across from the bathroom. I waited as Duffy moved from room to room, peeking in closets and looking behind doors.

"She's not here," I said when he'd finished.

"Nope. And there's a big fat suitcase sitting in her

closet. If you were on your way to see your boyfriend, wouldn't you pack a big suitcase?"

"I would," I said, coming farther into the living room.

"Here," Duffy said, pulling a small frame off the wall in the hallway. "This is Gina and Mark. Take a look and tell me what you think."

I took the photo and closed my eyes for a moment, trying to gather my radar before aiming it at the photo. I'm not great with photos, other than being able to tell if someone's died, but I was going to do my best. When I opened my eyes I focused all of my concentration at the photo. I got a foggy image in my head, but nothing really clear. After a minute I said, "Hold on," and headed into Gina's bedroom. I looked around the room and toward her dresser. There, in a small dish, was a wristwatch. I walked over to pick it up when I noticed a blue box to one side with TIFFANY & CO. across the top. I almost opened the box, but decided the watch was the better way to go. Crossing my fingers, I walked over to it and picked it up, then went to the bed and sat down on it, holding the watch and the photo. I then stared at the picture as I held the watch tightly and focused, trying to get a bead on Gina's energy. After a moment I looked up at Duffy and said, "I'm sorry, but I'm definitely getting the feeling she's dead. I just don't get the same thread of energy off her that I do for a living person."

"Can you tell what happened to her?" Duffy asked, watching me closely.

I closed my eyes and focused, holding on to the watch and wrapping my energy around it. After a moment I physically flinched. "Ow!"

"What?" Duffy asked, alarmed.

"Something happened to her here," I said, making a circular motion over my chest with my hand. "Something that hurt . . . a lot."

"A car accident?"

"Maybe . . ." I concentrated on the sharp pain that

had punctured my energy three distinct times. "I feel this sharp stabbing pain here"—pointing to my right breast—"then here"—indicating my breastbone—"and here," I finished, pointing to my heart. "Bang, bang, bang," I said, and repeated pointing to the three places.

Duffy was looking alarmed as he asked, "Did you say 'bang'?"

I nodded back at him. "Yeah. Bang. But more like *boom*! I keep hearing this explosion in my mind."

"She was shot," Duffy said gravely.

"Yes," I agreed. "But who would shoot her?"

"Abby, can you see where she is? She obviously wasn't killed here. Where is her body?"

I scowled. I hated this stuff. Now that I knew Gina had been murdered, it made my job so much more distasteful. Murder carries an energy that is heavy and thick and feels intuitively like being covered in slime. Still, if Gina and I had reversed roles, I would hope that she would do everything she could to find out where I was and bring me back for a proper burial. Squaring my shoulders, I closed my eyes again and thought, *Come on, crew! Show me where she is!*

Almost immediately I saw the color green and the image of a star. I felt moisture, then intense heat while an acrid smell filled my nostrils. I waited, but nothing else appeared in my mind's eye, even though I was pushing my guides for more. Finally I opened my eyes and sighed heavily. I had no idea what these images meant. "Do you have a pad of paper?" I asked.

Duffy reached into his jacket, pulling out a small pad and a pen. I took it from him and began to scribble on it. I wrote down "green," followed by "star," then "wet," then "hot" and finally "ash." Next I let the pen hover over the pad of paper, waiting for a shape to form in my mind. When I had it I began to draw a rough sketch. I began with a box in the center of the paper and on this I wrote "green" and "star." Next I drew a line that ran along the bottom of the page. This I labeled "black" and "hard." Finally I drew a fan on the side of the box that I'd labeled "green" and I wrote "heat." I handed the drawing to Duffy and said, "I'm sorry. That's the best I can do."

Duffy looked at the drawing intently for long seconds before closing the notebook and tucking it away. "You ready to go?" he asked me.

I nodded and walked the picture back over to Gina's dresser, where I laid it down. I was about to set the watch back in its dish when I thought better of it and turned back to Duffy. "Can I keep this?" I asked. Duffy cocked his head, giving me a questioning look, and I realized how that must have sounded. "Not forever," I quickly explained. "It's just that I'm getting a little residual energy off it and I want it close in case I try to tune in again later."

"You pick up her energy by using her jewelry?"

"Yeah. It's called psychometry. The basic theory is that objects can retain some of the energy of people they come into contact with. Metal objects are especially good at providing a sort of imprint of the person who wore them. The more you wear something, the more it becomes imprinted with your energy. I'm feeling like Gina wore this a lot."

"So why leave it behind?" Duffy said, giving me a pointed look. "Before we go let's take a thorough check of the place and see what she took with her. I didn't see her car in the driveway, so I'm assuming she drove somewhere."

"Good plan. You check in the kitchen; I'll look around in here. I'm probably better at being able to tell what a girl would take on a trip."

Duffy nodded and disappeared into the hallway. I rummaged around in Gina's closet and dresser drawers and noticed what a neat and organized person she seemed to be. Everything within her drawers was neatly pressed and folded. It also seemed like the drawers themselves were packed full. There were no missing piles of clothing. I looked inside her closet and noticed it was just as orderly. There wasn't a group of extra hangers where clothing would have been taken and packed. Her hamper also appeared empty. My guess was that she had just done laundry. I stepped back into her room, and my attention was called to her bed. I walked over and pulled up one of the pillows. There was a nightshirt neatly folded behind it. I frowned and set the pillow back into place.

Next I walked into the bathroom and looked around. Gina's toothbrush was in the holder on the side of the sink along with her contact lens case. I unscrewed the cap on the case and noticed the outline of one lens. I unscrewed the other and saw the same. I fished around inside her medicine cabinet and found an empty eyeglass case.

Just then Duffy appeared in the doorway. "Find anything?" he asked me.

"Wherever she went she left in a hurry," I said, picking up the contact case. "It doesn't look like she packed any of her clothing, and she wasn't wearing her contacts. Since her eyeglass case is empty I'm guessing she was wearing her glasses when she walked out of here. Also, her hamper's empty."

"Yeah . . . ?" Duffy asked, probing me to explain the relevance.

"You do your laundry naked?" I asked.

"Not usually."

"Me either. Usually I'm wearing sweats, which go into the hamper when I'm finished with the laundry and ready for bed."

"Maybe she wore the sweats to bed," Duffy said.

"Nope. Her nightshirt's under the pillow."

"So she was wearing sweats, which means she wasn't dressed for work. Kelly told Ellie that Gina called her around eleven o'clock last Tuesday night and said she was off to California."

"Can you check Gina's phone records to get a sync on the time?" I asked.

"You sure you're not a cop?" Duffy asked me with a grin. " 'Cause you sure talk like a cop."

"You hang out with them long enough, they rub off on you," I said by way of explanation.

"That's right. Ellie said you were dating a cop. Is he coming to the wedding?"

I looked down at my boots and nervously twisted a strand of my hair. "Uh, no. That ship has actually sailed," I mumbled, a pang in my chest making me wince.

"So you're single?"

I sighed and said, "Yep. Looks that way."

"Good. Save a couple dances at the reception for me, okay?" he said, and chucked me under the chin.

I looked at him and let one of my eyebrows drift up. "I do believe you're flirting with me."

"Damn straight," he said, winking. "Come on. Let's see if we can find anything out from Gina's coworkers before I have to give you back to Ellie."

As I followed Duffy out of Gina's apartment I couldn't help but feel we had overlooked the obvious. Looking back I blame myself, because if I hadn't been so caught up in the increasing attraction I felt for Duffy, I might have allowed myself to focus on the one clue that could have tied this whole case together in time to save my own life. But hindsight is like that—always twenty-twenty. And believe me, it's even more sharply focused from heaven.

Chapter Five

Before we returned Gina's key to her landlord, Duffy knocked on both her neighbors' doors but got no response. He left his card wedged into the doorjambs with a request for them to call him.

Our next stop was a large business complex in downtown Denver. We parked in a giant parking lot and hoofed it into the building. Duffy found the listing for Gina's work and we took the elevator up to the fifth floor, where Denver Fidelity Investments was located.

A young receptionist with short brown hair and apple round cheeks greeted us with a "Good morning and welcome to Denver Fidelity. Did you have an appointment with one of our financial planners?"

Duffy whipped out his sheriff's badge and explained, "We'd like a moment with Gina Russell's manager."

The receptionist looked rather shocked when Duffy flashed his badge, but she quickly regained her composure, picking up the phone and dialing an extension. After a moment she said, "Mr. Lindstrom? There is an officer here to see you about Gina." After a pause she said, "No, I don't know what it's about. He's just asking to speak to you."

After replacing the receiver and giving us a tight smile, she said, "Mr. Lindstrom will be right with you. Please have a seat in our lobby."

We walked over to a comfortable seating area and had to wait only a few moments before a tall, skinny man with blond hair, beard and mustache appeared. He looked first to his receptionist, who gave a short nod in our direction, then briskly walked over to us, extending his hand.

"Good morning, I'm David Lindstrom. Gina's former supervisor."

"Good morning, sir," Duffy said, taking his hand and giving it a good pump. "I'm Sheriff McGinnis and this is an associate of mine, Abigail Cooper. May we talk somewhere in private?"

"Of course, of course," Lindstrom said, his mannerisms fidgety and nervous. "Come this way to my office. We can talk in private there."

We followed Lindstrom through a maze of cubicles and side offices before being shown into a nice-sized office with a window view of the nearby mountains. Gesturing to two chairs, Lindstrom took up his seat behind a large wooden desk. "How can I help you today, Sheriff McGinnis?" he asked.

Duffy leaned forward in his seat, making eye contact with Gina's supervisor. He'd clearly picked up on the same nervous energy coming from Lindstrom that I had. "Gina Russell is a friend of my family's and we have reason to believe she may be in trouble," Duffy began.

"What sort of trouble?" Lindstrom asked.

"We're not sure," Duffy answered. "We have some facts in front of us that do not fit her behavior, and we're hoping you can shed some light for us."

"What kind of facts?"

"We haven't found anyone who's seen or heard from Gina since last week," Duffy said.

Lindstrom nodded. "I knew something must have happened to her."

"What do you mean?" Duffy asked.

"Well, I got a voice mail from her about a week ago, and all she said was that she was quitting and not to bother sending her stuff. That we could just toss it out with the trash."

"What stuff?" I asked.

"The personal items she kept at her desk. Pictures, a radio, some thank-you cards from clients, her day calendar. The whole thing was so unlike her. She was my most reliable employee here at Fidelity, and for her to up and quit without explanation or notice or even cleaning out her desk was so against her character that I was very concerned with her sudden departure."

"Was the voice mail she left you stamped with a time?" Duffy asked.

Lindstrom nodded. "Yes, it came in about two in the morning. I remember, because I thought it was an odd time to receive a voice mail; then I listened to it and I figured she really wanted to make sure I wouldn't answer my phone. I tend to work late a lot."

"I see," Duffy said. "Do you still have the voice mail?"

"No," Lindstrom said, shaking his head. "I'm sorry, but I deleted it a few days later. I tried calling her, of course, at least to talk things over, but she never called me back."

"Did she give you any reason for her resignation?" Duffy said.

"No. The voice mail simply said that she wouldn't be here in the morning because she was quitting, and there was no need to pack up her desk; she didn't want anything here, and that was that."

Duffy nodded his head for a moment, never breaking eye contact with Lindstrom. His body language suggested that he was on the fence about whether or not to believe him, but my radar said that the man was telling the truth. Finally, Duffy said, "Do you know where Gina might have gone?"

"I have no idea," Lindstrom said.

"She mentioned something to a friend of hers about heading to California to be with her boyfriend," I suggested. "Did she ever talk to you about him?"

"No," Lindstrom said, looking at me. "Gina was very professional. She didn't bring her personal life to work, and frankly we never discussed it."

"Would she have confided in anyone else here?" I persisted.

Lindstrom squirmed uncomfortably, collecting his thoughts before answering. "She and Jeff Yeats used to have lunch together every once in a while. You may want to check with him."

"Is he in today?" Duffy asked, reaching inside his jacket for notepad and pen to write down the name Lindstrom had given him.

"Yes. I'll get him and you can use my office to speak with him."

When Lindstrom left the room to get Yeats, I turned to Duffy. "Awfully squirmy guy, wouldn't you say?"

"Something's buggin' him," Duffy agreed. "My guess is he's holding back on info until he's sure nothing is going to come back to bite him in the butt."

A minute later the door opened and an extremely handsome man with chiseled features and broad shoulders walked in. "Hello," he said to the two of us. "Mr. Lindstrom said that you had some questions for me?"

"Yes, Mr. Yeats, please sit down," Duffy said, indicating the chair vacated by Lindstrom. When Yeats had settled himself, Duffy said, "I'm Sheriff McGinnis and this is my associate, Abigail Cooper. We're trying to locate a friend of ours, Gina Russell. We think she may be missing and we're trying to track her down. Do you know where we might be able to find her?"

Yeats went pale at the mention of Gina, and he didn't speak for several seconds. Finally, he said, "You gotta understand, I have a wife and a baby on the way."

"Are you saying you know where Gina is?" Duffy asked, leaning forward in his chair again to focus on Yeats.

"No," Yeats answered, and held his mouth open for a moment as if he were going to continue, but then snapped it shut and just stared at Duffy and me.

After another pause Duffy said, "Mr. Yeats, we are concerned for the well-being of our friend. If you have any information that could help us find her, I would strongly encourage you to offer it to us."

Yeats squirmed under Duffy's steady gaze, and with a heavy sigh he said, "I don't know where she's gone. We broke up and she split. That's all I can tell you."

"You were having an affair?" I asked as I looked at his energy and got the symbol of a triangle in my mind's eye.

"Yeah," he said, avoiding my eyes and looking at the desk. "It wasn't anything big. We started out going to lunch, and things got flirtatious. Then one night we were both here late and one thing led to another. . . ." Yeats's voice trailed off, his complexion now colored a slight pink.

"So you broke it off with her, but she wouldn't take no for an answer," Duffy supplied when Yeats fell silent.

"No," Yeats said, looking up at Duffy. "It wasn't like that. It wasn't that serious. About two weeks ago we were supposed to hook up, and I was gonna tell her it was over, but she beat me to it."

"She beat you to what?" Duffy said.

"She called me on my cell and said that she'd given it a lot of thought, but she didn't want to see me again."

"Kind of an uncomfortable working environment," I commented.

Yeats chuckled wryly. "You could say that. We avoided each other like the plague."

"Did Lindstrom know about you two?" I asked, thinking that he had been awfully quick to point to Yeats for information on Gina.

"I'm not sure. I mean, we were careful and all, but we've always suspected he reads our e-mails. He's like that—really suspicious of the staff, always thinking we're up to something."

"Except in your case he was right," I pointed out.

Yeats blushed again. "Yeah, I guess so."

Duffy asked, "So what did you think when you heard Gina had quit without notice?"

Yeats shrugged. "I guess I sorta felt relieved. I mean, I was considering leaving myself, so I was glad she stepped up before I had a chance."

"Do you know where she's gone?" Duffy pressed.

"No."

"Have you heard from her?"

"No. Not a word."

My lie detector remained silent, and I managed to catch Duffy's eye, giving him a slight nod that I believed Yeats. "Thank you, Mr. Yeats. We appreciate your help," Duffy said as he pulled a card out of his jacket and extended it across the desk. "If you should hear from Gina, would you please call me right away?"

"Sure," Yeats said, taking the card, then giving us both a pensive look. "Say, you don't think anything's *happened* to her, do you?"

"Happened?" Duffy asked carefully.

"Yeah. You said she was missing. You don't think she's hurt or something, do you?"

Duffy held his gaze steadily as he said, "That's what we're trying to rule out, Mr. Yeats. Again, if you hear from her, or if you can think of anything else that might help us locate her, please call the number on the card."

Duffy and I took our leave and headed out of Lindstrom's office. We passed Lindstrom in the hallway, and Duffy gave him a business card as well. He added that he would appreciate it if Gina's hard drive weren't wiped clean for the time being, until it was determined that Gina was safe. Lindstrom was quick to reassure Duffy that he would cooperate fully with the sheriff's department.

When we were back in the car Duffy asked me, "So what do you think?"

"I think this thing gets weirder by the moment. Was Gina the type to have an affair with a married man?" I asked, suddenly wondering if Ellie knew about her friend's affair.

"Not that I ever saw," Duffy said. "Gina was this really smart, dynamic, headstrong girl. She could have any guy she wanted, so I didn't think she was the type to waste her time on a married guy."

"So what happened to her?" I asked, more puzzled by this mystery than ever.

"That is the sixty-five-thousand-dollar question," Duffy said grimly. "I'll drop you off at Ellie's, then I'm going to head into the station and file a missing persons report."

"Should we tell Ellie?" I asked, feeling a sense of dread at the prospect.

"Not yet. Let me work this a little longer before we get her upset. She may hate us later for keeping it from her, but until we've got some evidence about what happened to Gina I think we should hold off."

I nodded. "You'll get no arguments from me. Where else are you going to look?"

"I'm gonna try to track down her neighbors and see if they've seen or heard from her since last week. Then I'll look for a bead on her car. That might give us some clues." Just then Duffy pulled into Ellie's driveway and parked behind her Lexus.

I got out but heard him call to me before I shut the door. "Yes?" I said, poking my head back in the car.

"Thanks for coming with me today, Abster. I'm glad I had you along."

"Anytime, Duffles," I said, using an ancient nickname for Duffy.

"Whoa!" Duffy chuckled at the mention of his old

moniker. "Don't let anyone else hear you using that; it took me years to shake off that baby."

"Be safe," I said as I shut the door and headed up the steps to Ellie's condo. Behind me I heard Duffy's car roll away down the drive and a soft toot on his horn. A moment later, as I was about to knock, the door was pulled open and a startled redhead stared at me. "Oh! Hi, Abby! We've been waiting for you."

"Hey, Sara, good to see you again," I said as I stepped over the threshold.

"Ellie's upstairs; she said she'd be down in a minute."

"Great. Are you coming with us to the bridal shop?"

"Absolutely. I'm the official fashion coordinator for the wedding. As maid of honor it is my duty to make sure that none of us looks cheesy."

I smiled as I took in Sara's outfit. She was fashionably put together in a light blue cashmere sweater, black skirt and spiky pointed-toe shoes. On her arm was a new Kate Spade, and I commented, "Well, I love your taste in pocketbooks."

"You can never go wrong with Kate," Sara said.

"Is that Abby?" we heard from the upstairs hallway.

"Yep," called Sara. "So let's get a move on already; I've got a hair appointment at three."

"I'm coming, I'm coming," Ellie said, making her way downstairs.

As she descended the staircase, my intuitive phone went haywire. I cocked my head as I looked at her, and as I picked up the intuitive message in my ear a small smile formed at the corners of my mouth. "How ya feelin'?" I asked.

"I'm fine," Ellie said as she swept a stray hair out of her face. "But I swear, this wedding has me completely nervous. My tummy's really been acting up."

"Uh-huh," I said, and gave her a wink.

Ellie eyed me for a moment, then seemed to make up her mind about something. She turned to Sara and said, "I think we should take separate cars."

Sara blinked in surprise and said, "But I thought we were all going in my car."

Ellie eyed me again and said, "Yes, but you have that hair appointment, and there's an errand that I have to run with Abby that might make you late. If you take your car and we take mine, we don't have to rush at the bridal shop, and I know you won't be late for your appointment."

"Oh," Sara said, looking a little dejected. "Okay, then. I'll meet you two at the bridal salon. Abby, don't let her drive like a maniac. It's also my responsibility to make sure she reaches the altar in one safe piece."

I saluted smartly and said, "Aye-aye, Madam Bridesmaid!"

"I can see why you like her," Sara said to Ellie as she headed out the door.

The moment the door closed Ellie turned to me and said, "You cannot breathe a *word*!"

I smiled, folded my arms like a cradle and sang, "It's a *girl*!"

Ellie seemed to look at me with a mixture of emotions that ran from excitement to relief to nervousness. "Abby, not even Eddie knows," she cautioned.

"I told ya so, I told ya so, I told ya so!" I sang, jumping up and down on the balls of my feet. Years earlier I had predicted that Ellie would have two children, and her firstborn would be a girl. I had also predicted that if she wasn't careful, she would walk down the aisle with a bun in her oven.

"You're sure it's a girl?" she asked as she grabbed my hand and squeezed it tight, an anxious look on her face. Ellie had always wanted a little girl.

I gave her a huge smile and said, "All I can hear in my head is the phrase 'pretty in pink,' so yeah, I'd bet it's a she."

"Eddie is going to be so excited," Ellie said as she grabbed her purse and waved me to the door.

"How come you haven't told him?" I asked.

"Are you kidding?" she answered. "That boy can

no more keep a secret than a sieve can hold water. He's the worst."

As we headed to Ellie's car I noticed another car coming down the driveway. I recognized it from the night before as Eddie's Jeep. "Hi, sweetheart!" Ellie called as he parked and opened his door. Turning quickly to me she said, "Remember, not a word!"

I nodded solemnly as Eddie walked up to us, still in his hospital scrubs and looking very tired. "Hey, babe," he said when he got close to Ellie, and reached around to grab her by the waist, pulling her in for a kiss.

"What're you doing home?" she asked. "I thought you had another fifteen-hour shift today."

"I switched with Calvin. I forgot my passport on the kitchen table, and I have to take care of my license today or we can't get married."

"You guys haven't applied for your marriage license yet?" I asked, shocked that they had left it for the last minute.

"No," Ellie explained over her shoulder as Eddie continued to hold on to her. "He lost his wallet and he's got to replace his driver's license."

"Must've slipped out of my back pocket," Eddie said right before he kissed Ellie's neck playfully.

Ellie giggled. "Your wallet wouldn't slip out if you'd grow a butt big enough to fill out a pair of jeans," she said as she gave his behind a playful slap.

As I watched the two of them banter back and forth I felt the most awful melancholy, and I realized how much I missed Dutch. I swallowed hard and turned slightly away, blinking at the tears that were forming against my will.

"Abby?" Ellie said as she noticed my shift. "You okay?"

"I'm fine," I said hoarsely. "Must be this altitude. How long does it take to adjust to this place, anyway?"

Eddie let go of Ellie and stepped close to me. "Why don't you come inside and let me check you out?" he asked, looking concerned.

I turned to him, and an intuitive message hit me with such blinding force that I stepped back quickly, as if I had just lost my balance.

"Abby?" Ellie said as she stepped forward, holding out her hand as if to catch me.

I looked at her, but her voice seemed far away. I tried to focus on her face but kept getting a feeling of being sucked backward, and then I really did lose my balance and nearly went down.

Eddie caught me and held me up, half carrying, half walking me to the steps. "Pants on fire," I said as the singsong chant reverberated so loudly in my head that I thought everyone could hear it.

"What?" I heard Ellie ask as Eddie set me down on the steps and tilted my chin to look in my face.

"Pants on fire!" I yelled as I looked at him, and jumped up, nearly knocking him back.

"Abby, it's okay," he said, watching me closely. "You'll feel better once you sit down for a few minutes."

I was breathing hard and my chest felt tight. Something was very, very wrong, and I was having a hell of a time trying to sort out what was going on. Every time I looked at Eddie, all I got were the chills. I didn't know what was happening. I'd never had an intuitive message this strong before. I felt as if I were coming unglued, as though some unseen force were pulling my soul right out of my body, but my conscious mind wouldn't let it go without a fight, and a kind of tug-of-war was taking place. I was aware of Eddie and Ellie, even able to register that they both looked alarmed, but I was unable to shake the feelings of disconnectedness.

With a thump I sat back down, and gripping the concrete stairs focused all of my energy on taking deep, easy breaths. After a few minutes the alarm and disconnectedness had passed and I began to feel a little better.

"How you doing?" Eddie asked when my breathing had returned to normal.

I felt my cheeks grow hot with embarrassment that I'd had such a reaction, and said, "Better. I don't know what is going on with me lately."

"It's the altitude," Eddie said. "It happens a lot with out-of-towners. They push themselves before their body's had a chance to adjust, and they get panic attacks that can feel pretty scary."

"I'll say," I said, standing up and brushing off my skirt. "Sorry about that," I said to Ellie, who still looked a little shocked and concerned.

"Don't apologize, Abby. My God, it's not your fault. I just want you to be okay. Do you want to skip the bridal salon and go lie down for a while?"

I thought about that for a minute but shook my head no. "I think I'll be okay. Maybe just a glass of water?"

"We've got bottled water in the fridge," Ellie said, and looked at Eddie, who moved quickly into the house and came back a minute later with his passport and a bottled water for each of us.

"Sip it slowly," he advised as he opened the top and handed it to me.

"She'll be okay?" Ellie asked him as he gave her a bottle.

"She'll be just fine. But go easy on her, which means don't drive so fast. Hey, where's Sara? I thought she was going with you."

"She has a hair appointment after the salon, so I suggested separate cars. We're meeting her there," Ellie explained.

Eddie nodded. "Okay then, gals, I'm off to stand in line at the DMV for the rest of my life. Abby, it might be a good idea to take a nap later on. Don't overdo it, okay?"

I nodded at him as I took a swig of water. After swallowing I said, "That's a great idea, Eddie. I'll think about taking a nap after we get back from the bridal shop. Good luck at the DMV."

Ellie kissed Eddie and sent him off to his car. After he pulled out of the driveway she sat down on the step next to me. "That wasn't just the altitude, was it, Abby?" she asked, a note of trepidation in her voice.

"I don't know what the hell it was, Ellie," I answered, avoiding her eyes.

"Liar, liar, pants on fire," Ellie said, her arm swinging companionably over my shoulders.

"You remember that, huh?" I said.

"Absolutely. Every time you were within hearing distance of a lie you'd repeat that rhyme and point your finger at the liar. It's how we knew Ricky Smith knocked down our fort, and how we knew Duffy was the one who broke Mom's favorite china plate."

"Yeah, I remember," I said, looking back at my bottled water.

"So what is Eddie lying about?" Ellie asked me point-blank.

I didn't answer her for the longest time. I was afraid that Ellie would see the fear I held for her friend Gina, and for something that had to do with Eddie that I couldn't quite place. "I don't know, Ellie," I whispered. "But when I do, I promise you, friend-to-friend, I will tell you."

Ellie took that statement in, then slowly nodded. "Good enough," she said, and squeezed my shoulder. "Come on, girl, let's go meet Sara before she throttles us for being so late."

Little did I know then that Sara had another engagement that would prevent her from meeting us at all.

Chapter Six

Ellie did her best to drive with care, which meant that I was still white-knuckling it, but at least I wasn't screaming, "Oh, God, look out!" every time she took a turn or changed lanes. Still, I was doing a lot of praying, and that must have been the trick, because we made it to the bridal salon in one piece.

We found "rock-star parking" as Ellie put it, which meant we were lucky enough to wait behind a little old lady as she backed her huge Buick out of a spot close to the mall's entrance. Once parked, we hurried out of the car and dashed across the lot; Ellie was anxious to meet up with Sara and apologize for our lateness.

The bridal salon was located on the ground floor of an elegant three-story mall, sandwiched between Coach and Bebe. When we entered the salon Ellie looked around the front area for Sara but didn't see her. "Huh. She's not here," she said.

"Maybe she's in back," I suggested.

"Yeah," Ellie said as she grabbed my arm. "She's probably by the bridesmaid dresses. Come on; let's go find her."

We walked to the back section of the store, and

again Ellie looked around, but there was no sign of Sara. "Where do you think she is?" I asked.

"Might be in the ladies' room. Let me show you the dress, and if she doesn't show up in a minute or two I'll ask around and see if anyone's seen her," Ellie said.

I followed her over to a group of absolutely gorgeous dresses. "Here we are!" she said, giving me a ta-da with her hands.

"Wow!" I said as I lifted the hem of one of the dresses to feel the fabric. Made of two layers of silk, the dress had an empire waist and long pleats of fabric that flowed softly down to a bell shape. The color was a kind of honeydew green that shimmered in the light of the salon. "Ellie," I said as I felt the fabric beneath my fingertips, "this is gorgeous!"

"I know," she said, beaming. "Sara picked these out, and they look absolutely fabulous on every single one of my bridesmaids. I just knew you'd like it too!"

"I do," I said as I nodded my head, very surprised that I actually liked a bridesmaid dress, because I'd been forced to wear some doozies in my time.

"Gina was a size six. What size are you?"

"I float between a four and a six," I said.

"Cool, that's perfect. We'll have to take up the hem, I think, because Gina's an inch or two taller than you, and maybe a little around the bustline—she is like a double-D or something bodacious like that—but the tailoring here is fabulous. It should be a quick fix."

Just then a pretty Asian woman approached us, "Hello, Ellie," she said warmly.

"Hi, Kim," Ellie answered. "Kim, this my good friend and substitute bridesmaid Abby Cooper. She's going to wear Gina's dress. It's still in the back, right?"

"Yes, it's here." Kim chuckled. "I'll go get it and we can see how it fits. If it needs a little tailoring we can get it done in time for the wedding."

After Kim had gone into the back I turned to Ellie and asked, "Is your dress here too?"

Ellie nodded and gave me a finger wag that suggested I follow her. We headed back up to the front and over to one of the mannequins. On display was a lovely satin dress of dusky eggshell. A basket-weave pattern formed the bodice, and a full skirt of satin and crinoline flowed out from the waist. Small beadwork dotted the skirt here and there, and I whistled in appreciation. "My God, Ellie, you are going to be one beautiful bride!"

"It's perfection, isn't it?" Ellie said, giggling with delight as her happiness bubbled over.

"Wow, I can't wait to see you in it," I agreed.

"Well, the countdown is already on," Ellie said with a grin. "It's T minus four days from today!"

"Here we are," came a voice from behind us, and we turned to see Kim walking with the bridesmaid dress dangling on her arm. As I took the dress from her and headed off to the fitting room, I felt a sudden and horrible pang of guilt. This was Gina's dress, after all. How could I be excited about wearing a dead woman's dress? I stepped into the changing room and shut the door. I placed the dress on a hook next to the mirror and sat on the small bench in the room for a moment, thinking about what to do.

Ellie would expect me to come out in the dress, but knowing Gina was dead and not being able to say anything to Ellie about it was making me feel so guilty my stomach hurt. I paced the floor for a bit, trying to work out what to do, when there was a soft knock on the door and Ellie entered.

"Abby!" she exclaimed when she saw me still fully clothed. "Come on, girl! Try that puppy on."

I looked at her for a beat or two, her eyes dancing with merriment and excitement over her impending big day, and I couldn't do it. I couldn't break her heart just yet. I'd do it later, when she was surrounded by family and friends. Sucking it up, I peeled out of my sweater and skirt and put on Gina's dress, silently sending up a prayer to her that I was sorry.

When I had the dress on I turned so Ellie could see me, and she squealed. "It's wonderful!"

"You think?" I asked, avoiding my own eyes in the mirror.

"Yeah! I mean, we definitely need to take it up an inch or two at the bottom and maybe tuck some in at the bust, but otherwise it looks so awesome on you! I knew it would go with your coloring."

"It feels weird to be wearing Gina's dress," I said as my discomfort grew.

"Why, honey? I mean, it's not like she's here to claim it."

I winced. "Ellie," I began carefully. "I don't think I feel right about taking Gina's dress."

"You'd rather buy your own?" Ellie asked me, her head cocking slightly to one side like a trusting puppy.

"Uh, yeah, I think I would," I said as I played that across my conscience.

"Okay, if that's what you really want. I'll have Kim pull out a size four and a size six, and you can try both of them on and see which one you like best."

"Perfect," I said, and hurried to take off the dress as Ellie disappeared out the door. I hung the dress up and stared at it as I waited. Somehow I knew that neither Gina nor I would ever get to wear the dresses outside of these walls, but that didn't stop me from acting like nothing was wrong and plunking down three hundred and fifty dollars for the thing. What we do for friendship.

A little later, as I was having my Visa swiped, I asked Ellie, "So what happened to Sara?"

"I have no idea. I asked Kim if she'd seen her and she said she hadn't, but that she'd been on her break until just before we got here. Knowing Sara, my guess is that she came in, waited a few, got mad and left."

"She's a by-the-clock kinda girl, huh?"

"You know the type?"

"Have you *met* my sister?" I deadpanned.

Ellie laughed. "How is Cat these days, anyway?"

"Think Julius Caesar meets Martha Stewart."

"Ouch! That's a wicked combo."

"You wait; you'll see," I said, wagging a finger at her. "Cat will show up and it will be all chaos and mayhem."

"I thought that's when your parents arrive," Ellie said.

"No, that's when the bridal party joins you for your elopement—which, trust me, you will be planning the moment they get here."

"So you're telling me Claire and Sam haven't mellowed with age?"

"Don't think fine wine. Think vinegar instead."

"Great," Ellie said as Kim handed me my wrapped dress over the counter. "Remind me to tell the ushers to seat your parents in the back row."

"You won't need reminding." I groaned.

Ellie's cell phone gave a small chirp as we headed out the door, and she pulled it from her purse. Looking at the readout she gave a small frown. "Well, crap," she said as she tucked the phone away.

"What's up?" I asked.

"That was a text message from Sara. She said she can't make the party tonight."

"What party?" I asked.

"Didn't I tell you? I'm such a bonehead. I'm having a bachelorette pajama-party for my bridesmaids and a few girlfriends."

"Sounds like fun." I smiled. If I knew Ellie, there would be good food, good drinks and good fun.

"Which brings me to my next question, and please feel free to say no."

"Sounds serious," I said.

"It's not; it's just that I would be imposing on you, but it would mean the world to me."

"You'd like me to do a reading for the girls," I said, already way ahead of her.

"Never could keep anything from you." Ellie grinned. "So what do you think?"

"Like you even have to ask," I said. "Of course, it would be my pleasure."

"I will pay you, of course—"

"Don't be ridiculous; consider it my gift to you," I said, cutting her off.

Ellie took a moment to give me a sincere look as she took my hand and squeezed it. "Thank you," she said solemnly.

"No sweat," I said, squeezing her hand back. "So, did Sara's message say why she couldn't make it?" I asked, something buzzing in the back of my brain.

"No. She just wrote 'count me out for party' and that's it."

"Do you think she's really mad?"

"Possibly. You know what they say about redheads."

"Where are we going, anyway?" I asked as I noticed we were heading away from the entrance we'd come through from the parking lot.

"This way," Ellie said giving me a coy look. "I have a surprise for you."

I followed along with her, looking for any sign of where she could be leading me, but within moments we had paused in front of Tiffany & Co. and Ellie turned to me and said, "Surprise!"

"Are we having breakfast?" I asked as I followed her through the door.

"Nope," Ellie said excitedly as she rushed to the counter. "Something better!" As a clerk behind the counter spotted us and came walking over, Ellie said, "Hi, Jan."

"Miss McGinnis! So good to see you. I have your package ready for you. Wait one moment and I'll be right back."

As the salesclerk darted behind a curtain I gave Ellie a questioning look, but she only winked back as she danced on the balls of her feet with excitement.

When Jan returned, she handed a small robin's-egg-blue box tied with a silver bow to Ellie, who promptly handed it to me. "Ta-da!" she said with relish.

I took the box and gave her a grin, then removed the ribbon and opened the lid. When I folded back the Tiffany tissue paper I sucked in a breath as I gazed down at a beautiful silver charm bracelet with one charm. A heart dangled from the chain, and as I lifted it out of the box I noticed it was engraved in script with my name—*Abby*—on one side and a small diamond inserted in the center of the heart on the other.

"Ellie . . ." I said breathlessly as I inspected the bracelet.

"It's my bridesmaid's gift to you, Abs. Thank you for being in my wedding," she said as she reached over and gave me an impromptu hug.

I was moved enough to give her a tremendous squeeze back, and then let her go and quickly put the bracelet on. I shook my wrist back and forth, showing it off to Ellie and Jan. I loved it.

"Thank you so much, El. This is just amazing," I said as I put the box back together and tucked it into the bag Jan held out for me.

"Ready to go?" she asked.

"Sure am. But I have one request."

"What's that?"

"Can we get some lunch? I'm starved!"

"Your wish is my command, girl! I know just the place. It's a bit of a hike from here, but well worth it," she said, and we trooped out of the mall.

Ellie and I chatted companionably once we were in the car, and I hardly noticed her driving now that I had a shiny new bracelet to look at. At some point my stomach rumbled, and Ellie looked over at me with a sly grin. "You really are hungry, aren't you?"

"Famished," I admitted.

"There's a protein bar in the glove box. Why don't you have that as a snack to tide you over?"

I dug around in her glove box and came up with a

Kashi Bar. I unwrapped the bar and took a bite. We fell silent while I munched on the snack, and with a contented sigh I looked out the window. We were on the highway now, and in the next lane was a blue sedan with a woman about my age behind the wheel. A man sat in the passenger seat next to her, and his attention seemed to be very focused on watching her. I was about to turn back to my snack when my intuitive alarm went absolutely haywire. I had the feeling that there was something terribly wrong with the scene in the other car. My eyes went back to the woman and I studied her intently, listening to the whisper of a thought that was circling in my head. *Kidnap! Kidnap! Kidnap!* pounded in my mind, and while I kept my eyes on the woman I said to Ellie, "Stay in this lane a minute and don't speed up!"

"What?" Ellie asked, startled by the panic in my voice.

"Just stay next to this car for a moment!" I commanded, my voice sharp.

Ellie did as I asked while I intently gazed at the couple in the other car. I noticed that the woman looked slightly disheveled. She also appeared to be crying, but her eyes were pinned on the road ahead and she had a very firm grip on the steering wheel. The man was watching her intently, and then he noticed me. I saw him mouth something to the woman, and their car began to move past us. Ellie was glancing at the car too, and she also began to move forward.

Then I saw the man mouth something again to the woman, and she increased her speed even more. "Ellie," I said, tearing my eyes away from the car, "swing behind them, and whatever you do, don't lose them!"

As Ellie held back slightly, then zoomed into the next lane to keep pace behind the blue sedan, I grabbed my purse from the floor and pulled out a pen. I wrote the license plate number down on my hand, then reached for my cell phone. I put my earpiece on and flipped open the lid to jam 911 into the display, then waited an anxious three seconds until the emergency dispatcher picked up.

"Nine-one-one dispatch, what is your emergency?"

"I need to report a kidnapping!" I shouted as Ellie looked sharply at me.

"What is your location?" the dispatcher asked.

"We're on . . ." I said, looking at my cell's display and following the red star moving across the screen, "I-Seventy headed east!"

"Just past Route Eighty-seven!" Ellie added, leaning in toward me so the dispatcher could hear.

"Who has been kidnapped?" the dispatcher asked me.

"A woman in a blue Chevy Malibu. License number Victor-Paul-tango-six-nine-five! I think she's being held against her will by a man in a dark brown shirt with brown hair, clean shaven, in his mid to late forties or early fifties!"

"Where are you in relation to the Malibu?"

"We're right on their tail, and we're not letting them out of our sight!" I said as Ellie gave me a firm nod and zipped to the right lane as the Malibu began to swerve in and out of traffic. I hesitated to look at the speedometer; we had to be going ninety by the way we were passing the cars around us. "We're in a black Lexus SC four-thirty, right behind the sedan!"

"I'm sending a dispatch now; will you hold on the line with me until they arrive or you lose sight of the car?"

"Affirmative!" I yelled, my adrenaline pumping. The man in the car in front of us appeared to be shouting at the woman. His face was dark and angry, and I prayed that he wouldn't hurt her until the sheriff had a chance to arrive. "Careful!" I screamed as Ellie had a very close call with a car on her left, barely missing it as we ducked in and out of traffic trying to keep up.

"Jesus!" Ellie grimaced as she gripped the steering

wheel and righted our path. "Abby, what if we hang back? This is starting to get really dangerous!"

"Ellie, please do not lose that car!" I begged her. "If we lose sight of them that woman's as good as dead; I can feel it! Just do your best, okay?"

Ellie glanced over at me quickly, her mouth forming a determined line, then back to the traffic in front of her as she lowered her shoulders and concentrated on not getting us killed or losing the sedan.

Finally we began to hear the sounds of sirens coming up behind us. I turned in my seat and felt a small sense of relief as I saw two approaching sheriff's cars coming up fast and furious. "Patrol cars behind us!" I said to Ellie and the dispatcher.

"Are you still in sight of the car?" the dispatcher asked.

"Yes! It's about ten yards in front of us. They're going about a hundred now, but we're keeping pace!" Just as I got those words out the blue sedan swerved too suddenly and began to fishtail. "Ohmigod!" I screamed as Ellie punched the brakes, and cars around us also tried to avoid the swerving sedan.

"Hang on!" Ellie screamed as she pulled the wheel sharply to the left and into the median. She had no choice, because we were going so fast we would have hit the car in front of us in the next second. In the rough terrain the Lexus held its ground, and we slowed enough to regain some control, but the sedan skidded and fishtailed until it ended up in the median about a hundred yards ahead, its nose dipping into a slight ditch and coming to a rather abrupt stop. As we came to a halt I saw the man in the passenger seat jump out of the car. A dark blotch of blood covered his right hand as he looked wildly around, then darted across the median, running through oncoming traffic that swerved to avoid him. Just then the two sheriff's cars arrived, and Duffy jumped out of one of them, running to us with an anxious look on his face.

"El!" he shouted as he got close to us. "What's going on?"

"That man!" Ellie said, pointing to the fleeing assailant. "Duffy, don't let him get away!"

Duffy took off running while another deputy arrived. My attention followed Duffy for a beat; then I ran toward the car. That blood had to come from somewhere. When I got to the sedan I yanked open the driver's-side door, and inside was the woman leaning forward, her face pale and sweaty, her shirt one giant stain of blood. An ugly knife protruded from her right side, and one hand was clutched painfully around the shaft as she gave a small moan. "I need help over here!" I yelled back to the deputy, who was lingering by Ellie and talking into his walkie-talkie.

Both Ellie and the deputy rushed to my side, and I stepped back so that he could assist the woman. Ellie stood next to me as we looked on, and it was then that I realized my cell phone was still clutched in my hand. I checked my ear phone and asked, "Dispatcher, are you still there?"

"I'm here," she answered. "Is the sheriff on scene?"

"They're here, but we need an ambulance right away! The woman's been stabbed!"

"I'm dispatching that now," she said as I heard computer keys tapping. "I have your location from the sheriff on scene. ETA is six minutes. Is the woman conscious?"

"Barely, and she's losing a lot of blood," I said as Ellie put a hand on my shoulder. It was only then that I realized I was shaking. The deputy was working with the woman, laying the seat back and talking gently to her. Traffic on both sides of the highway was slowing to a crawl as gawkers looked on. A minute or two later Duffy came back across the highway, empty-handed.

He puffed his way over to us, his look angry. "Lost the son of a bitch in the woods," he said as he turned his head slightly and depressed a button on the walkie-talkie secured to his shoulder. "Dispatch, this is car three-eighty-one at the scene of that eleven-forty-seven, can you confirm the eleven-forty-one?"

"Confirmed, three-eighty-one."

While Duffy called in his codes, I glanced back at the sedan and my heart went out to the woman inside. There was a moment of regret as I wondered whether, if we hadn't chased the car, perhaps she wouldn't have been hurt. Then my intuition weighed in and reassured me that the woman would recover and that she wouldn't have had a chance otherwise. We'd done the right thing.

A few minutes later the ambulance arrived, and Duffy and the deputy stepped aside while the woman was carefully loaded into the emergency vehicle. As I watched her go, I knew that even though she'd been badly injured, my intuitive alarm had saved her life. Why my trusty intuition failed to save my own life mere days later is something I'm still trying to work out.

Chapter Seven

Ellie and I waited inside her car, shivering even though the heat was turned up, until Duff came over and tapped on the window. Ellie lowered the pane and he peered in. "We'll need a statement from you two," he said.

"No problem," Ellie replied.

"My thinking is that you'll probably want to go to the hospital to see how she's doing though, huh?" Duffy asked. Ellie and I both nodded. "Okay, then, follow right behind me and I'll take your statement there."

We followed Duffy to the hospital, his siren blazing the way for us. We parked in the Emergency parking lot, then walked inside, and Ellie and I took a seat in the waiting room while Duffy headed over to the information desk to make sure the woman had arrived alive. Coming back a moment later, he said, "She's being prepped for surgery. We'll know more in a few hours, I think. In the meantime," he said, flipping open his notebook, "I'd like the two of you to tell me exactly how this happened."

Ellie looked at me and said, "You first, Abs."

I gave a detailed account to Duffy about how we had been driving along and I'd happened to glance over at the car next to us when my intuition went haywire and I'd known something was wrong.

"How did you know?" Duffy asked me. "I mean, did you see the knife and that's when you knew she was in trouble?"

I thought back and said, "No, I don't remember seeing a knife. I just knew she was in trouble."

Duffy nodded, "Okay, so go on."

I continued with my story, describing the man in as great detail as I could, trying to give the police as much as possible to hunt down the villain.

When I'd finished, Duffy said, "Well, we'll have the knife, at least, and hopefully the guy left his fingerprints on it. If he's got any priors, we'll know who he is. The woman we believe is Hadley Rankin from Mountain View; at least that's who the car is registered to. There was no ID on her, so we can't be sure, but we've got a deputy checking out her home, and he'll try the neighbors if he gets no response."

"Do you think the guy who stabbed her was a boyfriend or something?" Ellie asked.

"No," I said immediately. "He was a stranger to her."

"How do you know?" Duffy asked me.

I tapped my temple and said, "My sixth sense says they didn't know each other. It's also saying that he's done this before."

Duffy nodded. "The other deputy on scene, Garcia, called in a canine patrol. Maybe they'll have better luck tracking down the maggot than I did."

My left side felt thick and heavy. I'd known the moment I'd seen the assailant reach the woods that he wouldn't be found, and I worried about someone so dangerous loose in the world.

Just then a familiar face came down the hallway. "Eddie!" Ellie said, jumping up to greet him.

"I just got back from the DMV and one of the ER interns told me you were here," he said after he'd given her a big hug. "What's going on?"

Ellie filled him in, and I watched his expression turn from concerned to frightened. "Jesus, Ellie!" he exclaimed when she'd finished. "You could have been killed!"

"We were fine," I reassured him. "Really."

Eddie turned on me, his face angry. "You force my fiancée on a high-speed chase after a guy with a knife and you expect me to be okay with that?"

"Eddie!" Ellie said, rubbing his arm to calm him down. "It's all right. I promise. You know I'm a good driver."

"Ellie," he said, "we both know you are definitely *not* a good driver!"

"Well, I'm all right, after all," she snapped back. "And that woman needed us. There's no telling what that psycho would have done to her if we hadn't been there."

Eddie pouted for a long, tense moment as he looked from her to me to Duffy. Finally he said, "I gotta get back upstairs."

"Sweetheart, don't be like that," Ellie coaxed, and pulled him to one side, out of earshot. They talked in muffled tones for a few minutes as Ellie did her best to reassure him that there was no harm done.

I looked at Duffy to gauge his reaction, and he said, "He's got a point, you know."

"Now you're taking his side?" I asked.

"You two had no business chasing that car at those kinds of speeds. You could have been seriously injured or caused a major traffic accident."

A big part of me wanted to argue with him, but I knew he was right, so I left it alone. I was just happy that we'd been able to save the woman and that neither Ellie nor I had gotten hurt. A minute later Ellie joined us again and said, "I think I've calmed him down. He's just a little on the protective side."

"Wouldn't have any other type of guy marrying my sister," Duffy said as he pulled her close and gave her a kiss on the forehead.

She laughed and gave him a playful punch in the

stomach. "He's also going to see if he can find out anything about her condition for us."

"Great," I said, and took my seat again as my stomach gave a rumble. I had forgotten how hungry I'd been when this whole thing started.

Duffy got up and announced, "Sounds like your furnace is running low there, Abs. I'll head down to the cafeteria for some fuel. They have pretty good sandwiches here—any preferences?"

I brightened at the prospect and said, "Tuna or egg salad if they've got it."

"I'll take anything with turkey," Ellie said, and grinned at her older brother. After Duffy had headed in the direction of the cafeteria, Ellie turned to me and asked, "How you holding up?"

"I'm okay. You?"

"Shaken but okay."

We sat there side by side for a beat or two without speaking, when Ellie surprised me with, "I think you and Duffy should go out."

I did a double take as I looked at her. "Excuse me?"

"Seriously. You know he's a great guy, Abs. And he's lonely."

"Ellie," I said as I squirmed in my seat, "I *just* broke up with my boyfriend!"

"So, the timing is rather perfect, wouldn't you say?" she said, allowing her eyebrows to dance up and down.

"No. No, I wouldn't say that the timing is perfect. I would say the timing is bad."

"There is nothing like getting right back up on that horse again to make you forget about the last fall," Ellie advised.

I rolled my eyes and replied, "Ellie, you know I love Duff, but I love him like a *brother*."

"Yes, but he's *not* your brother; he's mine. Which is all the more reason you should consider going out with him. Think of it!" she said with relish. "If it worked out between you two, we could be sisters!"

"I think you need to eat, El; you're starting to hallucinate."

"I'm serious!" she insisted.

"That's what I'm afraid of," I replied. "Oh, look! Here comes Duffy with our food!"

"This conversation is not over, Abs."

"Mmmmm. I'm so hungry I could eat a horse!" I said, avoiding any more commentary on the subject.

Duffy came over to where we sat, carrying a tray of food and drinks, and Ellie jumped up and moved down one seat to allow him to sit between us. When he sat down she beamed me the full grille and I rolled my eyes.

Duffy handed out the sandwiches and chips and drinks and we all munched happily until Ellie jumped up midway into her sandwich, covered her mouth and bolted for the ladies' room.

Duffy watched her go, then turned to me. "What happened?"

Setting down my sandwich on a small table next to me, I said, "Prewedding jitters. Let me check on her and I'll be right back."

I found Ellie at the sink, gripping the porcelain and looking pale. "You okay?" I asked, coming up behind her.

"This nausea has gotta stop," she said as she eyed me in the mirror. "What if I get an attack during the ceremony?"

I chuckled as I patted her lightly on the back. "Aww, El, I'm sure it'll be okay. Can I get you anything?"

"No. Thanks, Abs, it should pass in a minute," she said as she turned on the faucet and splashed some cool water over her face.

Just then there was a knock on the restroom door. "That must be Duffy," I said as I trotted over to it. When I opened it up I saw Duffy and Eddie. "Hey," I said, a little startled to see Eddie again.

"Is she okay?" he asked.

"I'm fine," Ellie said, coming over to stand behind me. "Just all this excitement and the wedding count down has me a little nervous."

"Will you let me take you home, El?" Eddie asked her gently.

"That's a good idea," I chimed in. I had only to look at Ellie's energy to know that she was in desperate need of a nap.

"What about Hadley?" Ellie asked me. "Don't you want me to wait with you until we know that she's okay?"

"Duffy and I can handle it," I said easily.

Ellie brightened suddenly as she thought of something. "Yeah. You're right. That'll give you two a chance to spend some time together. Come on, Eddie; let's blow this Popsicle stand."

As Ellie zipped around me to grab Eddie by the hand, then over to retrieve her coat so that they could head out, Duffy asked me, "What was that about?"

"You know your sister," I said, shrugging my shoulders and leaving it at that.

After Ellie and Eddie had gone, Duffy and I sat back down in the waiting room. He had finished his sandwich, so I quickly polished off mine, then scooped up the trash and threw it away. When I got back to my seat Duffy had a thoughtful expression on his face. "What's up?" I asked him.

"Nothing. Just glad you came in for the wedding."

"Me too," I said, grinning at him.

"Tell me something, Abby."

"Shoot."

"How does a guy dump a girl like you?"

His words sliced into me like a knife, and my smile faded quickly. "To be honest, Duff, I'm not really sure."

"So what happened?"

I was looking down at my boots now, unable to make eye contact for fear that if I did, I'd start bawling. "I guess he got scared."

"Is it true he dumped you on Valentine's Day?"

"Yeah. He said he had a big case he needed to concentrate on and that we should slow things down a little."

"So he didn't really say, 'I want to break up with you'?"

I thought about that for a minute. "No," I said as I remembered looking into his energy and seeing no reflection of myself there. "He didn't have to. It was implied."

"How?"

"Well, it's hard to explain. But he hasn't called, and it's been several days, so what does that tell you?"

"That he's focusing on work," Duffy said. "You know, I told Rachel the same thing right before she started cheating on me. I had just gotten this sheriff gig, and I needed to have all my energy go into it. Next thing I know she's makin' out with some pilot in my own backyard. She told me later that she thought I was pulling away from her, but the truth was I just needed to focus."

"So what you're telling me is that you guys all stick together," I said, giving him a hard look.

"No more than you ladies," Duffy said, beaming me a bright smile.

"Well, trust me on this," I said firmly. "The way this is going, Dutch Rivers and I don't have a future together." Even as I said this I hoped I'd feel my left side go thick and heavy, confirming that I was making a false statement. Instead, there was nothing. No light, airy feeling on my right, nor thick and heavy on my left. That made me even more depressed, and I laid my head back against the chair and closed my eyes with a sigh.

"Tired?" Duffy asked.

"Yeah."

"Want me to take you back to Viv's?"

"No. I want to wait and see what happens to Hadley first."

Just then there was a whoosh of air by my face as

someone rushed past me. I opened my eyes in time to see what looked like a panic-stricken man hurry to the emergency information desk. The clerk behind the counter listened to what he had to say, typed something into her computer, then spoke in hushed tones to him, and he seemed to sag against the counter. She talked a little more, then pointed in our direction, and the man looked over at us. "Duffy," I said as I elbowed him, only then realizing he'd also laid his head back and closed his eyes.

"What's up?"

"That man coming toward us. I think that's Hadley's husband."

Sure enough, the man stopped in front of us and identified himself as Jackson Rankin, Hadley's husband. He looked ashen with worry, and I got up and coaxed him into the seat, sitting down in the chair next to him while Duffy began to gather some information.

"So you came home at what time?"

"About twenty minutes ago. I came home and found my house a wreck—"

"What do you mean by 'wreck'?" Duffy interrupted.

Rankin paused and blinked a few times as he tried to think of a way to explain. "In my front hallway the rug was all bunched up, like something heavy had been dragged across it. And in my living room there was an overturned table and a lamp was broken. That's when my neighbor tapped on my window and said the police were looking for me, and I needed to call the Denver sheriff's department right away. I headed to the phone and called, and they said they thought my wife had been brought here."

"May I borrow your house keys?" Duffy asked him.

"My house keys?" Rankin asked.

"Yes, I'd like to send a CSI team out to your house," Duffy explained.

"Yeah, here you go," Rankin said, giving over his keys with a shaking hand.

"Thanks," Duffy said, putting them into a small envelope that he'd pulled from his pocket, which he marked with Rankin's name and filed back into his shirt. "Mr. Rankin, do you know anyone who would want to hurt you or your wife?"

"No. No one. Everyone loves Hadley. She's the nicest woman you'd ever want to meet," Rankin said, his voice becoming shaky again.

"Okay," Duffy said, pausing a moment to allow Rankin to regain control. "Do you have a picture of your wife with you?" Duffy asked, probably wanting to identify that the woman in the hospital was indeed Hadley Rankin.

"Uh, no," Rankin said, his face growing red. "I should have one, though, shouldn't I?" he asked us, looking chagrined.

"Can you describe her?"

"She's about five-four, one hundred twenty pounds, with brown hair and hazel eyes."

Duffy nodded and asked, "Does your wife wear any jewelry that might identify her, Mr. Rankin?"

"She wears a wedding ring and a watch I gave her last year."

"Can you describe the watch?" Duffy asked, looking back through his notes.

"It's a silver Timex with a blue face."

Duffy nodded and snapped his notepad closed. "Yes, that all fits with the description of the woman we found at the scene."

"So what's happened to my wife?" Rankin asked, his voice breaking a little.

"I'm afraid she was assaulted and kidnapped at knifepoint. She and her assailant were observed by this young woman, who noticed something amiss and alerted the police. When we caught up to your wife's car the suspect had fled, but not before stabbing your wife in the abdomen. She's in surgery at this time, and we have no updates on her condition just yet."

"Oh, God," Rankin said, and his eyes filled with

tears; then he buried his face in his hands and began to sob.

Duffy's mouth was set in a grim line as he looked at Rankin. Even though he'd put on his cop face, I could tell it bothered him to have to tell the man that his wife had gone through a terrible ordeal. "Can I get you some water, Mr. Rankin?"

Rankin didn't reply, but kept sobbing. I nodded at Duffy, who got up to get the water, while I rubbed the man's back, leaning over to say, "She'll be okay, Mr. Rankin. I have a good feeling she's going to be all right. We just have to wait and see what her surgeon says, but I can't imagine it will be much longer."

As it turned out, we didn't have long to wait. Before Duffy returned with the water, a doctor in scrubs came down the hallway, stopped at the info station and was pointed in our direction. "Mr. Rankin?" he asked when he stopped in front of us.

"Yes?" Rankin said as he looked up, his eyes full of hope.

"I'm Dr. Hall. Your wife is out of surgery and doing very well. We were able to retrieve the knife and repair the damage to her bowel, which was the only organ that sustained any injury. Your wife was very lucky, because it could have been much worse."

"She's going to be okay?"

"We want to monitor her carefully for the next twenty-four hours, but her outlook is excellent."

"Can I see her?" Rankin asked.

"Yes. She's recovering in ICU and she's still very groggy, but if you'll wait over there by the elevator I will take you up in a moment after I speak to the sheriff."

Duffy had come back with the water in the middle of the conversation, but heard enough to know that Hadley was going to be okay. When Rankin had shuffled off to the elevators, Dr. Hall turned to Duffy and said, "I've got the knife in an evidence bag. I tried to be as careful with the extraction as possible. I'll have it sent down in a few minutes and hopefully your techs can get a good set of prints off it."

"Thanks, Doc," Duffy said. "While I was getting Rankin some water I called the station and told them to send some techs over to his house to see if they can pull some prints. I'm meeting them over there in a little while with the keys. When do you think you can give us the okay to talk with Mrs. Rankin?"

"As I told her husband, we want to keep a close watch on her for the next twenty-four hours, and, barring any complications, I would expect it would be all right to talk with her tomorrow."

"Great. I'll be back then. Abby, you ready to go after we get the knife?" he asked, turning to me.

"More than ready," I answered, and we headed over to the information desk to wait for the knife to come down from the upper floor. A few minutes later a young man in scrubs showed up with a tightly sealed envelope and a clipboard. Duffy signed for the package and we headed out the door.

Once in the car Duffy asked, "So where to?"

"Ellie's supposed to have a pajama party tonight for the bridesmaids, but I'm wondering if it's been canceled."

"Let's call her and find out," Duffy said, and reached for his cellular. Speed-dialing her number, he waited for her to pick up, then quickly filled her in on the details about Hadley's condition. After that he asked her, "So I've got Abby in the car and she was wondering if you were having your peeps over for a party tonight—no boys allowed."

I heard Ellie's laugh on the other end, then some muffled sounds as she gave him an answer. Winking at me, Duffy said, "El says to get your tuchus over to her house, 'cause you are not getting out of her party that easily."

"Should we stop at Viv's so I can change?" I asked.

Duffy repeated my request to Ellie, then turned

back to me. "She says she's got stuff you can wear if you don't want to make the extra stop."

"Cool."

"We'll be there in ten," Duffy said, and hung up the phone. Turning to me he added, "You done good today, you know."

I smiled tiredly at him. "Thanks. But it's been a long day. Where does Ellie get the strength to keep going?"

"At this point, I gotta believe it's pure adrenaline. She's excited about the wedding."

I nodded and we fell silent for a while. A thought swirled up into my mind as I mentally sorted through the events of the day. "Hey, Duffy?" I said.

"Yeah?"

"Do you think the guy who attacked Hadley had any connection to Gina's disappearance?"

Duffy cut me a look. "Is that what your radar is saying?"

I thought about that for a minute. "No. No, it's just that here's this woman who's doing her thing and some stranger walks in and kidnaps her and holds her at knifepoint."

"How do you know he was a stranger to her?"

I was surprised by his response. "You think she knew him?"

"Anything's possible, Abby. He could be her ex-husband. A guy she's cheating on her husband with. A neighbor or even a family member. Statistics are overwhelmingly in favor of some kind of relationship in cases like this. Point is, we won't be able to rule anything out until we know who he is."

"Huh," I said, thinking on that. "So you don't think there's a connection."

"I don't have enough to go on to make that conclusion yet. For one thing, we don't officially know that Gina's disappearance wasn't voluntary."

"Did you file the missing persons report?" I asked.

"Yep. Took care of that yesterday. And I also have an all-points bulletin out on her car."

"What did you find out about her phone records?"

"Well, Kelly was right about the time she said Gina called her. It was a little after eleven P.M. The odd thing is that the plane reservation was made at nine P.M., but not from Gina's home phone or cell phone."

"She probably booked it on the Web," I said.

"Not according to United's records. They confirm that Gina called the customer service line at approximately nine ten P.M. and got a reservation for the first flight out the next morning at six A.M."

"If she booked her flight for six A.M. at nine, wouldn't she start packing right away? I mean, she calls Kelly two hours later and says she's leaving for California, and she hasn't packed a thing. That's just weird."

Duffy was nodding his head. "The only thing I can figure is that she bought her plane ticket, then started doing her laundry so that she'd have clean clothes to take on her trip."

I thought about that for a minute—it sounded plausible. "What time did she call her boss to quit her job?"

"Lindstrom said two A.M., and I confirmed that through her cell phone records, which record a call to Fidelity at around that time."

I gave Duffy a confused look. "So she was up at least until two A.M. And all of her clothes were put away, not one item was packed, and she had a flight out at six A.M.?"

"That's the gist of it."

"Something is really not adding up here, Duff."

"I know, Abs. I know."

"Did you hear from her neighbors?" I asked.

"Not yet, but they've probably been at work all day. Hopefully there will be a message from one of them when I get back to the station. First, however, I have to check out things at the Rankin crime scene." As he finished this sentence we pulled into Ellie's driveway, which was lined with cars. The other bridesmaids and guests were here.

I squeezed Duffy's arm before I got out and said, "Thanks for the lift, and for the record you were pretty great today too."

"Just doin' my duty, ma'am," Duffy said with a smart salute and a broad grin. There was something so endearing about him in that moment that my heart gave a little flutter and I felt my cheeks grow warm. I got out of the squad car quickly before I made things really complicated. "See you tomorrow, Duff, and call me if you talk to Hadley." Then I shut the car door and rushed up the stairs to Ellie's front door, wondering how I could be having thoughts about another man while my heart was so freshly broken. "Trouble," I mumbled as I raised my hand to knock. "This can be nothing but trouble." Little did I know that I was right on the money.

Chapter Eight

I was met at the door by the very bubbly bridesmaid named Christina. "Hi, Abby!" she said happily as she shoved a margarita into my hand before I'd even had a chance to remove my coat. "We haven't had a chance to get to know each other yet. I'm Christina, bridesmaid number three. Come on in and join the party!"

"Thanks, Christina," I said as I set the margarita down to shrug out of my coat. "Ellie said she had some clothes I could change into. Do you know where she is?"

"She ran to the store a minute ago to pick up more tequila. She said when you got here to send you upstairs. She's already set aside some choices on her bed."

"Awesome, thanks," I said, and hurried up the stairs. I made a point not to glance at Ellie's photo gallery. I couldn't bear the thought of seeing the flat picture of Gina right now.

I headed into Ellie's room and approached her bed. There were three sets of clothes laid out for me. The first was a pair of jeans and a raspberry-colored sweater. The second was a gorgeous light blue cashmere tracksuit, and the third was a pair of black cotton sweatpants and a matching hoodie.

I opted for the cashmere tracksuit and changed. By the time I'd rejoined the party Ellie was walking in the door with a bag of goodies. "I got more tequila!" she called to the living room full of girls.

Cheers went up from the group gathered there, and I peeked into the room to see what they were up to. The girls were boisterously playing some game that involved dice and some figurines making their way around a board. "What're they playing?" I asked Ellie.

"Mystery Date, if you can believe it."

"I used to love that game!" I said with a laugh.

"How you doin'?" she asked me as I followed her into the kitchen.

"I'm fine. A little tired, but good."

"I'm just so glad that Hadley's going to be okay," Ellie said as she began to unload the groceries.

I picked up a bag of lime-flavored Tostitos that Ellie set on the counter and tore it open. "I love these," I said as Ellie shot me a smile.

"Help yourself." She giggled. "Will you still be up for giving us readings tonight?"

Crap! I thought. I'd forgotten about making that particular offer. "Sure. But how about we limit it to just a few? I'm beat and don't think I could do more than four or five tonight."

"That's perfect, Abs. I'll make everyone draw out of a hat to be fair, and when someone draws a number, then they'll get read."

"Great. But stack the deck, honey, so you get a reading," I said with a wink.

"Oh, I plan on it!" Ellie said with a grin. "I've got you all set in the guest room, so why don't you head there and I'll send the first victim up in a minute."

"Cool," I said, grabbing my margarita and the Tostitos. I trooped upstairs once again and made my way to the spare bedroom, where Ellie had prepared a small card table, some chairs and a cute little votive candle in between. I sat down in one of the chairs and closed my eyes as fatigue settled into my bones. I took a few deep breaths and shrugged the feelings off, then focused on getting into my zone.

Now, contrary to popular belief, psychics do not walk around in a state of constant awareness. We do not head out into the big wide world each day and get bombarded with information. If we did, trust me . . . we'd all be in the loony bin. Unless there is something of grave importance that our guides want us to pay attention to, like Hadley's circumstance, for instance, it takes a conscious effort to turn on our radar. It's a mode we go into. Think of how Tiger Woods walks onto the green at a big tournament. He is focused, centered and intense. He's all business, and you can tell simply by looking at him that he's in his zone.

It's pretty much the same with us. We focus, gather our energy and flip the old switch, so to speak. I know many psychics who, in order to do this, take an hour or two to meditate. I'm more of a Cliff's Notes kind of gal, so I need only a few minutes to prepare.

The routine is pretty much the same every time. First I run through my chakras, or energy points. I imagine them being turned on much like a lightbulb. There are seven of these in total, all a different color, running from my tailbone to the top of my head.

Once all my chakras are lit I call out to three of the archangels, Michael, Gabriel and Uriel, for protection, wisdom and clarity, then to my crew, who are my own set of metaphysical baby-sitters, if you will.

The crew consists of five spirit guides who have identified themselves to me through dreams and meditations. Collectively, they've made it known that their duty is to make sure that when I do my job, I get it right. Mostly they just try to keep me in line, which seems to require all five.

By the time I'd finished my meditation the first

party guest was peeking in the doorway. "Hi, Christina," I said. "Come on in and sit down."

"Thanks, Abby," she said, taking her seat. "I've never had this done before," she admitted.

"Ooooh," I said with a grin. "A virgin. Well, Christina, I promise to be gentle and still respect you in the morning, okay?"

Christina laughed and nodded. "What should I do?" she asked as she looked at me expectantly.

"I need your full name and your date of birth so that I can focus on your energy. You don't have to do anything other than that," I explained. "I get to do all the work."

"Christina Plimpton, January ninth, nineteen seventy-six."

"Perfect," I said as I closed my eyes. In my mind, I gathered my intuition like drawing back on a bow with an arrow, then loosed it at Christina. I waited to "feel" her energy before retrieving back my intuitive arrow, but as I searched I felt absolutely nothing. My brows lowered as I concentrated. This was weird. I couldn't get a handle on her energy. Finally, I pulled my intuitive arrow back, thinking I must be more tired than I thought, and reached out to my guides for assistance. No information was forthcoming. I asked for a topic, and got . . . zippo. I *insisted* on a topic . . . and still . . . zippo. Getting frustrated, I shot my arrow once again at Christina's energy, only to be disappointed.

Changing tacks, I asked a question in my head: *How is Christina's love life?*

No answer.

How is Christina's career?

No answer.

How is Christina?

No answer.

Finally I opened my eyes and looked at the anxious girl in front of me. She had no doubt watched my facial expressions and was wondering why I appeared so pissed off. "Christina—" I began.

"It's something bad, isn't it?" she asked me.

I smiled, making an effort to appear relaxed. "Not at all. It's just that I seem to be more tired than I expected, and your energy is so subtle I'm having a hard time making a connection. Why don't you send the next person up so I can warm up on them and then we'll try you again in a little bit, okay?"

"Uh . . . okay, I guess," she said, looking so disappointed that I almost held her back and tried again. But something told me to move forward to the next guest, so I waited while she got up and left the table, feeling truly crappy for letting her down.

A minute later a petite blonde made an entrance, seeming more nervous than she probably would have if I'd been able to connect with Christina's energy. I waved her in and she introduced herself as Michelle. After a moment I focused all of my energy on her and felt a connection right away. So relieved I could have laughed out loud, I began, "Michelle, do you have a brother?"

"Yes, I do."

"He's your older brother, right?"

"Yes, he is."

"Are you and your brother spending money on the outside of your mother's house?" I asked, puzzled by the message sequence coming to me.

"Uh . . ." she said as she thought through my question.

In my mind I kept hearing the word "mother," then seeing the image of a house, then a dollar bill. As I followed this sequence I was shown a LA-Z-Boy chair being set on the porch of the house, and I asked, "Are you and your brother buying some type of chair for the porch of your mother's house?" Odd as the image was, that was what I was compelled to say.

Michelle gave a hearty laugh as she replied, "Ohmigod! Abby, you are amazing! My brother and I are buying my mother a porch swing for her birthday at the end of March!"

I sat back in my chair relieved. Thank God, my radar was fine. There was something up on Christina's end. Michelle and I continued to have a terrific session for another fifteen minutes or so and I asked for the next in the group.

Because I was expecting Christina, I was surprised when Ellie appeared in the doorway. "Knock, knock!" she said coming into the room with a bottle of Pellegrino water.

"I thought Christina was coming back up," I said as she took her seat.

"She decided to wait until you finished with me. She's a little nervous to come back up here. What did you say to her?"

"Nothing, and that's the truth. Also the problem."

"You didn't get anything at all?"

"Nada," I said.

"Hmmm. Well, she thinks that you saw something terrible happening to her and you won't tell her what it is. She's waiting to come back until she sees what you have to say about me."

"You know I don't filter," I said defensively.

"That's what I told her, but she can get a little wiggy, Abby, so not to worry. Now enough about her. Let's focus on me!" Ellie said with a small clap of her hands.

I gave her a grin and closed my eyes, focused, shot my arrow, retrieved it back and began speaking. "Okay, El, the first thing I get is the image of a cradle, and we already know you're pregnant, but they're pointing to a pink blanket here."

"That's what you told me this afternoon, that I'd have a girl," Ellie said.

"Oh, yeah," I said, remembering. "Well, they're saying that this is the first of two. So I hope you like girls, because I'm definitely seeing another cradle later, and it's also got a pink blanket."

"Wonderful!" Ellie said. "Eddie will be thrilled!"

"And congratulations on the new house," I said, moving on to another topic.

"You are good," she sang back at me.

"You're moving closer to water," I said, seeing a FOR SALE sign in my head and a moving van parked next to a lake.

"There's a house we've fallen in love with about a stone's throw from Huston Lake and that wouldn't be as long a commute for either Eddie or me."

"Great! I'm feeling like you need to act before the end of March, because that property won't be available for long."

"We planned on making an offer after we got back from our honeymoon."

"Perfect. Now let me ask you about this legal thing . . ." I said as I focused on the next thought that came into my mind.

"What legal thing?"

I hesitated a moment before answering her, trying to piece together the string of thoughts and images my crew was sending. There was something not quite right here. "Did Eddie go see an attorney about a prenup?"

"Noooo . . ." Ellie said, drawing out the *O*.

I scratched my head and focused. "Are you sure? My crew is definitely saying that Eddie is seeing an attorney about something."

"We haven't even talked about a prenup," Ellie insisted. "Truly, it's never come up."

"Is he going to an attorney for any other reason? Like did one of his patients threaten to sue him?"

Ellie squirmed in her chair and began to look frightened. "Abs, he's got malpractice insurance up the yin-yang, and as far as I know no one is threatening a lawsuit. Is that what you see?" she asked me, tension making her voice tight. "Do you see him getting sued?"

I concentrated as hard as I could on Eddie's energy,

and the very next image did nothing to calm my fears. In my mind's eye I saw Eddie sitting on a bird swing, rocking back and forth. The image pulled back and the door to the cage banged shut. *Uh-oh.* Unless I was wrong, Ellie's fiancé was about to go to jail.

Now, I know most people would agree that I should filter a message like this and avoid telling my client what I'm seeing so as not to upset them. But long ago I took a vow never to do that. I'd broken that vow exactly once, and had no intention of ever doing so again. I gathered my courage and began, "Ellie, I want you to prepare yourself, because what I'm picking up isn't pleasant."

Ellie's face went stark white and her eyes opened wide. "What is it? What do you see, Abby?"

"Eddie's headed to jail."

"What?"

"I'm sorry, Ellie, but that's what I'm getting. Something bad is going down, and Eddie's going to need an attorney. And a good one."

It took Ellie a long time to speak. When she did she said, "You're sure?"

"Yes, honey. There are certain metaphors that are old standards for me. My sign for a jail cell keeps coming up in my head when I ask about Eddie. Moreover, my crew keeps saying 'lawyer' and pointing to Eddie. I don't know when, and I don't know why, but it's soon, whatever it is."

Ellie's eyes filled with tears, and she looked at me with a face that begged me to take it back. "But Abby, I love him. He's a good man. There's nothing he could be doing that would send him to jail!"

I looked at her with deep compassion, then closed my eyes and focused hard. *Why is Eddie going to jail?* I asked my crew. My crew answered by giving me a strange mix of signals. When I thought I had it figured out I opened my eyes and said, "I'm not sure what I've got here, Ellie, but I feel like Eddie may have done something to break the law, but there is also this feeling like he didn't do what they say he did. It's like he had no choice, like he was compelled or forced to do what he did, and that's why I believe a good attorney can help him."

"Do you know what it is that he's done?" she asked, her face still pale and frightened.

"No," I said as I dug hard for that. "All they'll tell me is that he was forced to do this thing that is against the law. He had no choice. There's also this sense of wanting to run away. I keep feeling like I want to hide, and it has to do with this issue of being forced into something."

"Abby, he's a good guy!" she burst out.

"I know, honey, but—"

"And besides that, *I'm pregnant*!"

"Ellie," I said, reaching across the table to take her hand. "I could be wrong. I can misinterpret on occasion."

" 'Liar, liar . . . pants on fire . . .' " Ellie whispered. She was openly sobbing now.

"No, really, it's true," I insisted. "I can be wrong—"

"Not you, Abby . . . Eddie. This morning in the driveway. That's what you said about Eddie. That he was a liar."

"Ellie, I'm a long way from home, here. And this altitude could really be screwing with my antennae. I didn't mean to upset you. I really am sorry about all this."

"I can't imagine what he's done," Ellie said. "I can't imagine what he'd be forced into that he would go to jail for."

"Maybe it's time you and Eddie had a heart-to-heart?"

Ellie nodded, the tears still flowing. "This is awful," she said as she put her head down on her arm to cry.

I reached out and stroked her shoulder when I heard, "Knock, knock," from the doorway.

"Oh!" I exclaimed, startled that someone else had entered the room. Looking up, I noticed a petite woman standing in the doorway. She was as little in stature as my sister, but with brown hair and big wide eyes, and I remembered her from the dinner the night before. I thought I remembered her name was Kelly, and she was also one of the bridesmaids. "Hi, there. What's up?" I asked, still patting Ellie's shoulder.

"Ellie said to send the next person up after twenty minutes. It was my turn, so I came upstairs and . . . Ellie, are you okay?" she asked, noticing for the first time that Ellie was crying.

"I'm fine. Just a little emotional these days," Ellie said as she raised her head and wiped her tears. "I think I just need to go lie down for a while. Can you please let everyone else know that I'm not feeling well, and if they want to stay they're welcome to, but I won't be joining the rest of the party?"

"Oh," Kelly said, coming into the room and putting a hand on Ellie's shoulder. "Is there anything I can do?"

"No, I'll be okay. Thanks," Ellie said, getting to her feet as her lip quivered and more water leaked out of her eyes. "I just really need to be alone right now." And with that she bolted for her bedroom.

I watched her go and felt like one hundred and twenty pounds of smelly caca. Goddamn it. This part of my job sucked.

"What did you say to her?" Kelly asked me.

"Nothing I can share, I'm afraid," I replied. "Listen, Kelly—right?"

"Yes."

"I know you were next, and I'm so sorry to do this to you, but I am not up for any more readings tonight."

"That's okay," Kelly said, quick to reassure me. "I didn't really want my fortune told anyway. You people scare me!"

I smiled tiredly at her as I mentally shut down my radar. "Thanks for understanding. Listen, can you do me one more tremendous favor?"

"Sure," she said.

"Could you drive me to Ellie's aunt Vivian's? I'm exhausted, and if I don't get some sleep soon I'm gonna drop where I'm standing."

"Of course, Abby. Let me just break up the party downstairs and we'll go, okay?"

"Thanks, Kelly. While you're talking to the girls I'll get changed."

As Kelly went downstairs I headed into the bathroom, where I'd left my clothes folded on the counter, and changed out of Ellie's cashmere tracksuit. Before going back downstairs I knocked on Ellie's door to see if she was okay, but she didn't answer, and my intuition suggested that I should leave well enough alone.

I met Kelly in the living room as the rest of the girls were packing their things and cleaning up so that Ellie didn't have to do it later. I'm not sure what Kelly had told them, but each one found a way to give me an evil look as I shifted uncomfortably from foot to foot while I waited for Kelly to grab her coat and keys. We were out the door a minute later, and I was supremely relieved.

"Vivian is over on Scottsdale, right?" Kelly asked me as we fastened our seat belts.

"Sounds familiar," I said, realizing I didn't really know where she lived. "Just don't ask me how to get there; I have no idea where I am in this city."

"I've been to her house once, last Fourth of July. I remember these big pink flamingos in her front yard. She's a bit of an odd duck, that one."

"Kooky," I agreed.

"So where do you know Ellie from?"

"We go way back. She was my neighbor when she lived in Michigan, which was a million years ago."

"Oh, yeah, I remember her saying that she was originally from there," Kelly said.

"How do you know her?" I asked.

"She used to date my older brother."

"Really?" I asked, looking at her. "How long ago?"

"Right before she dumped him for Eddie." Kelly laughed.

"Ouch," I said. "That's great that you two can remain friends."

"Yeah, if it were anyone else I'd hate her, but Ellie is my best friend. She's just the nicest person. I'm not even close to being a social butterfly, and the fact that someone like her can be nice to me . . . well, I can't help but love her, you know?"

"I'm right there with you, girlfriend. She is the nicest person I know. And she's always taking care of people and thinking of them. Do you know that for three Valentine's Days in a row when I was single Ellie sent me a huge bouquet of flowers with a card that said, 'Just because you're single doesn't mean you shouldn't get flowers today.'"

Kelly laughed. "She's been sending me giant boxes of chocolate for two years, and this year she added a big stuffed bear."

"I just wish I could have been as good a friend to her," I said.

"Are you talking about the reading you just gave her?"

"Yeah . . . it's bad enough giving tough news to a total stranger. When it's someone you love, it just makes it that much harder to deliver."

We fell silent for a bit as Kelly drove, and I looked out the window at the passing scenery. I could barely see the outline of the Rocky Mountains against the inky black sky. There was no moon tonight, and clouds seemed to cloak the night in a black mist. I leaned back in my seat and sighed, closing my eyes and listening to the radio, when I felt a familiar buzz in the back of my head—my crew had a message.

At first I tried to ignore them—I was too damn tired to tune in any more tonight—but the more I ignored it the stronger the buzz became. Finally, a little annoyed, I flipped my intuitive switch and got a forceful, *Call Duffy!*

Okay, I'll call him in the morning, I thought.

Left side—heavy feeling . . .

You want me to call him right now?

Right side—light, airy feeling . . .

Opening my weary eyes I reached for my purse, dug out my cell phone and Duffy's card, which he'd given to me at the hospital. "Who're you calling?" Kelly asked.

"Duffy," I said as I punched in his number.

"Reception out here might not be so good," she said.

"It'll go through," I said, not bothering to explain that my crew would make sure of it.

" 'Lo!" Duffy said as the line was picked up.

"Hey, Duff. It's Abby," I said.

"Hey, Abs. I'm glad you called. I've got some news. We found Gina's car."

"You're kidding," I said, sitting up straighter in my seat.

"Yep. About two hours ago."

"Where?"

"At the airport. Parked in international parking."

My intuition was humming at rapid speed now, and there was no way I believed Gina had taken a trip out of the country. This was a setup. "Duffy, you have got to believe me. She did not fly out of town."

"I'm with ya. The other reason I needed to talk to you was that we found something in her car that I'm a little bothered by."

"What?"

"Surgical scrubs. Size large. And they were soaked in blood."

"Surgical . . . ?" I didn't finish that thought, because immediately I thought about my reading tonight with Ellie and how I had seen Eddie being carted off to jail and requiring an attorney. "Duffy, we have to talk . . . *now*."

"Okay, where are you?"

"I'm with Kelly. She's driving me to Viv's."

"I'm a few blocks over from Viv's. Closer to you if you're coming from Ellie's, in fact. Have her drop you off at my place instead and I'll swing you over to Viv's when we're done talking."

"Cool, hold on." Turning to Kelly, I asked, "Kelly, instead of dropping me at Viv's could you please take me to Duffy's?"

"I guess," she said, looking slightly annoyed. "I don't know where he lives, though."

"Duffy, can you give her directions?"

"Sure, pass the phone to her," he said, and I did.

About twenty minutes later we pulled into Duffy's driveway. "Thanks, Kelly, I really appreciate the taxi service."

"You're welcome," she said in a tight, clipped tone. She hadn't spoken to me since I got off the phone with Duffy, and I couldn't figure out what I'd said to piss her off, so I just let it be for now. I gave her a smile and closed the car door. As I turned and headed up Duffy's walkway, I heard her zoom out of the driveway and accelerate down the street. Definitely pissed. Great.

The door opened before I had a chance to reach it, and a smiling Duffy greeted me. By the sight of him, I guessed he was freshly showered. His hair was still damp, and he smelled of soap and scented shampoo. He was dressed in a rust-colored knit sweater that molded itself to his toned torso. A pair of loose-fitting jeans hugged his hips, and even though it was thirty degrees outside, he was barefoot. "Hello, gorgeous," he said warmly. "I was about to send out a search party; did you guys get lost?"

"Hey, yourself," I said as I walked into his front hall. "I don't know; Kelly never said a word to me after she hung up with you, so we might have." Duffy waited next to me as I shrugged out of my coat, and while he hung it in the closet I had a chance to move into the interior and check out the digs.

Duffy's house was similar to Vivian's in structure—the same Tudor design, but that was where the resemblance ended. His beech hardwood floors were glossed to a high-polished shine. The walls were painted an off-white, and contemporary light fixtures added accents to the ceilings. After he'd put my coat away, he led me into his kitchen, which appeared newly updated with granite countertops and cherry-wood cabinets adorned with Art Deco pulls. The kitchen opened on the opposite side to the living room, which was decorated with a cream-colored couch and a matching love seat and thick shag throw rugs accented with a bleached-wood coffee table and matching side table. Here and there were Art Deco accents and artwork. Overall the home was warm and inviting, and matched Duffy's personality so well I had to smile. "Nice place," I said, nodding my head in approval.

"Thanks. It's a work in progress, but it's getting there. Have a seat," he said, pointing to a bar stool on one side of the kitchen island. "Want to join me in a glass of wine?"

"Love it."

"Chianti?"

"Perfect."

Duffy poured us each a glass, then came around to join me at the bar. "So what's up?"

I took a small sip of wine before answering him. The flavor was smooth and silky, with no bitter aftertaste. It was fabulous. "I gave your sister a reading tonight," I began, playing my finger around the rim of my wineglass.

"And by the look on your face I'm guessing the message wasn't good."

"Bingo."

"Another cheating girlfriend in my future?" Duffy asked, giving me a sideways look.

"Huh?" I said, looking up at him. Then I remembered that my last reading with Ellie had revealed his eventual breakup with his ex, Rachel. "No," I said, then added with a grin, "You know, it's not *always* about you."

Duffy laughed, lifting his wineglass in a "touché" gesture. "So what'd your little crystal ball reveal this time?"

"It's about Eddie. And it's bad."

"How bad?"

"Bad enough to send Ellie to her bedroom in tears."

"Can you tell me?" Duffy asked, his eyes intense with concern.

"Normally I would never betray your sister's trust like this, but I think you need to know. At least, my feeling is that I need to bring you into the loop."

"Okay," Duffy said.

"I think that Eddie's in trouble."

"What kind of trouble?"

"The legal kind. In Ellie's reading I got the strong feeling that he was going to need an attorney. A good one. I also got the distinct impression that he was going to be spending time in a jail cell."

"Well, hell, Abs. You really know how to breeze into town and ruin a good party," Duffy said, trying to make light.

"I'm serious, Duff," I said, no hint of a grin on my face.

"I know; I'm sorry. So did you get a feeling for what he's done or what he'll do to warrant internment?"

"Not exactly. But my gut says that it's heavy."

"How heavy?"

"Gina's-car-being-found-with-surgical-scrubs-full-of-blood heavy."

Duffy looked at me for a long, intense moment as he considered what I'd just said. "No way," he finally said. "I know the guy, Abs; it's not possible."

"And yet, Gina's vanished into thin air. She has a history of playing with unavailable men. Her car's discovered in an airport parking lot, and the only connection to what might have happened to her is the scrubs, which is the only outfit I've ever seen Eddie in."

Duffy rubbed his chin for a minute, his five-o'clock shadow giving him a roguishly handsome look. "Damn," he mumbled. "Fine. We're running the scrubs through some DNA testing right now, but we won't get those results back for a few weeks. In the meantime I'll start asking some questions about Eddie."

"Listen, for what it's worth, whatever Eddie's in trouble for, I know it was against his will. I got the strong feeling he was forced into a situation and he had little choice in the matter," I said. "And I've met the guy, and his energy does not feel like that of a violent murderer. Having said that, I have to admit that this altitude could be jumbling my radar, and I just think it's wise to be thorough here."

"Okay. Enough said. You want more wine?"

I nodded and Duffy got up to retrieve the bottle. I was in a hazy, sleepy mood at this point, feeling really relaxed. My eyes wandered to Duffy's rear as he went around the counter. He had a nice ass. Almost as nice as Dutch's. Thinking of Dutch made me suddenly melancholy, and I could feel the hurt beginning to burble up, so I shook my head and squared my shoulders, pushing back thoughts of him and focusing on the present.

"You okay?" Duffy asked me.

"Huh?" I said, startled by the question.

"You looked so sad for a second."

"Yeah," I said, nodding. My lip quivered in spite of my best efforts to push the hurt away.

"Hey, there," Duffy said as one tear formed, then leaked out of my eye down my cheek. "Come here, girl," he said as he set the bottle of wine down and pulled me up off my chair into his arms. The move was tender and so unexpected that it just about killed me. I fought for control. I would not give in to this sudden bout of sadness.

"I'm okay," I whispered, my voice shivering with emotion.

"Liar, liar . . . pants on fire . . ." Duffy chuckled into my hair. "Remember that?" he asked me. "You used to yell that at me every time I was trying to get away with something. I don't know how you did it, but you could always tell when I was lying."

Duffy was rocking me gently, stroking my back and holding me close. I swallowed hard. I didn't want to be a soppy mess in front of him. I wanted to be cool, together, laid-back. It wasn't happening. I closed my eyes and gave him a squeeze. It just felt good to listen to his throaty, masculine voice and rock in his arms.

He hugged me tighter, then wrapped his hands up into my hair and pulled my face up to look into his eyes. His expression was mixed. There were hints of a shared understanding of how it felt to get your heart trampled on, along with compassion and something else that was chemically charged. I realized this last part a moment before he lowered his lips to mine and kissed me.

He tasted like the wine we'd been drinking, and his mouth was soft and hungry. I felt a moment of guilt, because I'd been Dutch's girl for so long that this was like cheating. But an instant later Duffy's hand moved to my neck, and with his thumb he tilted my head back. Lowering his mouth to my neck, he worked his teeth and tongue expertly along my skin. I gave a soft moan, and thoughts of Dutch faded into one big, oozy feeling of need.

I wanted Duffy, and I wanted him badly. I gripped his sweater beneath my fingertips as the urge to absorb him into me intensified. Duffy must have sensed my increasing desire, because he pulled his lips up from my neck to look again into my eyes. His pupils were big, black, liquid pools of desire. Without a word he grabbed my hand and pulled me into his bedroom. He shut the door, and the only light left came in from a street lamp outside.

Again he curled his fingers into my hair and tilted my head up. "Do you realize what a knockout you are?" he asked me.

I grinned seductively at him and reached up to pull his lips on top of mine. I didn't want to talk right now. I had other things on my mind. My other hand reached under Duffy's sweater and played across his chest. He was built like the mountains in the distance. My fingers trailed over the landscape of his chest, hard, chiseled rock with valleys in between. My desire grew, and with one move Duffy's shirt was on the floor. My sweater joined it a moment later, and as I fumbled with his jeans zipper I felt his hands at my lower back, working the skirt from my hips.

Kicking off his jeans, he pulled me into him, and our skin felt hot where it touched. We were kissing each other in mad, hungry, devouring moves, the frenzy to quench our thirst for each other driving our desire. His hands touched every sensitive place I had, and I moaned with each new caress. My hands also found things to play with, and it wasn't long before Duffy inched back toward the bed, pulling me with him. Just before lying down he asked me, "Top? Or bottom?"

"Side to side," I said wickedly.

He nodded his head as he stuck out his chin thoughtfully. "This could be fun," he said as he pulled me down to the comforter. And God help, me . . . it was.

Chapter Nine

We both woke with a start as the phone rang at seven A.M. the next morning. Duff reached over me to grab it and said in a throaty whisper, " 'Lo?" I could hear the faintest hint of a voice coming through the receiver, and Duffy answered, "Good morning, Viv. What's wrong?"

I could hear Viv's voice more clearly now as Duffy held the phone slightly away from his ear. I thought I heard her say something like, "Ee's missing."

"No, she's here at my house. We were catching up with each other last night and it got late, so I put her up in my guest room."

I distinctly heard a snort come through the other end of the line, followed by something that sounded like, "Testing the swimmers out on her, huh?"

Duffy's face turned red as he sat up and scratched at his chin. "I'll bring her by later, Viv. Thanks for calling." And he hung up the phone.

"Uh-oh," I said with a giggle. "We're busted."

"Looks like it. If I know Viv she'll be on the phone with my mother in five . . . four . . . three . . ."

"She's going to tell *Nina*?" I said, horrified at the thought.

"Count on it, Abs. Sorry, but Viv lives to make my

mother miserable. She's gonna have a field day with this latest development."

"Ohmigod, I'm so embarrassed," I said, burying my face in my hands.

"Come on, go shower and I'll make us some breakfast. We'll work on getting our stories straight after we've had something to eat."

Duffy showed me into the bathroom and pulled out a clean towel for me to use. I took my time, allowing the hot water to wash away much of the guilt I was now feeling. Don't get me wrong: Last night had been wonderful. But in the clear light of day my conscience was having a hard time with the fact that a week after getting dumped I was hopping into bed with someone else. Was I a slut, or what?

I wrapped myself in Duffy's flannel robe and slippers and padded out to the kitchen, where the scent of French toast and coffee made my stomach grumble. "That smells fantastic," I said as I took a seat.

"I aim to please," Duffy said, setting a plate of steaming French toast and a cup of coffee in front of me. He then grabbed a second plate, flipped two pieces off the grill for himself and joined me at the bar.

"What are we going to tell everyone now that the word's out?" I asked as I cut into my breakfast.

"What would you like to tell them?" Duffy asked. Why did men always answer tricky questions with a tricky question?

"What would *you* like to tell them?" I answered. I could play that game too.

Duffy chuckled. "I get to go first, huh?"

"Age before beauty," I said with a wink.

"Ahh, that's how it's gotta be, huh? Okay, well, let me think," he said, and took a few bites of his breakfast, then gave me a rather serious look. "My guess is that you're fresh off the broken-heart tour, and probably need a little time to think about how you feel."

"Pretty much," I said, thankful that he understood how I felt.

"So, while you're thinkin' . . . how about we just keep it low-key to everyone else. We'll stick to the 'she slept in my guest room' story, and if anyone wants to assume something else happened, then that's their problem."

"Sounds good," I said, and reached over to squeeze his arm. "And thank you."

"For what?"

"For growing up to be such a great guy," I said, and meant it.

Duffy dropped me off at Vivian's an hour later, and luckily she wasn't home when I arrived. There was an envelope taped to her door with my name on it. It said that the back door was open and to let myself in. She'd gone to get her hair done and do some shopping for a dress appropriate for her grandniece's wedding. I headed around back and then inside and quickly changed, anxious to put on clean clothes. While I was applying my makeup I heard my cell phone give a little chirp. Hurrying over to it, I flipped open the lid and said, "Hey, Cat!"

"Hi, sweetie! We're here!"

"Denver?"

"Yep. We just checked into the Brown Palace. Tommy is tired and wants to take a nap, so I thought this would be a good time for us to catch up."

"Great, what'd you have in mind?"

"Well, the boys would love to see you. And I still need to buy a wedding present for Ellie and Eddie. How about I come pick you up and we can do some shopping with the boys?"

Cat was referring to my nephews, Mathew and Michael. They were five years old and full of mischief. "Absolutely, honey. Bring them by."

"Where are you now?"

"I'm at Viv's. Hold on and I'll get you her address."

Walking into the front hall I picked up an electric bill on Viv's side table and read off the address to Cat, who promised to be there post-haste. I rushed back into the bathroom and spent some time on my long hair. Next I changed into a pair of camel suede pants and an off-white V-neck shirt with a matching suede jacket. I completed the ensemble with a fabulous pair of brown leather boots I'd picked up at Nine West. As I was putting on some earrings I heard a beep outside. Hurrying to retrieve my purse, I bustled out of the house after writing a quick note to Viv.

In the driveway was a stretch limo the size of a small whale. A driver got out of the front seat and came around to get the door for me. The moment the car was opened a flurry of noise greeted my ears as Cat competed with her spoiled-rotten sons, who were bouncing around in the limo and making a commotion. Seeing me she yelled, "Look, boys, it's *Auntie*!"

Matt and Mike paused in their romp across the limo's seats long enough to take in the sight of me; then they continued as if they'd never been interrupted. "Good to see you too, monkey men," I said as I climbed in the limo and snatched Mikey off one of the seats, kissing and tickling him half a dozen times until he squealed with delight; then I moved on to his older-by-one-minute brother. After letting go of Matty, I turned to Cat and said, "Hello, sis! Wow, you look great. Have you done something to your hair or is it that you've been working out?"

"Ohmigod you've had sex!" Cat said, her mouth opening into a huge O of shock.

My own mouth dropped open at her declaration and I felt my cheeks grow hot. "I have not!" I said, working on a falsely-accused attitude.

"Mommy, what's sex?" Mikey asked.

"It's a game grown-ups play, sweetheart."

"I want to play!" Matty shrieked, and jumped over to sit by my side.

"I'm sorry, sweetheart; it's only for adults."

"I want to play sex!" Mikey yelled in full support of his brother.

"Now you've done it," I said to her. "See what throwing that word around does? It's just trouble."

"So, dish! Who's the lucky man?" Cat persisted as Matty picked up her purse and turned it upside down, allowing all the contents to scatter on the floor. I bent over and helped Cat pick up her belongings as two additional pairs of hands reached for anything interesting. "Matt, give Mommy back her cell phone," Cat demanded while my nephew flipped open the lid and punched in a number expertly.

With a growl of irritation, Cat reached for Matt, but he scurried to the other side of the limo and a moment later was yelling into the phone, "Hello, Daddy? Mommy and Auntie are playing sex and they won't let us play."

"Oh, God, will you stop him?" I said as I grabbed Mikey by the middle and clung to him while my sister got up and moved across the stretch limo to deal with Matty.

Giving him a dark look, she grabbed the phone out of his hand and said, "Tommy? Ha, ha, is that you?"

There was a reply, and Cat's face fell as her complexion paled noticeably. "Ah, sorry, wrong number!" she said, and clicked the phone closed.

"Uh-oh," I said. "Who was that?"

"Mr. Ling Hong. He's one of my top clients. But I don't think he recognized it was me," she said in a voice that wasn't convincing.

"Let's just hope he doesn't check his caller ID," I said before I could stop myself.

"Oh, *noooooo*!" Cat wailed. "I can't believe this is happening to me! Matty, you are a very bad boy!"

"I want to play sex!" Matt insisted, folding up his arms and screwing up his face into a really good pout.

"Fine, but we'll need to get it for you at the toy store. Driver? Take us to the nearest mall."

"*What,* exactly, are you going to buy him at the

toy store?" I whispered when she'd settled next to me again.

"The biggest, loudest humdinger of a truck I can find. Once he's got that to occupy his mind, he won't give S-E-X another thought."

"Parenthood One-oh-one by Cat Masters," I said, shaking my head.

"It'll work," Cat insisted. "Trust me."

Fifteen minutes later we were inside the same mall Ellie and I had ventured to just the day before. Fortunately I'd been spared any further grilling by my sister, as my two nephews had done a splendid job of keeping her attention focused on them. "Stay with Mommy!" Cat said as she tried to hold on to each of their hands. The twins were having none of it. Surrounded by sights and sounds and wide-open spaces, all they wanted to do was run pell-mell across the floor.

"And you didn't bring your nanny with you because . . . ?" I asked her as I picked a squirming Mikey up and carried him so he couldn't run away.

"She said she needed a few days off." Cat grunted as she did the same with Matty.

"Gee, can't imagine her wanting to spend any time away from these two little *angels,*" I said.

"They're hyper because they had a soft drink on the plane."

"Why would you give them a soft drink?" I asked, running out of patience for my sister and her two monsters.

"They were making a lot of noise, and I thought if they had something to sip on, it might calm them down."

"Ah, well, in that case—ow! Mikey don't kick Auntie—great thinking," I finished woodenly.

"Oh, look, Abby! There's a cute little shop. I wonder if there's anything for Ellie and Eddie in there," Cat said, pointing to a gift shop with plenty of things the boys could break.

"Why don't I stay out here with them while you

browse?" I said as I set Mikey down and took a firm grip on his hand.

"Oh, okay," Cat said, and handed Matty to me. "I'll just be a minute." And with that she dashed inside.

While I struggled with the boys, Cat took much longer than a minute and finally appeared in the doorway. "Oh, thank God," I said, and got ready to hand off one of the boys. My arms felt like they were being pulled out of their sockets.

"Can you come in and give me your opinion for a quick second?" Cat asked.

"What about these guys?" I asked.

Cat squatted down and looked intently at the twins. "M and M," she said sternly. "Mommy and Auntie need to go inside this store. Now, it's a grown-up store and you will need to be on your best behavior. If you're good then we'll go to the ice cream parlor right afterward. Okay?"

Magically, both boys stopped struggling and nodded their heads. I personally thought that the last thing they needed was more sugar, but what did I know?

We all trooped into the shop, and Cat zigzagged her way over to a beautiful glass sculpture of two figures embraced in a kiss. "What do you think of this?" Cat said, letting go of Matty's hand while she picked it up and showed it to me.

"I think that's gorgeous, and Ellie will love it," I answered, noting that the price tag put it upward of three hundred dollars.

"Or there's this piece over here," Cat said, trotting over to another sculpture that was etched in glass with a mermaid wrapping her long fish tail around a man sitting on a rock. "You know, because Ellie is a Pisces, it sort of fits."

"I like the first one better," I said, looking back to the sculpture we'd just come from.

"Good! Me too!" Cat said with a hand clap. "Now let me flag down—"

Cat never got a chance to finish her sentence, because at that moment a loud *Wonk! Wonk! Wonk! Wonk!* came from the front of the store, followed by, "Stop! Thief!" from one of the salesclerks, who dashed out the door.

"Oh, my goodness!" Cat said, turning to me. "Can you believe there was a shoplifter in this very store? I tell you, America is no longer safe! Where's Matty?" she said, looking around.

"He took that truck," Mikey said.

"What truck?" Cat said, alarmed.

"The one on that table over there," Mikey said, pointing to several model cars that were displayed neatly on one of the tables in the store. There was a space in between the other cars where obviously one had been.

"Mikey, tell Mommy where Matty went with the truck," Cat said, her eyes darting around the store as she looked frantically for her missing son.

"He ran outta the store and that lady ran after him," Mikey said, pointing to the front of the store.

"Oh, my God!" Cat shrieked, and dashed out of the store. I stood there with Mikey for a beat or two, wondering what to do. I decided to head over to the counter and wait for Cat to return.

As I stood by the counter and rocked with Mikey on my hip, the remaining sales girl gave me a dark look and asked, "Is that your son?"

"My nephew," I said.

"What about that other child? The one who stole that antique model."

"My other nephew."

"That was a very expensive model," the clerk said. "I may have to call the police."

"Cut him some slack, lady. He's only five years old."

"They turn to the dark side so young these days," she said, her eyes narrow and mean.

"What are you, Darth Vader?" I snapped, then

pulled in my horns and said, "My sister will make amends if any harm comes to the truck."

"Is that the woman who also ran out of the store?"

"She'll be right back," I growled.

"How can you be sure?"

"Because this is her other kid," I sneered. This idiot was seriously pissing me off.

"Well, she'll need to pay for the model. And if she can't afford to pay for it, then I will be forced to call the police," she snipped.

I rolled my eyes and turned away. This woman was coming close to deserving a bitch slap, and before I did anything stupid I figured it would be prudent to walk away. I decided to head over to the window with Mikey and look for Cat. Across the mall I spotted someone who looked very familiar. A man with dark, scruffy hair walked quickly through the mall, several packages in hand. He looked around shiftily, and something about him made the hair on my arms stand up on end. Then I had it: It was the man who had kidnapped Hadley Rankin. Setting Mikey down quickly, I reached inside my purse and pulled out my cell. Just as I snapped it open, Cat, Mathew and the other salesgirl came back in, all three out of breath.

Before Cat could even say a word to me I gently pushed Mikey at her and dashed out the door. Running toward the man who was very near an exit door, I hit my redial button and put the phone to my ear. "Come on, Duff: *pick up!*" I said as I closed the distance between the kidnapper and me. Just as Duffy's voice mail clicked on, the man turned around, obviously hearing my booted footsteps. As he spotted me barreling down on him he bolted through the mall's double doors.

"Son of a bitch!" I swore as I followed close on his heels. "I know who you are!" I yelled as he flew through the foyer, heading toward the parking lot. Still holding on to my cell, I tried to dial 911 into the display, but I couldn't do that and keep up with the scumbag I was chasing. I had no idea what I'd do if I caught up to him; I just knew I needed to keep him in my sights.

Suddenly the kidnapper flung one of his bags at me, catching me in the face. "Ugh!" I said as my head snapped back. "You bastard!" I yelled, my adrenaline kicking into overdrive, and I put on some serious speed. My feet were screaming in those heels, but I was determined not to lose this guy. Just as I was within grabbing distance, he hit the brakes and I slammed into his back. In one horribly quick move he had me by the scruff of the neck and plowed me head-first into a car.

I tumbled over the hood and onto the pavement, landing hard on my back. I barely had time to gather my wits when I looked up to see the creep reaching down to grab me with one hand, while pulling back with the other as he got ready to punch my lights out. At that exact moment someone right behind him yelled, "Hey! Leave her alone!"

Distracted, my attacker looked over his shoulder for a split second, and it was all the time I needed. Using every ounce of strength I had, I kicked up with my booted foot as hard as I could and got the bastard right in his jewels. He sank to his knees, clutching his johnson. In a flash I was up and throwing all of my body weight on top of him, pushing him to the pavement. I heard him moan as his cheek hit the ground, but couldn't care less if he ended up scratched and bruised. Wasting no time, I quickly sat on his head and reached for his arm. Yanking it up and back, I yelled, "If you move, I'll break your friggin' arm!"

My Good Samaritan squatted down beside me as I held fast to scumbag's arm. "You okay?" the young man asked.

"I'm fine," I puffed, slightly out of breath. "My cell is over there. Can you grab it and call the police?"

"On it!" he said, and ran to retrieve my cell. Coming back to me, he sat down on the fugitive's butt, giving me a small smile as he dialed the police.

Mall security was the first to arrive, and they had the man handcuffed and sitting in their Jeep until a Denver deputy showed up. While I was giving my statement, Cat's stretch limo passed by and came to a screeching halt as Cat realized I was at the center of the commotion. Rushing out of the car, she pushed her way through the small crowd that had gathered at my side. "Abby? What's going on here?"

"Just wrapping things up, Cat. I'll be with you in a minute."

Cat waited while I gave the rest of my statement to the deputy, and just then Duffy drove up. "Hey, Calvin," he said as he got out of his squad car.

"Hi, Sheriff," the deputy in front of me said. "We've got the suspect in the back of my car. This young lady says she knows you."

"Duffy?" Cat said from over my shoulder. "Is that Duffy McGinnis?" she asked.

"Catherine Cooper, as I live and breathe. You look fabulous, girl!" Duffy said as he reached over and gave Cat a hug.

"Thank you. My secret is eight glasses of water a day and a good Pilates trainer. You look amazing; how've you been?"

"Can we catch up with each other later?" I complained. I wanted to tell Duffy that I'd caught the kidnapper.

"Sure, sure," Duffy said with a chuckle. "So I heard over the scanner that this is the same guy you pegged for the Rankin kidnapping?"

"He's the guy."

"How sure are you?"

"One hundred fifty percent," I said, looking him in the eye.

"He carrying any ID on him?" Duffy asked the deputy.

"A Kansas license as Warren Biggins and some

credit cards that identify him as Mark Hopskins and Joel Nelson. I'm running those right now to see if they come up stolen."

"They will," I said, feeling my intuition chime in.

"Cal, haul him back to the station and take his prints. See if you can get a rush on a comparison to the ones we pulled off that knife yesterday from the Rankin assault."

"On it," Calvin said, and closed up his notebook.

After he'd gone and the crowd began to disperse Duffy pulled me aside and asked, "Did I really hear you took him down?"

"Got him right in the testes," I said with a grin. "That'll teach him to target women."

Duffy grinned and shook his head. "Abby, what the heck were you thinking? That guy knifed a woman yesterday; he could very well have done the same to you."

"I'm fine," I said. "I've just got a bad case of really sore feet. These boots were not made for walking."

"I can rub them for you later," he said, and I blushed.

"Ohmigod!" Cat squealed from behind us. *"You had sex with Duffy McGinnis!"*

"I want to play sex!" Matty called out the window of the stretch. "Mommy, I want to play *sex*!"

I felt my cheeks burn with embarrassment as several people in the parking lot turned to observe a five-year-old using the *S*-word. "Uh, Duffy?"

"Yeah?"

"Can I possibly get a ride home with you?"

"Not up for explaining yourself to your sister, huh?"

"What gave it away?"

A few minutes and one very short explanation later, I was riding shotgun in Duffy's squad car, thankful to have left Cat and the twins behind. Don't get me wrong; I love my sister and my nephews dearly, but the only way I can maintain that kind of devotion is in small doses.

"You up for some lunch?" Duffy asked as we drove.

"I could eat," I said.

"Great, you like pizza?"

"Who doesn't?"

On the way to the pizza joint I recounted for Duffy exactly what'd happened at the mall. I had him in gales of laughter as I told him about my nephew and his bolt out the door with an expensive model car. "Sounds like your nephew has a stubborn streak," he said.

"You don't know the half of it," I said, shaking my head in mirth.

"Reminds me of his auntie when she was little."

"Oh, he's *so* much worse than I ever was," I said.

"Sure, sure," Duffy said with a wink and a grin. "That's what they all say."

We landed at the pizza parlor and headed inside. The eatery was a quaint little dive with checkered red-and-white tablecloths and the smell of dough, sauce and cheese coating the air with an aromatic scent. We found a booth in the back and sat down. The first thing I did after sitting was to unzip my boots and take my feet out for a much-needed break.

As I rubbed my right foot, Duffy asked, "Why do women wear shoes that hurt their feet?"

"The same reason men splash on aftershave. It may hurt like a bitch, but there's no denying the opposite sex likes it."

"Got it," Duffy said, giving me a wink. Under the table I felt his hand at my calf.

"What the . . . ?" I asked.

"Give 'em here," he said gently, and pulled my foot out of my hands. Before I could protest, his magic fingers were returning feeling to my battered soles. By the time the waitress came over, I was in serious heaven.

"Oh, my God, Duffy, that feels so good," I said after we'd given our order.

"You can return the favor anytime," he said with a mischievous smile.

"Sure," I purred. "Bring your aftershave over to Viv's tomorrow and I'll slap some on for you."

Duffy chuckled, giving my feet a final squeeze. "Or you could spend the night at my place and help me shave in the morning."

I ignored the invitation and put my boots back on. Going for a change of subject I asked, "Have you heard from your sister?"

Duffy nodded his head and avoided my eyes. "Yeah, she called me right after I dropped you off. She's still pretty upset."

"I wish I could take it back," I said moodily.

"Abby, it's not your fault. You got a message and she needed to hear it. You were doing your job, and I think it's great that you didn't filter, because she obviously needs to know. I, on the other hand, am starting to feel a little guilty about running a background check on her fiancé."

"Has anything come up yet?"

"Nope. Zippo. Like I thought, Eddie is clean as a whistle."

"Is there anything new in your hunt for Gina?"

"Only that she didn't board a plane the night she left her car. When she called in her reservation she paid by credit card. I'm trying to get the credit card number just to confirm it was hers, but no boarding pass was issued under her name. Her parking ticket was left in the car, and it's stamped February twelfth."

"So the whole thing's a setup."

"What do you mean?"

"We're being tossed a bunch of red herrings here. We're being made to believe Gina left of her own free will, and might still be alive. I'm not buying it."

"I know, me either. But I still can't rule out that Gina wasn't grabbed in the parking lot of the airport. If she didn't drive her car there, who did?"

"Any word from the neighbors?"

"Yes, actually. Both of them tell the same story. On the night she disappeared, they didn't see or hear anything suspicious. Neither one has seen her since last Tuesday, and no one has seen anyone else enter or exit the property on a regular basis. When I asked if she'd had any male visitors lately, they mentioned a guy coming around a month or two ago, but depending on the exact dates, it could have been Yeats or her boyfriend, Mark, right before he left for California."

"We're missing something."

"Count on it. On the plus side, I spoke with Hadley Rankin this morning."

"You did? How is she? Will she be okay? What did she say?" I asked in rapid-fire succession.

Duffy laughed as he held up his hands in a timeout signal. "Whoa, there, girl! She's doing remarkably well. Even though it looked bad, there wasn't too much internal damage and she can be released as early as tomorrow. As for what happened, she said that she came home from her part-time job and there was a knock on her door. When she peeped through the eyehole no one was there. Curious, she opened the door to get a better look, and that's when her assailant jumped her."

"Biggins," I corrected. I just knew we'd caught our man.

"Probably. Anyhoo, she and he wrestled around for a bit; then he told her that if she didn't cooperate fully with him he was not only going to kill her, he'd wait for her husband and kill him too."

"Bastard!"

"In a word," Duffy agreed. "So she's forced into her own car and told to drive. She also said that she was convinced her kidnapper knew where he was taking her, but he wouldn't share their final destination. She said she knew the moment she got in the car with him that he was going to kill her, but she cooperated because she didn't want her husband to die as well."

"Men like that need to be strung up by their gonads," I said, unfolding my napkin and setting it in my lap as the waitress approached our table with a big pizza platter in hand.

"Don't worry; he'll get his," Duffy said, and my right side felt light and airy, so I knew he was right.

"So when do we tell Ellie?" I asked as the pizza was set on the stand and Duffy used the spatula to cut me a piece.

"I'm still going with when we know for sure."

"When 'we' as in you *and* me, or just you? 'Cause I'm already sure, Duff."

Duffy let out a sigh. "I know, I know," he said. "I just can't break her heart right now, Abs. Hell, she's been through enough this week. Let's just let her get past the rehearsal dinner tonight and then we'll talk, okay?"

"Okay," I said as I took a bite out of my pizza. It was so hot that I had to do a Coke chaser, and I fanned my mouth as I complained, "Jesus! This pizza's on fire!"

Duffy grinned as he blew on his slice before taking a bite. Then something seemed to occur to him and, setting his pizza down, he reached into his back pocket. He pulled out a folded piece of paper and, after looking thoughtfully at it, showed it to me. I saw then that it was the sketch that I'd drawn in Gina's apartment when Duffy asked me where her body was.

"See this?" he asked me, pointing to the section on my sketch where I'd drawn the shape of a fan and labeled it "heat." "Do you think that could be a fire?"

I stared at the sketch as my right side felt light and airy. "Yeah!" I exclaimed. "Duffy, that's exactly what that is!"

"So, if this is where we can find Gina's body, then I'm thinking that means someone tried to burn the evidence," Duffy said.

"Most definitely," I said.

"Okay, after lunch I'm gonna drop you off at Viv's. I gotta check out any local fires in the area in the past week."

"Good thinking," I said, then began to chow down in earnest. I didn't want to hold Duffy up.

Shortly after lunch Duffy dropped me back at Viv's, and I walked inside to find her and three other stately-looking women seated around her coffee table, each with a handful of playing cards and a small stack of poker chips. "Hi, Abby," Vivian called. "These are my poker buddies, Virginia, Eleanor, and Melba. You up for joining us?"

Now, I don't like to brag, but with my sixth sense I'm a killer poker player. I hesitated before answering her, my competitive streak wanting to kick some granny tail, but decided against it, primarily because I could just see Vivian pumping me for information about Duffy's swimmers. "Thanks, Viv, but I'm pretty bushed. I think I'm going to take a nap right now. Maybe some other time?"

"Your loss," Viv said with a grunt.

"Nice to meet you, ladies," I said as I began to walk down the hallway toward my room.

From behind me I heard Viv say, "That's my grand-niece's friend, the one I told you was sleeping with my grandnephew, Duffy. And good thing, that, because I hear if you don't get regular sex as a fertile man; your swimmers can shrivel up and die. . . ."

Oh, brother. I could only imagine what she'd say about Duffy and me tonight at the rehearsal dinner. I plopped on the bed face-first and lay there for a few minutes wondering how I got myself into such messes. Rolling over, I looked up at the ceiling. I was tired, but not sleepy. I thought about reading, but that meant getting up to dig around in my suitcase, and I was too relaxed for that. Instead I thought I'd check on my puppy, so I reached for my cell and dialed Dave.

"Yo!" he said when he picked up the line.

"Hi, Dave! It's me, Abby," I said, feeling really glad to hear his voice.

Squeeka! Squeeka! Squeeka! came noise in the background.

"Hi, Abigail! How's it hangin?"

Whonka! Whonka! Whonka! came another set of noises.

"Low and left, pal," I deadpanned. "What's with all the racket in the background?"

Cuckoo! Cuckoo! Cuckoo!

"Oh, that's Eggy. I bought him a few toys to play with."

Squiggy! Squiggy! Squiggy!

"A few?" I chuckled. "Geez, Dave. Sounds more like you bought him the store."

Whonka! Cuckoo! Whonka! Cuckoo!

"Yeah, well, I wanted to take his mind off missing you."

Squiggy! Squeeka! Squiggy! Squeeka!

"I think you've succeeded. How's your woman holding up with all that noise?"

Thump! "Ruff!" Eggy barked happily.

"Just threw him a ball. He loves those. Anyway, my old lady's fine with it. She's away at her sister's right now."

"Ah, so it's just the men this week, huh?"

Squeeka! Whonka! Squeeka! Whonka!

"Yeah, just us guys. Here, Eggy, try this out. Ah, that's a good boy. He loves those velvet chews. He'll be munchin' on that for hours. So how's it goin' with your wedding?"

"Uh, it's not exactly *my* wedding, Dave. It's my friend Ellie's."

"Yeah, that's what I meant. Speaking of which, I saw Dutch yesterday."

I sat bolt upright. "You did?" I asked, my heart picking up the pace.

"Yeah. Saw him and Milo out at Guzzoline Alley."

"Did he ask about me?" I said, only then realizing I was white-knuckling the phone.

"Uh . . . not exactly."

"What do you mean, not exactly?"

"Well, he didn't ask about you."

My heart sank. "Oh," I said as a tear formed in my eye.

"But I really didn't talk to him. Mostly it was pretty loud on account of the Red Wings game, and me and the old lady were seated way away from him and Milo."

"Dave, it's okay. You don't have to explain."

"It could be worse, Abby," Dave said kindly.

"How, exactly?" I asked, rubbing my eyes.

"He could have been out with a girl."

There was a very long moment of silence while I thought about that. Then, "Give Eggy a kiss for me, Dave. I'll call you in a day or so, okay?"

"Hang in there, girl," Dave said.

I disconnected and shut off the cell. Getting up to retrieve the charger from my suitcase, I plugged it in and stuck my tongue out at it. I'd had the damn thing on steadily since the night Dutch had given it to me, and he had not called once. And even though I was now quickly running down the path of getting involved with someone else, I still missed him. A lot. A *whole* lot.

I went back to the bed and took off my boots. With a heavy sigh I lay back and felt the tears coming. Before long I was having myself a good cry. Soon after that, spent and exhausted, I fell fast asleep.

Chapter Ten

I was walking on a path in the woods. All around me I felt the forest closing in, and panic coursed through my heart. Ahead I heard a voice I recognized, my grandmother's. She was reciting a nursery rhyme she said to me at bedtime when I was a child:

Now I lay me down to sleep . . .
I pray the Lord my soul to keep . . .
And if I die before I wake . . .
I pray the Lord my soul to take . . .

"Grams?" I called to her. "Grams? Where are you?"

"I'm here, Abby-gabby. Come on; you'll miss the movie," she called from somewhere up ahead.

I hurried through the forest, running now away from an increasing sense of danger. I came to a fork in the road, and in the middle of the fork was the crumbling ruins of a building. The mailbox read, ABBY COOPER, and I looked at it curiously, because I'd seen it before, but I couldn't place where. My grandmother stood, beautiful and radiant, on the steps of the crumbling ruin, a warm and inviting smile on her face. She pointed right, then left at each path in the fork and said to me, "Abby-gabby. Which way will you go?"

Before I could answer her I heard a voice behind me say, "Time's up!"

I turned toward the voice, but couldn't discern where it was coming from.

"Time to get up!" the voice said, and my eyes flew open.

"Huh? Wha . . . ?" I said, groggily sitting up and blinking around the room, trying to get my bearings.

"It's time to get up, Abby. You'll be late for the rehearsal dinner if you don't jump in the shower and get ready now," Vivian said from the doorway to my bedroom.

I shook my head, trying to clear the cobwebs, and said, "Thanks, Viv. Be right there."

She nodded and shut the door. I pivoted and put my feet on the floor but sat there to collect my thoughts for a second. The dream bothered me. This was the second time my grandmother had made contact with me, and I wondered about her message. I could feel it was important, that there was something about a decision to be made and it was vital to choose the right direction, but the decision involved was something of a mystery.

With a tired sigh I pushed off the bed and shuffled to gather my dress, makeup bag and hair supplies. Making my way to the bathroom I could hear Viv on the phone with the taxi company. "We'll need the cab to arrive by five thirty and not a moment later or there'll be no tip for the driver. . . ." Good ol' Viv. She was one tough cookie, all right.

An hour later I was dressed in a gorgeous black velvet gown that showed plenty of leg and played to my strengths (small waist and broad shoulders) while hiding my shortcomings (small boobs and a bubble butt). I'd taken extra care with my hair, curling it into lots of tight spirals that cascaded down past my shoulders. This style had been a gamble when I'd started in with the curling iron but came out perfectly, thank God. It'd been a really long time since

I'd had a good-hair day, so I suppose this made up for it.

I threw on a pair of three-inch heels and long silver earrings, and topped the look off with smoky gray eye shadow and a deep burgundy lipstick. Eyeing myself critically in the mirror when I was finished, I was quite pleased with the result. "Rrrrow," I mouthed at the mirror. Sometimes there is nothing better to assuage a broken heart than looking hot. Tonight I was on fire.

I came out of the bathroom and put my gear away, then joined Viv in the front hall. She eyed me with a smirk on her face for a moment before commenting, "You trying to reel Duffy in, or give him a heart attack?"

"Little of both," I said with a wink.

"That's my girl," she answered with a wink of her own. "Oh, look! Our cab's here. Good for him, right on time. I hate having to tip poorly. Come on, Abby, let's boogie."

Viv and I headed out to the waiting taxi and enjoyed a pleasant enough trip to the country club. On the way I couldn't help but notice Viv's extra-large pocketbook, and I could only imagine what she intended to pinch tonight.

A valet held the door open for us as we exited the cab, and even though I offered to pay, Viv shooed my efforts away and gave the cabbie a twenty. He gave her a dark look, as the fare had been nineteen dollars even, and while Viv's back was turned I slipped him a few extra bucks. "Come on, Abby!" Viv said. "Let's get inside out of this cold."

I pulled my own wrap closer around me as I hurried inside with her, noting that the temperature had dipped dramatically in the past few hours. Once inside we gave our wraps to the coatcheck girl and headed into the main dining room, which had been reserved for this occasion. I eyed the crowded room, looking for Ellie. I wanted to see how she was holding up and to offer my sincere apologies for what I'd said in her reading. Even though I knew I needed to tell her what I did, it didn't mean that I didn't still feel guilty for bringing so much worry down on her shoulders right before her wedding.

While I was taking in the room I felt an arm wrap around my waist. Startled, I looked up to see a man about my age with light brown hair and green eyes. "Excuse me," I said, moving away from him. "Do I know you?"

"Not yet, but the night's young," he answered with a cocky grin. "I'm Gary, Eddie's cousin and the best man. You wouldn't be Sara, would you?"

"No, I'm Abby," I said. "Are you walking with her on Friday?"

"Yeah, but I'd rather walk with you," he said as his eyes traveled from my ankles up and hovered overlong around my bosom. I noticed as I looked at him that he swayed slightly on his feet. There was a half-empty martini glass in his hand, and as I watched him watching my chest, he gulped down the rest.

"Yo," I said, snapping my fingers to get his attention. My radar told me this guy was about as sleazy as they came. "Have you seen Ellie? I need to talk to her."

"Ah, no," he said as his eyes came up to meet mine for a millisecond, then traveled back down to the twins.

"Okay, then," I said, and turned away. Gary made me want to take a shower. "I'd better go find her."

Gary put his hand on my shoulder to stop me. "What's your rush, sweetheart? Why don't you and I go somewhere private and get to know each other?"

I swiveled back toward him, and in a move that Dutch had taught me, I picked his hand up off my shoulder and turned his wrist palm-side up. He winced and bent at the knees, trying to relieve the sharp pain that was no doubt shooting through his wrist. "Let's get one thing straight, Gary," I whispered close to his ear. "I don't normally do this, but in your case I'm willing to make an exception and give you some free intuitive advice."

"Ah-aaah?" he said, his eyes finally coming to my face and holding steady there.

"In case you hadn't heard, I'm a professional psychic. And what I'm picking up from you is the following: You have a drinking problem, Gary. And I'm thinking your girlfriend, the tall blonde that you were pretty crazy about? Well, she left you because she thought you were never going to change. And there's now an issue at work, am I right; Gary?"

"Naaah-haa!" he said as I put a wee bit more pressure on his wrist.

"Yes, there's something about you getting creative with your accounting, and someone has caught on. Have you been fudging your expense reports?" I said with a narrowed look at him.

"How did you . . . ?" he said through gritted teeth.

"I'll ask the questions, Gary. Now, as I was saying, your guides are telling me that you are out of lucky chances. You need to straighten up and get yourself into rehab ASAP. As in the day after the wedding. But first you will need to own up to your employer about your expense reports, and admit that you are an alcoholic. If you don't, you're headed for rock bottom."

Gary nodded at me, his eyes wide and frightened. I let go of his wrist then and he straightened up and shook out his hand. "Don't tell anyone, okay?" he said, looking around to see if we'd been overheard.

"Do you promise to go into rehab and get yourself some help?"

"Yes!" he hissed. *Liar, liar . . . pants on fire . . .*

I scowled at him. "I'm disappointed, Gary. My radar says you're full of baloney."

Gary gave me a snarl. "Do you know how expensive those rehab places are?"

"Why don't you ask your cousin for some help? I'm

sure, as a doctor, he's bound to know of some good programs that may not cost an arm and a leg."

"You want me to go to Eddie?" He laughed. "I'm supposed to go to my perfect cousin, with his perfect medical degree and his perfect new wife, and ask him to help his loser cousin? No way."

"Fine. Don't get help," I snapped. "Hit rock bottom, pal, and enjoy the ride down!" And with that I turned on my heel and walked away. Nothing irritated me more than people who would not help themselves. I had no patience for it. Wanting to get away from Gary, I moved to the opposite side of the room, where I heard a woman's voice I recognized call my name. My spine snapped into an erect posture as I realized my very own Mommy Dearest was in attendance. Freezing the fakest, most plastic smile I could muster onto my face, I spun around to greet her. "Hello, Claire. Lovely to see you." *Liar, liar . . . pants on fire . . .*

"You as well, Abigail," she said, giving me her warmest head nod. My mother is outwardly very beautiful. She's an inch taller than me, with short-cropped silver hair, long legs, high cheekbones and deep-set eyes. Think Katharine Hepburn and you'd be close on appearance. Think pissed-off polar bear and you'd be closer on personality. "You've done something different with your hair," she said, looking at the top of my head, her eyes narrowing and her mouth turning down in a pout.

"Is Sam here?" I asked, trying to lure her away from the critique I knew was soon to follow.

"Of course he is; did you think I would come unescorted?"

"No, I just—"

"Only the most desperate woman would show up to something like this unescorted. Where is your date, dear?" she asked me with a glint in her eye, and I knew that she'd heard about my big breakup.

Just as my cheeks began to feel hot I heard, "I'm right here," and Duffy touched my elbow.

Turning gratefully to him I said, "Hey, there, I wondered where you'd gotten to."

"I had to bring you back something to drink. You wanted red, right?" he asked, placing a glass of wine into my hand.

I nodded and beamed him a smile. *Ha! Take that, Claire!*

"Hello, Duffy," Claire said, her nose wrinkling as if she were smelling a particularly nasty fart.

"Claire. You're looking well," Duffy said smoothly.

"Thank you," she replied, giving him the tiniest smile. "I understand your sister has landed herself quite a catch. Her fiancé is a doctor, correct?"

"Yes, Ellie's found herself a good guy who just happens to be a doctor," Duffy said, placing his hand on the small of my back, which sent shivers up my spine.

"We always knew she would marry well." Claire eyed me again. "Abigail, perhaps you should talk to Ellie about how to land a man with potential."

I bristled and opened my mouth to tell Claire exactly where she could stuff her advice when Duffy said, "Oh, trust me, Claire, Abby's doing very well of late in that department. Come on, Abby; there are some friends of mine I'd like to introduce you to. Claire, as always, it's been a pleasure." And with that he took my hand and guided me across the room.

"I owe you huge," I said when we stopped over by the appetizer buffet.

"You look amazing," he said, ignoring my remark.

"Thank you," I said, and blushed deeply. "Have you been here long?"

"No, I mean it," he said, grabbing me around the waist and pulling me close. "You've always been hot, but tonight—wow!" And with that he kissed me right there in public.

I swooned for just a moment, then pulled back and said to him, "Hey, we cannot do this *here*!"

Duffy grinned. "Abs, when you're right, you're right." Next thing I knew he had my hand and was weaving me through the crowd. I saw my father at the bar and passed within four feet of him, but he didn't seem to recognize me, which was typical for Sam. I noticed his hand was tightly gripped around a double shot of vodka on the rocks. I imagined he was well into his second or third at this point.

Duffy led me out of the dining hall and through a hallway to a set of stairs that had a rope across the entrance. He undid one end of the rope and waved me forward. I looked at him curiously but headed up the stairs.

At the top Duffy again took my hand and led me down another long hallway. Stopping in front of a doorway he put his fingers to his lips and said, "Shhhh." He then opened the door and waved me inside to another set of spiral stairs. Carefully we tiptoed up, and I worked hard to keep my heels from tapping on the metal. At the top of the stairs was a small circular room with windows all the way around. Even though it was dusk outside, the view was splendid. The golf course could be seen spreading out before us, and in the distance the Rockies stood tall and proud set against the fading sunlight. It was so beautiful I sucked in a breath as I turned in a circle to get the full view. I enjoyed the vista for a long moment, then turned to Duffy, who had a rather hungry look in his eyes.

I grinned at him, meeting his gaze, but didn't say a word. He was quite handsome himself tonight, dressed in a deep purple velvet jacket, so dark it was almost black, fitted over a blindingly white shirt open at the collar, black pants and leather boots. "I really want to kiss you," he said in a voice thick with desire.

"So what's stopping you?" I asked, raising one eyebrow in challenge.

"Not sure it's really a good idea," he said seriously.

"It was a minute ago."

"Yeah, but a minute ago I forgot that you're vulnerable right now, and I'd only be taking advantage of the fact that some asshole just broke your heart."

And just like that the spell was broken. "Ah," I said, backing up as if he'd slapped me. "I see. So last night was . . . what? Another lapse in memory?"

"No," he said, taking a step forward. "Last night was amazing. In fact, it was the first time in a long time I felt okay about spending the night with someone."

"Good for you," I snapped. My feelings were bouncing around wildly in my chest. "Glad to see you're making progress."

Duffy took another step toward me, "Yeah, but it's been tough, which is why I'm trying to be the good guy here."

"Congratulations," I said, moving away from him again when my back made contact with the wall behind me. "I'll make sure to send you a medal when I get back home."

"I don't want a medal," he said, moving ever closer, his voice barely a whisper.

"Then what the hell do you want, Duffy?" I asked, tears stinging my eyes.

"Right now," he said inches away from me, "all I want is to kiss every thought of that other guy right out of you."

My breathing was coming in short, quick pants, my fists were balled and I didn't know if I was pissed off, turned on or a little of both. "Like I said," I whispered as Duffy's lips hovered over mine, "what's stopping you?" and with that he melted against me, his lips soft, moist and hungry. I wrapped my arms around him as we slid down the wall and onto the hard floor. He kissed me until my lips felt hot and raw, while his hands found my breasts and I moaned as he unzipped my dress enough to kiss my nipples and arouse me into dizziness.

My hands found the buttons of his shirt. Itching to

touch his skin, I fumbled with them until I had them open and twisted my fingers into the hair of his chest. Duffy gave a guttural sound that was half purr, half growl as he nibbled my neck, and the sound sent shivers through me. A moment later he rolled over to his back, pulling me to lie on top of him, then cradled my chin with one hand as he swept a curly hair out of my eye. He lingered that way for a moment to stare into my eyes, and as I gazed back into his face I realized I didn't know how I felt, but I was desperate to stop feeling so torn up inside.

I wanted to stop hurting every time I thought about Dutch, and I wanted to feel safe in the arms of someone else, but as my fingers came out from under Duffy's shirt to rest on his shoulders I could see in his expression that he was unwilling to be my rebound guy.

"You're not ready, Abs," he said gently, his hand stroking my cheek as a single tear formed in my eye and leaked its way down to his fingertips.

I swallowed hard and nodded, not trusting my voice. He sighed and pulled me close to hug me sweetly and stroke my hair. "I'm sorry," I whispered, tears falling freely now.

"Hey, now," he said softly. "None of that. I know how it feels, remember?"

"When does it stop?" I asked.

"When you're ready," he answered, and kissed my hair. "The thing is, you can't force it. You can only wait for enough days to pass until your insides don't feel like they've been wrung through the garbage disposal."

"I feel like I've been unfaithful," I confessed.

"I know what you mean," Duffy said. "Two weeks after I kicked Rachel out, I slept with someone else. It was a shitty thing to do, being that I knew the girl would read more into it than I was ready to give, and I've regretted it ever since. But I know what you're going through right now. You just want to feel something other than sad, and sometimes a little intimacy is the only thing that can change the subject."

I pulled up from his chest and smiled ruefully, "Goddamn, Duffy. When did you turn into such a knight in shining armor?"

He grinned back, "I was promoted three weeks ago, up from stable boy."

"Congratulations," I said, sitting up and finger-combing my hair. "Your new post suits you."

"Thanks, but don't let the word get out. I've got a reputation to protect, ya know."

"So I've heard," I said with a grin as he helped me to my feet and I straightened my clothing.

"You really do look great tonight, Abby," he said, lifting my hand and kissing my palm.

"Isn't that how this whole thing started?" I asked, cocking my head.

"Yeah, come on," he said, and squeezed my hand. "Let's get back to the party before we start too many rumors."

We headed back downstairs, and I ducked into the ladies' room to touch up my makeup and hair after our little romp. When I got back to the dining room, everyone was seated and the waiters were serving dinner. I had a moment of panic as I looked around the room, wondering where I should sit. Gary was sitting next to Ellie and Eddie at the head table, and even though there was an empty seat next to him, there was no way I was going to sit there. Next, I saw Claire and Sam at the same table as my sister, my nephews and my brother-in-law. Fortunately, there were no extra seats there, and just about the time I'd resigned myself to eating with a group of strangers off to my right, I caught sight of someone waving to me from across the room. Duffy held a space at a table with some other members of the bridal party and Viv. I walked quickly over to him and waved at Cat, who mouthed, *Where were you?* to me as I passed her table.

Later, I mouthed back, and reached Duffy's table. Taking my seat just as a serving of roast chicken was laid in front of me, I smiled around the table. Duffy winked at me as he bantered fondly with Viv, who was asking him if his swimmers were getting a good workout.

I managed to stifle a giggle as I cut my meat and began to eat. Out of the corner of my eye I caught someone staring at me, and I glanced up at Kelly, who glared at me, then looked away. *Hmm. Wonder what her problem is?* "Hi, Kelly," I said, trying to break the ice.

"Hey," she said, not making eye contact.

Christina, who sat on the other side of me, leaned in and whispered, "Don't mind her. She's just pissed that you and Duffy have become an item."

"We're not an item," I whispered back.

Christina nodded, her eyes dancing with merriment. "Sure, honey. Whatever you say."

Thinking about what Christina had said about Kelly, I leaned in and whispered, "I didn't know Kelly liked Duffy."

"Oh, yeah," Christina whispered back. "Duffy jumped her bones a while back, then never called her again. I'd say she's still pretty hung up on the guy."

"Kelly was Duffy's rebound chick right after Rachel?" I asked, surprised that Duffy would poop in his own backyard.

"Yeah, how'd you know?" Christina said, looking at me in surprise.

"Uh . . ." I said while I searched for an explanation that wouldn't throw Duffy under the bus. "I'm psychic, remember?"

"Except where I'm concerned, right?" Christina said with a giggle and an elbow poke.

I smiled, embarrassed by the memory of the night

before. "Apparently," I said with a small shake of my head.

Just then the lights dimmed in the dining hall and a spotlight fell on Eddie from across the room. He was standing at a table where Ellie, her parents and a couple who were probably his parents were seated. "I'd like to thank you all for coming," he began, a glass of wine in his hand. "As you know, we're doing things a little backward this week. This is the rehearsal dinner before the actual rehearsal, which will be Thursday night, so all of you in the wedding party need to be at St. Sebastian's Church on Everwood day after tomorrow at six sharp."

In the dark I felt Duffy's hand reach over and grip mine. He held it while Eddie continued. "In three days I will become the luckiest man on the planet as I watch the most beautiful woman in the world walk down the aisle to become my wife . . ."

At that moment I felt my left side grow thick and heavy, and I gripped Duffy's hand in alarm. "What?" he leaned in close and asked me as he saw the look in my eye.

I shook my head and mouthed, *Nothing,* and tried to focus on Eddie's speech.

". . . so I've prepared a little something to entertain you all this evening. It's a slide show I've titled 'Eddie and Ellie, A Love Story,' and without further delay, let's get to it!" Eddie finished, and the spotlight dimmed while a light shone on a screen across the room where a baby picture of Ellie appeared with the accompanying music, "Isn't She Lovely" by Stevie Wonder.

Much as I tried to focus on the slide show, the feeling I'd had when Eddie talked about marrying Ellie in three days kept stealing my attention. I knew these two would not be getting married as planned. While I fought about what to do with this newest piece of intuitive information, Duffy leaned in and whispered, "Holy shit!"

I snapped out of my thoughts and turned to him. "What?"

"I know where Gina is," he said, and pointed to the screen.

On the slide was a picture of Ellie, Eddie and a whole troop of friends, dirty and muddied, with a football clutched in Eddie's hands. The group looked to be having a fantastic time. In the background was a large field, and at the edge of the field was a green shack with a slanted roof and a large white star painted on top.

That should have held my attention, but it didn't. I was too shocked and horrified to see Sara's face among the crowd as it stared smiling back at me, flat and plastic next to Gina, who appeared exactly the same. "Oh, God . . ." I moaned, and turned to face Duffy, my eyes wide and afraid.

"Abs?" he said turning to me as I put my head into my hands. "What is it? What's the matter?"

"Sara," I whispered as my mouth went dry. "Where is Sara?" I asked a little louder as my eyes darted around the table, searching for the redhead and not finding her.

"She's not here," Christina said. "She's mad at Ellie or something and she's off pouting somewhere."

I turned back to Duffy, my heart pounding in my chest and a feeling like I might be sick overwhelming me. "Come on," he said, taking me up out of my chair and winding me quickly through the crowded room. We hurried out through a back door, where I took huge gulps of the cold night air. "What's happened?" he asked me after a moment, when it looked like I was beginning to catch my breath.

"It's Sara," I puffed. "Duffy, her photo's the same as Gina's! Sara's been killed too!"

"What?" came a shocked voice to my left, and I turned in alarm to look at Ellie, who was standing frozen in the doorway, watching us with wide, horrified eyes.

Chapter Eleven

"Ellie . . ." I gasped. I hadn't heard her come to the door.

"What do you mean like Gina, Sara's been killed too?!" Ellie demanded walking over to me and Duffy, her face frightened, but looking determined to hear what we'd been talking about.

"I'm not certain, Ellie," I tried. "It's just my intuition—"

"El? What's going on?" Eddie asked, coming up to us, and I noticed with dismay that a small group of people had followed him and were staring at us from inside the doorway.

"Abby thinks Gina and Sara have been killed," Ellie said with a note of panic in her voice.

"What?" Eddie said, staring at me. "What's all this about?"

I looked between Ellie and Eddie as I wondered where to begin. Taking a big breath I said, "One of the little oddities that goes along with my sixth sense is my ability to look at a photograph of a person and tell if they are living or dead." I paused to see if they were following me, and both of them nodded, so I continued. "Ellie, when I first came to your house I noticed Gina's picture on the wall. I could tell that something had happened to her. That she had well . . . died."

I said it as gently as I could, but Ellie still sagged against Eddie and said, "Oh, my God, no!"

"That's impossible," Eddie said as he supported his fiancée. "Gina flew to California last week. If something had happened to her, we would have been notified."

"Gina never flew to California, buddy," Duffy said. "Abby and I have been investigating this for two days. Her boyfriend broke it off with her for good about a month ago, and hasn't heard from her since."

"Maybe she flew there, and she's just waiting for the right opportunity to see him," Ellie said hopefully.

"She never got on the plane, El. She's MIA. And, unfortunately, I think Abby's intuition is on target."

"But . . . how can that be?" she demanded as her head swiveled between Duffy and me. "And now you think that Sara's dead too?"

I couldn't take the look of horror and shock on Ellie's face. I looked at my feet as I felt all eyes on me. How could I explain this? As I was about to try I heard, "Is this a joke?" from the doorway.

I glanced up to see Gary, another martini glass in hand, wobbling on unsteady feet as he came forward to our group. "Of course it isn't," I snapped. "Do you think I'd upset my friend by making this up?"

"Oh, I think you get a kick out of upsetting people in general," Gary slurred. Even from four feet away his breath was fumy enough to be a fire hazard.

"This is none of your business," I said. "Why don't you go back to the dining room and attempt to sober up."

"I'm fine," he said, lifting a finger to point it in my direction. "It's you who's the problem."

"Gary," Eddie said in warning.

"Naw, naw, cousin," Gary said to Eddie. "I've got a point here. My thinking is that this *chiquita* is upset her friend is getting all the attention, so she's here to stir things up a bit. And what better way of stirring things up than by looking around to see who's missing and claiming something tragic has happened to them? Personally, I smell a fraud."

"Not sure how you could smell anything with breath like that," I said, waving my hand in front of my nose. "Ellie, you know me. I'm not making this up. Something *has* happened to Gina. And I'm fairly certain something's also happened to Sara."

"Phony!" Gary yelled, and pointed his accusing finger again. "If you're so psychic, why don't you tell me what I'm thinking right now!"

"That's enough," Duffy said, stepping in between Gary and me.

"Don't get in the middle of this," Gary said as he took a wobbly step forward and stood just inches away from Duffy.

"I'm already in the middle of it, pal," Duffy said evenly, pulling himself up to his full height. "I've known Abby a lot longer than you. And I believe her. If she says something's happened, then you can bet the farm on it."

Ellie began to cry. "Please!" she said as she let go of Eddie and reached for Duffy's shoulder. "Please don't fight!"

Gary and Duffy stared at each other for long seconds before Gary finally gave me one last, "Fraud," and headed back inside.

When he was gone I turned to Ellie and said, "Honey, I'm so sorry. Duffy and I wanted to have some proof before we told you."

"What could have happened to them?" Ellie asked as the tears trailed down her cheeks.

"That's what we're going to find out," Duffy said gently. Turning to me he said, "Come on, Abs," and led me out the door. We walked down the hallway past pairs of staring eyes as people had come out of the dining room to see what all the fuss was about. I could see Gary huddled by a good-sized group, telling everybody who would listen that I was a big, fat faker.

"Abby?" my sister asked as we passed her. "Why is that guy calling you a fraud?"

"I'll call you later," I said, and kept walking. The last thing I wanted was to have to explain all this to Cat and, even worse, to Claire and Sam, who would devour all the gory details like two hungry mountain lions.

Duffy paused at the coatcheck and retrieved our coats; then he hustled me outside and we waited for his car to be driven up by the valet. Without a word we hopped in and he began to drive. After a while I asked, "Where are we going?"

"To find Gina," he said.

"Oh." I stared at my hands, hating the havoc I'd caused.

"Hey," he said, noticing my downcast face. "I meant what I said back there, Abby. None of this is your fault."

"Then why does it feel that way?"

"Because it sucks being the messenger when the news is bad. I've known you too long not to trust that you're right. So has Ellie, and that's why we owe it to my sister to find her friend and deal with that reality rather than wondering if Gina's alive or not."

"What about Sara?" I asked in a choked voice.

Duffy was silent for a long moment, and I watched his hands grip and ungrip the steering wheel while he thought through his answer. After a time he said, "We'll deal with Gina first. Sara second."

The rest of the way to our destination was spent in silence. I stared out the window at the passing terrain and thought it ironic that I'd been on this very road the night before, feeling exactly the same way about giving Ellie the bad news about Eddie.

I didn't want to give her any more news that would make her cry. I wanted to be wrong about Gina and Sara. Mostly I just wanted to go home.

We reached a large meadow a short time later, and Duffy parked the Mustang on the side of the road, pointing down a hill and across a large, open field to the green shack from the photograph, which was barely discernible in the early evening twilight. He got out and grabbed a small toolbox, a pair of boots and a Denver Broncos windbreaker from the trunk. "Here," he said, setting the boots at my feet. "They'll be pretty big on you, but at least it's better than tramping through this field in those heels."

"Thanks," I said, my lips quivering as I bent to undo the buckle on my shoes.

As I was bent over I felt a heavy weight land on my back. I looked to my left and saw the arm of Duffy's dress coat dangling by my side. "That will keep you warm," he said.

I stood up once I had his boots on and shrugged quickly into his thick wool coat, noticing that he'd donned the lighter jacket, which looked slightly ridiculous over his velvet blazer. "Next time maybe we should stop at home first to change," he said, catching my eye and looking down at himself.

"What?" I laughed. "And miss this fashion-don't moment?"

"Come on, dollface," he said with a roll of his eyes as he handed me a flashlight and clicked on another he pulled out of the toolbox. "Let's see if your hunch is right." I followed after Duffy, trying to keep up in his long coat and giant boots while our beams bounced in unison over the thick foliage of the field.

While I struggled through the winter weeds, Duffy flipped open his cell phone and made a call to Information. He asked for a residence and was apparently connected, because in the next second he said, "Hey, there, Colonel. It's Duffy McGinnis." There was a pause while the colonel answered him, and then Duffy continued: "Thanks, I'll pass your congratulations on to my sister. Listen, the reason for my call is that I need to look at that old shack on your property. Can

I have your permission to check it out this evening, sir?"

Another pause while Duffy listened to the reply, then: "You don't say. Some kids lighting firecrackers about a week ago? Mm-hmm. Well, sir, I'd like to take a look if that's all right with you. I'll call you if we find anything. Thank you for your cooperation, sir, and have a good night."

Duffy flipped his phone closed and turned back to me. "That was Colonel Pentwater. He bought this property a couple years ago after he retired from the army. Kind of a crazy old coot. Has this love of army green. Paints all the structures on his property green and puts a star on top. You would have thought I'd remember that when I looked at your drawing, but I didn't connect the dots until I saw it up on the screen."

"What did the colonel say about kids with firecrackers?"

"He said about a week ago he heard some kids out here playing with firecrackers. He says he came down the road in his truck and chased them off, but one of the firecrackers had burned the side of his shack. It went out almost as soon as it was lit; apparently it was drizzling out that night, thank God. Otherwise this whole area could have gone up."

"That explains the heat section on my drawing," I said, thinking back to what I'd sketched.

"Sure does," Duffy said just as we reached the shack. I was huffing pretty good by this time, hampered by the thick foliage and the altitude, not to mention my awkward attire.

"You okay?" he asked, glancing back at me.

I waved at him as I bent over and took big breaths. Just as I was getting my breathing under control I noticed something foul in the air. "Jesus," I said as I shuffled away from the shack, which was the direction it was coming from.

"Yeah, I smelled it coming down the hill," Duffy said as he waved the flashlight at the wooden structure. The shack was about medium size, maybe six feet by nine by eight feet tall. It had a slanted roof, and the white star stood out against the dark army green. Duffy waved the flashlight over to the right, and we could both see where a small section had been burned. "Stay back, Abby," Duffy cautioned as he moved in a few steps toward the door.

Just then his foot slipped on something and he stumbled a bit. Backing up, he shone the light down on the ground and bent to examine the object. His expression clouded over as he reached into the toolbox he'd been carrying and pulled out some tongs.

Curious, I inched closer to get a better look at what he'd found and saw a small, square brown piece of leather on the ground. "It's a wallet," I said to him.

"Mm-hmm," he answered as he carefully pulled up the flap of the wallet and shone the light at the inside. I watched as his mouth dropped a fraction and his brow lowered while he reached over to his toolbox again and extracted a small plastic tent from inside and laid it next to the wallet. He stood up and looked back at me, his face a little frightening in its serious expression. Tossing me his phone he said, "Abby, hit speed-dial two; ask for Dan Jennings; tell him I said to get a unit over to the Valley Hill Country Club and take my sister into custody, pronto!" And with that he dashed forward to the door of the shack.

"What is it?" I asked as I caught the phone, but Duffy was already reaching for the handle. I hit the speed dial and listened to it ring just as Duffy opened the door to an odor so nasty it sent me reeling back a few paces.

"Hey, Duff," a male voice said from the cell.

"Hello," I said, and coughed into my sleeve. "Is this Dan Jennings?"

"It is," came the reply.

"This is Abby Cooper; I'm a friend of Duffy McGinnis's." My eyes were intent on the wallet Duffy had opened. Something about it had caused him to panic about Ellie, and I wanted to see what it was. Breathing only through my mouth, I moved forward while I was talking to Jennings, bending low to get a better look.

"What can I do you for, Abby Cooper?"

"Duffy needs you to go to the Valley Hill Country Club and take his sister into custody," I said.

"What?"

I shone the beam of my flashlight down on top of the license within the wallet and my heart began to thump loudly in my chest as panic coursed along my limbs. My eyes focused on the face that even in the dark I could recognize smiling out from the license inside. "You need to get Ellie McGinnis from the Valley Hill Country Club right now!" I said, my voice becoming shrill as I stood up and watched the light from Duffy's flashlight bouncing inside the shack. A moment later it lingered on the floor, and from where I stood I could very clearly make out the top of a blond head and beside it one hand curled into a tight fist. "We're at Colonel Pentwater's shack!" I squealed. "A woman's been murdered and Ellie's fiancé's wallet is at the scene of the crime! You need to take her into protective custody *now*!" I finished, and ran away from the shack into the weeds to throw up my dinner.

Hours later I was still sitting in Duffy's Mustang, the engine humming and the heater on high. I was shivering even though it must have been eighty degrees inside. Condensation was forming on the window I was looking through, and I kept having to wipe it away with my arm. Duffy's clock read a little after midnight, but it felt as if it were much later to me. I'd been watching the CSI techs come and go from inside the shack while Duffy and several other deputies worked the scene. Colonel Pentwater arrived in his army-green Jeep and gave his statement to one of them.

We now suspected that what he'd heard a week ago

hadn't been kids with firecrackers at all, but Gina's killer as he pumped three rounds into the center of her chest. Duffy had walked me back up the hill, and he'd told me that it was evident Gina had been shot. He said she was naked, and he suspected she'd been sexually molested, but it might be hard to tell given the condition of the body and the length of time it had been exposed. I'd taken a big gulp and tried not to imagine the mental picture he'd painted.

While we waited for the other deputies and CSI techs to arrive, Duff and I had talked a bit about the circumstantial evidence pointing to Eddie as Gina's killer. Neither one of us was ready to convict Eddie, but the fact that his wallet had been found at her murder scene and the bloody surgical scrubs found in her car made Duffy extra cautious about his sister's safety.

With sirens closing in from the distance he'd asked me, "Does your sixth sense weigh in on this?"

I paused before answering him, wanting to feel out the answer. "I would love to tell you that my intuition says there's no way Eddie could have shot Gina. But there was a part in Ellie's reading where my crew insisted he'd done something bad enough to land him in jail."

"Like murder?"

"In my gut I want to say no," I said as I got a heavy left-sided feeling. "But my feeling is that whatever Eddie did to break the law, he had no choice in the matter. It's like he was forced into it."

"Think I did the right thing by taking Ellie into custody?"

"Until we know for sure that Eddie had no part in this? Hell, yeah," I said.

Duffy nodded and gave my arm a squeeze, then headed off to meet the arriving cavalry.

Jennings had picked up Ellie from the country club, bringing her to the station, and word came back to us that she hadn't gone willingly. Another car had been dispatched to keep a close eye on Eddie until they could get a search warrant for his home, which one tired judge had signed not fifteen minutes earlier. While a separate team was sent to search Eddie and Ellie's condo, he was "asked" to accompany a deputy to county headquarters for questioning. I had learned all this from the radio squawking loudly in Duffy's car. Most of the police codes I couldn't decipher, but I'd learned some of the information from the comings and goings of deputies and other officials as they stood on the road near Duffy's car, taking a break in between gathering evidence and working the scene.

About an hour after the CSI techs arrived, Cat called me on my cell. She'd seen Jennings come to get Ellie, and she wanted to know what had happened. I filled her in on everything I knew, and her reaction had been horrified but strong. She'd told me to stick close to Duffy so that she could be sure I was safe and said she'd head over to the station to offer her support to Ellie and the McGinnises.

A while later she'd called me back to say that Ellie had been released to her parents' custody with instructions that she was not have contact with Eddie until Duffy had given the okay. Cat said Ellie had been quite colorful about what the deputy who delivered that particular message could do with himself. Still, Nina and Jimmy had convinced her to come home with them, and Cat learned that a patrol car had been dispatched to watch over the house for the time being. Cat left me, saying she was going back to her hotel and she'd call me in the morning.

Much later, and just as my eyes began to feel droopy, Duffy moseyed up the hill toward the car. He gave me a tired smile as he approached, and I returned it with equal enthusiasm. "Hey, kiddo," he said when he opened the door on his side and got in.

"Hey, yourself," I said. "You done or just taking a break?"

"I'm done," he answered with a sigh as he clipped on his safety belt. "Come on; let's get outta here."

"How's Ellie?" I asked as we pulled a U-turn and headed down the road.

"Mom's with her, but I doubt she wants to hear from me tonight. The timing of this thing totally sucks," he said with a growl.

"Poor Ellie. I feel so bad, Duffy. I mean, I feel like it's all my fault."

"Hey," he said, turning to look at me, his face hidden in shadow. "You did nothing wrong, Abs. Hell, if it turns out that Eddie was responsible for Gina's death, you may have saved Ellie's life."

"You know, I've been thinking about this, and I just don't think he murdered her."

"I hope you're right, Abs."

"You've known him awhile. Do you think he did it?"

Duffy sighed again, and this time it was a sad sound. "I don't know what I think. I want to believe that Eddie had nothing to do with this. I want to believe that some bad guy stole his wallet, then happened to come across Gina, thought she was really pretty and tried to get her attention but failed and then things turned ugly. I want to believe that she didn't suffer much, and that a total stranger did this, because as bad as it is that Gina's dead, it's a thousand times worse to me that the killer might be someone I know."

As he talked about some anonymous stranger happening across Gina, I felt my left side grow thick and heavy. "Damn," I said, realizing that Gina definitely knew her killer.

"What?"

"Nothing," I said, not wanting to add more of my two cents. "It's just I feel so bad for Ellie. I wish there were something I could do."

"There is," Duffy said, his voice barely more than a whisper.

"What?" I asked.

"You can help me find Sara next."

"Oh, yeah," I said, and my depression grew. "I had almost forgotten about her. How shallow is that?"

"You've had a long day. Cut yourself some slack, would ya?"

Just then we pulled up in front of Aunt Viv's house. All the lights were out, and it looked like no one was home. Duffy and I got out of the car and headed to the front door. He tried the handle but it was locked.

"Do you think she's home?" I asked, looking at my watch and noting it was almost one A.M.

"She's probably staying over at Mom's helping her comfort Ellie, and in the commotion she forgot all about you. Did she leave you a key?"

"No."

"Come on then," he said as he walked back toward his car.

"Where are we going?"

"My place. You can sleep there."

"Ah," I said, thinking about what that might indicate.

"I have a spare bedroom, or you can bunk with me, but if you bunk with me I can't be held responsible for any sleep-induced groping."

"Sounds good," I said as I trailed after him, and then felt my cheeks grow hot when he looked back at me over his shoulder and I realized what it sounded like I had just agreed to. "I mean, the spare bedroom. It sounds good. Not that bunking with you would be bad. Not that it *was* bad . . . What I mean is . . ." I stammered.

"Abby," Duffy said as he paused in front of the car.

"Yeah?"

"Shut up before my ego takes any more punches, 'kay?"

"No problem," I mumbled, and hurried into the car.

A few minutes later we arrived at Duff's and headed in. He sweetly helped me off with his coat and sat me on a chair in the kitchen, where he poured me a glass of wine, then hurried into the direction of his bedroom. A minute later he came back out with some sheets, a comforter and a pair of men's sweatpants and an oversize T-shirt. "Sorry, I don't think I have anything in your size," he explained as he lifted the clothes off the top of the pile.

"These will be fine, thanks," I said, still a little embarrassed by my faux pas earlier.

"Why don't you head into the bathroom to change and I'll set up your bed," he said as he began walking down the hall to a separate bedroom.

"Great," I said to his back, and got up off the bar stool with a tired sigh. I headed into the bathroom and tried on the clothes. They were huge on me, but I was secretly pleased to be wearing Duffy's things. I looked in the mirror at the oversize T-shirt that bore a Broncos logo, and a memory drifted up to my mind of a time recently when I'd been staying with Dutch and wore one of his T-shirts to bed. It had been just as large and felt just as comforting.

I turned away from the mirror as I felt that familiar pang of sadness over the loss of that relationship. What the hell was I doing getting involved with Duffy so soon after my breakup with Dutch? And on that note, *were* Duffy and I even involved? I shook my head as these thoughts tumbled through my mind. This was the last thing I needed to be thinking about right now. Ashamed of myself, I quickly washed my face, used my finger for a toothbrush and then gathered up my clothes and headed back to the kitchen, where I looked around for any sign of Duffy.

He came out of the bedroom a moment later in a pair of boxer briefs and a T-shirt similar to the one he'd given me. "Bed's all made," he said, grinning as he looked at me in his clothes.

"Thanks again." I tried to not ogle him in his undies.

"Anytime. Did you want to hit the hay or sit with me for a bit and talk?"

"I could sit," I said, hoisting myself back up onto the bar stool. "What's on your mind?"

"That sketch you drew of where we could find Gina. Do you think you could do it again to help us find Sara?" he asked as he went to the kitchen and poured himself a glass of wine.

"So you think she's dead too?"

Duffy nodded as he took a seat next to me. "While you were in the car I had a deputy go over to her house. One of Sara's best friends is a gay guy she's been rooming with since college. He said he'd been away at his boyfriend's for a couple of days and came home to find the house empty yesterday. He hasn't seen or heard from her in a couple of days, which he said is unusual for her, because she always checks in with him. He'd tried calling her several times but her phone went straight to voice mail. He told the deputy that tomorrow he'd planned on calling around to her friends to try to find her."

"Too bad he waited," I said as I thought about how much sooner we could have been alerted if we'd only known she was missing.

"Yeah, everyone wants to respect everybody else's privacy these days," Duffy agreed. "So back to this psychic sketch stuff. Do you think you could whip out another one of those?"

I smiled a little ruefully. He made it sound as if it were a piece of cake. "I could try," I said, taking another long sip of wine and closing my eyes. While I focused I asked, "Can you bring me some paper and a pen?"

"On it," he said.

While Duffy shuffled around in the kitchen to get my supplies, I concentrated on where I thought Sara might be. I called out to my crew for assistance and asked for their help in letting me see where she was and what had happened to her. After a moment a picture formed in my mind's eye. I clearly saw thick trees and undergrowth surrounding a small clearing. I looked around the clearing and noticed that to my left were cobblestones laid out in a cross. In front of the cross was a mailbox, and on the mailbox my first name, ABBY, was written. I waited for more clues to form but nothing else came into focus. I realized with a jolt that this was the second time a mailbox with my name on it had bubbled up from my subconscious. Deciding to dwell on it later, I then asked for a little direction on what had happened to Sara, and immediately felt three thuds to the center of my chest.

With a startled intake of breath my eyes flew open. "Oh, God," I said as my hand came up protectively to cover my heart.

"What is it?"

"She was shot too. Three times in the chest. Boom. Boom. Boom," I said, holding my hand like a gun and firing over my heart, under my right collarbone and then in my breastbone.

Duffy's jaw dropped a fraction. "Whoa," he said when I'd finished.

"What?"

"That's exactly where Gina was shot."

"Here, here and here?" I asked, retracing the pattern.

"Exactly," he said.

"Same killer," I said, feeling a little clammy.

"Sounds like it."

"Hang on," I said, and reached for the pen and paper. Quickly I jotted down my vision exactly as I'd seen it and swung it back to Duffy. "Here, this is where her body is," I said, pointing to the sketch.

Duffy examined it for long moments. "I don't know where this is," he said. "But the stones are in the shape of a cross. Maybe this is some religious nut?"

My left side felt thick and heavy. Nope. I shook my head and replied, "No. I don't think that the cross is literal."

"Huh?"

"I think it's a metaphor. I think it symbolizes a place, but is not the actual form of the place."

Duffy scratched his head and looked back at my sketch. "Why'd you write your name on the mailbox?"

I turned my head to look at the drawing again. "I'm not sure. I had this same image in a dream this afternoon, and I know it fits in this sketch, but I don't know how."

"Like the star on the roof of the shack," Duffy said, and I nodded. "Okay, I'll make some copies of this and pass it around. Maybe it will spark someone's memory and we can figure out where the heck it is."

I yawned and stretched my arms above my head. I was so tired I was ready to drop. "Can we pick this up again in the morning?" I asked.

"Sure, go get some rest. You deserve it."

"Peace," I said as I hopped off the bar stool, then shuffled down the hallway toward the spare bedroom.

"If you need anything," I heard Duffy call behind me, "like an extra blanket, or a glass of water, or a back massage . . ." He let that last bit trail off until I paused to look over my shoulder at him. "Just holler," he said with a wink.

Hoo-boy. I gave him the Boy Scout salute and sashayed away, afraid that if I opened my mouth I actually *might* do just that.

Chapter Twelve

My cell phone woke me the next morning. Climbing out of bed and trudging over to my purse, I pulled out the small device and took a quick peek at the caller ID. I was secretly hoping it was Dutch, but the indicator said my sister was trying to hunt me down. "Hey, Cat," I said, my voice sounding froggy.

"*Where* are you?" she demanded.

"Good morning to you, too," I said woodenly. "I slept well, thanks for asking. And yourself?"

"I'm serious, Abby. You have no idea what I've been through in the past twelve hours. After I got off the phone with you I was practically accosted by a mob at the hotel!"

"What? What mob?" I asked, a little alarmed.

"Several of the hotel guests are attending the wedding. They were gathered in the lobby when I got in last night and wouldn't let me go to bed until I'd told them everything I knew. I explained to them that your sixth sense had led the police right to Gina's body, and that there was some incriminating evidence that pointed to Eddie as a suspect."

"Cat," I moaned. "Why couldn't you have simply said, 'No comment,' and left it at that?"

"They were *relentless,* Abby! I had to tell them for fear of bodily harm!"

I rolled my eyes and asked, "So then what happened?"

"I thought that once the crowd had been given the details they'd disperse and go back to their rooms, but that awful man, Eddie's cousin Gary, was there. He started talking about how he's convinced you're some kind of witch and he thinks that you used your psychic powers to make the police believe Eddie killed Gina!"

"Whoa," I said, snapping my eyes wide. "That's crazy!"

"It gets worse," Cat said.

"The man's a drunk, Cat! How could people believe that pile of dung?"

"It wasn't that they believed him, Abby. I mean, it was obvious Gary had had one too many, so no one was really buying into his line of crap until one of the other bridesmaids—I think her name is Christina—told everyone about how you did a reading for Ellie yesterday. She said you kept telling Ellie that her fiancé had done something terrible and you wouldn't tell her what it was, but then you went and told Duffy and now everyone is mad at you for ruining Ellie's wedding."

My knees gave out and I sat down hard on the bed. "That is so far from the truth, Cat, that I can't even comment."

"Claire and Sam have been telling everyone how humiliated they are. I even heard Claire make the suggestion that perhaps you were switched at birth."

"What?! What do you mean she's *suggesting* that I was switched at birth?!" I said, outraged.

"Well, one of Nina's relatives was talking with Claire at the hotel, and I overheard Claire say that when you were born she didn't entirely trust the nurse who was assigned to care for you in the nursery and that she thought there was a distinct difference between the baby she gave birth to and the one who was brought to her from the nursery a few hours later."

I put my head in my hand as I felt the first hint of a really good headache begin above my eyebrows. "Maybe she's right," I said after a moment.

"Oh, come on, Abby. Of course she's not. You know Claire; she's just that shallow."

"No, I'm serious, Cat. Maybe I was switched at birth. If that were really the case it sure would explain the difference between Mommy Dearest and me."

"Abby, you were not switched at birth. Which is fortunate, because I'm still glad to be related to you, and that is not just because next to you I'm the cute one. . . ."

I smiled ruefully into the phone. "Gee, thanks," I said.

Cat chuckled. "So where are you, anyway?"

"I'm at Viv's," I said easily, as my lie detector went off in my head.

"Really?" Cat asked me, and I could tell by her tone she knew full well I was not where I claimed to be. "What room are you in? Because I'm here at Viv's and I haven't seen any sign of you."

"Uh . . ." I said as my brain searched for a backup story. "What're you doing at Viv's? I mean, here?"

"I came by to check on you and see if you'd heard anything else about what happened. Viv said she stayed over at Nina's last night and didn't get home until a little while ago. She said that she completely forgot to give you a key, and *she's* assuming you're at Duffy's."

"Uh . . ."

"Yes?" Cat said, the smugness in her voice evident.

I made several sounds into the phone that I hoped sounded like static. "Sorry, what did you say?"

"So *are* you at Duffy's?" my sister pushed.

"Sorry, Cat, *crrrrch*, I can't hear you, *crrrch*, I think I'm losing the connection, *crrrrrchhhh*!" and I flipped the lid to the phone closed.

"Morning," Duffy said from the hallway.

I jumped a little, as I hadn't realized he'd been standing there. "Hey! No fair sneaking up on me!" I groused as I worked to straighten out my bed-head.

"Your curls look good in the morning," Duffy said with a lazy drawl.

"Thanks," I said, pulling my hand down from my hair and standing up. "Have you been awake long?"

"Couple minutes. How about some breakfast?" he asked.

"You cookin'?" I said, my interest piqued.

"Depends on which room you'd like me to cook in. I could cook in here if you'd like," he said with another lazy drawl and a steady gaze.

"Ha!" I said, and began to move around the bed, straightening the covers nervously. "I like pancakes. You know how to make pancakes?"

"Yeah," Duffy said with a chuckle. "But if I make 'em you gotta do the dishes."

"Deal!" I said quickly.

"Naked," he added as he pushed away from the doorjamb and headed down the hallway.

I fanned myself as he walked away. That man was definitely a morning-sex kinda guy. Trouble was, he was incredibly cute when he was rumpled.

After I'd straightened up the room I grabbed my cell and called Dave. He answered groggily, "Hey, honey. How're you?"

"Morning, Dave. I'm fine. Did I wake you?"

"Naw," he said, yawning into the phone. "I been up most of the night."

"Yeah?" I asked my brows wrinkling. "You okay?"

Dave yawned again before answering. "I'm fine. Just can't sleep, is all."

"Missing your old lady?" I said with a smile.

"Naw. It's your little buddy."

"Eggy?"

"Yeah. He's got to bring all his new squeaky toys to bed, and about every hour he wakes up and squeaks one or two of them just to make sure they're working."

"Well, duh!" I said, laughing at him. "Now you know why I don't buy Eggy squeaky toys."

"Yeah, but he's so cute with 'em. He tries to carry like three or four at a time and he can barely walk. It's hilarious."

"We'll see how hilarious it is in another day when you still can't sleep," I said. "So otherwise he's okay?"

"Yeah, he's fine. So how's the wedding? You walk down the aisle yet?"

"Dave, I am not walking down the aisle. It's my friend Ellie who was supposed to get married."

"Hmmm. Sounds like now she's not."

"Looks that way."

"Let me guess. You predicted the groom would be a real scumbag and now she won't marry him."

I smiled at how well Dave knew me. "Not quite, but you're really close."

"So, does that mean you're coming home early?"

I paused for a moment, thinking about that. My flight wasn't for another three days, and knowing what I was about to face with Ellie and the rest of the wedding guests, the prudent thing might be to leave town early. But then I thought about Sara, and how we still didn't know where she was. Perhaps I needed to be part of the solution while I still had a little time left. "Naw, looks like I'm gonna stick it out here until Sunday. I need to wrap up some stuff and help out a friend if I can."

There was a long pause on the other end of the line, and finally Dave said, "Abby, you don't always have to be the hero, you know."

"What's that supposed to mean?" I asked.

"It means that when someone's in trouble you're the first person to march to the front lines on their behalf, and sometimes the better thing to do is wave the white flag and come on home."

"Jesus, Dave. Now you're getting all preachy on me."

"I'm just sayin', I know how you are."

"See you Saturday, pal," I said, and disconnected.

Padding out to the kitchen, lured by the fresh smell of pancakes on the griddle, I found Duffy on his own phone. "So, no confession, huh?" he said, and, noticing me, waved me over to a bar stool. "Yeah . . . uh-huh . . . okay. Well, give him a little rest and I'll be there in a couple of hours. I need to check on my sister first."

I took my seat at the bar and unfolded my napkin as I listened to Duffy. A moment later he disconnected and began piling hotcakes on a plate that he set in front of me. "Smells delicious," I said with a happy smile.

"When it comes to food, I don't mess around," Duffy answered, pouring the batter for his own portion onto the griddle.

"So Eddie didn't confess?" I asked as I swiped butter onto my breakfast.

"Nope. He steadfastly denies any and all wrongdoing. But he hasn't lawyered up yet, so I'm gonna head in and see what I can pull out of him. I'd like to know how his wallet ended up at Gina's crime scene, and why a set of bloody scrubs was found in Gina's car."

"Freaky coincidence?"

"Maybe. But I'd like to hear it from Eddie."

I cocked an eyebrow in his direction, "Kind of a catch twenty-two for you, huh?"

Duffy nodded and ran a hand through his thick brown hair. "You said it. If he can't give me a reasonable explanation, then I've got to push him on Gina's murder. If I can't get him to 'fess up, and we find more evidence from the crime scene linking him to Gina's murder, then it's a tougher trial. If he is guilty and cracks, then I risk my sister hating me for the rest of my life."

"You can't really believe he did this," I said. The more I pointed my radar at the question of Eddie's guilt, the more convinced I was that he was innocent.

"I can't afford to believe one way or the other, Abs. I have a murder to solve and a suspect in custody. Since I haven't talked to him yet, I couldn't tell you one way or the other how I feel about him."

"So, what are you going to do about Sara?" I asked, switching off the topic of Eddie.

"File a missing persons, then grill Eddie, see if he cracks. If not we'll just have to wait and see if she turns up or if we can track some more clues to her whereabouts."

"You've got my help if you need it—at least until Saturday."

Duffy smiled as he piled his pancakes on his plate and came to join me at the bar. "I appreciate that. Right now, if you're willing, I'd really like you to be there for Ellie. Before I talked to the station I put a call in to Mom, and Ellie's hurting something fierce."

"Do you think she'll want to talk to me? I mean, my sister tells me that the general consensus is that this is largely my fault."

Duffy stopped pouring the maple syrup long enough to look me directly in the eye. "Abs, right now Ellie's not pointing fingers. At this moment she's grieving the loss of one of her best friends, and she's also worried sick about her fiancé. If I want to work this case I can't let her grief allow me to overlook the facts. I owe this investigation my full attention, to either present her with the fact that I believe Eddie killed Gina, or that this was all one huge coincidence."

"Okay," I said with a nod. "I got ya."

"Good, now go get naked under the shower while I'm too distracted by my breakfast to join you, and I'll take you over to Viv's when you're done."

"Sure," I said, feeling my cheeks flush as I got up to deposit my dishes in the sink. "I'll get right on that."

"Better hurry," Duffy said, his mouth full of food. "I eat fast."

And with that I bolted to the bathroom.

An hour later we had pulled up in front of Viv's, which could be seen all the way down the street by the long line of cars parked in front. "Wow," I said, noting the cars. "Looks like a party."

"Viv's gathering the troops, I see," Duffy said coming to a stop. "Come on, time to face the music."

I didn't realize what he meant until we walked through the front door and Kelly and Christina met us in the front hallway. "Hi, Duffy! Hi, Abby!" Christina said with an elbow in the ribs to Kelly.

I smiled at them, but Kelly gave me a dark look. "Isn't that the same dress you wore last night?" she snapped.

Before I had a chance to answer, Viv came around the corner and announced, "It's just the lovebirds!" over her shoulder right after she saw us. "Abby and Duffy finally pulled themselves out of bed!" she yelled again.

I turned toward the door, intent on bolting, but Duffy caught me and whipped me back around. "Thanks for the bulletin, Viv. I don't think they heard you in China."

"Your swimmers gettin' a good workout, Duffy?" she asked, and I swore all conversation stopped in the house.

Duffy eyed her with a grin and took a big sniff of the air. "Mmmm. Viv, is that your special meat sauce I smell?"

I took my own whiff as he said that, noticing that there was something garlicky and deliciously aromatic filling the house. "It is," Viv replied.

"What time's dinner?" Duffy asked.

"Four thirty."

"Count me in for a helping," Duffy said, and kissed me on the cheek before turning and heading out the door.

When he was gone I gave a brief smile to Christina and Kelly and Viv, then bolted to my room. When I opened my door I saw my sister seated comfortably on my bed reading a magazine. "Ah, we meet again, Catwoman," I said with a flourish.

"Hello, Batgirl," she said, licking her fingers before flipping over the next page. "Did you have fun at the Batcave last night?"

"I will be so glad to get into something comfortable!" I said, ignoring her question and heading over to my suitcase.

"And Batman, is he well?"

"I know I have some yoga pants in here somewhere," I said, pawing through my clothes.

"Sworn to secrecy, huh, Batgirl?" Cat purred from the bed.

"Here they are!" I said, holding up my yoga pants in triumph.

"Abby," Cat said, her tone becoming impatient.

"Caaat," I said, mocking her as I turned back to my suitcase to fish for the matching top.

"You cannot torture me like this!" she wailed.

"Wanna bet?"

"I'm serious."

"Me too," I said as I located my top and began to shrug out of my dress.

"Give me one kernel, one tidbit, just one teeny-weeny little fact!" she said, throwing the magazine aside and batting her eyelashes at me.

I threw on my shirt and began pulling on my pants. "You know that theory you always had about Duffy's birthmark?"

"The one on his waist? The one I always thought went farther down?"

"Yep," I said, slipping on a hoodie and pushing my feet into slippers.

"Yeah . . ." she said, rolling her hands in an "out with it" gesture.

"It doesn't."

"It doesn't what?"

"Go farther down."

Cat squealed so loud I thought the paint was going to peel. "Will you keep it down! Geez!" I snapped as I hurried over to check the hall to see if anyone heard her.

I saw Viv come into the hallway and I waved at her from the door. She waved back, a large wooden spoon in her hand covered in red sauce. "Come help me with the sauce later," she said, then turned back toward the kitchen.

"Seriously, I cannot tell you anything," I said to Cat as I shut the door and moved over to the bed.

"Blah, blah!" Cat said, scooting over on the bed as I sat down. "So was it good for you?" she asked.

"We had a deal," I said as I crossed my legs and arms.

"You and Duffy had a deal?"

"No, you and I had a deal."

"What deal?"

"You asked for one teeny-weeny fact. And I just gave it to you, so the subject is dropped."

"You are no fun, you know that?"

"Crime fighting is no picnic," I said gravely. "Have you seen Ellie?" I asked, wanting to change the subject.

"No. She's at her mother's resting right now. Nina is going to bring her over later when Ellie feels up to it. I understand she didn't sleep a wink last night. The doctor tried to prescribe her some tranquilizers but Ellie refuses to take them."

Only I knew that Ellie would not risk her pregnancy by taking some heavy drugs. "She'll be all right," I said firmly. "She's a tough cookie, that one."

"You never answered my question from this morning."

"I'm not telling you anything."

"No, not that. About if there were any more details about Gina's murder."

"Yeah, like I'd fill you in now that I know you're working for the mob," I said, tongue in cheek.

"I *swear* I had to tell them!" she complained.

"You do remember I have an inboard lie detector, right?"

"Abby, you weren't there. You didn't see them. They were in a frenzy!"

I rolled my eyes and settled on the bed next to Cat. "The only thing I know is that Eddie is sticking to the story that he had nothing to do with it."

"Well, hell," Cat said with a pout. "I already knew that."

"It's all I got," I said, resting my head against the backboard and closing my eyes.

"Did Duffy find out anything else about Sara?" Cat asked.

"You heard about Sara too?" I asked lifting one lid. That was a detail I hadn't filled her in on.

"Of course. Everyone knows, and we're worried sick. Half the wedding party has been trying to track her down, and no one's seen her since you and Ellie told her to go to the dress shop. Nina called right before you two showed up to let everyone know they found Sara's car in the mall's parking lot. I understand a deputy has been dispatched to see if she ever made it inside or if she was perhaps overcome in the lot."

"Whoa!" I said as I sat bolt upright.

"What? What is it?" Cat asked, grabbing my arm.

"Eddie," I said as I thought back. "That day that we went to the bridal salon. Eddie came home and met us in the driveway. Ellie told him where we were going and who we were meeting. He left before us."

"Oh, my," Cat said, her fingers going to twist the necklace at her throat. "Do you think he might be connected with what's happened to her?"

My left side felt thick and heavy. "No," I said, thinking on it. "Still, it is another odd coincidence. I strongly believe there is a connection between what happened to Gina and Sara's disappearance, but how Eddie figures into this is the big mystery."

"Poor Ellie," Cat said, shaking her head.

"Poor Sara," I added as I lay back against the headboard again.

Cat then asked me, "Have you done your police psychic shtick on this case yet?"

"My what?" I asked, looking up at her.

"You know. Your psychic shtick. How you helped Milo and that rat-bastard ex-boyfriend who dumped you on Valentine's Day with that serial killer case in Royal Oak."

"You mean have I tuned in on this yet?" I translated, grinning at her nickname for Dutch.

"Yeah."

"Yes. And I've given Duffy my impressions, for all the good it's done," I added moodily.

"Hey, now, come on, Abby. Don't be like that. If Duffy is asking for your impressions then he must see value in what you're providing him, right?"

"I suppose," I said.

"And didn't I hear you'd drawn a sketch for Duffy that led him to Gina?"

"Man, is there anything you haven't heard about, Cat?" I asked with a big-eyed stare.

"I pride myself on rooting out useful information."

"Well, the sketch I drew for Sara doesn't look too promising. Duffy can't make sense of the landmarks."

"You drew a sketch of where Sara is?"

"Yeah."

"What did it look like?"

Instead of explaining it I got up to retrieve paper and pen, then quickly drew a similar sketch to the one I'd drawn for Duffy this morning. Handing this to Cat, I watched as she looked thoughtfully at it. "Hmmm," she said after a bit. "What is this mailbox-looking thingy over here with your name on it?"

"I have no idea."

"And these round circles in the shape of a cross. Do you think that's a grave?"

"If it is, then that's one large marker. I get the impression these are stones—like large stones laid out by hand."

"Odd . . ."

"I know," I said with a shrug. "Anyway, let's not talk about it anymore—this whole thing is giving me one serious headache."

"Sure," Cat said, scooting off the bed to put my sketch and pen back in my purse. "Why don't you get some rest? I have to go back to the hotel and rescue the boys from spending time with their grandparents. You know the Coopers; it's not a family gathering until someone's sobbing, and Matty and Michael are no match for Claire."

"You left the boys *alone* with them?"

"No. Tommy's there. If things get bad he will just scoot them back to the room. Anyhoo, I've got to run. I promised to be back an hour ago. We'll be at the hotel until tonight; then we're heading home."

"You're not staying for the wed—" And I stopped myself, realizing what I was about to ask.

Cat gave me a sad look; then she shrugged her shoulders and said, "I'll be back around four to give Ellie a supportive hug and dash off to the airport. Claire and Sam are headed out about an hour before us, thank God. I cannot wait to see the backside of them!"

"Way to put your foot down," I said with a grin, referring to the past two months, when my mother had been living at my sister's mansion in Boston and had steadfastly refused to leave.

"Sometimes it's better to be clever," Cat said with a small grin and a wink.

I walked Cat to the front door, noticing several wedding guests seated in the living room. Being a yellow-belly I didn't really want to engage a roomful of possible hostiles, so I meandered into the kitchen, my headache coming on strong. "Viv?" I asked as I came up behind her.

"Yes, dear?"

"Got any ibuprofen?"

"In that cabinet," she said as she took down a small vial with a weathered label and carefully extracted a tiny pinch of something brown from inside, then tossed it into the sauce.

I reached for the painkiller and a glass when out of the corner of my eye I saw Viv take another vial off the shelf. She took another pinch from the second vial and tossed that into the sauce as well.

When I'd knocked back the pills I turned to study her, curious about the vials that, I noticed, lined one shelf. Methodically she selected each vial, shook out a tiny pinch to toss into the huge saucepan and gave the meat sauce three quick stirs.

When she was finished I moved over to look at the bottles, noting that each one had a sticker with a woman's name typed across the center. Some of the vials were clearly older than the others, as their labels looked more worn and the glass was a different size and thickness. I stared at the slightly smudged label of the first vial and said, "Donna."

I looked to Viv for an explanation but she just bustled about the kitchen, pulling out serving plates before heading over to the fridge. I looked back at the vials and read the rest of the names: "Connie, Diane, Hazel, Carol and Edna." I turned back toward Viv when I'd finished reading off the list, really curious now, but Viv either hadn't heard me or was pretending not to notice.

I reached over then and picked up Hazel, wondering whether Viv packaged these herself, and if she did, why she would name them after women. With interest I pulled the small cork out of the bottle and sniffed the contents. The vial had no odor at all. "Hey, Viv?" I asked.

"Yes, Abigail?" she said with a small, knowing grin on her face.

"What are these?" I asked, holding up Hazel for her to see.

"My secret ingredient," she answered.

My brows pulled together in a frown. That didn't explain much. "Can I taste a teeny sample?"

"Help yourself," Viv said, her grin spreading.

Carefully I shook out a tiny bit into the palm of my hand. It looked like dirt. I licked my finger and placed it on the sample, then raised this to my tongue. *Hmmm.* It tasted like dirt too. "Blech," I said, and took a sip of the water. "This tastes like dirt."

"That's because it is, dear," Viv said, coming over to me and taking Hazel out of my hands to replace the stopper and put it back with the others.

"What? Why would you put dirt into your meat sauce?" I asked.

"Because it's special dirt."

"*Special* dirt?"

"Very special."

"Please do not tell me it's fertilizer," I said, ready to bolt to the bathroom and brush my teeth with vigor.

Viv chuckled. "Oh, I doubt that, Abby. No, this dirt was a gift from good old Mother Nature. A test of her temper and therefore worth its weight in gold."

I cocked my head at her for a long moment as she continued to smirk at me. My intuition buzzed as I puzzled over her riddle; it was obvious she wanted me to figure out her innuendos, but my headache was making that difficult. Finally I tuned in to what my guides were telling me and I had a vision of a storm. I looked back to the vials and the lightbulb went on. "Hurricanes!" I announced triumphantly. "These are all the names of hurricanes!"

"Bingo," she said, pointing her finger at me and giving me a wink.

I smiled at her, and secretly thanked my guides for helping me figure this out. Then something still nagged at me, and I asked, "So why do you put the dirt from hurricanes in your sauce?" I asked.

"These weren't any old hurricanes, Abby," she said, picking up Hazel and regarding it with a faraway look. "Hazel very nearly killed me," she said softly. "In fact, it was the storm that Jimmy lost his parents to."

My jaw dropped at that little tidbit. Ellie had once told me that her father's parents were killed when he was just a boy, but I never knew the cause. "Your brother and sister-in-law died in a hurricane?"

Viv nodded, a very sad look on her face. "Yes, the house they lived in just down the street from me collapsed, and only Jimmy survived. Beth, his mother, was four months pregnant at the time. It was awful."

I gasped when she said this. "Then I *really* don't understand why you would put dirt from that awful storm into our food. Don't you think that's a bad omen?"

"On the contrary," Viv said, and caressed the vial. "Hazel was the most powerful force I have ever seen. She was a category-four storm that battered at us for fourteen long and painful hours, pounded us into the ground until we begged for mercy, and some of us she challenged on that day lost their lives to her.

"It is that strength, that *resolve,* Abby, that colors this dirt. That's why I put it into the food. To feed us Hazel's strength, and give us her fierce courage."

"What doesn't kill you makes you stronger," I whispered, realizing what Viv was getting at.

"Bingo," she said, again and squeezed my hand. "And no telling everyone about the vials. Ellie's daddy doesn't go for eating the storm that killed his parents, pigheaded scamp that he is."

"Your secret's safe with me," I said with a smile. "Now, how can I help?"

I worked with Viv in the kitchen for a while, putting together a garden salad and some hors d'oeuvres and peeling apples for an apple crumb dessert. I avoided the living room as much as I could, because every time I went in there I got the evil eye from the entire room. It was obvious that everyone was convinced I had something to do with Eddie's arrest, and the only thing that kept me from fleeing the premises was the thought of what Ellie must be going through.

I wanted to help my friend, not slink out of town. Selfishly, I also wanted to make it better between us. I didn't know how Ellie felt about me right now, but I needed to make sure she understood that nothing that I'd gotten intuitively had been intentionally derived to hurt her.

At about three thirty, Ellie and Nina came by. Both women looked worn and tired, but each tried to put on a brave face nonetheless. Nina spotted me right away and hurried over to where I was standing in the front hall, waiting to greet her and Ellie. "Hello, Abby, how are you holding up?" she asked me kindly.

"I'm fine," I said, bending forward to give her a hug. "I'm more worried about you two. How's Ellie doing?"

Nina squeezed me tightly, then let go before answering. "She has her moments. Finding out about Gina was horrible. And that the police suspect Eddie . . . well, I don't even know how to process that yet. Ellie's convinced he's innocent, and I have to say I'm with her on that one right now."

"I wish I were convinced of that too," I said with a frown.

"Yes, Ellie told me about your reading with her. But it's so hard to believe our Eddie had anything to do with this," Nina insisted.

"I know," I said with a sigh. "The only thing I know for sure about this mess is that if Eddie had anything to do with it, he was forced into it."

"What do you mean?" she asked.

"I'm sure Ellie told you that in her reading I saw Eddie going to jail. Then I saw that he would need a lawyer, and a good one, and the reason was because he had done something to break the law, but it was something he had not done willingly. Intuitively it felt like he was forced into a situation he had no control over, and things just got out of hand."

Nina was looking at me with a very intense expression. After a long moment she whispered, "I never liked the way Gina acted around Eddie."

"What?" I asked, lowering my own voice so no one would hear us.

Nina looked over her shoulder to where Ellie was being hugged and supported by her friends; then she turned back to me and, taking my hand, pulled me into the kitchen. Nodding to Vivian, she led me out to the enclosed porch. "I know it's a little chilly out here, but at least we'll have some privacy."

"No sweat. So you were saying about Gina around Eddie?"

"Ah, yes," Nina said, nodding her head. "Gina was an absolutely beautiful girl. She used to turn so many heads, and Ellie and she were quite the pair when they went out. The men would trip all over themselves to say hello to them. They used to tell me some very funny tales about their nights out together.

"Then Ellie met Eddie, and things changed. You see, Gina dated a lot of men, but Ellie was more of a tagalong. She liked being in a relationship, while Gina liked to sow her wild oats. The more time Ellie spent with Eddie, the more Gina seemed to resent it.

"And last summer, just after Eddie proposed, we had everyone over for an engagement pool party. I remember going upstairs to get some more towels for the guests when through the upstairs window I could see Gina leading Eddie by the hand out behind the garage. He seemed to be going along grudgingly, and they disappeared from my view for a minute or two. Then suddenly Eddie came storming out from that area, and Gina was trailing after him, frantically telling him she was sorry. Eddie stopped at one point and I'll never forget what he yelled at her."

"What?" I asked.

"He said, 'If you ever pull a stunt like that again, I'll tell Ellie what a whore you really are.'"

"Whoa," I said breathlessly. "What do you think she did to him behind the garage?"

"I don't know, for sure, but I'm pretty positive that Gina made a pass at him and Eddie turned her down flat."

"Does Ellie know about this?"

"Absolutely not," Nina said. "I would never tell her something so upsetting. And as far as I know, Eddie kept his mouth shut too."

"So that's why you don't think he had anything to do with her death. After that incident he would have been careful to keep his distance with her."

"That, and I saw firsthand how dedicated to Ellie he really is."

Just then Viv poked her head out of the door. "You two gonna stay out there all day, or come in and be social?"

"Coming, Vivian," Nina said with the smallest hint of an eye roll.

I followed Nina through the door and into the kitchen, where the aroma of Viv's secret sauce became even more mouthwatering. "Man, Viv!" I said. "If that sauce tastes as good as it smells, count me in for seconds!"

Viv smiled ruefully at me and quipped, "And I'll be sure not to rule you out for thirds."

I laughed and helped her with the plates and silverware for the dinner she was preparing. There were about fifteen mouths to feed, and Viv showed me where she kept her extra flatware. "Nice stash," I said, referring to a large drawer in a bureau crammed into the dining room that was packed full of mismatched forks, knives and spoons.

"I like to collect this stuff from all over. You never know when you'll have a day like today with so many mouths to feed."

I smiled, thinking of the sets she'd swiped from the country club. "Comes in handy, I suppose," I agreed.

"It does. In the top drawer you'll find some extra salt and pepper shakers. Make sure there're enough to go around."

I pulled open the drawer and saw that there were more than enough. Everyone in attendance could have their own personal pair of salt and pepper shakers—with two more to spare if needed.

While I was working on getting the buffet ready, an arm slipped around my waist and a blond head tilted onto my shoulder. "Hey, there, girlfriend," Ellie said.

I nearly cried with relief that she didn't seem to be mad at me, and I turned toward her and pulled her into a huge bear hug. Not trusting my voice, I just squeezed her for a moment, then got a grip and said, "I can't tell you how sorry I am."

"I know," she whispered. "I'm so glad you're here, Abs. I don't know what I would have done if all of this had blindsided me. Thank God you told me that something big was coming. At least I had a day or two to prepare myself."

I sighed in relief and pulled away to arm's length. "Whatever you need from me, you've got it, okay?"

Ellie nodded, and I noticed the tears beginning to slip down her face. "I need you to help Duffy and find out who did this to Gina. And I need that as much for Gina's sake as for my own. I can't have the father of my baby and the man I love going to jail for something he didn't do." Ellie sobbed as she unconsciously rubbed her belly.

"I know, I know," I said, pulling her into a hug again. "There, there, girl. I promise you I will do everything I can to help Duffy with this. It is my solemn vow to you."

"Ellie?" a voice said from behind us, and we both turned to see petite Kelly in the doorway. "Sorry, I thought I heard you crying. Are you okay?"

"Hey, Kel," Ellie said, straightening up and putting on a brave face. "I'm fine. Just a little overwhelmed right now."

"Can I get you anything?" Kelly asked, the worry on her face intense as she stepped forward to stroke Ellie's arm.

"Some water would be wonderful," Ellie said.

After Kelly left to retrieve the water, I said, "It's good to have friends, huh?"

"I'm very lucky." Ellie smiled. "Come on; let's see if Viv is done stirring her sauce. I haven't eaten since last night, and I think for the baby's sake I need to."

A short time later we all had plates loaded with food, and the talking was reduced to a minimum, due to the fact that people couldn't seem to gobble down Viv's delicious meat sauce fast enough. I tried eating slowly to pace myself, as I was definitely serious about digging in for seconds. The doorbell rang shortly after we began eating, and Cat came prancing in to join us.

"Hello, everyone!" she announced to the group, then padded over to Ellie and gave her a quick hug. The pair chatted for just a minute or two, and Cat gave Ellie her personal business card and said, "Ellie, if you need anything—and I do mean anything—you just call me and I will make sure you have it. I've already placed a call to my legal team in Boston, and they have recommended someone fabulous here in the Denver area. They've made the preliminary phone call to the law office of Jim Watson, one of the best criminal defense lawyers in the state. He's willing to take the case, and all you have to do is call him at the number I've written on the back of my card. His initial retainer is on me; consider it a wedding gift."

Ellie took Cat's card and held it to her heart. "How can I ever thank you?"

"No need, Ellie. You're like family to me, and I take care of my family," Cat said with a wink. Just then the phone rang, and Viv hurried over to it. After saying hello she was silent for a long moment, and I noticed the color draining slowly from her face.

"Oh, no," I said as my intuition buzzed and I felt a familiar dread come over me.

"What?" Kelly, who was seated on my left, asked me.

"Something terrible has happened," I said as I waited for Viv to disconnect and tell us about the phone call.

Instead, with a shaking hand Viv handed the phone to Nina. "It's Duffy," she said, and Ellie stopped talking to Cat as she overheard her great-aunt. "I'm afraid it's bad."

"What is it?" Ellie said, jumping to her feet and rushing over with her mother to the phone. "Tell me!" Ellie demanded as Viv just looked at her with a pitying stare.

"There's been a fire," Viv said.

"Where?" Ellie asked.

"The jail. I guess it was pretty bad."

"Eddie?!" Ellie screeched, her voice panicked.

"They can't find him," Viv said, and reached with her hand for a chair to sit down in, the strength seeming to go out of her knees. "They're taking a head count of the prisoners who made it out. Eddie's not among them."

Chapter Thirteen

"Oh, my God," Nina said, and took the phone to talk to her son.

Ellie began to shake, and the paleness to her skin made me quickly pull out a chair for her. "Ellie," I said, trying to get her attention as she just stared out into space, the news too much for her. "Ellie!" I said again, and got right in her face. "Do you have a picture on you of Eddie?" Something was telling me that Eddie was still alive, and I had to know for sure.

"Wha . . . ?" Ellie said, looking at me but not taking in my words.

"I need a picture of Eddie!" I commanded. Then I stood up and said to the group, "Does anyone have a picture on them that Eddie is in?"

"In my wallet," Ellie said breathlessly. "Oh, God, Abby. Please look for me! Please tell me if he's still alive!"

Kelly leaped off her chair and rushed to the hall, returning a moment later with Ellie's purse. "Here!" she said as she shoved it forward.

All eyes were on me as I dug in for Ellie's wallet. Pulling it out, I handed it to her, and with shaking fingers she tore it open and retrieved a photo of the two of them. I looked at the photo and closed my eyes in relief. "He's alive, El," I said.

Ellie let out a long and painful sob. "Thank you, Lord!" she said, and began crying in earnest.

"So where is he?" Cat asked me.

"I don't know. Maybe we should head over to the jail and see if there's any word?" I offered.

"Come on, everyone," Cat said, taking charge. "I've got a limo outside. Viv, Nina, Ellie and Abby, you're with me. Everyone else, follow the limo."

Without delay, we all piled out of Viv's house. In the backseat, hopping up and down, were Matt and Mike and one very tired brother-in-law. "Hey, Abby," Tommy said as I sat down.

"Hey, guy. Cat left you all out here?"

"She said she'd be right back, and that was about fifteen minutes ago. Where's the party?" he asked as people began to pour into the car.

"We're headed to jail!" Cat announced, getting in after Vivian.

"What'd you do this time?" Tommy said like it was a question he asked all the time.

"Not *me*!" Cat said, giving him a dark look. "Ellie's fiancé."

"Okay," Tommy said as he scooted over to make room for his wife. "Have you thought about the fact that we will probably miss our plane?"

"They have other ones," Cat said impatiently. "Ellie, can you tell the driver where to go?"

"Yes," Ellie said, and headed up to the front of the cab.

I looked around the limo and noticed the absence of my parents. "Claire and Sam not up for a joyride?"

"They took an earlier flight," my sister announced joyfully. "My master plan worked."

"Which master plan was that exactly?" I asked.

"The one where leaving them alone with the twins for a few hours would ensure that they would want to get the hell out of here before I asked them to babysit again!"

"Good thinking." I nodded.

"I know!"

"Too bad you didn't think of that, like, two months ago," I added.

"Better late than never." Cat sniffed.

We arrived at the jail about fifteen minutes later. There were fire trucks, sheriff's cars and ambulances lining the street, not to mention the melee of people milling about made up of the curious, the press and emergency crews.

The limo came to a halt about one hundred yards from the county jail, unable to get closer due to barricades set up by the sheriff. Ellie was out of the car first, her eyes wide and scared as they caught site of the three-story building still ablaze. I followed close on her heels, along with several other members of our troop.

Taking Ellie's arm, I led her in the direction my radar was pointing. We found Duffy on the east side of the building, talking with a fireman as they pointed up to the third floor, where smoke still poured from one of the windows.

I shuddered at the sight. I'd been in a fire a few months back, and the memory still gave me nightmares. We approached the taped-off area right behind Duffy, and when we neared I called out to Duffy, who turned and came over to us in haste.

"Hey, baby girl," he said as he swept Ellie into a tight hug.

She cried a little into his chest as he held her, and after a moment she pulled away and said, "Please tell me you've found him."

Duffy's eyes told us before he even had a chance to speak that he didn't have good news, and Ellie seemed to wilt a little more. "We're still looking, El. I'm so sorry," he began.

Nina came up behind me and reached forward to touch her son's arm. "Your father's on his way. Let's get Ellie over there where she can sit down and we can talk."

I followed the trio as we headed to a curb and sat Ellie down gently. She leaned into her mother, who wrapped a protective arm about her daughter as she asked Duffy, "How did this happen?"

Duffy looked chagrined and had a hard time meeting his mother's eyes as he said, "We were tight on space, Ma, so they put Eddie in with Warren Biggins."

"You are kidding me!" I said, looking at Duffy like he needed his head examined. "Why would you put him in with that psycho?"

"We had no choice. I was on my way here when I got the word. It looks like the fire started in Biggins and Eddie's jail cell. Biggins was known to have arson on his list of priors. I have no idea how he got the accelerant, but he set his bedding on fire, and when the jail cells opened to evacuate the prisoners, he and Eddie overpowered one of the guards and the two of them made a run for it."

"Eddie is *with* Biggins?" I asked, shocked by the news.

"According to several eyewitnesses, yes."

"So Eddie's all right? He's just escaped?" Ellie asked.

Duffy looked back at his little sister. Holding her gaze he said in a voice thick with gravity, "I hope so. Both he and Biggins are still unaccounted for."

"What do you mean, you hope so?" I asked, knowing there was more to this story.

Duffy took a big breath, let it out slowly and said, "In their efforts to escape, Eddie and Biggins went back into the heart of the fire. Before disappearing into the smoke, one of the prisoners swears he saw Eddie's pants catch fire."

"Oh, God," Ellie said and she covered her face with her hands.

"Ellie," I said, remembering two things that could give her hope. "Remember, I saw his picture. He's *alive;* I *know* it."

Ellie gulped back a tremendous sob and peeked her

eyes out from her hands. "You're sure?" she asked me, her voice barely a whisper.

"Yes. Yes, I can feel it. He's alive. And now I know what happened in the driveway the other day. Do you remember when I was really dizzy? And I said something about Eddie?"

Ellie pulled the rest of her hands down from her face and her mouth formed a small O. "You said 'pants on fire.'"

I nodded. "Yes, I did. That's what my guides were trying to say. That his pants were *actually* going to catch on fire. And since I saw him getting a lawyer, then I think we'll find him, and he'll be okay." That was a small stretch, but I had to give Ellie some hope.

She reached up and grabbed my hand. "Thank you, Abby," she said as tears streamed down her face.

When she touched me I felt a familiar yellow warning light go on in my mind. Ellie was in danger, and as I focused on her energy I knew we had to get her home and into bed. "Nina," I said gently. "We need to get Ellie out of here. Will you take her home?"

"No, I want to stay!" Ellie insisted, and I noticed how pale and drawn her face had become. "Eddie may be hurt, and he'll need me."

"No!" I said sharply, noticing that the yellow light in my head beat more strongly. "Ellie, you have got to get some rest. I'll stay here with Duffy and see if my radar can't lend a hand, but only if you agree to go home and lie down immediately."

"Come on, my love," Nina said as she helped Ellie to her feet. "Abby's right. You need to go home and rest. Duffy, will you call us the moment you hear something?"

"Scout's honor, Ma," he said with a small salute.

"Please," Ellie said over her shoulder to me as Nina led her back toward the limo, "please find him for me, Abby."

"I'll make sure she gets home safe," Cat said as I realized she was next to me.

"Thanks, Cat. Are you guys staying in town or heading out now that you've missed your plane?"

"Oh, I think it's time to head home. I'll have Tommy phone the airport as soon as we get Ellie and Nina back to their house. Call me as soon as you hear anything, okay?"

"You got it. Safe journey, okay?" I said as I hugged her.

Turning back to Duffy, I asked, "So now what?"

"Now we wait until they've put out the fire and then search the building to find casualties. You're certain Eddie's alive?"

"Positive," I said, feeling it in my bones. Closing my eyes, I focused on him and let my radar fill my mind with intuitive information. "He's alive, but his right leg is injured. There's also a sense of panic about him. He's scared, Duffy."

"I don't doubt it," Duffy said. "Can you get a feel for where he is?"

I focused harder, allowing my intuition to go beyond Eddie's pain and state of mind and to feel his surroundings. "He's moving," I said as I felt a shift in the energy. "I think he's in a car."

"Can you describe the car?" Duffy asked.

I grimaced. That was a very tough question, but I asked it in my head and waited for a detail to surface. I got the thought "green" in my head, and opened my eyes. "Green. He's in a green car. A sedan, I'd say. Not an SUV or truck."

Duffy pulled the mouthpiece of his walkie-talkie off his shoulder. "Command, this is Sheriff McGinnis. I need a perimeter search of the area around the jail for a green sedan with possible escapees inside."

In the next fifteen minutes a preliminary search of the area was done, and no green sedan was spotted. Without a make or model of the car I suspected Eddie was in, there was no telling where he might be. About the time the last of the patrol cars had reported in that there was no sign of a green sedan on the streets surrounding the jail, I got an idea and said, "Duffy, have some deputies go to the hospital."

"Something's going to happen at the hospital?" he asked me.

"No, have them go and look around the hospital. Remember? Eddie's been hurt. He's bound to have friends there, colleagues who might be willing to help him without alerting the police."

"Now you're thinking," Duffy said with a grin, and reached for the mouthpiece of his walkie-talkie again.

After that, we did a whole lot of waiting. A few people I'd seen at Viv's house came over to see if there'd been any word. Most of them eventually went home after Duffy promised to update everyone once he heard something.

The fire was put out, and crews began the slow, methodical search for people who couldn't be accounted for. I listened to the chatter on Duffy's radio as room after room, then floor after floor was carefully searched. By this time it was very close to ten P.M., and out of the corner of my eye I spotted Christina making her way over to me. "Hey," she said when she got close.

"You're still here?" I asked with a shiver. Duffy had lent me a blanket, which I'd wrapped around myself while I waited in the cold with him, and I shivered underneath it.

"Yeah, my uncle owns a restaurant just down the street, and I went there right after we arrived. He's usually got better dirt on what's going on than the police. Say, have you seen Kelly? She and I drove together, and she went to the car to grab her purse, like, hours ago and I haven't seen her since."

An alarm went off in my head as my heart skipped a beat. "No, Christina, I haven't seen her. Which one of you drove?"

"She did," Christina said, searching the much-thinned crowd. "Damn, and she was my only way home. Maybe Duffy can give me a ride?" she asked hopefully.

"Uh, sure," I said as the alarm continued to gong in my head. "I'll ask him. . . . Say, just out of curiosity, what kind of car does Kelly drive?"

"A Saturn, why?"

Warning! Warning! Warning! flashed through my head so strongly that I blinked as I tried to focus on our conversation. "What color is the Saturn?"

"Light green—have you seen it?"

My breathing quickened, and I grabbed Christina's hand and pulled her over to Duffy. "I know where Eddie is," I said when I caught his attention.

"Where?" Duffy asked, and Christina looked at me in shock.

"I think he's kidnapped Kelly. They're in her car and I think she's in big trouble."

Duffy put an APB out for Kelly's light green Saturn, and motioned for us to join him in the search. We piled into his patrol car and headed away from the county jail.

"Do you really think he'd kidnap Kelly?" Duffy asked me.

"It's weird," I said as I focused my energy on the thought. "I remember when Ellie and I were chasing after Hadley Rankin's car, when she'd been taken by Biggins, and that word, 'kidnapped,' kept racing through my mind. It's the same intuitive thought with Kelly. I know she's been kidnapped."

"Do you think Eddie's responsible, or Biggins?" Duffy asked me.

I grimaced. I hadn't considered that. I focused again on Eddie and tried to extend the energy outward. My feeling was that he wasn't alone, and that he too was in some kind of danger. "I think Biggins is with him," I said, and my right side felt light, confirming the statement.

"Any ideas where they may be, Abby?" Duffy asked.

I closed my eyes and focused with all my heart on Kelly. I had a sense of darkness, and for a moment I was terrified that she might be dead, but as I felt her energy, I had a sense of confinement. I felt trapped and enclosed and scared, and it was such an intense feeling that I moved back from it. "I think she's in the trunk," I said after a moment.

"The bastards," Duffy said, his grip on the steering wheel tightening and a determined look on his face. "Can you tell where they're taking her?"

"No, but give me a little time and I'll keep working on it."

We drove around the streets near the jail for about twenty minutes, and I waited for the energy around Eddie to change. Finally, I felt a subtle shift, and about ten minutes later I said, "He's not with her anymore. . . ."

"Where is he?" Duffy asked.

"He's someplace warm. There's a smell," I said as the faintest whisper of a scent floated to my nostrils. "He's someplace that smells like . . . like . . . bleach."

"Bleach?"

"Someplace big," I said, feeling the expanse of a building surrounding me. "There are many levels, and he's on the lowest one."

"Is he out of the city?" Duffy asked me.

"I can't tell."

"You said before you thought he was in the hospital. Do you think that's what you're getting?"

My eyes snapped open. "Yes! Yes, that has to be it! I'm not sure where he is in the hospital, but I really think that's it!"

"He's not with Kelly anymore?"

I focused, playing that against my radar. "No. He's left her."

"So the son of a bitch leaves Kelly in the trunk of a car with Biggins while he heads off to the hospital to get fixed up?" Duffy grumbled. "I'm gonna wring his neck when we find him. Jesus!" And with that Duffy grabbed his radio and began to shout instructions into it. He ordered a complete search of the hospital and flipped on his lights and siren as we raced through town to get there.

When we arrived, we searched the parking lot for Kelly's light green Saturn, but there was no sign of her car. Duffy got back on his radio and asked for the deputies already inside to report in. The hospital had eight floors. His team had started in the basement and they were still working their way up, with no sign of him yet.

Duffy parked, and Christina and I followed him into the hospital. Stopping inside the lobby, Duffy turned to me and asked, "Can your radar tell us if he's near?"

"Doubtful. It's not the same as a dog with a scent."

"Can you at least try?" he asked.

I hesitated for a minute, unsure; after all, there was a lot at stake here. "Yes," I said finally. "But try not to expect too much." Heading over to a bank of chairs, I sat down and got situated, then focused again. Intuition is a tricky thing. It has its own language, which, for me, is made up of metaphors, whispers of thoughts and feelings that must be interpreted. I've found that as a tool, it's important to ask the right questions when trying to get an answer. For instance, if you ask the wrong question on a subject you're trying to learn about, you can become diverted by the answer. It's very important to be as specific as possible.

Knowing this, I took a moment to formulate a question that I thought would point me to the exact location we needed to go. In my head I asked, *Where is Eddie's hiding place located in this hospital?*

Immediately I got the scent of bleach again, then a sense of spinning movement and loud noises all around. I waited and told my crew that I needed more clarity and was rewarded with a visual of a washing machine. My eyes flew open. I knew exactly where he was. "He's in the laundry room!" I said excitedly.

Duffy wasted no time calling out to the other deputies in the hospital, ordering everyone to meet him down in the laundry room. He ordered Christina and me to stay put, while he went off to meet his men.

After a few minutes Christina said, "That's some gift you've got there, Abby."

I smiled shyly at her. "Thanks. It comes in handy every now and again."

"I'll bet. So, why do you think it didn't work during my reading the other night?"

I cocked my head, thinking about the answer to that. Truth was, I had no idea. "I'm not sure, Chris, but since it seems Ellie's bridesmaids keep disappearing, it might be a good idea to try again before I go home."

"Sounds good. Not tonight though—you look bushed."

"You said it, girlfriend," I said with a sigh as I laid my head back against the wall.

Christina and I stared at the television set up in the hospital lobby for what felt like an eternity. I checked my watch several times, and noticed that nearly an hour had already passed, with no sign of and no word from Duffy.

Tired as I was, I got up and paced the floor. What had happened? Had they found Eddie? Was I wrong? Maybe I'd led the police in the wrong direction? Maybe Eddie wasn't here at all.

As these thoughts ricocheted around my head, I became increasingly agitated. I decided that I had been wrong. That in my effort to help, I'd really hurt the situation because I'd diverted two deputies and one sheriff from trying to find Kelly and her car. I could only imagine what must be happening to her right now. She was probably cold and frightened. Taking another glance at my watch, I decided I'd had enough of the wait. I had to go down and find Duffy and apologize for sending him on a wild-goose chase.

Just as I was about to tell Christina to stay put, he came down the long corridor followed by two other deputies, holding a plastic bag and leading a doctor in a white coat by the arm.

Duffy's expression was grim, and my heart sank as I studied his face. Pausing at the desk he spoke to a clerk on duty, then nodded to the other two deputies as they escorted the doctor and the plastic bag out of the hospital. Finally he headed in our direction. "So far, Abby," he said stopping before me, "you're getting high marks on the bloodhound exam."

"You found him?" I asked.

"No. Not exactly."

"Then what did you find?" Christina asked.

"Well, for starters we found the orange jumpsuit Eddie was wearing, and we know it was his because one of the legs has a big burn hole in it. Then we found one of the doctors who helped bandage him up. Looks like he sustained mostly second-degree burns to his right leg—just like you said," Duffy added, looking at me with a small grin.

"Was he alone?" I asked. I wondered if I'd been right and that Biggins wasn't with him.

"As far as I can tell. The doc who helped him was Dr. Shevat, one of Eddie's resident buddies. All he'll tell us is that Eddie was here, and he was by himself. No sign of Biggins and no sign of Kelly. Shevat says Eddie called him from the laundry room and convinced him to help patch him up. The wound was pretty serious, and will need further attention if it's going to heal right.

"Shevat says that he treated the wound; then Eddie asked for some food. Shevat went upstairs to the cafeteria to get him some, and when he came back down Eddie was gone."

"So he's left the premises," I said, looking up the long corridor as if I would spot him hiding in a doorway somewhere.

"Looks like it. He took a set of scrubs from one of the bins and bolted. One of the laundry workers says his winter coat, hat and gloves are missing too. We've taken Shevat in for further questioning. Maybe he's hiding Eddie's whereabouts; maybe he's telling us the truth. Hopefully Eddie told him something while he was being patched up that will help us find him."

My left side felt thick and heavy. "Not likely," I said.

"You think Shevat's telling the truth?"

I nodded. "He's not going to lead you to Eddie," I said firmly. "And at this point, I don't see how you're going to track him if his wound is covered and he's in warm clothing. He could be anywhere."

"Can you get a hit on him again?"

My shoulders drooped a little. "Duffy, I'm exhausted," I said. "Plus, anything that I get is bound to be pretty general. My feeling is that you're not going to find him before he's ready to be found, so we'll just have to hope that he comes to his senses and turns himself in."

"But what about Kelly?" Christina asked quietly.

I gave her a grave look, my intuition buzzing in the back of my mind. "I wish I could tell you that I wasn't worried about her, that Eddie would never let anything happen to her. But the truth is that when I focus on her energy I can sense that she's surrounded by danger. I think that Eddie left her with Biggins."

"Man!" Duffy said as he balled his fists. "You think you know someone! How could he leave her with that maniac?"

"He may not have had a choice," I said, and then I remembered the reading I'd given Ellie, and a few pieces of the puzzle started to click into place.

"So what now?" Christina asked.

"We get you two home, and I put out an Amber Alert on Kelly's car. With any luck, we'll find them in the next few hours."

Wearily Christina and I allowed ourselves to be herded out of the hospital and back to Duffy's patrol car. Before pulling out of the lot, Duffy authorized the Amber Alert and told his dispatcher to call him at home if there were any new developments. After that, we sat lost in our own thoughts as he drove to

Christina's apartment. We were almost there when my intuition buzzed in and I said, "She's alone."

"What?" Duffy and Christina asked me at the same time.

"Kelly. I think she got away. I feel like she's out of danger," I said.

"So where is she?" Duffy asked me.

"I don't know," I said, shaking my head. "I just feel this sense that she's on foot and far from home but she knows where she is."

Duffy sat back in his seat, his fingers drumming on the steering wheel for a moment before he called in to his deputies and told them to be on the lookout for a single white female fitting Kelly's description on foot. "It's cold out," he said after he'd called it in. "I hope she gets to a phone soon."

"If she calls anyone, she'll call me or Ellie," Christina said. "Oh! That's my building, Duffy. I'll run in and check my messages. If I hear anything I'll get in touch you guys right away."

"And vice versa," Duffy said with a small wave as she got out of the car. We waited until Christina made it safely into her apartment, then pulled away and drove toward the other side of town. I stared out the window, thinking grave thoughts and looking blankly out at the dark. "Penny for your thoughts," Duffy said.

I gave him a tiny grin and said, "Do I look that cheap?"

"Okay, how about ten million dollars for your thoughts?" Duffy asked, giving me a handsome smile.

I laughed in spite of myself. "Always there to boost my ego, aren't you?"

"I try," he said. "So, really. Where were you just now?"

"Honestly? I was back home. I miss my house, Duff. I miss my dog, my friends, my clients, and yes, I even miss the thought of returning to a town where I know I might run into my ex."

Duffy nodded, taking in what I'd just said and allowing a moment of silence to grow between us before he said, "So, asking you to move here is out of the question, huh?"

I did a double take. "What?"

Duffy ran a hand through his hair and, staring straight ahead at the road, he said, "You were pretty amazing today, Abby. In fact, you've been pretty amazing throughout this whole investigation. The Denver sheriff's department could absolutely use someone with your skills and abilities."

I cocked my head at him and narrowed my eyes. "Ah. So you'd like me to move out here for professional reasons, huh?"

Duffy took another moment before he answered. "Not entirely."

"Not entirely what?"

"Not entirely in that I'd also like to have an opportunity to take you out to dinner," he said.

"Uh-huh?" I said, smiling again.

"And give you a proper tour of the city," he added.

"Uh-huh?"

"And maybe, down the road, when you're ready . . ." he said, letting the thought trail off.

"Yes?"

"I'd like the chance to jump your bones again," he finished, turning to give me the full grille.

"I see. My, how romantic. How could a girl resist an offer like that?" I deadpanned.

"Don't fight it, sweetheart," Duffy said, giving me a sideways glance. "I'm irresistible."

I rolled my eyes but laughed all the same. "Or so you've been led to believe," I said. "Uh, we're at your house?" I asked as we pulled into his driveway.

"Yeah. I may need you to play bloodhound again if I get a call in the middle of the night. It'll be more convenient if you're here at my place. I called Viv from the hospital and told her you were staying with me."

"How thoughtful of you," I said woodenly while I got out of the car. "I'm sleeping in the spare bedroom," I added, just in case he thought otherwise. He gave me a sad look over his shoulder but didn't protest, then turned to unlock the door.

I stood behind him, watching his back and thinking about what he'd said in the car. Truthfully, I wasn't sure how I felt about Duffy's overtures. I liked him. I liked how he looked, I liked how he smelled and, God help me, I even liked how he tasted, but I was an emotional basket case right now. The breakup with Dutch was still a little too fresh for me. What I really needed was time and some distance to sort out my feelings. To mourn the death of the relationship I'd had with Dutch, then see how I felt about Duffy. Trouble was, while I was here in Denver, there was no way I'd have the opportunity to get the space I really needed.

As I followed Duffy into his house, I decided that I would change my itinerary and try to catch a flight out either tomorrow or the day after. I couldn't stay here and think with a clear head, so going home early would be just the thing to do.

Chapter Fourteen

"Dearly beloved, we are gathered here today to mourn the tragic loss of one of our own," a deep male voice from behind me said.

I looked away from the spaghetti sauce I'd been stirring for Viv and, lured by the voice, went into her living room. There, dozens of people were squished into the space, which had been removed of all its furniture and replaced by church pews. A priest stood at the back of the room. A silver casket lay to his right. I looked toward the casket but couldn't make out who was inside.

The crowd wore black. Many of the women had veils that obscured their faces. The men all had their heads bowed low as the priest continued. "She was a member of our community. A friend to many. A woman who provided comfort and counsel to many of you here."

A sob interrupted the priest, and I turned toward the noise. Ellie was consumed with grief. Her shoulders were shaking, and great gasps came from her hunched form. I was drawn forward by her grief. I wanted to comfort my friend, but at that moment a great howl erupted from beside the casket. The sound was piercing, and I winced as I turned toward the noise. There sat Eggy, next to the casket, his nose in the air and the most pitiful sound coming from his mouth. It was as if he were in some kind of terrible agony, and I rushed to him as I called out, "Eggy! Baby, what's the matter?"

His howling paused for the briefest moment, and he seemed to look about the room in earnest, but then he lifted his snout once again and howled even louder. I reached his side and began to stroke his fur, cooing to him and checking him over to see where he might be hurt. Eggy paid no heed to my touches and soothing words. He just continued to cry and whine.

I was really concerned now. I couldn't figure out what was wrong with my dog. I looked up to see if anyone else knew what to do and saw Dave in the pew right in front of me. He sat with the most forlorn look on his face I'd ever seen. A thin line of tears welled out of his eyes as they stared open but unseeing straight ahead. "Dave!" I called, and snapped my fingers in front of him. He didn't even blink. "Dave!" I yelled at the top of my lungs. Again, no acknowledgment from him.

Eggy stopped howling at that moment and turned in a circle, where he lay down in a tight ball and whimpered in small bursts of pitiful noise. I was still trying to get Dave's attention when I noticed Cat sitting just down from Dave. She was sobbing hysterically. Her face was red and puffy, her hair unkempt, and the clothes she wore looked rumpled. Tommy had his arm draped over her shoulders and was whispering gently to her. He too had a rather heartbroken look about him.

Something terrible had happened, and the realization was sinking in that whoever was in that casket had left by tragic means. I began to stand as a leaden feeling filled my chest. I was connected to this, but I was slow to make out how. I stood as the priest droned on and on. I surveyed the crowd, realizing that I knew every single face in it. My blood ran cold as I began to turn, and I gripped the side of the gurney the casket rested on as my eyes slid down the silver box to the body of the soul peacefully resting there.

My own face stared back.

"Oh, God . . ." I said, and I felt my knees grow weak. "No, no, no, no no!" I stammered. "How did this happen?" I screamed as I turned to the crowd. "How did this happen?!" I yelled again, and felt hands on my shoulders, shaking me gently.

"Abby," someone said.

"What happened!" I wailed, shoving those hands away. *"Who did this to me?!"*

"Abby!" Duffy shouted, and my eyes snapped open. "You're dreaming, honey. Come on, wake up, girl."

"I'm awake," I said as I stopped struggling.

"Jesus, what were you dreaming about?"

My eyes were trying to focus on Duffy's face. I was shivering with fright, and wet tears were cold on my face. "I dreamed that something terrible happened to me," I whispered, holding back the full details.

"Ah. Well, that's understandable," Duffy said as he sat down on my bed. "It's been a pretty eventful week. But you're okay; you're here and you're safe . . . well, as safe as any girl can be at two o'clock in the morning sleeping in the room next to mine," he said, trying to make light.

I wasn't in the mood to be kidded with. The dream had been too real, too vivid for me just to chalk it up to my subconscious. "Duffy?" I asked as I reached out to hold possessively on to his arms.

"Yeah?"

"If I asked you if I could sleep in your bed, but didn't want any hanky-panky to go on, would you be offended?"

"Definitely," he said, then pulled me into his embrace, snuggling his chin into my hair and kissing the top of my head gently. "But for you, I'll try to overlook it this one time. Come on. Grab your pillow and follow me."

We padded into his room, and I got under the covers quickly while he turned off the light. When he climbed into bed and lay on his back I curled myself around his arm and tried to stop shivering. "You okay?" he asked after a bit.

"Yeah. Just shaken. It was one of those dreams that sticks with you."

"It was just a dream, Abs. I promise, you're safe and sound."

I lay awake the rest of the night, feeling the weight of my left side, as it had grown thick and heavy the moment Duffy spoke about being safe and sound. Sometimes being psychic simply sucks.

Light broke through the curtains around seven thirty. Duffy stirred next to me as a ray hit his face, and he let out a groan as his eyes drifted open. "Hey," he said when he saw me.

"Hey, yourself," I said back.

"You didn't sleep a wink, did you?" he asked as he scanned my eyes.

"Maybe half a wink," I said. "Your phone didn't ring."

"Nope," he said on a yawn. "That means they haven't found Kelly yet."

"She's alive, Duff," I said, knowing somewhere down deep she was still with us.

"Good to know," Duffy said as he smoothed a hair out of my eyes. "Come on. Let's get you up and showered so I can drop you at Viv's and head to the station."

I got up and zoomed into the shower while Duffy rustled up some raisin toast for both of us, which I ate while he took his turn. While he was shaving his phone rang, and I rushed it into the bathroom for him. He answered it and looked at me the moment someone began speaking on the other end. "Where?" he asked the caller. "How long ago?" he said after a pause. I looked at him with my eyebrows raised. Maybe he'd mouth a clue for me. "Where is she now? Uh-huh. Okay, I'm on it. See you in fifteen."

Duffy clicked off the phone and picked the razor back up, making three strokes in very quick succession, then wiped the rest of the cream off his face. "Hello?" I waved at him. "Waiting for details here. Who was that?"

"They found Kelly," Duffy said.

"Ohmigod! Is she all right? Where was she? Did they find Eddie too? Are you going to go see her now?"

Duffy grinned at me as he threw on his shirt and started buttoning it. "If this psychic gig doesn't work out for you, you could always be an auctioneer, you know," he said. I rolled my eyes and began tapping my foot impatiently. "Okay, okay. They found her walking along Highway Eighty-seven. I have no details other than she was walking under her own power and was transported to the hospital, where I'm headed right now."

"Great. I'll get my coat and we'll be on our way."

"I'm dropping you at Viv's," Duffy called as I sprinted out the bathroom door.

That stopped me. "Why can't I come along?" I demanded as I spun around and gave him a look.

"You can't come along because this stuff is starting to affect you. You didn't sleep last night, did you?" he asked.

"There are lots of nights I don't sleep," I said defensively.

"Yeah, well, tonight won't be one of them. I think it's time you took a step back, Abby."

"No way," I said, standing my ground in the hallway. "I'm *going* to the hospital. I've come this far, Duffy. You can't leave me out now."

Duffy gave me a look that said he would if he could, but I held his stare until finally he shook his head and said, "Fine. Come on. But you'll wait in the lobby until I'm done talking with her."

"Deal."

"We'll call Ellie and have her meet us there. Kelly may want her close by."

"Should we also call Kelly's parents?" I asked as we walked out the front door.

"She's an orphan," Duffy said, rounding to his side of the patrol car.

"What?"

"Yep. Her mom died of cancer when she was real young, and her daddy died about three years ago. The guy committed suicide. He hanged himself in the bathroom. Kelly found him."

"Man! That girl has been through it all, hasn't she?"

"Yeah, she really has. And she's never been the strong will-of-steel type. You blow on her, I think she'd fall over."

"Poor thing," I said, my heart going out to her.

Duffy called Ellie; she and Nina agreed to rush immediately to the hospital to lend Kelly some support. He tucked his cell away, and just as we turned onto the street where the hospital was his radio bleeped to life, and a dispatcher rifled off some codes that didn't make sense to me. Duffy looked startled by the announcement and immediately reached for the radio. "Dispatch, this is car three-eighty-one, over."

I was watching him as we cruised toward the hospital, and that was when my intuition chimed in and I knew we weren't going to make it into the parking lot.

The dispatcher rifled off another set of codes, and all I caught were the words ". . . escapee in State Bank building on Lincoln," and, "all units in the area please respond."

Duffy slowed the patrol car as he took a quick glance in the rearview mirror, then pulled a U-turn and hit the lights and the siren. "Hang on," he said as he punched the accelerator, and my body jerked back into the seat as we sped down the street. He slowed only slightly as he made a sharp right, and I glanced at his face as he concentrated on weaving in and out of the downtown traffic.

"It's Eddie," I said as my intuition buzzed.

"Yep," Duffy said, taking another hard right.

"Don't let him get hurt, Duffy," I said as we screeched to a halt in front of a large brown building with the nameplate COLORADO STATE BANK on the front.

"Stay put," he said, his face rigid and firm as he reached over and hit the release for the shotgun next to the radio.

I gasped a little as he lifted the gun from its perch. "Duffy," I said, "do you really need *that*?"

"I mean it, Abby," he said, giving me a hard, firm look. "You stay put until I get back. You hear?"

"I hear," I groused, and with that Duffy was out the door and running into the building.

I crossed my arms and sat back in my seat, watching as other patrol units surrounded the building and escorted people out. I hated to think about the explosiveness of the situation happening inside. Heaven forbid if Eddie were hurt—or worse—by the police. I shuddered to think what it would do to Ellie, especially if her brother were involved.

Just then I noticed a large van pull up to the building, and when the back doors opened half a dozen men in blue windbreakers with the initials FBI jumped out and jogged into the building.

I grimaced as I realized that if Eddie pulled any kind of stunt inside Denver's State Bank he'd be committing a federal crime on top of all the other things against him. I looked up at the building, squinting in the morning light to see if I could make out anything happening through the windows, then up toward the roof. There I got a little lucky, as I saw the barest glimmer of movement, but nothing solid. Curious, I got out of the car and headed over to a curb, hoping to catch a glimpse of the action.

I was walking with my hand held salute style above my eyes, peering up at the roof, when I bumped into someone on my left. "Excuse me," I apologized as I looked to see who I'd bumped into. I gasped as I recognized the face staring panicked and wide-eyed back at me.

"Come with me," Eddie said, and grabbed my elbow in a viselike grip. "And don't even think about sounding an alarm," he added menacingly.

"Uh . . . uh . . . uh . . ." was all I could blubber out.

"*Move!*" he hissed, and yanked on my elbow.

Scared by his wild eyes, I didn't resist, and we moved along briskly down the street and away from the safety of the police. "Why are you kidnapping me?" I asked him in a shaking voice.

"They're searching for a single white male. They're not going to think twice about a couple walking down the block," he answered. He groaned as we stepped up onto a curb and I noticed that he was working very hard to hide a limp.

"I heard your leg was burned," I said. If I could get him to converse maybe I could talk some sense into him.

"I'm fine," he said, and moved me into an alley.

"Eddie," I said, trying to reason with him. "Why make things worse for yourself? If you turn yourself in now, I'm sure they would go easier on you than if they capture you later."

"They're not going to go easy on me, Abby. You said so yourself when you did that reading for Ellie. You said you saw me in big trouble. They think I murdered Gina, and I'm not going to jail for something I didn't do."

We came to a stop then, and Eddie pulled me behind a Dumpster in back of a restaurant. He shoved me against a wall as he peered up and down the alley, waiting to see any sign of law enforcement. "No," I said in an even and calm voice. "What I said to Ellie was that you would need a good attorney. Which, let's face it, you now need more than ever."

"I had no choice," Eddie barked, then quickly lowered his voice. "My cell mate, Biggins—you know him as the guy who attacked Hadley Rankin—started a fire in our cell. I was asleep when he pulled that little party trick, and the next thing I know there's a lot of smoke and yelling and the doors fly open. I start running with the other prisoners when Biggins grabs me and pulls me in another direction. We were almost to an exit when one of the guards spotted us and came after us. That was when Biggins jumped him and almost got his gun. The guard got free and came up shooting—at both of us. I didn't hang around to explain, and followed Biggins."

"We know you were severely burned, Eddie," I said, pointing to his leg. "Why did you guys head into the fire?"

"Because I was being shot at, Abby, and it was the only way out."

"So you got clear of the building, and what? Saw Kelly and kidnapped her?"

Eddie blanched. "We got clear and I started to head to the front of the building. My leg was bad and I needed to get to a hospital. That's when Kelly saw me, and also when Biggins jumped her. He grabbed her keys and threw her into the trunk. I got in the passenger side when he got in the car and told him I was coming along. I figured it was the only way I could protect Kelly."

"So how did you end up at the hospital?" I asked.

"Biggins saw my leg and said I was more liability than help to him. He pulled up within a block of the hospital and told me to get out. I said I wasn't leaving without Kelly, and that's when he kicked me in the leg until I fell out of the car."

Eddie's face was contorted with guilt, and I knew he was telling me the truth.

"She got away from Biggins," I said to him. "She's at the hospital right now, she's alive and she's safe."

"She is?"

"Yes. Duffy and I were on our way over there when we got the call that you were in the neighborhood."

"Thank God," Eddie said as he let out a sigh. Just then we heard voices at one end of the alley, and Eddie pushed my head down as we ducked low behind the Dumpster. When the coast was clear he stood up again, keeping a firm grip on my arm as he looked nervously around.

"Did you have anything to do with Gina's disappearance?" I asked.

Eddie swiveled his head around to look me right in the eye and said, "No, Abby. I had nothing to do with it."

"I believe you," I said, as I now understood what my guides had been trying to tell me all along about Eddie's crime. He had nothing to do with Gina's murder. The breakout was what my crew had been hinting at. "And in my reading for Ellie, I didn't see you going to jail forever. Maybe it's better if you turn yourself in and explain what happened."

"I'm not taking that risk," he said firmly. "They may not have been able to prove that I murdered Gina, but I'm positive they can pin the breakout on me."

"But what about your career? You've worked your whole life to be a doctor. Why would you throw that away?"

"There are plenty of rural communities out west that would welcome a local doctor and not ask a lot of background questions. I'd have to give up a lucrative living, but that's not why I became a doctor anyway."

"What about Ellie?" I asked.

Eddie cut me a look, his lower lip quivering just a bit as he said, "She's better off without me."

"But what about the baby?"

Eddie released the grip he had on my arm, his mouth dropping open slightly as he asked, "What baby?"

"The one Ellie's carrying. Congratulations, it's a girl," I said, giving him a smile.

"You're lying," he said, even as tears formed in the corners of his eyes.

"Eddie," I said in a soft, soothing voice. "Haven't you noticed all the signs? The way Ellie's been bolting to the bathroom lately? And the little extra weight she's put on recently? And when was the last time she had a cycle? You two live together, so I'm sure you know when it's her time of the month."

"She's pregnant?" Eddie asked me as his eyes searched mine for any hint of a lie.

"Yes. She's almost three months along now. But I'm terribly worried about her. She's been under so much stress that if you disappeared too it could put her right over the edge. She wants to stand by you. She needs the father of her baby, even if he's on trial. Even if he's in jail. She needs you."

Eddie stepped away from me, and I noticed his breathing had quickened slightly. His hands were balled up in fists, and his face showed so much agony that my heart went out to him. "Why didn't she tell me?" he murmured.

"I don't know," I said to him. "Maybe because she was so nervous about the wedding, she just wanted to handle that until it was over, then surprise you with the news on your wedding night. Personally I can't think of a nicer wedding present, can you?"

"Shit!" he swore as he paced painfully up and down in front of me.

"Come on, Eddie. Do the right thing here. Let's walk back to Duffy's car and get inside and wait for him to come back. He'll make sure you don't get hurt."

"I didn't kill Gina, Abby."

"I believe you," I repeated, looking him dead in the eye. "I know it wasn't you. And I will do everything I can to help you. My sister has even retained the best criminal defense lawyer in the state on your behalf. I have a really good feeling about him. I think he's going to be able to help you. But you have to take the first step here."

Eddie paused and looked down the street, lost for a moment in his own thoughts. "What the hell am I doing?" he asked.

"Going back to the car with me," I said gently, and moved to take his arm. "Come on. You can do this."

Eddie hung his head then and allowed me to lead him out of the alley. We walked slowly, because I knew his leg must hurt something fierce. We made it without incident back to the patrol car. Duffy was still inside the bank building with the other police, searching for Eddie.

I opened the back door for Eddie and he got in, gentle as a lamb. I climbed into the front and we waited patiently as we listened to the chatter on the radio.

"I should probably call him," I said to Eddie as I reached for my cell.

"Can you hold off on that?" Eddie asked. "I'm not officially back in police custody yet, and I'd like to savor these last couple minutes of freedom if you don't mind."

"You got it," I said, and tucked my cell away.

About fifteen minutes later we saw Duffy come out of the bank building. He looked frustrated as he trotted over to the car and got in without looking in the backseat. "Son of a bitch got away from us," he groused a he locked the shotgun back into place.

"You don't say," I said casually.

"Damn it!" Duffy swore. "When I catch up to Eddie, I'm personally going to open a can of whoop-ass on his butt for being such an idiot! He should know better!"

"Uh, Duffy?"

"Jesus, you'd think those brains would come with some common sense, but nooooo!"

"Duff," I said again.

"My sister can sure pick 'em," Duffy continued, paying me no heed. "If I had a dime for every loser she dated, I'd retire!"

"Yo—Sheriff McGinnis," I said waving, my hand at him.

"This one I thought had some potential! He sure got one over on me, though," Duffy complained as he put the car into gear and pulled away from the curb. "Must've been the résumé. The guy graduates from Harvard and I'm suckered in."

"Yale," a voice from the backseat corrected. "I graduated from Yale, not Harvard."

The patrol car's tires screeched as they came to a sudden halt, and Duffy's head whipped around as he stared in shock at his newest passenger. "Holy shit!" he said when he spotted Eddie. "How the . . . ?" he said, turning to me. "What the . . . ?"

"I must confess, Sheriff," I said, grinning at the look on his face. "I may not have *exactly* stayed put when you went inside the bank."

An hour later I was still waiting for Duffy in the lobby of the sheriff's station. I had tried calling Ellie twice, but her cell kept going to voice mail. I knew she'd want to know that Eddie was safe and back in jail. Well, maybe not the "back in jail" thing, but at least he was safe.

When we'd gotten to the station Eddie had announced that he would talk only to Duffy. He further stated that he was willing to give a statement about his escape, but he would wait for his attorney before he even commented on Gina's murder. Except, of course, to say that he didn't do it.

While I waited for Duffy to take Eddie's statement,

I fished around in my purse, looking for something that could entertain me. I came across the small manual that came with my phone and, bored out of my gourd, I began to read it. "Huh," I said as I came across a section marked SPEED DIAL. "So that's how you do that." I got out my phone and plugged in everyone I knew into the speed-dial phone book. That was only about eight entries, and I sighed heavily as I thought about the small social world I lived in.

The truth was that ever since my best friend, Theresa, moved to California some months back, I'd been something of a hermit. I'd lived vicariously through my boyfriend and hadn't pushed myself to get out there and make new friends.

It occurred to me that if I wanted to move to Denver, I could take advantage of the social scene around Ellie. She knew lots of people, and she was always telling me of the parties she threw, the luncheons she had, and the get-togethers she was planning.

Maybe hanging out with someone like that was exactly what I needed. Maybe if I had Ellie as a mentor I could work on expanding my social group. After all, there really wasn't anyone left to hang out with back in Michigan, now that Dutch and I were *finito*.

Speaking of which, I mused, if I entered his number into my speed dial I'd have at least nine people in my phone book. I frowned at the idea. That might be too much temptation. However, what if I were hit by a bus and the authorities went looking through my cell phone trying to find a name to contact, and they saw that I knew only eight people? Granted, one of those eight was my ICE and was the same number as my sister, but still, wouldn't they think I was pathetic for having so few friends?

That did it. For vanity's sake I entered the number to his cell and hit the 9 button to encode the speed dial. "Who you calling?" I heard a voice ask to my right.

Tilting my head up, I smiled as I saw Duffy walking

toward me. "Hey, guy. No one," I said, and snapped the phone closed. "Everything squared away?"

Duffy sat down in the chair next to me, a file held loosely in his hands. "For the moment. We've got him back in the clink, and we've sent for a doctor to take another look at that leg. He may need a graft."

"A skin graft?"

"Yeah, there's a small section on his leg that doesn't look so good."

"Ouch," I said, wincing as I put my cell away. "So did he tell you how Biggins forced him to break out?"

"Yes, and the tape from the cameras in that section of the jail back up his story."

"The tape survived the fire?"

"The cameras record to a DVR located off premises. I can access them via our intranet."

"Technology," I said, shaking my head in awe. "So that means that once Eddie's cleared of Gina's murder, he'll be free to go?"

"You're convinced he didn't murder Gina?" Duffy asked me.

"Yep. He had nothing to do with it. The whole intuitive message about him being forced to commit a crime was the breakout."

"I hate to burst your bubble there, honey, but we've got another link between Gina and Eddie."

"What?" I asked as my intuition buzzed in that I wasn't going to like it.

"The credit card used to reserve Gina's plane reservation to California was issued to Eddie O'Donnell, and it was in the wallet we found at the crime scene."

"No!" I said, and my heart sank. "How can that be?" I murmured, puzzling over it, because my intuition insisted Eddie was innocent. Then, I thought of something. "What if Gina stole Eddie's wallet, and used his credit card to book her reservation? That could also be why it was found at the crime scene!" I said excitedly.

Duffy nodded as he thought that through. "Perhaps, and I'm sure that will be the tactic his lawyer uses. But that doesn't explain the other evidence found at the scene."

"What?" I asked as my heart dropped again. This looked worse and worse for Eddie.

"The scrubs we found in Gina's car had some short blond hairs on them. They look about the same color and length as those on Eddie's head."

"Have you run a DNA test yet?"

"I've got the paperwork started on a warrant for a lock of Eddie's hair. I'll have to wait for his lawyer to get here. He'll file a motion to suppress. The judge will rule in our favor, but it'll still take some time."

"So what's next for Eddie?"

"His bond hearing is being held later today. Given his flight risk, it should be substantial enough to keep him put until trial. I don't even want to think about how Ellie's gonna take this news," he said with a heavy sigh. After a moment he said, "Come on. Let's get over to the hospital and find out what happened to Kelly. You ready?"

I followed behind Duffy as we exited the station. We got into his patrol car again and headed back across town. "I tried calling your sister," I said to him as we drove. "She didn't answer her cell."

"It's probably better we tell her in person anyway," Duffy said with a sigh. "Man, I am getting so sick of giving my sister bad news."

"But at least she'll know where Eddie is," I said, trying to look at the bright side.

"Yeah, still, for the biggest week of her life it sure is turning out to be a shitter." I smiled in spite of myself. Duffy knew how to sum things up, all right.

We arrived at the hospital and headed inside to find Ellie and Nina. Instead we found Jimmy in the lobby, and Duffy greeted his father with a warm smile. "Hey, Pop," he said.

"Duffy! Where have you been, son? We've been waiting for a couple of hours now for you to show up."

"Sorry about that; we got sidetracked," Duffy said. "So where's Ellie? I need to talk to her right away."

"She and your mother are in with Kelly. Is there news?"

"Yeah, but I should let Ellie know first. Hey, Abby?" he said, turning to me.

"Yes?"

"Can you fill in my dad about Eddie while I go talk to my sister?"

"Absolutely," I said, and smiled at Jimmy.

After Duffy trotted off to find Ellie and Nina, I filled Jimmy in on the details, leaving out the part about Ellie being pregnant, of course. That was Ellie's news to tell, and I'd shared it with Eddie only because I'd been desperate to get him to see reason.

I also left out the part about Eddie's credit card connecting him to Gina's disappearance. Something about all this wasn't adding up. My intuition wasn't buying the latest evidence pointing toward Eddie as Gina's killer, and I didn't want to comment on it until we knew more.

Just about the time I finished, Nina came down the corridor looking tired and worried. Jimmy got up immediately and helped his wife into a chair next to me, where she seemed to sag when she sat down. "How you holding up?" I asked as I stroked her arm.

"I'll be fine," she said with a tired smile. "I'm more worried about Ellie."

"How'd she take the news?" I asked.

"Better than I thought she would. Now that she knows Eddie is accounted for, and that he did his best to save Kelly, she's taking it in stride. Especially since Kelly can back up Eddie's story."

"Kelly's backing up Eddie?" Jimmy said.

"Yes. She says that last night, right after we'd all

arrived at the jail, she was told by a firefighter that she had to move her car. When she was getting in it, she saw Eddie and another prisoner come out of the back entrance. She called to him, and that's when the other prisoner grabbed her, took her keys and threw her in her trunk."

"That matches what Eddie told me," I said.

"Later Kelly heard an argument coming from the front of the car, and shortly after that the car stopped. She said she heard more yelling; then Eddie howled in pain and the car took off."

"She must have been terrified," Jimmy said.

"She was. But that girl is smarter than she looks. She said that awful man you helped capture, Abby—what was his name?"

"Warren Biggins," I said.

"That's right; that's the name Duffy said when he filled us in on Eddie. Anyway, she says this Biggins character took her to the woods, where he told her he was going to make a real woman out of her, just like he'd done for the other girls."

"Other girls?" Jimmy and I said together.

"Yes. Apparently that horrible man had kidnapped and raped several other women, and he bragged to Kelly the whole time he made her march through the woods."

"How did she get away?" I asked.

"She said that Biggins had a hold of her collar and, when he tripped over a root and fell down, she rolled away from him and faded into the darkness. She then managed to make her way out of the woods and walked for several miles before finding help."

My intuition buzzed, and I almost tuned out on Nina for a moment, but then she said something that caught my attention. "Jimmy," she said, turning to him. "I think that this horrible man might have been the one who murdered Gina."

Jimmy nodded. "That could be why Eddie's wallet

was found near her body. Didn't you say that when they arrested Biggins he had stolen credit cards on him?" he asked me.

I nodded. "Yes. All the merchandise he'd purchased from the mall had been with stolen credit cards."

Nina and Jimmy nodded. "He's got a pattern then of pickpocketing. He could have easily stolen Eddie's wallet off of him and left it behind after he'd murdered Gina," Jimmy said.

I puzzled on that for a minute, thinking that was one explanation. But then why was Gina's plane ticket purchased with Eddie's credit card? And why was Eddie's hair found on the bloody scrubs in Gina's car? Biggins, I recalled, had dark brown hair, not blond. Something else bothered me too, and that was Sara's disappearance and—my guess—murder.

Intuitively I knew the two crimes were linked, and it seemed an extraordinary coincidence that three women, all close friends, had been targeted by Biggins, a total stranger to them. Granted, Kelly's abduction seemed a definite wrong-place-at-the-wrong-time scenario, but that still didn't explain the randomness of Gina's and Sara's murders.

"Well, I've told Duffy my theory," Nina continued, interrupting my troubled thoughts.

"What did he say?" I asked.

"He said that he'd check into Biggins's record a little deeper when he got back to the station after he takes Kelly's statement."

"And how is Kelly?" I asked.

"The poor thing looks a little worse for wear—she's sporting a black eye and a few other cuts and bruises and she had a slight case of hypothermia—but the doctor said she's suffered more emotionally than physically."

"At least she's safe and warm and surrounded by people who care about her," I commented, thinking that Kelly was one lucky girl.

"Yes. They're releasing her in a little bit, and Ellie

and I are taking her back home with us. She can stay in Duffy's old room while she's recovering from her trauma."

"That's a nice idea, honey," Jimmy said.

"The least we can do. Besides, we'll have room now that all the wedding guests are leaving," Nina added, her shoulders drooping and tears forming in her eyes.

"Awww, honey, don't cry," Jimmy said as he threw a protective arm around her shoulders and squeezed her gently.

"I just wanted Ellie's big day to be perfect. And instead it's become a nightmare!" Nina sobbed.

I felt terrible and helpless all at the same time. Nina and Jimmy had been more like parents than my own parents, and seeing them in so much anguish over their daughter made my own eyes water. Getting up, I headed for a tissue box and brought it quickly back to them. "Here, Nina. Please don't cry. It'll be okay; I swear it will."

"Thank you, Abigail," she said taking a tissue. "I'm so happy you could come into town. You've been such a comfort to Ellie. I suppose, however, you're going to head back home soon, like everyone else?"

I nodded, thinking that it was best to be totally honest with her. "Yeah, I've decided that tomorrow I should go home. I mean, Eddie's accounted for, Kelly's accounted for. . . ."

"But we're still not sure about Sara," Nina reminded me, an unasked question in her eyes.

"I know," I said, stroking her hand and giving her a small smile. "But I don't know what else I can do for her, Nina. I've tuned in as much as I can. The rest is up to your son and the other sheriff's deputies to figure it out. My feeling is that eventually she'll be found."

"But you're convinced she's dead, aren't you?" Nina pressed.

I took a moment to gather the courage to be totally honest with her. "Yes," I said, and took it one step further. "And I believe that Gina's and Sara's murders are connected."

Nina gasped and squeezed Jimmy's hand. "Biggins," she said slowly. "He's killed them."

Jimmy looked very worried as he glanced from his wife to me to Nina again. "All the better that Kelly and Ellie are staying with us, dear. We'll keep an eye on them as long as there's a killer on the loose."

"Well, this is just terrible," Nina said. "It's awful to think of someone out there, close to our friends and family, doing these horrible things. I don't know what I'd do if something like this ever happened to Ellie."

"I see nothing like that in her future," I said to Nina, trying to ease her mind the only way I knew how.

Nina nodded to me, her eyes filling with tears again as she said, "Yes, she's told me. Thank you for giving her that gift."

"You guys ready to bust Kelly outta here?" we heard Duffy call from behind us.

Jimmy, Nina and I all stood to greet him and Ellie as they came down the hall. "They're releasing her?" Jimmy asked.

"Drawing up the paperwork right now. I hear she's gonna be staying in my old room," Duffy said, looking at his mother with a playful grin.

"I can't very well put her in the garage, Duffy," Nina said.

"That's where we should have put Duffy when he was still living there," Ellie said, and gave a poke to her brother.

"Ouch! Hey, El, careful with the merchandise there."

"Sorry, didn't know it was so easily bruised," Ellie said.

I laughed and chimed in by saying, "It's not bruising he's worried about. He's got this real sensitive spot right under his rib cage, and if you push on it he squeals like the Pillsbury Dough Boy!" Four sets of eyes turned toward me, three of them quite shocked at my statement, and then I realized what I'd actually admitted to. "Uh . . . not that I would actually *know* he's got a sensitive spot. . . . I mean . . . uh . . . Duffy, didn't you tell me a story about your tickle spot or something?" I stammered, feeling my cheeks flushing.

Three sets of skeptical eyes swiveled back to Duffy, who looked at me and shook his head ruefully. "Wow. Man, when you open your mouth and insert your foot, you really shove it in up to the hip, don'tcha?"

"Ahem," I heard behind Duffy, and we all parted to see Kelly in a wheelchair being pushed by an intern. "I'm ready to go now," she said meekly.

"Kelly!" I said, thoroughly relieved to see her. "Hi, there, girlfriend! Let me just help you out," and I rushed to shoo the intern away as I grabbed her wheelchair and began heading for the exit. Behind me I could hear chuckling.

"What was that about?" Kelly asked, tilting her head back at me.

"You saving my tuchus."

"Huh?"

"Nothing. I'm glad to hear you're okay," I said.

"Thanks," she said, and turned back to stare out at the approaching door.

"Hey," I said, trying to melt the ice between us. "Maybe if I move here we can do lunch sometime?"

Her head tilted back again and she asked, "You're going to move here?"

"I'm thinking about it," I said as we got to the door and I punched the button that automatically opened it. "Say, do you know of any apartments for rent?"

"There's one in my building that's nice," she said amicably. "If you moved here we could be neighbors."

I smiled down at her, glad that she seemed to be coming out of her shell a little with me. "That would be cool," I said, and waited on the curb for everyone else to catch up.

When Jimmy went to get the family car, I had time

to look up at the skyline and think about what I'd just said. It sure was beautiful here. Maybe moving wasn't such a farfetched idea after all. With that, I decided to head home tomorrow and really think about it. Strongly consider a change of scenery. As I looked at those purple mountains in the distance, I had no idea how much of a change in scenery I actually had coming.

Chapter Fifteen

That evening found me at Viv's house busily packing my things and making the arrangements for my flight out the following morning. Viv came in and out of my room, dropping off little tidbits of things she thought I would need on my journey, like a pretty packet of monogrammed stationery she "found" among some old things. Or a first-aid kit she'd "picked up" from a friend. Or a pen she'd "rescued" from the counter at her bank. I was beginning to see quite clearly that Viv had a penchant for pinching.

With that in mind I made sure that I could account for all my belongings, then had to go about the house looking for my eye shadow, silk scarf and the silver heart bracelet Ellie had given me. Viv was very helpful in my search, suggesting that perhaps the bridesmaid's gift had fallen off my wrist over at Duffy's when I took his "boys" out for a "swim." I found it by consulting my radar, which kept pointing me toward the piano in the back corner of her living room. I finally discovered it by opening the lid of the thing and seeing it lying there on top of one of the piano keys.

"How'd that get there?" Viv asked me over my shoulder as I extracted the bracelet.

"Some little gremlin, perhaps," I said, giving her a look.

"Hmph," she said, and shuffled away.

Rolling my eyes, I headed back to my room and rechecked my luggage. I was still missing a sock, but figured I could live without it. I then took out my cell and called Dave to let him know I'd be home in the early afternoon.

"Hey, there, honey. How's it hanging?"

"Low and left like always, Dave." I laughed into the phone. It was good to hear his voice again.

"Glad to hear it. So, what's the word? Was the wedding a great party?"

"Not exactly," I said.

"Someone got drunk and puked on your shoes?" he said.

"Ewwww!" I replied, pulling the phone away from my ear as I made a face. "That is just . . . Ewwww!"

"Happened to me at a wedding once."

"You've been to a wedding?" I asked, my tongue in my cheek.

"Yes, young lady. As a matter of fact I have."

"Gee, Dave, I thought you avoided those like the plague."

"I only avoid my own. Someone else's I'm more than willing to attend," he said.

"Good to know," I said with a chuckle. "Listen, I'm headed out of Dodge in the morning, which puts me home about three. Will you be around so I can pick up Eggy?"

"Uh, sure," he said, the air going out of his voice. "I guess. . . ."

I smiled at his lack of enthusiasm. "You're gonna miss my little buddy, aren't you?"

"He kinda grows on you," Dave said.

"You can come visit anytime," I said.

"Yeah, I know," Dave groused. He was taking this harder than I'd expected. "I just got used to sleeping with him, is all."

"I thought he kept you up at night?"

"Only a little. And he still makes less noise than my old lady. That woman can snore."

I chuckled again. I was going to miss Dave when I moved. "Say," I said, thinking of something. "Why don't you and your sweetheart come over for dinner tomorrow night? I'll cook and we can hang out, watch a hockey game or something."

"You're going to cook?" he asked warily.

"Good point," I said. "How about if I order pizza?"

"Now you're talkin'," Dave said. "Except my old lady's still outta town, so it'll be just me, you and Eggers."

"Eggers?" I asked, my eyebrow cocking at the nickname.

"He knows who I'm talking about," Dave said defensively.

Just then my cell phone gave a sharp beep. "Ooops," I said. "Gotta go, Dave. My cell phone's about to die. I have to make sure it's charged before I split town."

"See you tomorrow, Abby," he said, and clicked off.

Before charging up my cell I checked it for voice mails. "You have no messages," the voice said. *Damn.* I got the charger out of my suitcase and walked over to a plug. It had officially been a week since Valentine's Day, and not a peep out of Dutch.

To tell the truth, I was actually surprised. I hated to think that I was so utterly forgettable as to not allow for one weak moment where he'd leave me some kind of "Hey, I was just thinking of you" message. Hell, he could have even left the old, "Can we arrange for a time to exchange our stuff back?" kind of call and it would have felt better than no message at all.

I wanted to be angry at him—for his outright dismissal, and for breaking up with me in the first place. But the reality was that I wasn't there yet. I was still in the heartbroken-please-handle-with-care stage. In fact, that Dutch seemed able to get over me so quickly only made my heartache a little worse.

Padding back to the bed, I plopped backward and just stared up at the ceiling for a while. Just as I could feel a really good cry coming on, I heard Viv's phone ring and then her soft footfalls in the hall. She knocked on my door and I said, "Come on in, Viv."

"It's Duffy; he's on the phone for you."

"Thanks," I said, sitting up and extending my hand as she handed me the phone.

"Let him down easy, Abby," she suggested as I lifted the phone to my ear.

"Thanks, Viv, I'll do my best," I said with my hand over the mouthpiece.

"First Rachel, now you," Viv muttered as she turned to walk out of the room. "That poor boy has no luck with women."

I waited for Viv to close the door before removing my hand from the mouthpiece and saying, "Hi, Duff. Calling to wish me a bon voyage?"

"Can I talk you into staying?"

"No." I smiled. "But you may be able to talk me into coming back."

"Kelly says that you're thinking of moving here."

"The thought had crossed my mind," I said.

"So how do I make the idea stick?"

I laughed. "By being nice to me, and calling me every once in a while when I get back to Michigan."

"Doable," he said. "What time's your flight?"

"Ten A.M."

"Did you need a lift to the airport?"

"I've got a cab lined up," I said. Truthfully, my thought had been that if I asked Duffy to take me I'd chicken out of flying home and send Dave a wire to ship my things and Eggy here.

"Okay. Listen," he said, and his voice grew serious. "They found Kelly's car."

"They did?"

"Yeah. They found it about a quarter mile from the colonel's place."

"Any sign of Biggins?"

"None. But his prints are all over the inside of the car. You know, I'm liking my mom's theory that Biggins might have killed Gina, and that he's a likely suspect in Sara's disappearance."

"Did you check into his record?"

"Yep. And it's ugly. Among other things, the guy's a serial rapist. He's been locked up three times for that beginning in the mid-eighties. His last incarceration was an eight-year stint in the Kansas State pen for raping twin sisters. One of them he beat badly enough to cause permanent brain damage."

I winced and asked, "How long ago did he get out?"

"He was released six weeks ago, on parole."

My intuition buzzed, and something about Biggins as the killer didn't seem to fit. "So, now he's changed his method, and he's killing his victims?"

"One of those really nasty statistics about repeat offenders says that serial rapists who've been caught and incarcerated before learn not to leave witnesses behind the next time they rape, and they quickly go from serial rapists to serial killers."

"Ah," I said with a shiver as I absorbed that factoid. Thinking about what Duffy said, I asked, "If we play this through, then how does Eddie tie in? I mean, how was it that Gina's ticket was purchased with Eddie's credit card, which was found in his wallet at the scene of the crime? And what about the bloody scrubs in Gina's car, and the hair? Biggins has brown hair."

There was an audible sigh on Duffy's end of the line. "If I had to shoot a theory I'd say that Gina used Eddie's card number to book her flight. I checked her credit history and she was maxed out to the limit. In fact, she had three cards already in collection. Also, her bank account wasn't more than a couple of hundred bucks, and Gina had a reputation for borrowing money from friends and not paying it back."

"Really?" I said, a little surprised by that. "I thought she made a good living at Fidelity. Where'd all her money go?"

"You saw her closet. The girl loved to shop. And she had expensive taste."

"So, she steals Eddie's credit card number; then what?"

"We already know Biggins is a pickpocket. He could have gone to the hospital, dug around in Eddie's locker, stolen his scrubs and the wallet and attacked Gina later."

"That would be a remarkable coincidence," I said as I tried to make the jigsaw puzzle pieces fit. "The fact that Gina and Eddie know each other as friends, and a total stranger steals his wallet and targets her as his next victim?"

"Maybe Biggins was stalking Gina, and saw her with Eddie. Maybe that's what led him to steal Eddie's wallet and scrubs. Maybe Eddie was framed."

My right side felt light and airy. "You know, Duffy, I think you're on to something there."

"And if Biggins was stalking Gina, he'd have ample opportunity to scope out Sara as well."

"Ellie's gang does hang out together a lot," I mused. "So, you really think Biggins is the guy?"

"If I put those pieces together like that, then yes."

Something still nagged at me, and after a moment of silence I reached out to my guides for some advice. With a powerful jolt I had an insight and said, "If Biggins had time to scope out Sara, he also had time to scope out the other bridesmaids."

"Which is why you'll notice a patrol car cruising periodically up and down Viv's street. I've also got one posted at my parents' house and another paying close attention to Christina's."

"Have you told her about Biggins?" I asked.

"Right before I called you I gave her a jingle and left her a voice mail. I'm waiting for her to call me back."

I wanted to relax after he told me about the patrol cars, but my crew was still flashing a warning. "Thanks for looking out for me," I said to him.

"Part of my new duty as knight in shining armor," Duffy replied.

"Night, Duffy," I sang with a smile.

"Bon voyage, girl."

I lay awake for several hours in the dark that night, unable to stop the restless thoughts zipping around in my brain. Beyond my making the big decision to move to Colorado, there was something else that was nagging at the edges of my mind. The only way I can describe it is to say that it felt like I was on the verge of some huge decision that was even greater than the idea of moving twelve hundred miles to the west.

It felt as if I were standing at a crossroads of immense importance. Go right and my destiny would shape one way. Go left and it would form a completely different future. As I examined the root of this, I came up with several theories, most having to do with whether to move or not to move. But none of those quite fit. I puzzled about it long into the night, never really coming to a sense of peace with it.

The next morning I was up very early and feeling a bit sluggish from lack of sleep. I took a long, hot shower, careful not to make too much noise, as I didn't want to wake Viv. My efforts were fruitless, however, because by the time I came out of the shower she was already hustling about the kitchen. "Morning, Viv," I said as I walked out of the bathroom.

"Abigail," she said. "Duffy called while you were in the shower. He and Ellie are on their way over. I guess something else awful has happened."

"What?" I said, halting in my tracks. "Did they say what it was?"

"No, but I could hear Ellie crying in the background."

"Oh, my God, maybe they've found Sara," I said, and ran into the bedroom to throw my things into the suitcase and finish getting dressed before they arrived. I pulled my jeans and sweater from the chair I'd draped them over and got them on, then dashed to grab my cell phone from the charger and push any other belongings into my suitcase. Just as I zipped it closed I heard people in the front hall. Shoving my boots on, I headed out to greet Duffy, Kelly, Ellie, Nina and Jimmy. "What's happened?" I asked as they all filed in. Ellie looked so gaunt and distraught. It had to be news about Sara.

"It's Christina," Duffy said. "We think she's been taken by Biggins."

"What?"

"I hadn't heard from her," Ellie choked out with a sob. "So Kelly and I went over to her place, and she wouldn't answer, but I just knew something was wrong. One of Christina's windows was open a little, so I hoisted Kelly through it, and it looked like the place had been torn to pieces!"

I looked back to Duffy. Ellie wasn't making sense. "I don't understand," I said.

"Ellie called me from Christina's a few hours after I got off the phone with you. I headed over, and her apartment looks like a tornado's been through it. There are definitely signs of a struggle, and a brutal one. We found evidence of blood on one of the curtains. We think it's Christina's."

"Oh, my God," I said, and felt my knees grow weak. "This cannot be happening," I said to Duffy, my eyes pleading with him to tell me something different.

"We need you, Abby," he said to me. "We need

you to try to draw one of your sketches again. Maybe Christina is somewhere we can recognize."

I looked at him blankly for a beat or two before saying, "You also want me to look at her photo, don't you?"

"We need to know," Nina said gently as she pulled out a photo of several girls, three of whom stared back at me in a plastic, flat way.

I looked at the photo for only a second, then back up into Nina's eyes. She obviously read my expression, because she gave me a pinched look and pulled her hand across her mouth as tears formed, then streamed down her face.

Ellie gave a tight sob and turned to her father, who then wrapped her in his arms and stroked her hair.

"I'm so sorry," I said as I reached out to her. But she was inconsolable.

"Will you draw your sketch?" Duffy said, his expression tight and hard as he handed me his pen and notebook.

"Yes," I said, and walked over to the table. I sat down and stared at the paper. This was awful. I closed my eyes, wishing I could start this whole trip over again. Wanting to go back in time to when these girls were still alive and tell them about the danger they were in. Instead I had to focus on where their bodies lay.

Ellie continued to cry in the background as I dug deep, willing myself to focus and concentrate. These people needed my help, and maybe, if we were lucky and found Christina, then there might be a clue that would help us nail this son of a bitch too. I concentrated on the question I had to ask my guides, and finally I said, *Show me the area where Christina's body is hidden. Give me landmarks to go by.*

Immediately I had an image in my head and opened my eyes and began to draw on the paper. I made a small square in the center and then some long lines above the square. To the right I drew what looked like a very tall mushroom, and to the left I drew a cross. Moving back to the center of my sketch I drew another square within the first square, and on top of that I placed a star.

I stopped then and turned the paper toward Duffy, who examined it carefully, then said, "Holy shit!"

"What?" Jimmy said. "What is it, son?"

"I know where this is!" Duffy said, and moved the sketch over toward his father. "See this? That's the colonel's field. And this is the water tower on the edge of his property. Abby, this makes sense. Biggins hid Gina's body in the colonel's shack. Then he left Kelly's car a quarter mile away from here. This must be where he takes the women he kidnaps!"

"Sara's close by there too," I said dully. I was still reeling from the shock of Christina's death.

Ellie gasped. "We have to find them," she said. "We have to find them and bring them home."

Duffy pulled the mouthpiece of his walkie-talkie off his shoulder and began rifling orders into it. When he was finished he looked at all of us and said, "You all stay here. I've got a search party gathering, and we'll call you with any news."

"No way," I said as I walked over to grab my coat. "I'm going with you."

Duffy cocked his head at me. "You can't. You have a plane to catch."

"There will be other planes," I said, quoting my sister. "Besides, you'll need me out there in the field."

"Forget about it, Cooper," Duffy said, puffing out his chest at me. "By all accounts Biggins is likely armed, dangerous and lurking in those woods. I'm not risking having another one of you kidnapped."

"He's not there," I said defiantly, my voice steady and calm, my resolve firm.

"How do you know?"

"My spidey sense is telling me he's not hanging out on the colonel's property, just hoping to nab another woman. Besides, you need me to act as bloodhound. You'll find them a whole lot faster if I'm around."

Everyone looked at Duffy while he weighed what I'd said. Finally, he said, "Okay, but you are to sit in the car, and this time you are to stay put, hear me?"

I saluted, and just as I shrugged into my coat Ellie said, "I'm going too."

Duffy cut her a glance. "No friggin' way," he said.

"She was *my friend,* Duffy!" Ellie screamed, the sound of her voice making us all wince.

"El," he said calmly, looking into her slightly wild eyes. "You've been through too much. Why don't you just go home and rest?"

"I have to be there for them!" Ellie shouted, the volume only slightly lower this time.

"I could go for you," Kelly said meekly. "I could be there for them, Ellie."

Ellie looked at Kelly, and her emotions broke again as tears streamed down her cheeks.

"You know," Duffy said, looking at Kelly appraisingly, "that's not such a bad idea. I mean, if you're up to it. Biggins probably took you there the night he kidnapped you. Maybe if you come with us you'll remember something?"

Kelly nodded, her large brown eyes fixed on him. "I could try," she said.

"Then it's settled. Mom, Dad, take Ellie home and keep an eye on her. Abby, Kelly, you're with me."

"What about me?" Viv shouted as we all began to troop toward the front door.

"Come on, Aunt Viv, you can come home with us," Nina said with uncharacteristic gentleness for the old woman. I had to hide a smirk at the look of surprise on Viv's face as she eyed Nina.

"Well, as long as I'm not a bother," Viv said.

"Exactly, and I'll hold you to that," Nina replied.

On the way over to the colonel's, Duffy called in the troops, then gave us the ground rules. "So the drill is that when we get to the field, you two will stay put in the car until we've made a preliminary search of the area." We were riding in Duffy's Mustang, and I strained to hear from the backseat as the police radio he had up front crackled with static. "We're going to do a grid search of the area to try and flush out Biggins. If we flush him, or find Christina, then we won't need your radar, Abs. If we don't find him or Christina, then I'll come back and get you, and we can see if you can pick up anything in the field. We cool?"

"What about me?" Kelly asked from the front seat.

Duffy smiled at her like a big brother. "You are to remain safe and sound in the warmth and comfort of my sweet little chariot, young lady," Duffy said with a wink. Kelly giggled, and I had to work at keeping my eye roll to a minimum. "Besides, it's colder than a penguin's butt out. Trust me, by keeping you in the car I'm doing you a favor."

When Duffy had finished, he got back on the radio and checked the status of the other deputies. I sat in the backseat and shuffled through my purse, looking for something to write on. I found the sketch I'd drawn for Cat when she had asked about where I thought Sara was, I looked at it for a moment, turned it over and began to duplicate what I'd just drawn in Viv's kitchen. I stared at my newest drawing for a long time.

I had an odd feeling about the area. A mixture of trepidation and anxiety was crawling along my senses, and the closer we got to the colonel's field, the more my stomach seemed to develop butterflies. I didn't like it, and I didn't quite know why.

A short time later Duffy parked in almost the same spot he had the night we found Gina. There were three other patrol cars already there, and in short order four more unidentified patrol cars joined us. I noticed that the men who got out of these wore blue windbreakers with FBI stamped in bright yellow across the back.

"You called in the Feds?" I asked Duffy.

"Biggins is wanted across state lines, and if he's turned from serial rapist to serial killer, like I think he has, we need as much support on this as we can get," he answered as he took a clipboard from the dash and some ammo from the side compartment next to the gearshift. He then turned sideways in his seat and gave both of us a stern look as he said, "Remember, stay in the car until I come back to get you. We'll be on our walkie-talkies when we do the grid, so if you want to know what's going on all you have to do is listen to the chatter," he said, indicating the radio. "I'm leaving the keys in the car so you can keep the heat on, okay?"

"Roger wilco," I said, and saluted smartly.

"Dodger that," Kelly said, following my lead.

Duffy's eyelids drooped in a look that said we were testing his patience, but he added a smirk as he got out of the car.

Kelly and I watched Duffy as he gathered the other deputies and FBI agents around him and showed them my crude map. We saw him point toward the right end of the field, and in the distance we could just make out the top of the water tower Duffy had referred to. The men walked as a group down the small embankment. Once they cleared the shack, they fanned out and began to walk in one line, sweeping their eyes right and left as they searched the field. After a while they entered the woods, and the group disappeared from sight.

Kelly turned in her seat when the last deputy vanished and said, "It's pretty creepy now that they're out of sight, huh?"

"Very," I said, as a ripple of unease flowed along my spine. "I don't really like it here," I added.

"Me neither. Thank God you're along. If he makes me wait in this car when he gets back and takes you, I don't know what I'll do."

"At least it's daylight," I said with a small shiver.

"You cold?" she asked me, and reached for the heat to turn it up. As she did so I noticed a reflection from the sun on her wrist.

"Is that the bracelet Ellie gave you?" I asked.

Kelly turned up the heat and said, "Yep. I love it. Ellie gave it to me," she said as she toyed with the bracelet. I noticed it also had a heart on the chain. "She's always thinking of me."

"I know," I agreed. "She gave me one too," I said, holding mine up for Kelly to see.

"Ooooh," she said. "Yours is gorgeous. She made each heart a little different, something unique for all of us."

I pulled my wrist back after Kelly had inspected it, and another silence passed between us. Searching for topics of conversation I asked, "What do you do for a living, Kelly?"

She giggled and said, "I'm a hairstylist. I was supposed to do Ellie's hair for the wedding. It's so sad that it looks like it's not going to happen now."

"Yes, it really is," I said. "At least, not until Eddie gets out of jail."

Kelly opened her mouth to comment, but just then there was an explosion of sound over the radio and she and I turned as an excited voice said, "Over here! I got him! He's over here!"

"Whoa," I said as I leaned closer to the front seat to listen. "I think they found Biggins!"

Kelly and I strained to understand the excited chatter lighting up the airwaves as police codes spoken in excited tones sparked from the radio. After a little while we heard Duffy's voice say, "Abby and Kelly, if you're listening, we've found Biggins. We've got some cleanup to do, but sit tight and we'll be on our way back soon."

"Phew!" Kelly said, sitting back in her seat. "I am so relieved they caught that son of a bitch!"

I gave a small look of shock as the expletive came out of her mouth. She just didn't seem the type to swear. Still, I watched the field intently, waiting for Duffy to reappear with his team and Biggins in cuffs.

"Hey, is that your sketch?" Kelly asked, eyeing the piece of paper still clutched in my hand.

"Yeah," I said absently, watching for movement. Even though Duffy claimed to have caught Biggins, the unease in my stomach hadn't lessened.

"Mind if I take a look?" she asked.

"Here," I said, and handed it to her. While she looked at my sketch I reached into my purse and pulled out my cell and earphone. I needed to call Dave and let him know I wasn't going to make my plane.

As I was about to put on the earphone, Kelly gave a gasp and said, "Ohmigod! I know where this is!"

I looked up to see her pointing to the stones laid out in a cross that I had drawn at the top left corner of the page. "You do?" I asked, the feeling of disquiet becoming a little stronger as she tapped the page.

"Yes! Why haven't you shown this to Duffy?"

"I did show it to him. I drew it the day we knew Sara had been killed."

Kelly sucked in a breath. She stared at me wide-eyed for a split second before she was out the car door and running as if her life depended on it down the embankment and across the field.

"Kelly!" I shouted as I rushed out of the car. "*Kelly!* Come back!" To my amazement she ignored me and just kept running. After a moment of indecision during which I considered picking up Duffy's microphone and telling him that Kelly had run out of the car, I figured that by the time he got back here, she'd be long gone. With a growl I pushed open the car door and ran after her as fast as I could, resigning to call Duffy on my cell when I caught up with her.

Kelly had a really good lead on me already, and for someone so tiny, she could run like the devil. As I chased after her, I managed to clip the earpiece to my ear and I flipped open the phone, searching with stolen glances through my speed-dial directory for Duffy's number. I couldn't remember which digit I'd assigned to him, and the more I tried to run, look at my phone and keep from losing sight of Kelly, the dizzier I became.

I had no idea what had gotten into her, but if she beat me to the woods, Duffy wouldn't know what had happened to us if I didn't call him. Aggravated, I raised the phone in front of me, hoping to get a longer look at my directory, but tripped on a stick and went down with a thud. Swearing like a sailor I picked myself up and looked to see Kelly's coat already fading into the forest.

I was panting heavily as I got up and charged after Kelly again. Holding tight to my cell, I decided to wait until I caught up with her to call Duffy. Trying to look for his number and running pell-mell across a field just didn't work with my already challenged coordination.

Ten yards from the woods, I lost sight of Kelly altogether. Cursing in between puffs I entered the woods and immediately tripped again. "Goddamn it!" I yelled as I picked myself up and glanced down at what I had tripped over. A woman's stylish high-heeled shoe lay under my leg, and while my frenzied brain tried to figure that one out I got up again and headed in the direction I thought Kelly had run toward.

The brush was thick here, and the woods were dark and menacing. "Kelly!" I managed as I slowed my pace a little. My lungs couldn't take this. "Kelly! Stop this! Come on! Come out and stop running!" Ahead, I heard a bloodcurdling scream. "Jesus!" I said, and ran toward the noise as branches scratched at my face and hands. *"Kellly!"* I yelled again. No one answered.

Puffing and panting, I crashed through the brush, deeper into the woods toward the sound of Kelly's scream. My heart was pounding so loudly in my chest I thought it would permanently push out my rib cage. My eyes darted wildly about as I searched for any sign of her black coat or brunette head. Finally I had to stop. I just couldn't go forward another foot until I caught a little breath. Wheezing with effort, I doubled over and held my hand to the stitch in my side. I managed one hoarse "Kelly!" in between breaths, but that took so much effort that I decided to give it a break until I had leveled my breathing again.

While I was doubled over, something shiny caught a small ray of sunlight and reflected in my eye only two feet in front of me. Reaching forward I picked up the object and noticed immediately that it was one of the hearts off the Tiffany bracelets that Ellie had given out.

"Oh, no," I whined as I panted and tried to stand up straight. I did so with effort; my side was killing me. I blinked a few times as stars swam in front of my eyes, but regained my balance and looked closely at the heart. I knew Kelly's name would be there. Her scream had been that panicked. She'd been taken by the same person who'd taken all the other girls, and was probably, even now, fighting for her life, if not dead.

I was utterly wrong. The elegant name on the bracelet read, *Christina.*

"You know, for a psychic, you sure suck," a voice said behind me at the same instant something metallic went *click.* I knew that noise. I'd been around Dutch on the practice range enough times to know the sound of the safety being pulled back from a big, bad gun.

"No," I said breathlessly. "Not you!"

"Yes."

"Why?"

"I'll fill you in, but first drop the heart." I did, and a second later felt the barrel of a gun in my back as I heard the killer bend slightly to retrieve it. "I've been looking for this; thanks for finding it." A second later the pressure of the barrel left my back and then the voice said, "Now move."

My back was ramrod straight, the stitch in my side completely forgotten as I obeyed orders, knowing there was a gun pointed at my back, and no help in sight this far into the woods.

"Which way should I go?" I asked.

"A little left, then straight ahead. And don't try anything," the voice said as I felt the metal poke me hard in the middle of my back again.

My mind began racing. How to get out of this? I clenched my fists and realized I still held my phone in my hand. As discreetly as I could, and using my body as a block, I felt the keys with my thumb and went for 911. Pretending to trip a little, I managed to click on the SEND button and waited for the line to be picked up in my ear.

My heart beat even faster, and adrenaline coursed through my legs, leaving them wobbly and shaken as I heard the line ring once, twice, and in the next instant a deep baritone said, "Rivers."

I grabbed a tree branch for support at the sound of the voice, a flood of emotions shooting up and down my nerves. "Rivers," Dutch said again, growing impatient when his first announcement was met with silence. I had two choices: I could discreetly hang up and go for 911 again, or I could try to alert him to what was going on. I opted for the latter.

"Where are we going, exactly?" I said loudly. "I mean, you have a gun to my back; I think I deserve to know where we're going."

"Edgar?" Dutch asked.

"You'll see."

"So why did you kill them?" I asked. "Why did you kill your friends, Kelly?"

"Abby, this isn't funny," Dutch said. "Come on, what gives?"

"They weren't *my* friends," Kelly said.

"But you killed them," I insisted, my voice shrill and shaking. "You killed them for no reason. In cold blood. And then you tried to frame Eddie. Why?"

Dutch was silent in my ear as we marched forward. I could feel him trying to decide if I was playing some joke or if I was serious. "Ellie is *my* best friend!" Kelly said. "She and I are so much closer than any of *you*! She understands me! She needs me! She doesn't need *any* of *you*! So I got rid of all the distractions in her life. I simplified things. Now she and I can focus on each other. We're sisters, or we will be once I marry Duffy."

"So it was you who lured Gina out of her apartment that night."

Kelly laughed, delighted that I was putting the pieces together. "And you and Duffy couldn't figure it out. I instant-messaged her to call me, because I knew that Duffy would search her phone records. It worked brilliantly. She calls, I tell her that Ellie is planning on fleeing the country because she doesn't want to marry Eddie, and Gina bolts for the airport, where I meet up with her in the parking lot."

"You killed her there?"

"Nope, just planted a little evidence. I'd hung out at Ellie's that weekend. While Ellie was out on an errand, Eddie came home, got out of his scrubs and asked me if I could cut his hair. While I was cleaning up he hit the shower. I snagged his scrubs and a little hair, and only after I got home did I realize he'd left his wallet in the pants pocket. He made it way too easy for me."

"So you lured her out of her apartment; then what?"

"I got her in my car and managed to get her all the way out here without much effort—of course, I did have my trusty gun here to help me."

"But she wouldn't go into the woods with you," I said. "She knew you were going to kill her."

"Yep. That bitch tried to make a run for it, so I shot her in front of the shack and hid her in it. I wanted to make it look like Eddie had tried to cover up the evidence, so I thought of burning down the shack, but it was too wet that night. I settled for dropping Eddie's wallet close by, rubbing the scrubs with her blood, then headed back to the airport to leave them in her car."

"And somehow you found out that Sara was on her way to the bridal shop and lured her away too," I said.

"She actually called me on the way over. Said she was meeting you guys. That stupid redhead."

"And Christina?" I asked, thinking about the heart I'd just found.

"I made it back to Christina's house after Biggins had kidnapped me. She let me in and was all, 'You poor thing! You've been through so much trauma!' Dumb bitch. She goes into her room to get me a warm sweater, and when she comes back I've got my gun out. I'm thinking she'll go as easy as Sara, but that cow decides to tackle me. Maybe she didn't think I'd shoot her. She was dead wrong," Kelly said with a little chuckle.

"That's how you got beat up," I said with a gasp. "It wasn't Biggins who attacked you; it was Christina!"

"Yep. I shot her a couple of extra times for that."

"And the night you took me to Duffy's," I said, thinking back as another realization slammed into place. "You weren't taking me to Viv's! You were taking me here, weren't you? That's why you were so annoyed when I called Duffy and told him I was with you. You would have had too much explaining to do if I didn't show up at his house, and why we were so late getting there!"

"You're not as dumb as you look." She snickered. "Now stop!"

I halted. Dutch had remained silent in my ear the whole time we were walking. My eyes watered as I wondered if he had hung up on me. "So now you're going to kill me too," I said dumbly as I looked ahead at a small stone structure, old and crumbling. It was the remnants of a tiny abbey. And now I knew why, in my dreams, the mailbox in front of the stones formed into a cross had had my name on it. In the middle of the crumbling ruin I saw two legs lying on the stone floor. One foot was covered with a stylish shoe. The other was barefoot, and I trembled as I realized that I was looking at Christina's final resting place.

"Ellie doesn't need any more distractions. And neither does Duffy," Kelly said simply.

"Kelly," I said, trying to keep my voice even. "He's out here with a dozen law enforcement agents! He's bound to find us! He'll know it was you!"

Kelly laughed. "Oh, I doubt that. Right now that group is half a mile away dealing with Biggins. They aren't even within earshot. Now turn around," she ordered, and I knew my time was up.

It's a strange thing that happens when you know you're about to die. There is this feeling of time stopping, and sound being muted. It is a feeling not so much of peace, but acceptance. I turned slowly around, and while the sound of Dutch's voice burst forth loudly in my ear again, I didn't register any of what he said next. I was too intent on looking Kelly in the eye.

When I did, I wondered at it. I wondered why I hadn't known about her earlier. I wondered why my guides hadn't warned me and prevented me from coming here in Duffy's car. True, I'd felt a sense of unease, but nothing like the major alarm bells that should have gone off.

I looked hard at Kelly. I took in her small, petite stature. Her girlish face. The way she still looked so fragile, even holding that monster gun in her tiny hand, and I realized I'd been swayed by the look of her. Still, that didn't account for why I hadn't known on some intuitive level how evil she really was. After all, I was a professional. I should have known it was her.

And that was when Kelly pulled the trigger, and before I could really register what was happening I was flying backward through the air. The bullet punched me with a force that boggled the mind. I felt my breath expel from my mouth with a heavy "Uhn!"

The world spun as fire erupted in my chest, the pain unlike anything I'd ever felt in my life. My hand came up protectively to the wound in my chest as a crimson stain spread through my fingers and I writhed in agony.

Dutch was yelling now, his voice loud with panic, but my mind was too consumed with my own pain to reach out to him. It was too late anyway. Kelly stood over me, pointing that gun straight at my heart. Our eyes met, and she hesitated for a split second as I nodded. I knew it was over, and there was nothing I could do about it.

Kelly smiled evilly at how quickly I caved. "You're just like Biggins," she said. "After I rolled away from him, I snuck back around for an ambush. He begged and begged me not to shoot him, but when I shot his balls off, he was singing a different tune a few octaves higher." Then her eyes narrowed and she took aim. I felt my limbs go numb, a paralysis of sorts stopped my writhing, and suddenly the pain was gone. I seemed to lift off the ground and float upward a few inches, and the last sound I heard was a second explosion as it echoed through the woods.

Chapter Sixteen

Floating up and up I saw the branches, then the tops of the trees, then the blue sky, when finally a tunnel formed around me. As I traveled into the tunnel I viewed the last week of my life as if I were in a darkened theater, and when that stopped, I became aware of the tunnel and the light again. It was an eerie feeling, drifting through space in a hollow tube that felt alive with energy. At the end was a bright white light, and it was so blinding that I had to shield my eyes.

I blinked several times, waiting for my eyes to adjust, and when they did I noticed that I was no longer in the tunnel but in a huge open garden. My mouth dropped a little at the sudden change in scenery while I ogled the beauty of the place. The grass was the most brilliant green I'd ever seen. It felt light and ticklish under my feet, which I noticed were bare. I pulled my head back up and looked around the garden. There were exotic-looking flowers I was sure I'd never seen before in the most gorgeous and vivid colors that seemed to glow with an inner light.

In the background I saw a waterfall so blue it looked aqua as it ran over its rocky edge and into a large crystal-clear pool. "Wow!" I said as my eyes tried to take in the sounds, sights and smells of the place.

"It's beautiful, isn't it?" a voice beside me said.

I jumped, both at the suddenness of the voice appearing beside me and the fact that I recognized to whom it belonged. "Grams!" I said when I'd recovered myself, and threw my arms around my grandmother.

After squeezing her tightly, I pulled back to look at her, drinking in the sight of my favorite grandparent. I sucked in a breath; she was so radiant and beautiful, and looking like she wasn't a day over thirty. The last time I'd seen her was when I was six years old, and she had been so frail then at the end of her battle with cancer.

Here she looked amazing. Her face was young and fresh, her hair a beautiful chestnut color instead of the gray I remembered. Her dress was gorgeous, a white-and-pink concoction of flowers and silk. "I can't believe it's you!" I said as I squeezed her in a tight embrace again.

She laughed in my ear and held me tight, and I felt a love so intense it filled me from head to toe.

"Hello, Abby-gabby, my dear, sweet, wonderful girl!" she said. "I've been waiting for you."

I pulled my head back. "You look beautiful!"

Grams laughed and gave me a big kiss on the cheek. "Come," she ordered, taking my hand. "There are things I need to show you."

I followed happily after her, loving the feel of her hand in mine. I had missed my grandmother so much since her death. She'd been one of my fondest childhood memories, and being reunited with her now was such a gift! "Where're we going?" I asked as I tagged along.

"This way," she said as she paused in front of a white wall that seemed to materialize out of nowhere. I blinked once or twice and said, "Where did that come from?"

"When you first arrive it can be difficult to see

what's right in front of you," Grams said as we walked down the length of the wall and paused in front of a beautiful walnut-colored door with a stained-glass window and a golden handle.

"What's in there?" I asked while she reached for the handle.

"Come in and you'll find out," she said, giving me a reassuring smile as she stepped through the doorway.

I followed after her, and to my surprise I found that we were in a long hallway. The walls were a soft yellow color that seemed to vibrate and shimmer with energy. Hanging on the walls in front of us were gilded frames carved with ornate designs. Some were gold, some were silver, and all housed portraits of people I recognized. I stepped forward to touch one of the frames. "This is Candice Fusco. She's a client of mine."

Grams gave me an encouraging smile as she waved her hand toward the other photos. I walked to the next and said, "Nora Brosseau, Joan Rogers, Kristen Laprade and Debbie Huntley. These are all my clients too."

Grams laughed and clapped her hands. "Yes!" she said.

"So, why are they here?" I asked as I looked down the length of the corridor.

Grams stepped forward to my side as I studied the portraits. "These are not only your clients, Abigail. These are the people you've assisted along their life paths. Many of these souls would still be at a crossroads if not for the clarity you've brought to them through your work and devotion to delivering the message."

I felt my cheeks grow warm. I was embarrassed by the praise Grams was giving me. "They would have gotten there on their own . . . eventually," I said.

"Don't sell yourself short, lovey. The role you've played in their lives is quite important."

I shuffled my feet a little. "Yeah, yeah. But why are their portraits here?"

"They will miss you when you're gone," Grams said.

"Huh?" I said, looking at her. I wasn't understanding her point.

"If you don't go back, Abigail, these people will have to fend for themselves."

"You mean I can go back?" I asked.

"Certainly."

"But if I'm here, doesn't that mean I've died?" I asked, scratching my head.

"There are many faces to death, dear. This is but one of the more temporary ones."

"But, Grams, it feels so great here! I mean, whoa! I feel like I've just had a giant espresso of love java. I feel awesome! And nothing hurts. I can feel things, the grass on my feet, your hand, the coolness of this wall," I said as I reached out and touched the wall, noticing with surprise that it didn't feel cool at all, but warm and vibrant. "Okay, scratch that, the warmth of this wall. Wow! This place is *so* awesome!" I said, really noticing how happy I felt. It was weird: From the depths of my soul I felt love and warmth and a happiness that felt intoxicating. I was light, and free, unbound by worry or anger or pain. In short, I felt simply euphoric.

"It is an amazing place, Abigail. But I wonder if it is truly your time to come."

"I'm here!" I announced, waving my hand with a flourish in front of me. "It must be my time."

Grams smiled at me the way she had when I was a little kid pushing her for a cookie right before dinner. "It is an important matter to think on. Not one to make without considering all things."

I looked at my grandmother for a moment, a bit confused. It almost sounded like she didn't want me here. "Grams," I said, "you trying to get rid of me? 'Cause I gotta tell ya, I'm thinking of hanging. I mean, did you get a load of that garden out there? Have you ever seen anything so beautiful?"

Grams was nodding and giggling as I went on and

on about how great it all was. "So your mind is pretty much made up, is that correct?" she asked me.

I paused as I looked at the portraits lining the walls. I would miss all my clients, that was true, and certainly I would miss my sister, and Eggy, and all my friends. But, truth be told, I felt I could also look out for them from up here. I had often felt my grandmother's energy around when I was back on Earth. Why couldn't I do the same for the people I cared about? "Grams, I'm just telling you, I have never felt this . . . this . . . *alive*! Is this how you feel all the time?"

My grandmother laughed. "Yes, it is one of the many perks to being here. But I want to make sure you understand what you're giving up. Your sweet pooch, Eggy, will not join you for many years."

My heart sank, and then I thought of something and said, "Yeah, but Dave will look after him."

"And your sister, she will be quite devastated by your passing."

"Cat's a tough cookie, Grams. You remember how much of a brat she was when she was little?"

"I remember she was a very *determined* child," Grams said with a smirk.

"Determined ain't the half of it. Her nickname is Patton."

"Ah," Grams said, as she eyed me the way a mother does when she's trying to decide whether her child is old enough to make her own decisions. "Still, I want to make sure you have all the information you'll need to truly make your choice."

"What do you mean?" I asked.

"Follow me," she said, crooking one finger and leading me down the corridor of portraits. We got to the end, and Grams stopped before another door. She rested her hand on the door handle for a moment as she turned to me and said, "In this room, whatever you decide will be final, and you will not only be sealing your own fate, but that of many others as well."

"Sounds heavy," I said, trying to make light of the serious look in her eyes.

"It is, Abigail. It most definitely is." And with that, Grams opened the door and I filed in after her.

When I came through the doorway I noticed a small, cozy room colored robin's-egg blue. On the wall were a few more portraits; not nearly as many as were outside in the corridor, but enough for me to pause and look at the faces. The first portrait was of a woman I didn't recognize. I racked my brain trying to place a name to the picture, but I simply couldn't. "Do I know her?" I asked as I studied the portrait.

"No," Grams said. "Not yet, anyway."

I turned around and gave her a look that said, *Huh?* but she just smiled and nodded toward the second portrait. I moved over one and stared at a beautiful painting of Dutch. He looked so handsome staring out from the canvas at me. His midnight-blue eyes were perfectly captured, and the smirk he seemed to always wear around me was expertly painted. "God, I miss him," I whispered.

"Yes. We know. Which is why none of us can figure out why you dumped him."

"Excuse me?" I said, whipping around. "What do you mean, *I* dumped *him*?"

"On Valentine's Day," she said, looking at me quizzically. "Remember? You asked him to leave and then you never called him again."

"Wait, wait, wait!" I said, putting up my hand in a stop motion. "*He* was the one who broke up with *me*!"

"Really?" she asked with that small smile again. "Your grandfather and I remember quite clearly that all Dutch said was that he needed a little more time to devote to his work. He is working on an extremely difficult case right now, and wanting to concentrate on it seemed highly reasonable to us."

I stared at her wide-eyed, and I realized belatedly that my mouth was hanging open. "Grams," I said after I had processed what she said. "Dutch was the one who wanted to cool it between us. Besides, it wasn't just me who didn't call him. He didn't call me either!"

"I see," Grams said, the smile growing. "And just how do you know that Dutch wanted to break things off with you?"

"Because when I looked into his energy, there was no reflection of me there!" I sputtered. I could not believe she'd gotten this whole deal so wrong.

"Ah," she said, nodding now. "So just because you couldn't see your own reflection in Dutch's energy anymore, that's why you thought you two were finished?"

"Well, what else could it mean?" I asked.

"Did you bother to look into the energy of your sister?" Grams said.

I did a double take, blinking at her. "No, why?"

"Because you would have seen your absence there too. You are no longer reflected in anyone's energy. Not Dave's, not Dutch's, not Eggy's. No one who was close to you has had you in their energy for a little while now."

And then it hit me, and the weight of it tugged my mouth open again. "Because I was going to die? That's why I wasn't in Dutch's energy?"

Grams nodded. "Yes, I'm afraid so."

Then something else dawned on me and I said, "And *that's* why I couldn't read Christina! She was going to die, and there was no future for me to see!"

"Exactly," Grams said.

"So if that's all true, then I can't possibly go back," I reasoned, and a small part of my heart felt heavier with the conclusion.

"Oh, there is still a choice open to you, my love. I just wanted to make sure you had all the information available before you made that choice. Now, as you see, there are some faces here. Some you recognize, and some you don't, but they have all been placed here because the fate of these people rests on your shoulders in a far greater way than those out in the hallway."

"Okay . . ." I said, waiting her out.

"If you choose to stay here with us," Grams said as she stepped forward to take up both of my hands and look me straight in the eye, "then these people will have their lives cut short, and they will join you here very soon."

I sucked in a breath and turned to Dutch's picture, fear gripping my heart. "No," I said.

"Yes," Grams insisted. "If you choose to go back and reclaim your life on the earthly plane, then these are the lives you will save."

Tears welled in my eyes and dribbled down my cheeks. I looked at all the paintings in the small room and wept, because if I made the selfish choice, the choice that I really, really wanted to make, I would tear apart families, and I would let down friends and loved ones.

I looked back at Grams, who held the most compassionate gaze for me. "Oh, Grams!" I wailed. "I'll miss you!" And I lunged forward, wrapping myself around her and squeezing her tight.

"So you'll go back?" she asked into my hair as she hugged me.

I nodded into her shoulder and blubbered, "I have to."

"That's my Abby-gabby." She chuckled softly. "Come on, my love. Let's go back to the garden." She took my hand and led me out of the little room into the long hallway and then out into the garden.

We walked the path back to the waterfall in silence, our arms entwined as I worked very hard to imprint all of my senses with my grandmother: how she smelled, how she felt, how she walked. And even though I was sad enough to still be crying, there was an underlying warmth filling my heart, and I knew I would never truly feel it again until the next time my earthly body ceased to function.

As the waterfall came into view I saw movement off to the side and turned my head. There were three tall men standing by a large hole that seemed to materialize out of thin air. After a moment a childlike figure came through the hole. A woman with brown hair, no taller than a young girl, stood wide-eyed and scared in front of the men, and as we drew closer I could see her tremble. I felt like I knew her, but my head was beginning to feel foggy. I shook it, trying to recognize the woman, but the fog only intensified.

"Don't stare at her, dear," my grandmother said. "She will have a tougher time of it if you do."

Heeding my grandmother's warning I pulled my eyes away. We walked a little farther when Grams stopped and turned to face me. "Now, remember," she said, holding my shoulders at arm's length. "You do not need your parents' approval to know you are a wonderful woman, and someone to be very proud of."

I blushed and pulled my head down, shuffling my feet. "Thanks, Grams," I said.

"I mean it, Abigail. Claire always did have her priorities mixed up. Even as a child that one never could stand it if one of her other siblings outshone her in any way. The fact that you are so special only means she cannot compete with you, and that is the basis of her resentment. You were a gift to her that she never realized, and threw away. You were given to her so that she could learn her great karmic lesson, one she hasn't yet grasped and, I'm afraid, is not likely to learn now that her time is winding down."

"I get it," I said, looking up at her. "But it sure wasn't easy growing up with Princess Iceberg for a mother."

"I know, dear, I know," she said with a chuckle as she swept a lock of my hair behind my ear. "Just remember what I told you every time you came over to my house after Claire was mean to you."

"Don't let the turkeys get you down?" I laughed, remembering one of her oldest and fondest phrases.

"Indeed. And if you ever need me, remember to look in your heart, and I'll be right there." With that she poked me in the chest, and as she did so, an electric pain gripped my heart.

"Owww!" I said, rubbing my breast bone. "It hurts when you do that!"

"This?" she asked, and gave me another poke that felt like a thousand needles stabbing right through my chest.

"Stop!" I said, and jumped back, trying to block her next poke, but Grams was too quick for me and got one more in, which hurt like hell. "Will you quit it?" I said, as I tried to raise my arms to fend her off, but they were suddenly like lead, and my body was frozen with cold. My eyes were droopy and I couldn't form any more words.

"We have a sinus tach!" someone yelled to my left. "Her stats are coming up and I've got a good rhythm!" they added.

"She's back!" said another voice. "Call in the chopper; we'll meet them in the field!"

There was movement all around me, and without warning I felt air being forced into my lungs and something wickedly uncomfortable was in my mouth and down my throat. I wanted to pull whatever it was out, but I couldn't move. There was a huge collar around my neck and I was strapped down. Again I felt my lungs expand, and I tried to scream out my discomfort, but all that came out was something like a moan.

"Hang in there," a man said above me. "Hold on, Abby. You can make it," he encouraged. Then I felt some hands lift the left side of the stretcher I was strapped to, and my whole body tilted sideways.

I winced, and stared straight into Kelly's lifeless

face. She was just a few feet away as she lay on the ground on her side. Her eyes were wide and surprised. Her childlike complexion was decidedly corrupted by a large hole gaping grossly out of the center of her forehead, while a thick pool of blood formed about her head.

A moment later I was eased back down as another whoosh of air was pumped into my lungs; then the stretcher was lifted again and I felt myself being hustled through the woods. I closed my eyes, feeling very weak and unable to take in everything that was happening to me. I no longer felt the agony in my chest that I had earlier, which was good, but everything seemed distorted and disconnected, which was still a creepy feeling.

"Agent Rivers, are you still there?" a man's voice said. "She's got a heartbeat again, but this chest wound is pretty bad. We're airlifting her to Denver General, and I honestly don't know if she'll make it."

"She'll make it," another voice barked, and it was a voice I recognized. "You hear that, Abby?" Duffy said. "I *order* you to make it!"

I wanted to nod my head, because of course I would, and there was no need to worry, but I was restricted by the collar and frankly too tired to move. I settled for the smallest of hand waves as I opened my eyes and winked at Duffy, who looked as pale as I'd ever seen him. But then something caught my attention and I focused on it in a sort of dreamy delirium for a moment as my eyes swam in and out of focus. Over Duffy's shoulder was the faintest image of a redhead. I couldn't see her face, but she was evident in Duffy's energy, and I wondered dizzily if this was a leftover reflection from Rachel.

Pulling my eyes back into focus I looked intently at him and gave another wink. When he noticed that I was looking at him, and that I had winked, his mouth scrunched together and he yelled, "Let's move!" to the other men as they picked up their pace to reach the chopper.

I settled for closing my eyes again and letting the darkness take me into its warm, but still very much alive, embrace.

Chapter Seventeen

". . . we repaired that along with the damage done to the right atrium. She was very lucky, actually to have gotten hit on the right side of her chest. A point-blank shot like the one she sustained on the left side of her chest would certainly have killed her," a woman's voice I didn't recognize said.

"What can we expect from her recovery, Doctor?" a baritone voice asked.

"We will want to keep her intubated for at least the next twenty-four to forty-eight hours. She'll be under heavy sedation that will paralyze her—"

"*Paralyze* her?" my sister's voice asked.

"Yes, but only medically. The vent is extremely uncomfortable, and the last thing we want is for her to try to use her energy to fight it. She will need a little time simply to heal. After we are assured that she will be able to breathe well on her own, we will remove the vent and monitor her for at least the next two weeks; then if you'd like to take her home, we can release her at that point, barring any other complications."

"So, she'll be able to come home in just a few weeks?" another male voice asked, and after a moment I realized it was Dave.

"Yes, in all likelihood."

"What about after that?" Dutch again.

"After that she will need some time to recover. A terrible trauma has occurred to her body, and it is not unusual for a woman of Abigail's size and stature to require three months of bed rest."

"That long?" my sister asked.

"That's typical," the doctor replied. "Sometime down the road she may also want to see a plastic surgeon about the scar on her chest. But other than that, she will most likely make a full recovery."

"Thank you, God," another man said across the room. Duffy.

"Oh, poor, Abby," a woman wailed. "It's all my fault, Duffy!" Ah, Ellie was here too. *Geez,* I thought, *how many people do they let into a hospital room, anyway?* With effort I tried to move. Nothing happened. I thought about moaning, but the thing in my throat hurt something fierce, and I decided against it. Finally I settled for fluttering my eyes open—it appeared this was the only part of my body I could actually move.

No one seemed to notice that I was awake, so I had no choice but to try to make a sound. I waited until the air had been pushed into my lungs to try an "Unh!"

A very pretty woman with deep red hair and eyes the color of brandy stepped forward. "Ah," she said as she pulled the stethoscope from around her neck and plugged it into her ears. "I see our patient has woken up. Abigail," she said to me, "I'm Dr. Amstadter, and you're in Denver General Hospital. We've got you on a machine that is pushing air into your lungs to help you breathe. If you can understand me, please blink your eyes once."

I blinked.

"Very good," she said with a smile. "Now I'm going to give you some medicine that will make you very sleepy and will let you get some rest so you won't have to feel the tube in your throat while you're asleep, okay?"

I blinked again.

"Good," she said, and reaching into her lab coat she pulled out a vial and a syringe, drew some liquid with the needle, then walked around to the other side of my bed. She picked up the IV cord snaking its way from a metal hook to my arm and slowly inserted the liquid into a plug on the line.

While she was fiddling with that I looked around the room at everyone I loved in the world as they stared back at me with that same emotion reflected in their eyes, and in an instant I knew I'd made the right decision to come back and see things through. I put every ounce of energy into the tiniest of hand waves, and the room broke into a grin. A few seconds later I was off to la-la land.

If ever anyone tells you how fast time seems to be flying for them, suggest they check into their local hospital for a two-week stay and see if they don't die of boredom. The good news about lying around all day with nothing to do but channel surf was that I was awake for only a small portion of each hour of daylight. I'd never felt so exhausted in all my life, and everything seemed to tire me.

I'd been taken off the vent about thirty-six hours after my operation. It was a painful extraction, and I was given sorbet to soothe my raw throat. Dutch, Cat, Duffy and Ellie had each taken turns sitting with me, around the clock. I was incredibly humbled by the fact that they were all willing to take so much of their time to spend with me. Dave had stayed until I'd been taken off the vent; then he'd gone back home to get Eggy out of the kennel and continue to take care of him until I recovered.

I'd learned from Duffy that a frantic call had come in from the Bureau to one of the agents out in the field with him. He had answered it, and learned that a Michigan-based FBI agent needed assistance right away. What I hadn't understood when Dutch had given me his Valentine's Day present was that these phones weren't just standard-issue to the agents in the field; they could also be set to receive direct GPS tracking signals from one another. Dutch had received my exact location from the phone I'd used to call him. To his amazement and relief he'd learned that other agents were a mere quarter mile away.

Word had spread through the group gathered under the water tower, where they found Biggins's body, that I was being held at gunpoint, and Duffy, his deputies and the FBI agents had hightailed it over to me as fast as they could run.

They'd heard Kelly shoot me and honed in on our location. One of the agents, a sharpshooter, had taken her out a nanosecond before she could pull the trigger again, which explained why I thought I'd heard her gun go off second time. It wasn't her gun after all.

I'd also learned that it was Kelly who had booked Gina's flight to California, knowing that if Gina's body was never recovered, Ellie might think her friend had simply abandoned her.

Kelly had also been the one to text-message Ellie from Sara's phone that Sara wouldn't be attending the bachelorette party. It looked as if Kelly had intended to make it appear as if all of Ellie's friends were abandoning her, at least until we found Gina; then she changed tactics to make it look like she was the only one to survive. It didn't matter to Kelly who got blamed for murder, be it Eddie or Biggins. Duffy said he'd learned all this from the journal Kelly kept in her apartment, amidst dozens and dozens of pictures of Ellie. The poor girl had been obsessed with her friend. As he dug deeper, he discovered that Kelly's mental illness stemmed back to when she'd discovered her father's body after he'd hanged himself. Her fragile brain hadn't been able to handle it, and Duffy learned that she'd had two mental breakdowns in six years.

Kelly's brother had also told the police that he hadn't had anything to do with her in quite some time, suggesting that she'd "gone over the edge" when he and Ellie broke up two years earlier.

I'd also learned a few things in my own personal life that gave me lots of time to reflect and make a few more key decisions. It started with the second day I came off the ventilator, when Cat burst into my room with a suitcase that was almost as big as she was. "Surprise!" she said as she came in the door.

"Hey," I said from the bed. "What's all that?"

"Things to cheer you up," Cat announced, and she flung open the lid to the suitcase and began removing little knickknacks from my home. There were three pictures of Eggy (these made me cry; I missed him!), along with a photo of Cat and the twins, and a mug shot of Dave. She also included some of my favorite DVDs, along with a brand-new portable DVD player to play them on, a figurine of an angel that I'd had for years and years, and my favorite afghan from Dutch's house. "Awww," I said as she piled the frames and knickknacks around the room. "Cat, you shouldn't have!" I said, hugging the picture of Eggy with my left arm.

"It's important to keep your spirits up. I flew to Detroit this morning, packed this stuff as quickly as I could, then came back lickety-split!"

"Thank you," I said, my eyes very moist.

"Oh!" she said. "And I almost forgot about this!" She thrust my old cell phone into my hand. "It was in your study, still plugged in from the last time you went to charge it. I think you have voice mail, because it keeps making these little beeping noises."

I looked at the display, which held a small envelope in the right-hand corner. Flipping open the lid I hit the 1 button, which was preprogrammed for voice mail, and waited for the messages to come in. "You have eight new messages," the robotic voice said. Surprised, I clicked the 1 button again and listened. "First message," the voice said. Then I heard, "Hey, there, Edgar. Sorry I haven't called you in a couple of days. Listen, I don't like how we ended our evening the other night. I really want to talk to you. Will you call me? Soon?"

The message was stamped the day I flew to Colorado.

"Next new message," the voice said again.

"Edgar," Dutch said. "It's me. Come on, babe. Call me, okay? I meant to write down your new number the other night, but I didn't get a chance before I left, so when you get this message call me on your new cell phone so I can record it into my speed dial. Seriously. Call me."

"Next new message," the voice said.

"Abby Cooper," Dutch again, his voice singing my name. "Sweethot, this is silly. I miss you! I want to talk about this, okay? You can't just dump me like that and not talk about it, so please call me on your new cell."

"Next new message," the voice said.

"Abigail. Dutch. Listen, Milo and I are headed to Guzzoline Alley tonight. How about if you meet us there and we can talk in person about this? Milo said he'd be willing to take your side," Dutch joked. "I told him, 'So what else is new.' " And he chuckled. "Come on, babe. Please meet me up there. I don't want you to go to your friend's wedding hating my guts. Maybe I can get a night off and meet you in Denver. Come on out and we'll talk about it, okay? Please?"

I flipped the phone closed and looked up at my sister, who was studying me with a steady gaze. "Dutch?"

"He didn't know my new number," I said as the

tears that had formed in my eyes spilled over. "Jesus, Cat! It was all a huge misunderstanding!"

"Mercury retrograde," my sister said as she came over and tucked a hair behind my ear. In that moment I saw my grandmother reflected in her face and mannerisms.

"I'm glad you're here," I said to her.

"I'm glad you are too," she said, and her own eyes misted. "You gave us quite a scare, you know."

"Gotta keep you on your toes," I said with a smile.

Later, Duffy came by and pulled up a chair to keep me company. "How goes the channel surfing?" he asked me.

"It goes. What have you been up to?"

"Making sure Eddie's acquittal is swift and soon."

"They're still charging him with Gina's murder?" I asked, thunderstruck.

"No, but the county prosecutor has to decide if they're going to proceed with the case for escaping incarceration. My guess is that, given the circumstances, they won't pursue it. He's also got a hell of a lawyer, and the DA has never won a case against him. Eddie should be cleared of everything pretty soon. And then it's off to the islands for him and Ellie."

"Too bad they didn't get to have their ceremony," I said.

"They're eloping, which, if you ask me, is the only way to go."

"Good afternoon, Abigail; how are you feeling?" Dr. Amstadter said as she breezed into my room. I was again taken by how pretty she was, with her gorgeous red hair and her glorious eyes. I noticed a moment later that I wasn't the only one taken with her.

"Hello, Doctor," Duffy said, standing up when she entered.

"Ah, Sheriff McGinnis. Good to see you again. How is our patient doing?"

"She's fine, just fine. I'm keeping an eye on her, though."

I smiled as I watched the two of them. Sparks practically flew between the pair. And then I remembered back in the woods the outline of the redhead in Duffy's energy. Amazing how some stuff works out, ain't it?

After Dr. Amstadter left, I turned to Duffy and said, "Sheriff, we need to talk."

Twenty minutes later I'd put a permanent end to the Duffy and Abby variety show. Being the swell guy he is, Duffy actually pulled off looking disappointed. Still, he said that he understood, and knew the moment he met Dutch that he was the one for me. I'd tell him later that the moment I met Dr. Amstadter, I'd known she was the gal for him.

Much later that evening I was groggy from the little catnap I'd had when I heard the door open and soft footfalls come across the tile floor. I opened my eyes and they were met with those of midnight blue. "Evening, Edgar," Dutch said.

"Hi," I said shyly. "How're you?"

Dutch smiled as he pulled up a chair to sit with me. "The question is, how are you?"

"Better, now that you're here."

"Ditto," he said as he reached up to stroke my hair. "I've missed you, ya know."

"Double ditto," I said, flashing him a grin.

"You still intend to give up on us?" he asked me after a long moment.

"Would you believe I never really did?"

"You wouldn't return my calls," he said. I called your house, your cell, your office. . . ."

"I didn't know you made any of those calls until this afternoon. I left my old cell at home when I came to Denver, and I never got a chance to check my other voice mails."

Dutch looked surprised, then shook his head with a grin. "Kind of stupid of me to give you a cell phone for Valentine's Day and not jot down your new number."

"Is the stupid part you're referring to about the cell phone for Valentine's Day, or not jotting down my new number?" I said with a grin.

"Probably a little of both, although, one of those two things saved your butt in the end."

"Best damn present I ever got," I said quickly, and then we both grew silent.

After a bit Dutch said, "I want you to come home and stay with me while you get better, Edgar."

"You do owe me after I played nursemaid to you when you got shot," I said, picking up my hand to stroke his arm. "But are you sure you really want to?"

"Take care of you? Absolutely."

"It won't ruin your powers of concentration?" I asked.

"I guess I deserved that."

"I guess you did."

"So are you gonna take me up on my offer?"

I took a big breath. There was something I needed to tell him, because I couldn't go to his home, let him take care of me and pretend like something hadn't happened that could very well be the final straw between us. "First, I have to confess something," I began, and despite my best efforts my voice shook.

"What's that?"

"See, I really thought you and I had broken up. So when I came out here, I was under the impression that I was single. And I was so torn up inside that I just wanted some comfort, if you will. Just a body to—"

"Edgar," Dutch said interrupting me as his big blue eyes bore into mine.

"Yeah?" I asked.

"What happens in Vegas, stays in Vegas. *Capisce?*"

"You don't hate me?" I asked, and my eyes filled with water again.

"No, you silly little do-do," he said with a grin as

he leaned in and hovered his lips over mine. "I love you, babe. I really, really love you." And then he kissed me tenderly.

When he pulled back to look at me, all I could manage was, "Ditto, cowboy."

Read on for a sneak peek at the
next book in the Psychic Eye series

Crime Seen

Coming from Signet in June 2007

As I look at it, there are two kinds of people in this world: cat people and dog people. And as a general rule, you'd be better off mixing oil and vinegar.

Or so I thought as I lay on the couch in my boyfriend's house, recovering from a bullet wound to the chest I'd received three months earlier. My sweetheart, Dutch, owns a fat, annoying, allergy-producing tomcat named Virgil. I own a cute, cuddly, hypoallergenic dachshund named Eggy. I guess you can see which side of the dog vs. cat smackdown I fall on. Yes . . . I'm biased—so sue me.

On this particular day, however, as Eggy and I were snuggling on the couch, easing into a really good nap, my nose wrinkled. Something smelled off . . . *really* off. "Ugh," I said as I took a sniff. "What *is* that?"

"Abby?" I heard Dutch call from his study. "Did you say something?"

I sat up on the couch as Eggy gave me an annoyed grunt. "There is really something foul around here," I said as I sniffed again.

"What?" he asked, coming into the living room. "Did you need something?"

"What is that smell?" I asked him as I looked around and caught Virgil trotting over from behind an end table to twirl figure eights around Dutch's leg. It was then that I spotted something foul and smelly on my purse, which was lying near where I'd seen Virgil come from. "Oh, no, you *didn't*!" I said aloud.

"What's the matter?" Dutch asked me.

I pointed with a growl and snapped, "Your cat just pooped on my purse!"

Dutch turned to look where I was pointing, and I swear I caught a small smirk on his face before he turned back to me and said in a calm, soothing voice, "I'm sure he didn't mean to."

"Of course he didn't mean to, Dutch!" I said angrily as I got up off the couch and headed into the kitchen for some paper towels. "Just like he didn't mean to pee on my side of the bed the other night, or hurl his hair balls on top of my clean laundry, or use my backpack for a scratching post. I'm sure it's all just a big fat *coincidence*!"

"Edgar," Dutch said, using his favorite nickname for me, after famed psychic Edgar Cayce. "Come on, he's just a cat. He doesn't have a malicious bone in his body."

"Tell that to the dead chipmunk he showed up here with yesterday," I groused as I came back into the living room and scrunched up my face as I wiped up the poo. "I'm sure those two had a bunch of laughs before Virgil *ate him*."

"Try and look at it from Virgil's perspective, Abs. He ruled the roost until you and Eggy moved in, so he's had to make a pretty big adjustment."

With the wadded-up paper towel in my hand, I glared at my boyfriend, letting him know what I thought about Virgil and his "adjustment." "Eggy's had to make some concessions too, you know, and you don't see him walking around pooping on everything."

Dutch sighed and picked Virgil up protectively. "Can we not fight about this?" he asked me.

I rolled my eyes and stomped into the kitchen. Normally I like cats. I mean, I like them as long as they don't defecate on my things and generally keep to themselves. But ever since I'd come here to recover from my wound, Virgil had been the bane of my existence, and Dutch refused to believe that his feline was out to get me.

I strolled back into the living room, about to continue the argument, when the phone rang. Dutch gave me a "saved by the bell" smile. Looking at the caller identification, he said, "It's Candice. That's the third call this week. Think you'd better talk to her this time?"

I sat down heavily on the couch. I wasn't ready for this yet. I make my living as a professional psychic, and three months earlier I'd had a booming practice. All that changed one early spring morning when I'd been shot at close range and I'd very nearly died. Okay, scratch that—I actually *had* died, but only for a moment or two.

So for the past three months I'd been laid up here in my boyfriend's home, tucked away in a lovely little city called Royal Oak, Michigan. For the first month I'd done little more than sleep. I'd been told that when you're recovering from a major trauma like mine, your body slows down considerably, and mine was no exception.

But the past two months I'd steadily gotten stronger, and I'd become more active. Mentally, however, I just couldn't seem to get a grip. The prospect of going back to work actually terrified me, and even though my bank statements continued to show a decline in my liquid assets, I just couldn't seem to get up off the couch and go back to work. I'd reasoned that I'd probably already lost most of my clients anyway—as a psychic, if you stop working, you stop eating.

Dutch, who's an FBI agent, recognized what I was going through, and labeled it post-traumatic stress disorder, which sounded to me like a nice tidy way of calling me loo-loo.

Now here I sat, not having done a single reading in

three months, and one of my best clients was on the phone again. I looked up at Dutch and gave him a winning smile. "Can you tell her I'm out and take a message?"

Dutch smirked and answered the phone. "Hi, Candice, you looking for Abby?" I breathed a sigh of relief and sat back on the couch, thinking what a great boyfriend I had after all. "Sure, sure," he said, nodding his head. "She's right here, hang on." And with that he extended the phone.

I mouthed, "I'll get you for this," and took the receiver. "Hi, Candice!" I said, going for breezy. "Long time, no talk-to."

"Abby!" she sang. "Man, girlfriend! It is so great to finally hear your voice. How are you feeling?"

Dutch was still hovering nearby, and I cut him a look of death but continued to keep my voice light. "Oh, you know, taking it slow and easy. I still get tired quickly, but what can you do?"

Candice made a concerned sound into the phone and said, "You poor thing. I expect you haven't gone back to work yet, have you?"

"No," I said as I fiddled with the tassel on one of the couch cushions. "I'm easing into the idea. I don't want to push it just yet."

"I would imagine that's got to be a bit of a drain on your finances, then," she said. "It must be hard to maintain your mortgage and the rent on your office."

I wasn't sure where Candice was going with this. She and I had never really had the normal psychic/client relationship. Candice was a private detective and had a home base in Kalamazoo, about ninety miles west of Royal Oak. On occasion she would call me and drive over to get my feelings on a case she was working on. We'd made a great team on the few cases we'd worked, and I'd come to consider her a friend as well as client. "Yeah, but I've got a few pennies saved, so I should be okay for a little while yet."

I couldn't see Candice's reaction, but I could have

sworn she was disappointed when she said, "Oh, I see."

There was a bit of a pause before I asked her straight out, "Want to tell me what's up?"

Candice giggled. "I never could be subtle with you. Here's the deal, Abs. I've decided to hang out my own shingle."

"Really?" I asked with a smirk. "Gee, now, where have I heard that idea before?"

Candice's giggle turned into a laugh. "Yes, I know, you were right—again!" I had given her a reading about six months before, and in that reading I'd told her that she was going to entertain the idea of going it alone, and that it was worth considering. "But here's the catch. . . ." she added.

"Yes?" I asked when she paused.

"I need to find cheap office space to work out of."

"Have you tried the classifieds? I'm sure there's plenty available in Kalamazoo."

"No, not in Kalamazoo," she said. "I'm moving in with my grandmother, so I'll need to find a space close to her place."

"You're moving here?" I asked. I'd met Candice's grandmother a few months before. She also lived in Royal Oak.

"Yes. Just like you, I need to watch my pennies, and when Nana offered that nice big house of hers, I couldn't pass it up."

That's when the light bulb went on in my head. "And you were thinking I could sublet you some space in my suite?"

"I know, I know," she said quickly. "I shouldn't have asked; it's just that I know you have that extra office in your suite, and I heard you'd all but quit the business, so I thought I could help you out until you got back on your feet as well as give myself a little head start."

"It's a terrific idea," I said—my right side felt light and airy, which is my sign for yeppers.

"Really?" she said. "Oh, Abby, that's awesome!"

"Absolutely." I grinned. It had been a long time since I had shared my office with anyone. The extra office in my suite had once been rented by my best friend, Theresa, who had moved to California almost exactly a year ago. I'd entertained the idea of a suite mate since then, but no one had ever seemed quite right. Until now. "When would you like to move in?"

"This weekend, if that's okay?"

"It's fine," I said. "Come on over when you get into town and I'll give you the spare key. We can talk rent then, if you like."

"Perfect. Thanks again, Abby. And I'm so glad you're feeling better."

I clicked off with Candice and trotted into the study in search of Dutch, who had stopped his eavesdropping around the time I'd agreed to let Candice rent the office. "That was a dirty trick you pulled," I said as I handed him back the phone.

"Needed to be done," he said gravely. "Now have a seat. I want to talk to you."

"Sounds serious," I said as I plopped down into one of the leather chairs across from his desk.

He looked at me for a long moment, and, like always, I felt my breath catch at the beauty of the man. Dutch is tall, blond and incredibly handsome. But the most riveting thing about him is his eyes. They're midnight blue in color, and whenever they stared me straight in the eye like they were doing now, I knew I was in for a lecture. "I'm worried about you," he began.

"Here we go," I said, and got comfortable. Dutch was big on worry, but usually only where I was concerned.

"I'm not kidding," he said. "It's time for you to think about getting your feet wet again."

"But I took a shower this morning," I said lightly.

"Edgar," he sighed. "You know what I mean."

"I'm not ready," I said as I looked down at my hands.

Dutch didn't say anything for a long minute. Finally he said something startling. "Not even if it's to help me?"

"What?" I asked, lifting my eyes. "What are you talking about?"

Dutch picked up three folders on his desk and waved them at me. "When you were in there talking to Candice, it gave me an idea. These are the three cases I've been working this past month, and I'm at a roadblock on all three. I need a break, Abby, and I was really hoping that you could do for me what you usually do for Candice."

My jaw dropped a little. Dutch had *never* asked me for help on a case. In fact, he'd all but fought me off every time I'd tried to assist with an investigation. For him to ask me this meant he'd turned a corner of sorts, and the sneaky bastard did it knowing full well I could hardly turn him down. Still, I was a bit doubtful that he was for real. "Are you fooling with me? Because if you are, that would be a low move on your part."

"I'm dead serious," he said, holding my eyes.

"I see," I said, weighing my decision. Half of me really wanted to help. After all, my boyfriend was legendary for his skepticism. I'd seen him try to run to the aid of a ghost who'd disappeared before his very eyes, and still try to deny what he'd seen. He was also the type of guy who liked to be the hero, and asking for help wasn't something he'd ever been comfortable with.

But if I was honest with myself, I had to admit that the trouble wasn't so much on his end as on mine. I hadn't used my radar in nearly ninety days, which was an all-time record for me. In fact, I'd worked hard not to use it. The truth was that it had failed me at the moment in my life when I had most needed it. I'd been sucker punched by a bullet to the chest, and I'd had no idea it was coming.

That's what was really eating away at me, the fact

that when I'd relied on my intuition the most, it had been silent. Now here I was, faced with a decision that was as tough a choice as any I could face right now. Should I take my boyfriend up on his offer and accept that he'd extended a bridge to bring us closer together, or blow him off and continue to sit in my stink? "Okay," I said grimly. "I'll help, but only on the condition that you take my input seriously, no matter how far-fetched it sounds."

Dutch smiled and extended his hand. "Deal," he said, and we shook on it.

FROM

VICTORIA LAURIE

The Psychic Eye Mysteries

Abby Cooper is a psychic intuitive. And trying to help the police solve crimes seems like a good enough idea—but it could land her in more trouble than even she could see coming.

AVAILABLE IN THE SERIES

Abby Cooper, Psychic Eye
Better Read Than Dead
A Vision of Murder
Crime Seen
Death Perception

Available wherever books are sold or at penguin.com